HIGH
NOON

HIGH NOON

NORA ROBERTS

G. P. PUTNAM'S SONS
New York

G. P. PUTNAM'S SONS
Publishers Since 1838
Published by the Penguin Group
Penguin Group (USA) Inc., 375 Hudson Street, New York, New York 10014, USA • Penguin
Group (Canada), 90 Eglinton Avenue East, Suite 700, Toronto, Ontario M4P 2Y3, Canada (a division
of Pearson Penguin Canada Inc.) • Penguin Books Ltd, 80 Strand, London WC2R 0RL, England •
Penguin Ireland, 25 St Stephen's Green, Dublin 2, Ireland (a division of Penguin Books Ltd) •
Penguin Group (Australia), 250 Camberwell Road, Camberwell, Victoria 3124, Australia (a division
of Pearson Australia Group Pty Ltd) • Penguin Books India Pvt Ltd, 11 Community Centre,
Panchsheel Park, New Delhi–110 017, India • Penguin Group (NZ), 67 Apollo Drive, Rosedale,
North Shore 0745, Auckland, New Zealand (a division of Pearson New Zealand Ltd) • Penguin Books
(South Africa) (Pty) Ltd, 24 Sturdee Avenue, Rosebank, Johannesburg 2196, South Africa

Penguin Books Ltd, Registered Offices:
80 Strand, London WC2R 0RL, England

Library of Congress Cataloging-in-Publication Data

Roberts, Nora.
High noon / Nora Roberts.
p.   cm.
ISBN 978-0-399-15434-8
1. Hostage negotiations—Fiction.   I. Title.
PS3568.0243H54   2007   2007001054
813'.54—dc22

Printed in the United States of America
1   3   5   7   9   10   8   6   4   2

BOOK DESIGN BY AMANDA DEWEY

This is a work of fiction. Names, characters, places, and incidents either are the product of
the author's imagination or are used fictitiously, and any resemblance to actual persons, living or dead, businesses, companies, events, or locales is entirely coincidental.

While the author has made every effort to provide accurate telephone numbers and Internet addresses at the time of publication, neither the publisher nor the author assumes any
responsibility for errors, or for changes that occur after publication. Further, the publisher
does not have any control over and does not assume any responsibility for author or third-
party websites or their content.

For Amy Berkower,
the negotiator

INITIAL PHASE

Do not forsake me, oh, my darlin'.

—"HIGH NOON"

1

Jumping to your death was a crappy way to spend St. Patrick's Day. Being called in on your day off to talk someone out of jumping to his death on St. Patrick's Day wasn't exactly green beer and bagpipes.

Phoebe weaved and dodged her way through the crowds of Savannahians and tourists thronging streets and sidewalks in celebration. Captain David McVee thought ahead, she noted. Even with a badge, it would've taken precious time and miserable effort to get through the barricades and mobs of people in her car. But a couple blocks east of Jones, the revelry thinned, and the booming music was only a throb and echo.

The uniformed officer waited as ordered. His gaze skimmed over her face, down to the badge she'd hooked on the pocket of her khakis. Cropped pants, sandals, shamrock-green T-shirt under a linen jacket, Phoebe thought. Not the professional look she worked to foster on the job.

But what could you do? She was supposed to be standing on the terrace of MacNamara House, with her family, drinking lemonade and watching the parade.

"Lieutenant MacNamara?"

"That's right. Let's move." She slid in, flipping out her phone with one hand, dragging the seat belt on with the other. "Captain, I'm en route. Fill me in."

The siren screamed as the driver punched the gas. Phoebe yanked out her notebook, taking cursory notes.

Joseph (Joe) Ryder, suicidal. Jumper with gun. Twenty-seven, white, married/ separated. Bartender/fired. No known religious affiliation. No family on scene.

WHY? Wife left, fired from job (sports bar), gambling debts.

No criminal, no previous suicide attempt on record.

Subject alternately weepy/belligerent. No shots fired.

"Okay." Phoebe let out a breath. She'd get to know Joe much better very soon. "Who's talking to him?"

"He's got his cell phone on him. The first on scene wasn't able to engage. Guy just kept clicking off. We've got his employer here—former employer, who's also his landlord. The subject's been talking to him off and on, but there's no progress."

"You?"

"I'd barely gotten here when I pulled you in. I didn't want to throw too many people at him."

"All right. My ETA's five minutes." She glanced at the driver, got a nod of affirmation. "Keep him alive for me."

Inside Joe Ryder's fourth-floor apartment, sweat rolled down Duncan Swift's back. A guy he knew, a guy he'd had beers with, joked with, had pissed with, for God's sake, in adjoining urinals, was sitting on the ledge of the roof overhead with a gun in his hand.

Because I fired him, Duncan thought. Because I gave him thirty days to get out of the apartment. Because I didn't pay attention.

Now, it was a very strong possibility that Joe was going to put a bullet in his own ear or take a header off the roof. Maybe both.

Not exactly the kind of entertainment the crowds expected on St. Patrick's Day. Not that it was keeping them away. The cops had barricaded the block, but from the window Duncan could see people pressed against the barriers, faces turned up.

He wondered if Joe was wearing green.

"Come on, Joe, we'll work it out." How many *times,* Duncan asked himself, would he have to repeat that same phrase the cop kept circling in his notebook. "Just put the gun down and come inside."

"You fucking fired me!"

"Yeah, yeah, I know. I'm sorry, Joe, I was pissed off." You stole from me, you stupid dick, Duncan thought. You screwed up, stole from me. You took a damn swing at me. "I didn't realize how upset you were, or what was going on. You come inside and we'll work it out."

"You know Lori left me."

"I . . ." No, not I, Duncan remembered. His head was pulsing with the mother of all headaches, but he struggled to remember the instructions Captain McVee had given him. "You must've been feeling upset."

Joe's answer was to start sobbing again.

"Just keep him talking," Dave murmured.

Duncan listened to Joe's sobbing complaints, tried to repeat key phrases as he'd been directed.

The redhead shot into the room like a sleek bullet. She shrugged out of a light jacket while she talked to the captain, then shrugged into a bulletproof vest. All her movements lightning quick.

Duncan couldn't hear what they were saying. And he couldn't take his eyes off her.

Purpose was the first term that came to his mind. Then energy. Then sexy, though the third was mixed into the first two in equal portions. She shook her head, looked toward Duncan—long, cool stare with cat-green eyes.

"It's got to be face-to-face, Captain. You knew that when you pulled me in."

"You can try to bring him in via the phone first."

"Been tried." She studied the man currently making soothing noises over the subject's weeping. Former employer and landlord, she deduced.

Young for it, she mused. Very cute guy who looked as if he was trying hard not to panic.

"He needs a face. He needs personal contact. Is that the employer?"

"Duncan Swift, owns the bar street level of the building. He called the nine-one-one after the subject contacted him and said he was going off the roof. He's—Swift's—been on scene since."

"All right. You're the commander on this one, but I'm the negotiator. I need to go up. Let's see how the subject feels about that."

She walked over to Duncan, gestured for him to pass her the phone. "Joe? This is Phoebe. I'm with the police department. How you doing out there, Joe?"

"Why?"

"I want to make sure you're okay. You hot out there, Joe? Sun's pretty strong today. I'm going to ask Duncan to get us a couple bottles of cold water. I'd like to bring them up, talk to you up there."

"I've got a gun!"

"I hear that. If I come up with a cold drink for you, are you going to shoot me, Joe?"

"No," he said after a long moment. "No, shit. Why would I do that? I don't even know you."

"I'll bring you out a bottle of water. Just me, Joe. I want you to promise you won't jump or fire that gun now. Will you promise to let me come on out, bring you a bottle of water?"

"Rather have a beer."

The wistful tone in his voice gave her a little edge. "What kind of beer would you like?"

"Got Harp in the bottle in the fridge."

"One cold beer coming up." She walked to the refrigerator, found there was little else but beer. Even as she took one out, Duncan moved beside her to open it. She nodded, pulled out the single Coke, popped the top. "I'm coming on up with the beer, all right?"

"Yeah, a beer'd be good."

"Joe?" Her voice was as cool as the bottles in her hand as one of the cops fitted her with a wire, removed her weapon. "Are you going to commit suicide?"

"That's the plan."

"Well now, if that's your plan, I don't know as it's a good one."

She followed one of the uniforms out of the apartment, then up the stairs to the roof.

"Got nothing better to do."

"Nothing better? You sound like you're feeling pretty low. I'm at the roof door now, Joe. Is it all right if I come on out?"

"Yeah, yeah, I said so, didn't I?"

She'd been right about the sun. It was strong enough to bounce off the roof like a hot red ball. She looked to her immediate left, and saw him.

He was wearing nothing but what looked like black boxers. Sandy-haired guy with fair skin—and that skin had already turned a painfully bright pink. He squinted at her out of eyes swollen from crying.

"I guess I should've brought out some sunscreen along with the beer." She held the bottle up so he could see it. "You're getting toasted out here, Joe."

"Don't matter."

"I'd sure appreciate it if you'd put that gun down, Joe, so I could bring you your beer."

He shook his head. "You might try something."

"I promise not to try anything if you put the gun down while I bring you the beer. All I want to do is talk, Joe, you and me. Talking's thirsty work out here in the sun."

With his feet dangling over the roof ledge, he lowered the gun, laid it in his lap. "Just put it down there, then step back."

"All right." She kept her eyes on his as she walked over. She could smell him, sweat and despair; she could see the misery in his bloodshot brown eyes. She set the bottle down carefully on the ledge, stepped back. "Okay?"

"You try anything, I'm going off."

"I understand. What happened to make you feel so low?"

He picked up the beer and, closing his hand over the gun again, took a long pull. "Why'd they send you out here?"

"They didn't send me, I came. It's what I do."

"What? You a shrink or something?" He snorted on the idea, drank again.

"Not exactly. I talk to people, especially people in trouble, or who think they are. What happened to make you think you're in trouble, Joe?"

"I'm a fuck-up, that's all."

"What makes you think you're a fuck-up?"

"Wife walked out on me. We hadn't even been married six months and she walks. She told me she would, over and over. If I started betting again, she was out the door. I didn't listen; I didn't believe her."

"It sounds like that makes you feel awful sad."

"Best thing in my life, and I screw it up. I thought I could score— just a couple of good scores and that would be it. Didn't work out." He shrugged. "Never does."

"It's not enough to die for, Joe. It's hard, and it's painful when someone you love walks away. But dying means you can't ever make it right. What's your wife's name?"

"Lori," he mumbled as tears filled his eyes again.

"I don't think you want to hurt Lori. How do you think she'll feel if you do this?"

"Why should she care?"

"She cared enough to marry you. Do you mind if I sit here?" She tapped the ledge a few feet away from him. When he shrugged, she eased a hip onto it, sipped her drink. "I think we can figure this out, Joe. Figure out how to get you help, how to get you and Lori help. You sound like you want to find a way to fix things."

"Lost my job."

"That's hard. What kind of work did you do?"

"Tending bar. Sports bar down below. Lori, she didn't want me to work in a sports bar, but I told her I could handle it. But I didn't. Couldn't. Started making bets on the side. And when I started losing, I shorted the till so Lori wouldn't find out. Bet more, lose more, steal more. Got caught, got fired. Behind on the rent, too."

He picked up the gun, turned it in his hand. Phoebe braced, and fought back the instinct to duck and cover. "What's the point? I got nothing."

"I understand how you might feel that way right now. But the fact is, Joe, there are plenty of chances left. Everybody deserves more than one of them. If you kill yourself, it's just done. It's just over all the way. No coming back, no making it up to Lori, or to yourself. How would you make it up to her if you got the chance?"

"I don't know." He looked out over the city. "I can hear music. Must be from the parade."

"There's something to live for. What kind of music do you like?"

Inside the apartment, Duncan turned to Dave. "Music? What kind of music does he like? What the hell is she doing?"

"Keeping him talking. She's talking him down. He's telling her." Dave nodded toward the speaker. "As long as he's talking about Coldplay he's not going off the roof."

Duncan listened as they talked music for the next ten minutes, a conversation he might've heard in any bar or restaurant in the city. When he pictured Joe on the roof, it seemed surreal. When he pictured the redhead with her cat eyes and tight little body holding what smacked of small talk with a mostly naked, armed, suicidal bartender, it seemed impossible.

"Do you think I should call Lori?" Joe asked wistfully.

"Is that what you want to do?" She already knew they'd tried to reach Joe's estranged wife, without success.

"I want to tell her I'm sorry."

"That's good, telling her you're sorry. But you know what works better with women—and I know as I am one. Showing her. We believe it when you show us. You can show me right now if you give me the gun."

"I figured on shooting myself before I jumped. Or maybe on the way down."

"Look at me, Joe." When he turned his head, she kept her eyes straight on his. "Is that how you're going to show her you're sorry? By making it so she has to bury you, so she has to grieve? Are you punishing her?"

"No!" His face, his voice, registered shock at the idea. "It's my fault. It's all my fault."

"All your fault? I never believe anything is all one person's fault. But let's fix it. Let's find the way you can make it up to her."

"Phoebe, I owe almost five thousand gambling."

"Five thousand's hard. It sounds like it scares you to owe that much. I understand what it is to have money problems hanging over your head. Do you want Lori to have to pay your debt?"

"No. If I'm dead, nobody pays."

"Nobody? But she's your wife. She's your legal wife." Phoebe doubted there was any legal liability, but she could see the idea of it strike Joe. "She could be responsible for your debts."

"God. Oh God."

"I think I know how to help you with this, Joe. Joe? You know your boss is inside. He's inside there because he's worried about you."

"He's okay. Dunc's a good guy. I screwed him. Stole from him. I don't blame him for firing me."

"I hear you say that, and know you understand you're responsible for your mistakes. You're a responsible person, and you want to fix those mistakes. Dunc's a good guy, you tell me, then I'm going to believe he understands that, too. I'll talk to him for you if you want. I'm good at talking. If he'll give you an extension on paying back the money, that would help, wouldn't it?"

"I . . . I don't know."

"I'll talk to him for you."

"He's a nice guy. I stole from him."

"You were feeling desperate and scared, and you made a mistake. I sense you're sorry for that."

"I am sorry."

"I'll talk to him for you," she repeated. "You need to give me the gun, and come back off the ledge. You don't want to hurt Lori."

"I don't, but—"

"If you could talk to Lori right now, what would you say?"

"I . . . I guess that I don't know how it got this far, and I'm sorry. I love her. I don't want to lose her."

"If you don't want to lose her, if you love her, you have to give me the gun and come back off the ledge. Otherwise, Joe, all you're leaving her with is grief and blame."

"It's not her fault."

Phoebe eased off the ledge, held out a hand. "You're right, Joe. You're absolutely right. Now, show her."

He stared at the gun, stared as Phoebe slowly reached out to take it. It was slippery with his sweat as she flipped on the safety, secured it in her belt. "Come on off the ledge, Joe."

"What's going to happen?"

"Come on off the ledge and I'll explain it. I won't lie to you." Once again, she offered her hand. Shouldn't, she knew. Negotiators could be pulled off by a jumper. But she kept her eyes on his, then clasped her fingers tight on his hand.

When his feet touched the roof, he simply slid down to the floor to sob again. She went with him, draped her arm around him, and shook her head fiercely at the cops who came through the door.

"It's going to be all right. Joe, you're going to have to go with the police. You're going to need to have an evaluation. But it's going to be all right."

"I'm sorry."

"I know you are. Now you come on with me. Come on with me now." She helped him up, took his weight as they walked to the door. "Let's get you some clothes on. No cuffs," she snapped. "Joe, one of the officers is going to go get you a shirt, some pants, shoes. Is that all right?" When he nodded, she gestured one of the officers toward the bedroom.

"Am I going to jail?"

"For a little while. But we're going to get started on that help right away."

"Will you call Lori? If she'd come I could . . . I could show her I'm sorry."

"I sure will. I want that sunburn treated, and he needs some water in him."

Joe kept his eyes downcast as he pulled on jeans. "Sorry, man," he mumbled to Duncan.

"Don't worry about it. Listen, I'll get you a lawyer." Duncan looked blankly at Phoebe. "Should I?"

"That would be between you and Joe. You hang in there." She gave Joe's arm a light squeeze.

He was led out, a cop on either arm.

"Nice job, Lieutenant."

Phoebe pulled out the gun, opened it. "One bullet. He was never going to shoot anyone but himself, and the odds are fifty-fifty he'd have done that." She handed the gun to her captain. "You figured he needed to talk to a woman."

"It leaned that way for me," Dave agreed.

"All in all, looks like you were right. Somebody needs to track down his wife. I'll talk to her if she balks at seeing him." She swiped at her sweaty brow. "Is there any water in this place?"

Duncan held out a bottle. "I had some brought up."

"Appreciate it." She drank deep as she studied him. Rich, dense brown hair, tousled around an angular face with a good, strong mouth and soft blue eyes that were currently pinched with worry. "Are you pressing charges?"

"For what?"

"For what he nipped out of the till."

"No." Duncan lowered himself to the arm of a chair. Closed his eyes. "Christ, no."

"How much was it?"

"A couple thousand, a little more, I guess. It doesn't matter."

"It does. He needs to pay it back, for his own self-respect. If you want to help him, you'll work that out."

"Sure. Fine."

"You're the landlord, too?"

"Yeah. Sort of."

Phoebe lifted her brows. "Aren't you the busy one? Can you manage to float the rent another month?"

"Yeah, yeah, yeah."

"Good."

"Look . . . all I got was Phoebe."

"MacNamara. Lieutenant MacNamara."

"I like Joe. I don't want him to go to jail."

A good guy, Joe had said. He'd likely been right on that one. "I appreciate that, but there are consequences. Paying them will help him.

He was crying for help, and now he'll get it. If you know where he owes the five thousand, he needs to make that right, too."

"I didn't know he was gambling."

This time she let out a short laugh. "You own a sports bar, but don't know there's gambling going on in it?"

His back went up. His gut was already in knots, and now his back went up. "Hey, listen, Slam Dunc's a friendly place, not a mob den. I didn't know he had a problem, or he wouldn't have been working the stick there. Some of this was my fault, but—"

"No. No." She held up a hand, rubbed the cold bottle over her damp forehead. "I'm hot, I'm irritable. And none of this was your fault. I apologize. Circumstances put him out there on that ledge, and he's responsible for those circumstances and the choices he made. Do you know where to find his wife?"

"I expect she's at the parade like everyone else in Savannah, except us."

"Do you know where she's living?"

"Not exactly, but I gave your captain a couple numbers. Friends of theirs."

"We'll find her. Are you going to be all right now?"

"Well, I'm not going to go up on the roof and jump." He let out a long sigh, shook his head. "Can I buy you a drink, Phoebe?"

She held up the bottle of water. "You already did."

"I could do better."

Hmm, a quick flicker of charm now, she noted. "This'll be fine. You should go on home, Mr. Swift."

"Duncan."

"Mmm-hmm." She gave him a fleeting smile, then picked up her discarded jacket.

"Hey, Phoebe." He made a bead for the door when she walked out. "Can I call you if I feel suicidal?"

"Try the hotline," she called back without looking around. "Odds are they'll talk you down."

He moved to the rail to look down at her. Purpose, he thought again. He could acquire a strong taste for a woman with purpose.

Then he sat on the step, pulled out his phone. He called his closest friend—who was also his lawyer—to sweet-talk him into representing a suicidal bartender with a gambling addiction.

From the second-floor balcony, Phoebe watched the green sheepdog prance. He seemed pretty damn proud of himself, matching his steps to the fife and drum played by a trio of leprechauns.

Joe was alive, and while she'd missed the curtain, she was right where she wanted to be for the second act.

Not such a crappy way to spend St. Patrick's Day after all.

Beside her, Phoebe's seven-year-old daughter bounced in her bright green sneakers. Carly had campaigned long and hard for those shoes, Phoebe recalled, whittling away at any and all resistance to the price or impracticality.

She wore them with green cropped pants with tiny dark pink dots, and a green shirt with pink piping—also a long and arduous campaign by the pint-sized fashion diva. But Phoebe had to admit, the kid looked unbelievably sweet.

Carly's sunset red hair came down from her grandmother, through her mother. The curls came from her grandmother, too—skipping a generation there, as Phoebe's was straight as a stick. The brilliant and bright blue eyes were from Essie as well. The middle generation, as Phoebe often thought of herself, settled for green.

All three had the pale, pale redhead's complexion, but Carly had inherited the dimples Phoebe had longed for as a child, and the pretty mouth with its dip deep in the top lip.

There were times Phoebe looked at her mother and her daughter, and through the impossible waves of love wondered how she could be the bridge between two such perfectly matched points.

Phoebe brushed a hand over Carly's shoulder, then bent to press a kiss on those wild red curls. In answer to the gesture, Carly shot out a mile-wide grin that showed the gap of two missing front teeth.

"Best seat in the house." From behind them, one short stride outside the door, Essie beamed.

"Did you see the dog, Gran?"

"I sure did."

Phoebe's brother turned to their mother. "You want a seat, Mama?"

"No, sweetie." Essie waved Carter off. "I'm just fine."

"You can come up to the rail again, Gran. I'll hold your hand the whole time. It's just like the courtyard."

"That's right. That's right." But Essie's smile was strained as she crossed the short distance to the rail.

"You can see better from here," Carly began. "Here comes another marching band! Isn't it great, Gran? Look how high they're stepping."

See how she soothes her Gran, Phoebe thought. How her little hand holds tight to give support. And Carter, look at him, moving to Mama's other side, running a hand down her back even as he points to the crowd.

Phoebe knew what her mother saw when she looked at Carter. Having a child of her own, she understood exactly that hard and stunning love. But it would be doubled for her, Phoebe thought. Mama had only to look at Carter, at the rich brown hair, those warm hazel eyes, the shape of his chin, his nose, his mouth, and she would see the husband she'd lost so young. And all the might-have-beens that died with him.

"Fresh lemonade!" Ava wheeled a cart to the doorway. "With plenty of mint so we've got the green."

"Ava, you didn't have to go to all that trouble."

"I certainly did." Ava laughed at Phoebe and flipped back her sassy swing of blond hair. At forty-three, Ava Vestry Dover remained the most beautiful woman of Phoebe's acquaintance. And perhaps the kindest.

When Ava lifted the pitcher, Phoebe hurried over. "No, I'll pour and serve. You go on and watch awhile. Mama'll feel better with you standing with her," Phoebe added quietly.

With a nod, Ava walked over, touched Essie on the shoulder, then moved to stand on Carly's other side.

There was her family, Phoebe thought. True, Ava's son was off in New York in college, and Carter's pretty wife was working, but this was the foundation, the bedrock. Without them, she wasn't sure she wouldn't just float off like a dust mote.

She poured lemonade, passed around the glasses, then stood beside Carter. Leaned her head on his shoulder. "I'm sorry Josie can't be here."

"Me, too. She'll be here for dinner if she can."

Her baby brother, she thought, a married man. "You two ought to stay the night, avoid the holiday traffic and the insanity of revelry."

"We like the insanity of revelry, but I'll see if she'd rather. Remember the first time we stood up here and watched the parade? That first spring after Reuben."

"I remember."

"Everything was so bright and loud and foolish. Everyone was so happy. I believe even Cousin Bess cracked a smile or two."

Probably just indigestion, Phoebe thought, with lingering bitterness.

"I felt, really felt, maybe everything would be all right. That he wasn't going to break out and come for us, wasn't going to kill us in our sleep. Christmas didn't do that for me, not that first year, or my birthday. But standing here all those years ago, I thought maybe everything was going to be all right after all."

"And it was."

She took his hand so they were linked, right down the line of the rail.

2

Cleaned up and hungover, Duncan sat at his kitchen counter brooding over his laptop and a cup of black coffee. He'd meant to keep it to a couple of beers, hanging with some of the regulars at Slam Dunc before heading off to catch the music, another beer or two at Swifty's, his Irish pub.

When you owned bars, he'd learned, you were smart to stay sober. He might bend that rule of thumb a little on St. Patrick's Day or New Year's Eve. But he knew how to coast through a long night with a couple of beers.

It hadn't been celebration that put the Jameson's with a bump of Harp back into his hand too many times. It had been sheer relief. Joe wasn't a smear on the sidewalk outside the bar.

I'll drink to that.

And it was better to be hungover due to good news than hungover due to bad. You still felt like shit, Duncan admitted as the horns and pipes throbbed in his abused head, but you knew it would wear off.

What he needed to do was get out of the house. Take a walk. Or a nap in the hammock. Then figure out what to do next. He'd been figuring out what to do next for the past seven years. And he liked it.

He frowned at the laptop another moment, then shook his head. If he tried to work now, even pretend to work, his head would probably explode.

Instead, he carried his coffee out to the back veranda. The mourning doves were cooing, bobbing heads as they pecked along the ground under the bird feeder. Too fat and lazy, Duncan thought, to bother to fly up into it. Rather take leavings.

A lot of people were the same.

His gardens were thriving, and he liked knowing he'd put a little of his own sweat and effort into them. He considered walking through them now, winding his way under the live oaks and the thick spider-webs of moss to the dock. Take a sail maybe, cruise the river.

Damn pretty morning for it, if you paid attention. One of those sparkling clear, hint-of-a-breeze mornings you'd wish you'd prized come July.

Or he could just go down and sit on the dock, look out toward the salt flats and watch the sun play on them. Take the coffee down and just sit and do nothing on a pretty spring morning—a damn good deal.

And what was Joe doing this fine morning? Sitting in a cell? A padded room? What was the redhead up to?

It was no use pretending it was just an ordinary day in the life when he couldn't get yesterday out of his head. No point thinking he wanted to sit on the pier nursing a hangover and pretending everything was just fine and dandy.

So he went up the back steps to his bedroom, hunted out clean jeans and a shirt that didn't look like it had been slept in. Then he pulled his wallet, keys and other pocket paraphernalia out of the jeans he *had* slept in after he'd dragged his half-drunken ass to bed.

At least he'd been smart enough to take a cab, he reminded himself as he scooped his fingers through his shaggy mass of brown hair.

Maybe he should wear a suit. Should he wear a suit?

Shit.

He decided a suit was a kind of showing off when worn to visit a former employee in Joe's current situation. Besides, he didn't feel like wearing a damn suit.

Still, the redhead might like suits, and since he had every intention of tracking her down, a suit could play to his advantage.

Hell with it.

He started out, jogged down the sweeping curve of the main staircase, across the polished sea of white tiles of the grand foyer. When he opened one of the arching double doors, he saw the little red Jag zip down the last curve of his drive.

The man who folded himself out of it was wearing a suit, and it was sure to be Italian—as would be the shoes. Phineas T. Hector could manage to look perfectly groomed after mud wrestling in a hurricane.

Duncan hooked his thumbs in his front pockets and watched Phin stroll. He never looked to be in any particular hurry, Duncan mused, but that mind of his was always running on high speed.

He looked like a lawyer, Duncan supposed, and a high-dollar one. Which was exactly what he was now. When they'd first met—had it been ten years now?—Phin had barely been able to afford the cab fare to court, much less an Armani suit.

Now he wore it like he'd been born to, the pale gray an excellent choice against his dark skin, his gym-hammered body. Sun flashed off his dark glasses as he paused at the base of the white steps to study Duncan.

"You look a little rough there, friend of mine."

"Feeling the same."

"Imagine so after the amount of adult beverages you poured into your sorry self last night."

"Felt good at the time. What're you doing out here?"

"Keeping our appointment."

"We had one of those?"

Phin only shook his head as he climbed the stairs. "I should've known you wouldn't remember. You were too busy drinking Irish and singing 'Danny Boy.'"

"I did not sing 'Danny Boy.'" Please, God.

"Can't say for sure. All those Irish tunes sound the same to me. You heading out?"

"I was. I guess we should go inside."

"Out here's fine." Phin settled down on the long white glider, laid his arms out over its back. "You still thinking of selling this place?"

"I don't know. Maybe." Duncan looked around—gardens, trees, pits of shade, green, green grass. He could never decide how he felt about the place from one day to the next. "Probably. Eventually."

"Sure is a spot. Away from the action, though."

"I've had enough action. Did I ask you to come out here, Phin? I'm blurry."

"You asked if I'd check in with Suicide Joe this morning, then come out to report to you. After I agreed, you embraced me and gave me a sloppy kiss. I believe there's now a rumor going around that my wife is our beard."

Duncan considered a moment. "Did I at least kiss her, too?"

"You did. You want to hear about Joe?"

Duncan jingled the keys in his pocket. "I was about to drive into the city, check in on him."

"I can save you the trip. He's doing better than I expected considering the shape he was in yesterday when I first saw him."

"Was his wife—"

"She was there," Phin interrupted. "She was pretty damn pissed, but she was there. He's got a violent sunburn, which they're treating, and I've approved, as his attorney, the court-appointed psychiatrist. As you're not pressing any charges, he's not going to do any serious time. He'll get help, which is what you wanted."

"Yeah." So why did he feel so guilty?

"If you hire him again, Dunc, I'll kick your ass."

"You can't kick my ass." Duncan gave him a slow and crooked grin. "You don't fight dirty enough, black boy."

"I'll make an exception. He'll get help. His wife will take him back or she won't. But you've already gone beyond what most would, and you hired him the best counsel in Savannah."

"Better be, for what you charge," Duncan mumbled.

Phin only grinned. "Got yourself to blame for that. Well, I'm going to head back and overcharge a few other clients."

"What about the redhead?"

"What redhead?" Tipping down his sunglasses, Phin frowned at Duncan over them. "There were a couple of blondes and one delicious brunette trying to move on you last night, but you were too busy brooding into your beer to intercept the passes."

"No, not last night. The redhead. Phoebe MacNamara. Lieutenant Phoebe MacNamara. God." On a long, exaggerated sigh, Duncan patted his heart. "Just saying that gets my juices up, so I believe I'll repeat myself. Lieutenant Phoebe MacNamara."

Phin rolled his eyes up to the white ceiling of the covered veranda. "You're a case, Swift, God knows. What are you going to do with a cop?"

"I can think of all kinds of things. She's got green eyes, and that snug little body. And she went out on that roof. Guy's sitting out on the ledge with a gun, a guy she's never met in her life, but she goes out."

"And you find that attractive?"

"I find it fascinating. And hot. You met her, right? What did you think?"

"I found her brisk and to the point, well bred and canny. And in possession of an excellent ass."

"I got her stuck in my head. Well, I think I ought to go see her, try to figure out why. You can give me a ride in, I need to pick up my car anyway."

After running a two-hour training session, Phoebe sat down at her desk. Her hair was pulled back, rolled at the nape of her neck, mostly to keep it out of her way. In addition, she thought—hoped—the style lent her some authority. A lot of the cops she trained—the male ones—didn't start out taking a woman very seriously.

They all took her seriously by the end, or they were out on their ass.

She might have had an inside man in Dave to help crack the door open for her in the department. But she'd shoved the door wide, and earned her rank, her position.

Now, due to that rank and position, she had a pile of paperwork to push through. And she had to spend the afternoon in court, testifying on the circumstances of a domestic dispute that had gone south into a hostage situation.

After that, she needed to come back and finish up what she could. And after *that,* she needed to go by the market.

And after things settled down at home, she needed to hit the books, to prep for a lecture she was due to give on crisis negotiation.

Somewhere in there she needed to squeeze out time to balance her checkbook—long overdue—and see if there was any way she could afford a new car without robbing a bank.

She opened the first file, and got down to managing her little corner of the Savannah-Chatham PD.

"LT?"

"Mmm?" She acknowledged Sykes, one of the negotiators in her unit, without looking up.

"Guy out here wants to see you. Duncan Swift."

"Hmm?" This time she looked up with a frown. She looked through the window of her office, saw Duncan studying the squad room as if it were a foreign planet.

She thought of her workload, of the time crunch, and nearly passed him off. Then his gaze shifted, met hers. And he smiled.

"Ah well." She pushed up from her desk, stepped out to the doorway of her office. "Mr. Swift?"

He had a damn effective smile, she decided. Something about it said it was easy and often used. And his eyes, soft and dusky blue, looked right at you. In her experience a lot of people weren't comfortable making that solid eye contact. But this man let you know he wasn't just looking at you, he was thinking about you while he did.

"You're busy. You look busy," he said when he reached her. "You want me to come back when you're not?"

"If what you came by for can wait about a decade, that's fine."

"I'd rather it didn't."

"Then come on in."

"Wow. It's sort of like on TV, but not exactly. Do you get weirded out sitting here where everybody can see what you're doing all day?"

"If I do, I can always pull the blinds."

He hooked his thumbs in the front pockets of worn jeans. There were long legs in those jeans, she noted.

"Bet you hardly ever do."

"I spoke with the attorney you hired on Joe's behalf. He seems very competent."

"And then some. So . . . I wanted to ask you if I should visit Suicide Joe—"

"Excuse me? Suicide Joe?"

"Sorry, we got to calling him that last night. It stuck in my head. Should I visit him, or is it better for him if I step back?"

"What do you want to do?"

"I don't know. It's not like we were pals or anything. But yesterday's loop keeps running through my head."

"It's more to the point what's running through his."

"Yeah. Yeah. I had this dream."

"Did you?"

"I was the one sitting out on the ledge in my underwear."

"Boxers or briefs?"

It made him laugh. "Boxers. Anyway, I was sitting on the ledge and you were sitting there with me."

"Are you feeling suicidal?"

"Not a bit."

"It's called transference. You're putting yourself in his place. It was a traumatic experience, for you as well as Joe, even though it ended well."

"Have you ever had one that didn't?"

"Yes."

He nodded, and didn't ask for details. "What do you call me having you stuck in my mind? Wishful thinking?"

"That would depend on what you're wishing for."

"I started to Google you."

She sat back now, raised her eyebrows.

"I thought, sure it's a shortcut, a curiosity-satisfying one. But sometimes you want to go the long way around. You get to find out about somebody from the source, maybe over some type of food or drink. And if you're wondering, yes, I'm hitting on you."

"I'm a trained observer. I don't have to wonder when I know. I appreciate the honesty, and the interest, but—"

"Don't say 'but,' not right off the bat." He bent down, picked up a hairpin that must have fallen out of her hair earlier, handed it to her. "You could consider it a public service. I'm the public. We could exchange life stories over that some sort of food and drink. You could name the time and the place. We don't like what we hear, what's the harm?"

She dropped the hairpin in with her paper clips. "Now you're negotiating."

"I'm pretty good at it. I could just buy you a drink. That's what— thirty minutes? A lot of people spend more time than that picking out a pair of shoes. Half an hour after you're finished work, or off-duty, whatever you call it."

"I can't tonight. I have plans."

"Any night in the foreseeable future you don't have plans?"

"Plenty of them." She swiveled gently back and forth in her chair, studying him. Why did he have to be so cute, and so appealing? She really didn't have time for any of this. "Tomorrow night, nine to nine-thirty. I'll meet you at your bar."

"Perfect. Which bar?"

"Excuse me?"

"You don't want to go to Dunc's—weird after yesterday, and it's loud and full of guys arguing over sports. Swifty's."

"You own Swifty's?"

"Sort of. You've been there?"

"Once."

His brows drew together. "You didn't like it."

"Actually, I did. I didn't like my companion."

"If you want to pick somewhere else—"

"Swifty's is fine. Nine o'clock. You can spend part of the thirty min-utes explaining how you 'sort of' own a couple of bars and an apartment building."

He used the smile again when she rose to signal his time was up. "Don't change your mind."

"I rarely do."

"Good to know. See you tomorrow, Phoebe."

A mistake, she told herself when she watched him walk away. It was probably a mistake to make any sort of a date with a lanky, charming man with soft blue eyes, especially one who had those little tugs going on in her belly when he smiled at her.

Still, it was only half an hour, only a drink.

And it had been a long time since she'd carved out half an hour to make a mistake with a man.

Phoebe dragged into the house just after seven with a bag of groceries, a loaded briefcase and a serious case of frazzled nerves. The car she wasn't at all sure she could replace had limped to a shuddering halt a block from the station house.

The cost of having it towed would eat a greedy chunk of the monthly budget. The cost of having it repaired made the possibility of bank robbery more palatable.

She dumped her briefcase just inside the door, then stood staring around the elegant and beautiful foyer. The house, for all its grandeur, cost her nothing. And though nothing was a relative term, she knew even if it were possible to move, she couldn't afford it, on any terms. It was ridiculous to live in a damn mansion and not know how to manage to pay to repair an eight-year-old Ford Taurus.

Surrounded by antiques, by art, by silver and crystal, by beauty and grace—none of which she could sell, hock or trade. To live in what could be construed as luxury, and have a tension headache over a goddamn car.

Leaning back against the door, she shut her eyes long enough to remind herself to be grateful. There was a roof over her head, over her family's head. There always would be.

As long as she followed the rules laid down by a dead woman.

She straightened, buried the anxiety deep enough so it wouldn't show on her face. Then she carried the grocery bag through the house to the kitchen.

There they were. Her girls. Carly at the kitchen table, tongue caught in her teeth as she struggled over homework. Mama and Ava at the stove putting finishing touches on dinner. Phoebe knew the rule of thumb was that two women couldn't share a kitchen, but these two managed just that.

And the room smelled of herbs and greens and females.

"I told y'all not to hold dinner for me."

As Phoebe stepped in, all three heads turned. "Mama! I'm almost done with my spelling."

"There's my girl." Setting the bag on the counter as she went, Phoebe walked over to give Carly a smacking kiss. "Bet you're hungry."

"We wanted to wait for you."

"'Course we waited." Essie moved close to rub a hand down Phoebe's arm. "You all right, baby girl? You must be so tired, having the car go out like that."

"I wanted to take out my gun and shoot it, but I'm over it now."

"How'd you get home?"

"I took the CAT, which is what I'll be doing until the car's fixed."

"You can use mine," Ava told her, but Phoebe shook her head.

"I'd feel better knowing there's a car available here at home. Don't worry. What's for dinner? I'm starving."

"You go on and wash up." Essie waved her away. "Then sit right down at the table. Everything's ready, so you go on."

"Don't mind if I do." She winked at Carly before slipping out to the powder room off the parlor.

More to be grateful for, she reminded herself. There were dozens of tasks and chores she didn't have to heap on her plate because her mother was there, because Ava was there. A thousand little worries she could brush aside. She wasn't going to let herself get twisted inside out over something as annoying as transportation.

She studied her face in the mirror as she dried her hands. She looked tired, and tight, she admitted. There would surely be lines on her face in the morning that hadn't been there yesterday if she didn't relax a little.

And at thirty-three, there would be lines sneaking in anyway. Just a fact of life.

But she was having a big glass of wine with dinner regardless.

It did relax her, as did the pretty food prepared by hands other than her own, the soft light, the easy music of female voices.

She listened to Carly talk about her school day, and her mother talk about the book she was reading.

"You're so quiet, Phoebe. Are you just tired out?"

"A little," she said to Ava. "Mostly I'm just listening."

"Because we can't keep quiet for five minutes. Tell us something good that happened today."

It was an old game, one her mother had played with them as long as Phoebe could remember. Whenever something hard or sad or irritating happened, Essie would ask them to tell her something good.

"Well, let's see. The training session went well."

"Doesn't count."

"Then I guess satisfying the prosecutor with my testimony in court this afternoon doesn't count either."

"Something good that happened to you," Essie reminded her. "That's the rule."

"All right. She's so strict," Phoebe said to make Carly grin. "I don't know if it's good, but it's different. I had a good-looking man come into my office."

"It only counts if he asked you out to dinner," Ava began, then gaped at Phoebe's expression. "You have a *date?*"

"Well, for God's sake, don't say it as if we've just discovered a new species."

"It's practically as rare. Who—"

"And it's not a date. Not really. The suicide I talked down yesterday? This is the man who he used to work for. He just wants to have a drink."

"Ava said it had to be dinner to count," Carly reminded her.

"He brought up dinner, we negotiated it to drinks. Just half an hour tomorrow." She tapped Carly's nose. "After your bedtime."

"Is he cute?" Ava demanded.

The wine and the company had done its job. Phoebe flashed a grin. "Really cute. But I'm just meeting him for one drink. Over and out."

"Dating isn't a terminal disease."

"Listen to who's talking." Phoebe forked up a bite of chicken and looked at her mother. "And listen to who's not. Mama?"

"I was just thinking how nice it would be if you had somebody to go out to dinner with, to the movies, to take walks with." She laid a hand over Phoebe's. "Only time there's a man's voice in this house is when Carter's over, or a repairman comes in. What's this really cute man do?"

"I'm not entirely sure, not altogether sure." She sipped more wine. "I guess I'll find out tomorrow."

Whenever she was home and could manage it, Phoebe liked to tuck Carly into bed. With her little girl at seven and counting, Phoebe knew the tucking-in stage wouldn't last much longer. So she prized it.

"Past your bedtime, my cutie." Phoebe bent to kiss the tip of Carly's nose.

"Just a little bit past. Can I stay up until any-o'clock on Friday night?"

"Hmm." Phoebe brushed her hand over Carly's curls. "Any-o'clock could be arranged. Let's see how you do on your Friday spelling test."

Bright-eyed with the idea, Carly pushed to sitting, gave a butt bounce. "If I get a hundred, can we rent a DVD, have popcorn *and* stay up till any-o'clock?"

"That's a lot of reward." Gently, firmly, Phoebe put the heel of her hand to Carly's forehead and nudged her back down. "You have an arithmetic test on Friday, too, don't you?"

Carly's gaze went to her Barbie sheets. "Maybe. It's harder than spelling."

"I always thought so, too. But if you do well on both your tests, we have a deal on the DVD, the popcorn and the any-o'clock. You get some sleep now, so your brain's ready to study tomorrow."

"Mama?" Carly said when Phoebe turned off the bedside lamp.

"Yes, baby."

"Do you miss Roy?"

Not Daddy, Phoebe thought. Not Dad, not even—very often—my father. It was a pitiful commentary. Phoebe sat on the side of the bed, stroked her fingers over Carly's cheek. "Do you?"

"I asked *you.*"

"So you did." And honesty was a linchpin of her relationship with her little girl. "No, sweetie, I don't."

"Good."

"Carly—"

"It's okay. I don't miss him either, and it's okay. I was just wondering because of what Gran said at dinner about having somebody to take walks with and stuff."

"I can take walks with you."

Carly's pretty mouth curved. "We could take a walk on Saturday. A long walk. Down to River Street."

On to the ploy, Phoebe narrowed her eyes. "We are *not* going shopping."

"Looking isn't shopping. We can just look and not buy anything."

"That's what you always say. And River Street'll be jammed with tourists on Saturday."

"Maybe we should just go to the mall then."

"You're tricky, kid, but you can't win this one. No shopping this weekend. And no talking your grandmama into buying you something online either."

Now Carly rolled her eyes. "Okay."

With a laugh, Phoebe snuggled down for a major hug. "Boy, oh boy, I sure do love you into little, bitty pieces."

"I sure do love you. Mama, if I get A's on my next *three* spelling tests, can I—"

"Negotiations are closed for the night, and so, Carly Anne Mac-Namara, are you."

She tapped a finger to her lips as she rose. And when she went out, she left the door open a couple of inches so the hallway light slanted in, the way her baby liked it.

She needed to get her work started. There was a good two hours of it waiting for her. But instead of angling toward her home office, Phoebe veered off toward her mother's sitting room.

Essie was there, as she was most evenings, crocheting.

"Got an order for a christening gown," Essie said, looking up with a smile as her fingers continued to ply thread and hook.

Phoebe moved over, sat in the pretty little tapestry chair that matched the one her mother used. "You do such beautiful work."

"I enjoy it. Satisfying. I know it doesn't bring in a lot of money, Phoebe, but—"

"Satisfying's most important. The people who buy your work, why, they're buying heirlooms. They're lucky. Mama, Carly asked about Roy."

"Oh?" Essie's hands stilled now. "Is she upset?"

"No. Not at all. She wanted to know if I miss him. I told her the truth, that I don't, and I have to hope that was the right thing."

"I think it was, if you're asking me." Concern filled Essie's eyes. "We've had us some lousy luck with men, haven't we, baby girl?"

"Oh yeah." Leaning back, Phoebe let her gaze wander to the ceiling, the beautiful plaster work of an old, grand home. "I'm wondering if I shouldn't cancel this sort-of date I've got tomorrow."

"Why would you do that?"

"We're doing all right, aren't we? Carly's happy. You've got your satisfying work, I've got mine. Ava's content—though I do wish she and Dave would stop pretending, now that they're both single, that they're not attracted to each other. So, why mix anything else in with having drinks in some pub with a man I don't even know?"

"Because you're a lovely young woman, with so much of her life ahead of her. You've got to step out of this henhouse sometimes. Which may sound silly, coming from me, but it's true." Essie's hands started moving again. "The last thing I want is for you to start boxing yourself in, holing up in this place we've made here. You have that drink and that conversation tomorrow with this good-looking man. That's an order."

Amused, Phoebe angled her head. "So it's do what you say, not what you do?"

"Exactly. Mother's privilege."

"I guess I will, then." She rose, walked to the door, turned back. "Mama? No online shopping for Carly this weekend."

"Oh?" The single syllable resounded disappointment.

"Mother's privilege," Phoebe echoed, then headed off to work.

3

Phoebe took her place at the front of the room. She had twenty-five cops in this training session, a mix of uniforms and plain-clothes of varying ranks.

A good portion of them, she knew, didn't want to be there.

"Today, I'm going to talk about the tactical role of the negotiator in a crisis or hostage situation. First, are there any questions regarding yesterday's session?"

A hand shot up. Phoebe swallowed her instinctive annoyance. Officer Arnold Meeks, third-generation cop. Bullheaded, belligerent and bigoted, in Phoebe's opinion, with a thick layer of macho over it.

"Officer Meeks?"

"Yes, ma'am." His smile usually started out as a smirk, and often stayed there. "You talked down a jumper the other day, St. Patrick's Day?"

"That's correct."

"Well, ma'am, I was interested in some of the particulars, seeing as we're in this training session with you. Now, I was curious, as it appears you broke some of the rules of negotiation during this incident. Unless being FBI-trained, as you are, things are different for you. Is that the case?"

Her early federal training would always rub some of the rank and file the wrong way. They'd just have to live with it. "Which rules did I break, Officer Meeks?"

"Well, ma'am—"

"You can use my rank, Officer, as I do yours."

She watched annoyance flicker over his face. "The subject was armed, but you engaged him face-to-face, without cover."

"That's correct. It's also correct that a negotiator should avoid, if possible, any face-to-face with an armed subject. However, circumstances may call for it, and we'll be covering that area of crisis situation in the role-playing sessions in the second half of this course."

"Why—"

"I'm getting to that. In my opinion, the incident on St. Patrick's Day called for a face-to-face. In point of fact, most jumpers respond better to this method. The subject had no history of violent behavior, and had not fired the weapon. In a situation such as the one on St. Patrick's Day, I, as negotiator, had to assess and weigh the advantages and disadvantages of going face-to-face. In my opinion, the advantages far outweighed the risks. As we've already covered the other considerations regarding face-to-face in a previous session—"

"Ma'am—Lieutenant," Arnie corrected, with just enough hesitation to make sure she knew it was deliberate. "Is it also correct you provided the subject with alcohol?"

I bet you have a really little dick, Phoebe thought, but nodded. "I provided the subject, at his request, with a beer. Providing alcohol to a subject during negotiations is not encouraged, but neither is it forbidden. This tack would be up to the negotiator, his or her sense of the situation and evaluation of the subject."

"Get him drunk enough, maybe he'd just fall off the roof." Arnie's comment got a few snickers. Phoebe inclined her head, let them die off.

"Next time you're on a ledge, Officer, I'll remember you get drunk off one beer and bring you a nice Coca-Cola instead."

That got more than snickers, and noting the angry red wash over Arnie's face, Phoebe cut through them. "As I've said, repeatedly, while there are guidelines for negotiations, the negotiator must be flexible, be able to evaluate, to think on his or her feet."

"But you agree providing alcohol or drugs is risky?"

"Certainly. My gauge in this case was it was low risk. The subject did not demand alcohol; he very politely asked if he might have a beer. Bringing him one gave him something he wanted, and allowed him some control, allowed him to exchange that beer for his word not to use his weapon on me, to allow me to come out and speak with him. Just you wait," she ordered Arnie before he could open his smirking mouth again.

Then she paused to make certain her tone would be calm and cool. "The preservation of life is and always will be the primary goal of negotiation. Everything, absolutely everything else, is secondary to that. Therefore, in this instance—as every single instance is different—I elected a face-to-face, elected to provide the subject with a single beer because I believed those choices would assist me in talking him down. As he's alive, as there were no injuries, as the weapon he held was never discharged but given to me by him, I believe—in this instance—my choices were the correct ones."

"You also used a third-party intermediary."

Now Phoebe smiled, sweet Southern sugar. "Officer Meeks, it appears you have several questions and problems with this particular incident and my handling of it. I wonder if you'd be more satisfied if the subject had just jumped."

"Seeing as he was only sitting up four stories, he'd only have a couple broken bones if he had. Unless he shot you and himself beforehand."

"There's an interesting train of thought. Disbelieving a subject is serious about suicide, or could indeed cause his own death."

Casually, she reached up to secure a stray wisp of hair that had escaped from its pins. And kept her voice just as casual. "I was acquainted with a negotiator who had this train of thought over a jumper who was about twelve feet off the ground, unarmed. Mostly being a nuisance, from my acquaintance's point of view, one that was keeping him from doing more important things with his valuable time. And he allowed that opinion to show. The subject jumped, headfirst, crushing his skull on the sidewalk. He was very dead, Officer Meeks.

"Anybody know why this nuisance ended up with a toe tag?"

"Negotiator screwed it up," someone called out.

"That's right. The negotiator screwed it up by forgetting the prime directive: Preserve human life.

"If you have any more questions or comments about the incident, please feel free to write them up for me. But for right now? We're moving on."

"I'd like to—"

"Officer." The temper Phoebe rarely set free strained on the leash. "You may be mistaken about who is running this session. I am. You may also be confused about the order of rank here. I am your superior."

"It seems to me, *ma'am,* that you don't want to address your questionable decisions during a crisis negotiation."

"It seems to me, *boy,* that you are unable to take no for an answer, by a woman who happens to outrank you, and that you're both rigid in your thinking and argumentative in attitude. These are very, very poor qualities in a negotiator. I'll so note to your captain, and hope that we'll be relieved of each other before much longer. Now, I want you to close your mouth and open your ears. That's an order, Officer Meeks. If you choose to ignore it, I'll write you up for insubordination here and now. Clear?"

His face had gone an angry red, and his eyes spoke furious volumes. But he nodded curtly.

"That's fine. Now, tactics, teamwork and the negotiator's role."

The minute the session was over, Phoebe headed straight for the women's room. She didn't beat her head against the wall, though she considered it. Instead, she turned to the mirror, gripped the sink below it.

"Arnold Meeks has a dick the size and width of a baby carrot, and his smirky, *insulting,* juvenile behavior is a pathetic attempt to compensate for his pinkie-sized weenie."

She nodded, relaxed her shoulders. Then dropped her head when she heard a toilet flush. How stupid could she be to mouth off to the mirror without checking the stalls first?

Phoebe knew the woman who stepped out, but that didn't negate the mortification. Detective Liz Alberta was a solid cop, a strong-willed brunette who worked in sex crimes.

"Lieutenant."

"Detective."

Liz ran water in the sink, turned her own face right and left as if checking her reflection. "Arnie Meeks is a fuckhead," she said casually.

"Oh." Phoebe sighed. "Well."

"He tells tits-and-ass jokes in the break room. I like a good joke same as the rest, and boys will be boys and all that. But I took some exception, and made my exception known after he told me the majority of rapes are bogus, pulling out the old chestnut about how a woman can run faster with her skirt up than a man can with his pants down."

"The fuckhead said that?"

"Oh yes, he did. And I filed a complaint on him. He isn't a fan of mine." Liz fluffed at her short, dark hair. "And I dislike him right down to the tip of that teeny weenie of his." She offered a sunny smile as she dried her hands. "Lieutenant."

"Detective," Phoebe returned as Liz tossed the paper towel into the bin and strolled out.

She didn't like it, but she went to Dave. As was her habit, she jogged up the two flights of stairs from the lecture area to her own section. He was striding out of his office, swinging on his jacket as she popped out the stairway door.

"Oh, you're heading out."

"I've got a meeting. Problem?"

"Maybe. I'll come back."

He glanced at his watch. "I can give you two minutes." He jerked a thumb, stepped back into his office. And said nothing when Phoebe closed the door behind her.

He was still so much the same as the day she'd first met him. A little gray dashed his temples, and those lines people called character in a man and age in a woman fanned out from his eyes. But those eyes were still clear and blue and, for her, drenched in quiet wisdom.

"I don't like having to do this, because for one thing, it means I've failed. But I'm asking you to consider removing Officer Arnold Meeks from my training sessions."

"Because?"

"I can't teach him anything. And, in fact, may be prejudicing him against any of the basic tactics and guidelines in the field."

Dave leaned back against his desk, a gesture that told her she'd get more than the two minutes now if she needed them. "Is he stupid?"

"No, sir, but he is small-minded. In my opinion."

"His father's still on the job. He's a son of a bitch."

Phoebe relaxed fractionally. "I'm shocked and amazed to hear that."

"I want all officers assigned to the sessions to complete them. You can relate your opinions of Officer Meeks, in this area, in your evaluation. I want all of them to get through it, Phoebe. You know as well as I do that at least some of what you teach them will work its way in, even into small minds."

"I dressed him down in the session."

"Did he deserve it?"

"And then some. But he's only going to be pissed off at me now, and even less likely to listen."

"Minimize the damage and move on." He gave her a pat on the shoulder. "I'm going to be late."

"Minimize the damage," Phoebe muttered, but reached up to straighten Dave's tie.

He smiled at her. "You're the best I've ever worked with. You remember that, and handle small-minded Meeks."

"Yes, sir, Captain."

She walked out with him, and when she peeled off, spotted Arnie loitering with a couple other cops outside her squad room. Her belly might have clenched, but her face was serene as she walked up to him. "Officer Meeks, the captain wishes all assigned officers to complete the negotiator training. I'll expect to see you Monday morning, as scheduled. Is that understood?"

"Yes, ma'am."

"Now I'm sure the three of you have more important things to do than stand around here. Go on and do it."

"Yes, ma'am," he repeated, in a tone that had her hackles rising. Minimize the damage, she reminded herself. "I expect we can both learn something from these sessions."

She couldn't hear what he said when she walked away; the words were low and indistinguishable. But she heard the snickers clearly enough.

She let it go. A woman who'd pushed through Quantico, who'd slogged through police training, through negotiation training, sexually outnumbered ten to one, had heard snickers before.

She also knew when eyes were trained on her ass, and while it might infuriate her, Phoebe reminded herself to pick her battles. And that she had a damn fine ass.

When she entered her office, saw the message from the mechanic, she understood she had bigger problems than a smart-mouthed cop and ass ogling.

Her car was going to cost seven hundred and fifty-nine nonnegotiable dollars.

"Ah, hell."

Giving up, Phoebe laid her head down on her desk for a moment of pure self-pity.

She caught the bus home, and the moment she was inside deeply regretted the prospect of going out again. Even the idea of going out again—the bus ride, sitting in a bar making small talk, only to ride yet another bus only to get back to square one—seemed overwhelmingly stupid.

She should dig up Duncan's number, cancel. Agreeing to the thirty-minute drink had been a moment of weakness anyway—that damn dimple. Hadn't she thought of a dozen other things she could do with thirty minutes on the ride home?

A bubble bath. Yoga. Give herself a facial. Clean out the junk drawer in her desk.

All were a better use of her time. But a deal was a deal.

Carly sprinted into the foyer to take a flying leap into Phoebe's arms. No outside irritations could stand up against a Carly hug.

"You've been in Gran's perfume." To make Carly giggle she sniffed elaborately at her daughter's neck.

"She let me have a spritz. Dinner's all ready, and I finished my homework." Leaning back, Carly beamed into her mother's face. "You get to be excused from doing the dishes tonight."

"Wow. How come I rate?"

"So you can get ready for your date. Come on!" Wiggling down, Carly took Phoebe's hand to drag her toward the dining room. "Gran thinks you should wear your blue sweater, and Ava thinks the white blouse that ties in the back. But *I* think you should wear your green dress."

"The green dress isn't really the thing for a quick evening meeting."

"But you look so pretty in it."

"She should save it," Ava commented as Carly dragged Phoebe in. "For when he takes her out to dinner. Sit right down, it's all ready. We wanted to give you plenty of time to primp."

"It's a drink. It's only a drink in an Irish pub."

Ava set her hands on her hips. "Excuse me? Tonight you represent every dateless woman in this city, every woman who's about to sit down to a lonely meal of Weight Watchers pasta primavera she's just nuked in the microwave. Every woman who'll get into bed tonight with a book or reruns of *Sex and the City* as her only companion. You," she said, pointing her finger at Phoebe, "are our shining hope."

"Oh God."

Essie patted Phoebe's shoulder before she sat down. "But no pressure."

She didn't want to be a shining hope. But she got on the bus. She had to refuse Ava's offer of her car three times, and disappoint Carly by choosing a black sweater and jeans over the green dress. But she put on the earrings her daughter picked out, and redid her makeup.

Life, Phoebe knew, was full of compromises.

She got a wolf whistle from Johnnie Porter—all of fifteen and full of sass—as he circled her on his bike.

"You sure look pretty tonight, Miz MacNamara. Got a hot date?"

Now she worried she looked as if she were expecting a hot date. "Why, thank you, Johnnie, but no. I'm off to catch a CAT."

"You going somewhere, you can just hop on here with me." He popped a little show-off wheelie. "I'll give you a ride."

"That's neighborly of you, but I believe I'll stick with the bus. How's your mama?"

"Oh, she's fine. She's got Aunt Susie over." Johnnie rolled his eyes elaborately on his next circle. "Talking about my cousin Juliet's wedding. So I lit out. Sure you don't want to boost on up on my handlebars?"

How a fifteen-year-old boy could turn that into a sexual innuendo was puzzling. "I'm sure."

"See you later, then."

Off to find some trouble, Phoebe thought with a shake of her head as he zipped down the wide sidewalk. God help the neighborhood when he was old enough to drive.

It was just cool enough she was grateful for the sweater as she walked from the bus stop along East River Street. Plenty of others enjoyed the evening and the stroll, wandering in or out of restaurants and clubs, pausing to window-shop or just gaze out over the water.

So many couples, she thought, hand in hand, taking in that balmy air. Mama had a point, she supposed. It was nice—could be nice—to have someone to hold hands with on a pretty spring evening.

And it was better, given her personal situation, not to think about that sort of thing. Especially when she was about to have a drink with a very cute man.

She had plenty of hands to hold. So many, in fact, that a solitary walk along the river was a rare indulgence. Take the moment, she advised herself and, because she had a few minutes, slowed her pace, turned toward the water, and enjoyed the indulgence.

And see, she mused, she wasn't the only one on her own. She saw a man, solitary as she, standing spread-legged in a pool of shadow and watching the water. The bill of his ball cap angled low over his face while a pair of cameras were strapped bandolier style over his dark windbreaker.

Not everyone was a couple.

Maybe she would bring Carly down for a long walk on Saturday, she thought as she tipped her head back, let the breeze take her hair. The kid got such a charge out of wandering around down here, looking at everything, at everyone.

They'd have to set the rules first. Lunch, yes. Fabulous prizes, no. Not with her car currently hostage at the mechanic's.

Probably a smarter idea to make that a nice walk through one of the parks away from retail outlets.

They'd work it out.

Gauging the time, she turned away from the water and didn't notice the solitary man lift and aim one of the cameras in her direction.

At Swifty's a shamrock dotted the *i* in the name on the sign. The stained glass panel in the door was a rather beautiful Celtic knot design. The doorknob was brass, and the outside walls were done in a dull stucco yellow, a shade she remembered seeing in postcards of Irish villages. Hanging pots dripped with airy flowers and green, green vines.

Little details, she thought. The man paid attention to little details.

When she stepped inside, it was as she remembered from her single previous visit. A big, burly bar set the tone. This was not the venue for airy ferns and apple martinis. But if you wanted a pint, or a glass of Irish, conversation and music, belly right up.

Leather booths were deep and cushy, the tables dark, polished wood. Shadow and sparkle played from the colored glass shades of hanging lamps, while a red-eyed turf fire simmered in a quaint little stone hearth.

The mood was warm welcome.

At one of the booths, its table loaded with drinks, sat the musicians. A girl with a shock of red-tipped black hair sawed a bow over the fiddle strings with a speed and energy that made the movement as blurry as the music was clear. A man old enough to be her grandfather pumped out rhythm on a small accordion. A young man with hair so pale it reminded Phoebe of angels' wings piped out the tune, while yet another set down his pint glass, picked up his fiddle, and slid seamlessly into the song.

Happy, Phoebe thought. Happy music, happy chatter under it. Cheery lights and color, with clever little touches sprinkled through.

Old tankards, a bowen drum, bits of pottery she imagined came from Ireland, an Irish harp, old Guinness signs.

"There you are, and right on time."

Even as she turned toward him, Duncan had her hand in his. That smile of his, she realized, it had a way of making her forget she didn't really want to be there.

"I like your place," she told him. "I like the music."

"Sessions nightly. I've got us a table." He led her to the one in front of the quiet fire where she could sink down on the cozy little love seat.

Take the moment, Phoebe thought again. "Best seat in the house."

"What can I get you?"

"Glass of Harp, thanks."

"Give me a minute." He moved over to the bar, spoke to the girl running the near end. A moment later he came back with a glass of golden beer.

"Nothing for you?"

"I've got a Guinness in the works." Those soft blue eyes zeroed straight in on hers. "So how are you?"

"Well enough. How about you?"

"Let me answer that by asking if you've got a stopwatch on me."

"Sorry, left it in my other purse."

"Then I'm good. I just want to get this out of the way, so it doesn't keep distracting me. I really like the way you look."

"Thanks. I'm okay with it myself most of the time."

"See, I've had you stuck." He tapped a finger to his temple, then paused to flash a smile at the waitress who brought over his pint of Guinness. "Thanks, P.J."

"You bet." The waitress set a bowl of pretzels on the table, gave Duncan a wink, Phoebe a quick once-over, then carted her tray off to another table.

"Well, *sláinte.*" He tapped his glass to Phoebe's, sipped. "So, I kept asking myself were you stuck in there just because of Suicide Joe or because I thought you were hot. Which was my second thought when I saw you, and was probably inappropriate given the circumstances."

She sipped more slowly, watching him. That tiny dimple that flick-ered at the corner of his mouth when he grinned just drew the eye like a magnet. "Your second thought."

"Yeah, the first was sort of: Thank God she's going to fix this."

"Do you always have that kind of confidence in total strangers?"

"No. Maybe. I'll think about it." He angled so their knees bumped companionably with a little whoosh of denim against denim. "It's just I looked at you and it struck me you were someone who knew what to do, knew what you were doing—a really hot woman who knew what to do. So I wanted to see you again, maybe figure out how come you're stuck. I know you're smart—also a plus—not only because of what you do, but hey, Lieutenant, and you seem young for that."

"I'm thirty-three. Not so young."

"Thirty-three? Me, too. When's your birthday?"

"August."

"November. Older woman." He shook his head. "Now I'm sunk. Older women are so sexy."

It made her laugh as she tucked up her legs, shifted a little toward him. "You're a funny guy."

"Sometimes. But with serious and sensitive sides, if you're counting points."

"Points?"

"There's always a point system in this kind of situation. He's clean. She has breasts. Points added. He has a stupid laugh, she hates sports, points subtracted."

"How'm I doing?"

"I'm not sure I'm going to be able to add that high without my calculator."

"Clever, too. Points for you." She sipped at her beer, studied him. He had a little scar, a thin, diagonal slash through his left eyebrow. "Still, it's risky to assume I'm smart and competent—if those are included in the final total—with so little actual data."

"I'm a good judge of people. On-the-job training."

"Owning bars?"

"Before that. I tended bar and drove a cab. Two professions where you're guaranteed to see all types of people, and where you get to peg them pretty quick."

"A cab-driving bartender."

"Or bartending cabdriver, depending." He reached over, tucked her hair behind her ear, gave the dangling silver at her lobe a little tap. The gesture was so casual and smooth, she wondered at her own quick jolt of intimacy.

"Easy to juggle hours on both sides," he continued, "and I figured I'd sock away enough to open myself a sport's bar."

"And so you did, fulfilling the American dream."

"Not even close—well, the American dream part—but I didn't earn the ready to open Slam Dunc riding the stick or driving a hack."

"How then? Robbing banks, dealing drugs, selling your body?"

"All viable options, but no. I won the lottery."

"Get out. Really?" Delighted, fascinated, she lifted her glass in toast before stretching out a hand for a pretzel.

"Yeah, just a fluke. Or, you know, destiny, again depending. I picked up a ticket now and then. Actually, hardly ever. Then one day I went in for a six-pack of Corona, sprang for a ticket."

"Did you pick the numbers or go with the computer?"

"My pick. Age, cab number—which was depressing since I hadn't planned to still be hacking—six for the six-pack. Just that random, and . . . jackpot. You know how you hear people say if they ever win, or even when they do, how they're going to keep right on working, living pretty much like they have been?"

"Yeah."

"What's wrong with them?"

She laughed again, snagged another pretzel. "Obviously, you retired as a cab-driving bartender."

"Bet your ass. Got my sports bar. Very cool. Only funny thing, and I may lose man points here, but I figured out after a few months I actually didn't want to be in a bar every night of my life."

She glanced around Swifty's, where the music had gone slow and dreamy. "Yet you have two. And here you are."

"Yet. I sold half interest in Dunc's to this guy I know. Well, almost half. Figured, hey, Irish pub."

"Hence Swifty's."

"Hence."

"No travel, no flashy car?"

"Some travel, some flash. Anyway, how did you—"

"Oh no, the question begs to be asked." She wagged a finger at him. "It's rude, but it has to be asked. How much?"

"A hundred and thirty-eight million."

She choked on her pretzel, holding up a hand when he tapped her on the back. "Jesus Christ."

"Yeah, that's what I said. You want another beer?"

She shook her head, gaped at him. "You won a hundred and thirty-eight *million* dollars on a lottery ticket?"

"Yeah, go figure. Best six-pack I ever bought. It got a lot of play at the time. You didn't hear about it?"

"I . . ." She was still struggling to absorb. "I don't know. When?"

"Seven years ago last February."

"Well." She puffed out a breath, pushed a hand through her hair. *Million* replayed through her mind. "Seven years ago last February I was busy giving birth."

"Hard to keep up with current events. You got a kid? What variety?"

"A girl. Carly." She saw his gaze shift down to her left hand. "Divorced."

"Okay. Lot of juggling, single parent, high-octane career. I bet you've got excellent hand-eye coordination."

"It takes practice." Millions, she thought. Millions stacked on top of millions, yet here he was, nursing a Guinness in a nice little pub in Savannah, looking like an average guy. Well, an average guy with a really cute dimple and a sexy little scar, a killer smile. But still.

"Why aren't you living on an island in the South Pacific?"

"I like Savannah. No point in being really rich if you can't live where you like. How long have you been a cop?"

"Um." She felt blindsided. The cute, funny guy was now a cute, funny multimillionaire. "I, ah, started with the FBI right out of college, then—"

"You were with the FBI? Like Clarice Starling? Like *Silence of the Lambs*? Or Dana Scully—another hot redhead, by the way. Special Agent MacNamara?" He let out a long, exaggerated breath. "You really are hot."

"Due to this, that and the other thing, I decided to shift to the Savannah-Chatham PD. Hostage and crisis negotiator."

"Hostage?" Those dreamy eyes of his sharpened. "Like if a guy barricades himself in some office building with innocent bystanders and wants ten mil, or the release of all prisoners with brown eyes, you're the one he's talking to?"

"If it's in Savannah, chances are good."

"How do you know what to say? What not to say?"

"Negotiators are trained, and have experience in law enforcement. What?" she said when he shook his head.

"No. You have to *know*. Training, sure, experience, sure, but you have to know."

Odd, she thought, that he'd understand that when there were cops— Arnie Meeks sprang to mind—who didn't. And never would. "You hope you know. And you have to listen, not just hear. And listening to you, here's what I know. You live in Savannah because there wouldn't be enough to do on that island in the South Pacific, or enough people to do it with. You don't discount the sheer luck of buying a winning ticket along with a six-pack, but neither do you discount that sometimes things are simply meant. Telling me about the money wasn't bragging, it was just fact—and fun. Now, the way I reacted to it mattered, in as much as if I'd suddenly put moves on you, we'd end this evening having sex, which would also be fun. But I'd no longer be stuck in your mind."

"Something else I really like," he commented. "A woman who does what she's good at, and is good at what she does. If Suicide Joe was still working for me, I'd give the son of a bitch a raise."

She had to smile, and by God, she was charmed right down to the balls of her feet. But . . . "That's quite a bit for one drink," she decided. "Now I've got to get on home."

"You love your kid—that's first and last. Your eyes lit up when you said her name. The divorce still bothers you on some level. I don't know which, not yet. Your work isn't a career, it's a vocation. Cab-driving bartender," he said. "I know how to listen, too."

"Yes, indeed. That's quite a bit, on both sides, for one drink."

He rose when she did. "I'll walk you to your car."

"It'll be a hike. It's in the shop. I'm catching a CAT."

"Jeez. I'll drive you. Don't be stupid, 'cause you're not." He took her arm with one hand, signaled a goodbye to the bar with the other on the way to the door.

"You're the second man who's offered me a ride tonight."

"Oh yeah?"

"The first involved hopping onto the handlebars of his bike. As I told him, I don't mind the bus."

"Take you just as long to walk to the bus stop as it will for us to walk to the lot down here. And I can promise you a smoother ride home." He glanced down at her. "Nice night for a drive."

"I'm only up on Jones."

"One of my favorite streets in the city." He strolled now, sliding his hand down her arm to link it with hers. "So's this one."

And here she was after all, Phoebe thought, half of a couple wandering on River Street, hand in hand. His was warm, the palm hard and wide. The sort of hand, she imagined, that could wrench the top off a pickle jar, catch a fly ball or cup a woman's breast with equal ease.

His legs were long, his stride loose and lazy. A man, Phoebe judged, who knew how to take his time when he wanted to.

"Nice night for a walk, too, especially along the river," he commented.

"I have to get home."

"So you said. Not cold, are you?"

"No."

He walked into the lot, hailing the attendant. "How you doing there, Lester?"

"Doing what comes, boss. Evening, ma'am."

A bill passed from hand to hand so smoothly Phoebe nearly missed it. Then she was standing, staring at a gleaming white Porsche.

"No handlebars." Duncan shrugged, grinned, then opened the door for her.

"I'm forced to admit this will be better than the bus—or Johnnie Porter's Schwinn."

"You like cars?"

"If you'd asked me that a couple hours ago, I'd have given you several reasons why cars and I are on nonspeaking terms currently." She brushed a hand over the side of the buttery leather seat. "But I like this one just fine."

"Me, too."

He didn't drive like a maniac, which she'd half-expected, and had to admit had half-hoped. He did drive, however, like a man who knew the city the way she knew her own bedroom—every nook and cranny.

She gave him the address and let herself enjoy the sort of ride she'd never imagined experiencing. When he pulled up in front of her house, she let out a long sigh. "Very nice. Thank you."

"My pleasure." He got out, skirting the hood to take her hand again on the sidewalk. "Great house."

"It is, yes." There it was, she thought, rosy brick, white trim, tall windows, graceful terraces.

Hers, whether she liked it or not.

"Family home, family duty. Long story."

"Why don't you tell me about it over dinner tomorrow night?"

Something in her actively yearned when she turned toward him. "Oh, Duncan, you're awfully cute, and you're rich, and you've got a very sexy car. I'm just not in a position to start a relationship."

"Are you in a position to eat dinner?"

She laughed, shook her head as he walked with her up to the parlor level. "Several nights a week, depending."

"You're a public servant. I'm the public. Have dinner with me tomorrow night. Or pick another activity, another day. I'll work around it."

"I have a date with my daughter tomorrow night. Saturday, dinner, as long as it's understood this can't go anywhere."

"Saturday."

He leaned in. It was smooth, but she saw the move. Still, it felt fussy and foolish to stop it. So she let his lips brush over hers. Sweet, she thought.

Then his hands ran down from her shoulders to her wrists, his mouth moved on hers. And she couldn't think at all. Deep, penetrating warmth, quick, hard flutters, a leap and gallop of pulse.

She felt it, all of it, as her body seemed to let out a breath too long held.

Her head actually spun before he eased back, and she was left staring, staring into his eyes. She said, "Oh, well, damn it."

He flashed that grin at her. "I'll pick you up at seven. 'Night, Phoebe."

"Yeah, 'night." She managed to unlock the door, and when she glanced back, he was standing on the sidewalk, still grinning at her. "Good night," she said again.

Inside, she locked up, turned off the porch light. And wondered what the hell she'd gotten herself into.

4

She'd no more than reached the top of the stairs when her mother and Ava slipped out of the TV room with big, expectant smiles.

"So?" Essie began. "How was it?"

"It was fine. It was a drink." If she'd been wearing socks, Phoebe thought as she aimed for her bedroom, they'd have blown clear across Jones Street during that good-night kiss.

Behind her back, Essie and Ava exchanged a look, then headed off in pursuit.

"Well, what's he like? What did you talk about? Come on, Phoebs." Ava clasped her hands together as if in prayer. "Give us dateless wonders the scoop."

"We had a beer in his very nice pub. I enjoyed it. I'm going to work out."

Another look was exchanged when Phoebe went to her dresser to pull out yoga pants and a sports bra.

"What'd you talk about?"

Phoebe glanced at her mother in the mirror, shrugged. She began to strip and change. She'd lived among women too long to worry about nudity. "This and that. He used to tend bar and drive a cab."

"Hmm. So he's enterprising, isn't he?"

"You could say."

"Where does he live?" Ava pressed. "In the city?"

"I didn't ask."

"Well, for goodness sake." Essie cast her eyes to the ceiling. "Why not?"

"It didn't come up." Phoebe reached in the little silver trinket box on her dresser for a tie, whipped her hair back into a tail.

"What about his people?" Essie demanded. "Who are his family, his—"

"That didn't come up either. I sort of got distracted."

"Because he was charming," Essie decided.

"He was—is—very charming. But I was distracted, considerably, when he told me he won the lottery several years ago, to the tune of a hundred and thirty-eight million."

She sailed out on that, automatically peeking in to check on Carly before moving to the stairs and up to the third floor.

She'd commandeered what had once been a maid's room for a little home gym. An indulgence on her part, Phoebe knew, but it also saved a health club fee and meant she could get an hour in early in the morning or at night, after Carly was in bed.

Work kept her away from home enough without adding gym time to it.

She'd sprung for an elliptical machine, a few free weights, and even a small TV to play exercise tapes. Carly often practiced her gymnastics while she worked out, so that was the big benefit of more mother-daughter time. Her mother and Ava used the equipment, so it paid for itself.

In the end it wasn't only more convenient but more economical. At least that's how she'd justified the expense.

Phoebe smiled to herself as she set the machine and climbed on. Her mother and Ava were already at the doorway, gaping.

"Did you say *million*?" Essie demanded.

"I did."

"I remember that, I remember something about that." Ava laid a hand on her heart. "Millionaire cabdriver. That's what they called him. Local boy. Single ticket. Oh my God! That's *him*?"

"In the flesh."

"Well. God. I think I'm going to sit down." Essie did so, right on the floor. "That's not just rich, not even just wealthy. I don't know what it is."

"Lucky?" Phoebe suggested.

"And then some." Ava joined Essie on the floor. "He bought you a beer."

Amused, Phoebe kicked her warm-up to the next level. "Yeah. And pretzels. Then he drove me home in his Porsche."

"Is he slick?" Essie's brows drew together, and the frown line Phoebe had inherited instead of dimples creased between them. "That much money, he's likely slick."

"He's not. Smooth," Phoebe decided after a moment. "He's pretty damn smooth, but I have a feeling that's innate. He talked me into having dinner with him Saturday night."

"You're dating a millionaire." Ava nudged Essie with her elbow. "Our little girl's dating a millionaire."

Because the idea made her nervous, Phoebe bumped the resistance up another notch—on the machine, and in her. "I don't know about dating. I'm not interested in dating anybody. It's too damn much trouble. What are you going to wear, what are you going to talk about? Is he going to want to have sex—and there I say: Duh. Are you going to want to have sex, which actually does require some thought and consideration."

"Dinner," Ava reminded her. "Saturday night."

"Yeah, well, he's smooth," Phoebe muttered. "He's pretty damn smooth."

The scene was a little storefront operation. Jasper C. Hughes, Attorney at Law. The intelligence Phoebe had indicated that Hughes, one Tracey Percell and an armed individual named William Gradey were barricaded inside.

The tactical team continued setting up outer and inner perimeters. Phoebe grabbed her ready box and headed for the first on scene. She was already unhappy knowing it was Arnie Meeks.

"Situation."

Arnie wore dark glasses, but she could feel the derision in his eyes as he stared down at her. "Guy's got two hostages. Witnesses heard gunfire. When I arrived, the subject yelled out that if anybody tried to come in, he'd kill them both."

Phoebe waited a beat. "That's it?"

Arnie shrugged. "Subject claims the lawyer cheated him out of six thousand dollars and he wants it back."

"Where's the log, Officer?"

The way his lips curled, Phoebe wondered if he practiced the sarcastic look in the mirror.

"I've been trying to keep this asshole from killing two people. I haven't had time for a log."

"At what time was gunfire heard?"

"Approximately nine A.M."

"Nine?" She could feel both temper and fear knot up inside her. "Nearly two hours ago, and you've just decided to send for a negotiator?"

"I have the situation under control."

"You're relieved. You—" She pointed to another uniformed cop as she pulled a log sheet out of her ready kit. "Everything gets written down. Time, activity, who says what and when." She took out a notebook.

Arnie grabbed her arm. "You can't just walk in here and take over."

"Yes, I can." She wrenched free. "The captain's on his way, and Commander Harrison is in charge of Tactical. Meanwhile, I'm in charge here, as negotiator. Get the hostage-taker on the phone," she ordered the cop she'd drafted as second negotiator.

"I'm the one keeping this from blowing up."

"Is that so?" She whipped around to Arnie. "Have you spoken to either hostage? Have you ascertained that they're still alive? If they've been harmed? If anyone requires medical attention? Where is your situation board? Your log? What progress have you made toward ending this situation without loss of life in the damn near two hours before you deigned to call this in?"

She grabbed the phone, checked her notebook where she'd already written down names.

"I don't want to talk to you!" The voice that answered screamed with emotion and fury. "I said I'm through talking to you."

"Mr. Gradey? This is Phoebe MacNamara. I'm a negotiator with the police department. You'll be talking to me now. You sound upset. Is everyone all right in there, Mr. Gradey? Does anyone have medical problems I should know about?"

"Everything's gone to hell. It's all gone to hell."

"Let's try to work all this out. Is it all right if I call you William? Is that what people call you?"

"I'm through talking!"

"I'm here to help." She heard it in his voice, he was through talking and poised to act. "Does anyone need anything in there? Medical attention? Water? Maybe something to eat."

"I needed my money."

"You need your money. Why don't you tell me about that, Mr. Gradey? Let me see if I can help you with that." She wrote down *used past tense.*

"I said it all already. Nobody listened."

"Nobody listened to you. You sound angry about that. I understand, and I apologize if you feel your problem wasn't given attention. But I'm listening, Mr. Gradey, I'm listening to you now. I want to help you resolve all this."

"It's too late. It's over."

She heard the gunshot in her head a second before it blasted the air. She'd heard it in his voice.

The lawyer had a mild concussion, some bumps and bruises. The secretary was hysterical but unharmed. William Gradey was dead from a self-inflicted gunshot wound to the head.

"Nice negotiating," Arnie said from behind her.

She turned, very slowly, until her eyes burned into his. "You arrogant son of a bitch."

"He took himself out while you were on the line. Not me." With his trademark smirk in place, Arnie swaggered off.

She forced herself not to go after him, not now, not now when her rage was so full and sharp and deep she could—would—do something she'd regret later.

It would wait for later. She promised herself that later she would deal with Officer Arnold Meeks. For now, Phoebe stood and watched Crime Scene walk in and out of the building. A hand dropped on her shoulder.

"Nothing more for you to do here," Dave said to her.

"I never had a chance with him. A minute, maybe two. It was over before I got here. I couldn't bring it back."

"Phoebe."

She shook her head. "Not now, please. I want to debrief the hostages, and take statements from any witnesses." She turned around. "I want all debriefing and statements recorded, and I want you to witness them."

"You and I both know sometimes things go south."

"What I don't know is if this one had to." The rage wanted to make her tremble. She refused. "I'm going to find out. The hostages are en route to the hospital, but the woman didn't seem to be hurt. She can talk. I'd like you to go with me, now, talk to her."

"All right. You may want to talk to the counselor. When you lose one—"

"I didn't lose him, and that I know." She bit off the words, so they both knew how close she was to snapping. "I never had him."

She didn't speak on the way to the hospital, and Dave didn't push. In the silence, she stared out the window and outlined the questions she'd ask, the tone she would take, to build the foundation for what she needed to prove.

Tracey Percell rested on a gurney in the ER's exam room. She was young, Phoebe noted, barely old enough to drink. A well-endowed young blonde who needed her roots done.

Red-rimmed, swollen eyes were weepy yet as she gnawed on her thumbnail.

"He shot himself. He shot himself right in front of us."

"You had a horrible experience. It may help you to talk about it, and it would certainly help us. Do you think you could do that, Tracey?"

"Okay. I hyperventilated, they said. Passed out. They said I should lie down awhile, but he didn't hurt me. I'm really lucky he didn't hurt me. He punched Jasper, and he stuck the gun right in his face. And—"

"You must've been scared." Phoebe sat beside the bed, patted Tracey's hand before she took out her tape recorder. "Is it all right if I record what we talk about?"

"Sure. They said they were going to call my boyfriend. Brad? My boyfriend Brad's going to come."

"That's good. If he doesn't come before we leave, I'll check on Brad myself. How's that?"

"Thanks. Thanks." Tracey stopped biting her thumbnail as if the mere thought of having her boyfriend come was enough to settle her. "I feel so weird. Like I watched a scary movie, but I was in it."

"I know. But it's over now. You work for Mr. Hughes?"

"Uh-huh. I'm a legal secretary. It's not much, but it's okay."

"And you went to work today, just like usual."

"I go in to open the office at, like, ten to nine. Jasper got in at the same time today. Lots of times he's later, but we got there right before nine today. We'd barely opened when he came in. Mr. Gradey. He pushed right in the door and punched Jasper in the face. Knocked him down. I screamed because he had the gun. He looked crazy."

Tracey's eyes watered again as she snatched out two tissues from the box nested on her lap. "He looked just crazy."

"What happened then?"

"He said for me to get up and lock the door. He said he'd shoot Jasper dead if I tried to run. He had the gun right to his head, and I was scared; I just did what he said. He said for us to push the desk in front of the door, and when we didn't move fast enough, I guess, he shot the gun."

"He shot at you?"

"No. He shot it into the floor, put a hole in the carpet. I guess I screamed again, and I was crying. He said to shut the hell up and do what he said. So we did. Then he hit Jasper again and started yelling that he wanted his money. His six thousand five hundred twenty-eight dollars and thirty-six cents. Every penny." She started on her thumbnail again. "Um, I guess you could say Jasper sort of talked him out of the money, for, you know, expenses and costs for this suit. And, um, the suit didn't really go anywhere."

"He was a client?"

"Well, I guess Jasper didn't really put him on the books. So to speak." Her gaze skidded away. "I don't know all the particulars, really."

"We'll get to that later."

"Okay. It'd be better if you asked Jasper about all that anyway. Jasper told him he didn't have the money, and he said Jasper better get it or else. They were talking about going to the bank, then the cop came."

"The first officer arrived on scene at that time."

"Well, yeah. Sort of. You could hear the sirens, and Mr. Gradey made me go with him to the window and peek through the blinds. Mr. Gradey yelled out something like: 'Get the hell away. You try to come in and I'll kill everybody.' How he had two people in there and a gun, and he'd use it. Gradey told me to yell out, too, so I did, like, please, he means it."

She knuckled her eyes. "Gosh."

"You must've been scared."

"Oh my God, ma'am, I've never been so scared in my whole life."

"Did Mr. Gradey hurt you then?"

"No. No. He made me lie down on the floor, on my stomach. Jasper, too. Then the cop, I guess he had one of those what-do-you-call-it? Bullhorns? He called out how he was Officer Arnold Meeks, and how Mr. Gradey was to put down his weapon and come out with his hands up. Right quick, too, he said, like he meant business. And Mr. Gradey, he just yelled back he was William Gradey and we could all go to hell unless he got his six thousand five hundred twenty-eight dollars and thirty-six cents back.

"Then they just yelled at each other awhile."

"Yelled at each other?"

"Yelled and cursed at each other for I don't know how long. Mr. Gradey wanted to know where the cop was, where the law was when Jasper stole his money. And the cop's like, 'I'm not concerned with your money, and you better get your ass out here, boy, with your hands up.'"

Phoebe glanced at Dave. "How did Mr. Gradey react to that?"

"He got really pissed, you know, 'specially when the policeman said how Mr. Gradey didn't have the balls to shoot us. Honest to God, I thought he'd do it then and there just to prove the cop wrong. I couldn't stop crying."

"You heard the policeman say that?"

"Yes, ma'am. Only he didn't say Mr. Gradey didn't have the balls, he said 'you asshole.'"

Phoebe looked at Dave as Tracey began to shred one of her tissues into bits of fluff. "And so Mr. Gradey, he told the cop to come on in and get him, and he'd shoot him, and us, too. How he needed his money. He had to sell his car, and he didn't have anywhere to live, and the cop's saying he'll be living in a cell and won't need a car. After a while, it seemed like a long while, more cops came.

"Do you think Brad's here yet?"

"I'll go find out in just a minute. What happened next, Tracey?"

"Well, Mr. Gradey, he got more upset. I thought, I really thought he was just going to shoot us and get it over with. I started crying again, loud I guess. He told me not to worry, it wasn't my fault. Cops and lawyers, he said. It was cops and lawyers, and they always fucked over regular people. I think . . ."

"What do you think?" Phoebe prompted.

"I think he was going to let me go on out. I just got the feeling. Me, not Jasper. 'Cause he asked if he let me go out, would I tell the cops about the money, and I said I would. Sure I would. Then the phone rang. That cop Meeks yelled for Jasper to answer. 'Pick up the phone, you son of a bitch.'"

Tracey let out a sigh. "I know it sounds stupid, but that policeman scared me about as much as Mr. Gradey and the gun." She swiped at her eyes. "I wish he'd just shut up. I wish he had because I think Mr. Gradey was going to let me go, and maybe he wouldn't've shot himself in the head right in front of me. I don't know."

"Okay, Tracey. All right now," Phoebe soothed as Tracey began to sob.

"It was so *awful* to see. He said how I could sit up when he was asking me if I'd tell the police about the money. So I was sitting there on the floor when the phone rang and all. I couldn't hear what the other guy said, but I was watching Mr. Gradey. I was watching and thinking if he lets me go, I'm never coming back to this office. I'll go back, take some more business courses, get me a better job. Mr. Gradey didn't say much, but he looked sad. Scared. Sad and scared like I was, and he hung up the phone. Next time it rang, I didn't think he was going to answer. Then he looked at me and said how he was going to put it on speaker so I could see how y'all treated people like us. So I could see how we didn't have a chance. There was a woman on this time. It was you," Tracey said after a moment. "Sure, it was you. So you know what happened next."

"Yes. I know what happened next."

Phoebe waited until they were outside, away from people, in the balm of spring air. "He incited the suicide. He risked the lives of two hostages with his posturing. He ignored procedure, trampled over every guideline of negotiation. And for what?"

"Not every police officer has negotiation skills, or understands how to handle a hostage situation from that standpoint."

She rounded on it, couldn't stop herself. "Goddamn it, Dave. Are you defending him? Are you, for one second, defending what he did?"

"No." Dave held up a hand. "And I'm not going to argue with you, Phoebe. Not when you're right. Officer Meeks will be debriefed."

"I'll be debriefing him. It's my purview," she said before Dave could deny.

"And you and Arnie Meeks already have considerable friction. You were on the line with the subject when he terminated."

"If I don't debrief Meeks, it undermines my authority. He didn't call it in for nearly two hours. Right there, he's earned a rip. This isn't a matter of him having a problem with me. It's a matter of him being a problem, with a badge."

"You be careful it doesn't smell like payback."

"A man's dead. There's no paying it back."

Phoebe took her time, in fact took the rest of the long day, to gather statements, information, to write up her notes and complete the incident report.

Then she called Arnie into her office.

"I'm going off shift," he told her.

"Close the door. Sit down."

"I'm on eight-to-fours. I go past four, I put in the OT." But he swaggered over, took a seat. Lifted his jaw at the recorder on her desk. "What's this?"

"This conversation is being recorded for your protection, and mine."

"Maybe I need my delegate."

"If you want your delegate present, you're free to call him." Deliberately, she nudged the phone across the desk toward him. "Be my guest."

Arnie shrugged. "You got five minutes before I start clocking OT."

"At oh-nine-eleven this morning you responded to reports of gunfire at the offices of Jasper C. Hughes, Attorney at Law. Is that correct?"

"That's right."

"You responded to this location, running hot, approached the building in question. At that time, an individual inside the premises informed you he was armed, with two hostages. Is this correct?"

"If you're going to go through the whole report, we're wasting time."

"Did you call for backup or for a negotiation team at that time?"

"No. I had it handled. Until you got there."

"You identified yourself as a police officer, via bullhorn."

"I took cover, as procedure, and ID'd myself, sure. I told the guy to put down the gun, to come out. He refused."

Phoebe sat back. "You're right. We're wasting time. The reports are here, including witness statements, statements from both hostages, statements from the officers who arrived on scene subsequently. Which include the fact that you did not follow procedure, did not call for a

negotiation team, did not follow any of the guidelines in hostage negotiation and instead threatened and berated the hostage-taker into an
agitated state."

"Guy shoots up an office, he's already in an agitated state."

"And there, you're correct. You never tried to talk him down."
Though her eyes flashed fury, her voice stayed flat, cold, utterly calm.
"You told him you didn't care, you told him he was going to jail."

He sent her that tight, smirking smile. "Not supposed to lie in negotiations."

"You're going to want to wipe that smirk off your face, Officer. You
pushed and you pushed." She snatched up a page from a report. "'Officer Meeks then engaged the subject via telephone and advised the subject he'd be better off just putting the gun to his head and pulling the
trigger.'"

"Reverse psychology. It was under control until you got on the line.
Hostages made it out, didn't they? No loss of life."

"There were three people in that office. Only two walked out."

"Only two mattered."

"In your opinion, yes, which I assume is why you felt entitled to call
the hostage-taker a worthless fuck. Although I see nothing in the report
that indicates the hostages mattered to you. You never asked for or ascertained their condition, and took actions that endangered their well-
being—including telling the armed hostage-taker he didn't have the
balls to shoot the hostages."

"You want to blame somebody for your screwup, *ma'am*—"

"My actions will hold up, Officer, I promise you. Yours, on the other
hand, don't. You're suspended for thirty days."

He came up out of the chair. "Bullshit."

"The incident will be investigated, as will your actions during it.
Meanwhile, you are ordered to report to the departmental psychiatrist
for an evaluation within the next seventy-two hours."

The ugly red spread over his face, as it had in the lecture room.
"You're not running over me this way."

"You're free to protest the suspension, but I can tell you you'll find
Captain McVee, who has copies of all statements, in agreement with my
decision."

"He'd agree to flap his wings like a chicken seeing as you're blowing him."

She got slowly to her feet. "What did you say to me?"

"You think it's some secret you're sitting here because you let McVee bang you? We'll see who's fucking suspended when I'm done with you. Bitch."

"You're suspended, thirty days, and the tag for insubordination is going in your jacket. You're going to want to get out of here, Officer, before you make it worse."

He stepped to her desk, planted his hands on it, leaned forward. "It's going to get worse, for you. That's a promise."

She felt the clutch in her throat. "You're dismissed. Badge and weapon, Officer."

His hand moved to his sidearm, his fingers danced over it, and Phoebe saw something in his eyes that told her he was more than just an arrogant son of a bitch.

The quick rap on the door had her fighting not to jolt. Sykes poked his head in. "Sorry to interrupt. I need a minute, Lieutenant, when you've got one."

"I've got one. Officer Meeks? I gave you an order."

He unclipped his weapon, tossed it and his badge onto her desk. When he turned and stalked out, Phoebe allowed herself one shuddering breath.

"You okay, LT?"

"Yes. Yes. What do you need?"

"Nothing. Things looked a little heated in here, that's all."

"Okay. Yeah. Thanks." She wanted to sink down in her chair, made herself stand. "Detective? You've been around here a long time."

"Twelve years."

"Hear a lot of the gossip, the buzz?"

"Sure."

"Detective, is it common belief that Captain McVee and I have a sexual relationship?"

He looked so stunned that her stomach instantly smoothed. "Jesus, Lieutenant, no." Sykes closed the door behind him. "Did that asshole say that?"

"Yeah. Let's leave it inside here, please. Let's leave the whole thing inside this office."

"If that's what you want." Sykes nodded down at Arnie's badge and gun. "I'll say one more thing I'd like to stay in this office. It doesn't break my heart to see that. You interested in my opinion, between you and me?"

"I am. Yeah, I'm interested."

"He'd never have had those in the first place without family connections. Guy's a loose cannon, boss. You watch your back."

"I'll be doing just that. Thank you. Thanks, Bull."

Sykes twinkled a little at her use of his nickname. He started for the door, stopped with his hand on the knob. "I guess some of us think of you as the captain's favorite niece. There were grumbles when you came in from the feds and took over here. Some of them were mine. Grumbling stopped pretty quick, from most. You're a good boss, Lieutenant. That's what counts around here."

"Thanks."

When he went out, she let herself sit. Let herself shake.

5

What didn't suck, Phoebe decided, was to come home after a viciously bad day and find two dozen stargazer lilies waiting for her. Essie had arranged them into quite a show in Cousin Bess's big Waterford vase, culling out a trio from the field for Phoebe's bedroom.

"You can have the whole lot up in your room, of course, but I thought—"

"No, this is fine. This is lovely." Phoebe leaned over for a sniff of them where they stood elegant and splashy on the piecrust table in the family parlor. "We can all enjoy them here."

"I didn't read the note." Essie handed it over. "And I have to admit, it was a bitter war of conscience and curiosity. Even though I know who sent them."

"I suppose he did. Well." Phoebe tapped the little envelope on her palm.

"Oh, for God's sake, Phoebe, read it!" Ava stood behind Carly, rubbing the girl's shoulders. "We're dying here. I considered wrestling your mama to the ground for that note."

Phoebe supposed when a man sent flowers to a house with four females, he sent them to all. She opened the envelope, and read.

" 'See you Saturday. Duncan.' "

"That's it?" Disappointment dragged through Ava's voice. "Not
much of a poet, is he?"

"I'd say he's letting the flowers speak for themselves," Essie corrected. "That's poetical enough."

"Mama, is he your boyfriend?"

"He's just someone I'm going to have dinner with tomorrow," Phoebe
told Carly.

" 'Cause Sherrilynn's big sister has a boyfriend, and he makes her
cry all the time. She lays across the bed in her room and cries *all* the
time, Sherrilynn says."

"And I bet Sherrilynn's big sister enjoys every minute of it." Phoebe
reached down to cup Carly's face. "I'm not much of a crier myself."

"You cried when you called Roy last time."

A mother could never hide tears from a child, and a mother who
thought she could was delusional. "Not so very much. I'm going to go
up and change. I heard a rumor it's pizza night around here."

"And DVD and popcorn night!"

"I heard that, too. I want to go take off my work, and put on
my play."

Upstairs, Phoebe sat on the side of the bed. Could a mother ever
really protect her child from her mistakes, or the ripples from them that
spread all through a life?

Weren't they in this house now because of a single event from more
than twenty years before? Weren't they all who they were, with their
lives tangled together under this roof, because of that steamy summer
night when she was twelve? Decisions she made, actions she took, even
words she spoke would affect her daughter forever. Just as her mother's
had affected her.

Mama had done her best, Phoebe thought. But trusting a man with
herself, with her children, had changed the course of their world.

And she remembered it all, every movement, every moment, as if it
were yesterday.

The room was a box of heat, stained with the grease of his sweat. He'd begun to swig whiskey straight from the bottle of Wild Turkey Mama kept up high in the kitchen cupboard, so the stench of whiskey added another smear to the trapped air.

Phoebe hoped he'd drink enough to pass out before he used the .45 clutched in his free hand that he'd taken to waving around like a mean little boy with a pointy stick.

Put your eye out, you're not careful.

He'd already fired off a few rounds, but just to kill lamps or bric-a-brac and put holes in the walls. He'd held it to Mama's head, too, screaming and cursing as he'd dragged her across the floor by her long red hair.

But he hadn't shot Mama, not yet, or made good on his threats to put a bullet in Phoebe's little brother Carter, or Phoebe herself.

But he could, he could, and he made sure they knew he would if *they gave him any goddamn lip.* So fear lived in the box, too, a terrible, helpless fear that hung in the trapped air like blackflies.

Though all the shades were drawn or the curtains pulled tight over the windows, she knew the police were outside. He talked to them on the phone, Reuben did. She wished she knew what they were saying to him because he mostly calmed down afterward.

If she knew, for sure, what they said to calm him, maybe she could say it, too, in the in-between times he got tired of talking to them and hung up the phone and before he stirred himself up hot again and they had to try to cool him off, one more time.

He called the person on the other end of the phone Dave, as if they were friends, and once he'd gone on a long ramble about fishing.

Now, he'd gone back to pacing and drinking and cursing. The terrible in-between time. Phoebe no longer flinched when he swung the barrel of the gun toward the sofa where she and Carter huddled.

She was too tired to flinch.

He'd broken in just after supper, when the sun had still been up. It had been down a long time now. So long, she thought maybe it would be coming up again before long.

Reuben had shot the pretty little clock with the mother-of-pearl face that had been a wedding present to Mama and Daddy, where it sat on the dropleaf table, so Phoebe couldn't be sure how many hours had passed since its death at five minutes past seven.

Mama loved that clock. Phoebe knew that's why Reuben had killed it, because Mama set such store by that sweet little clock.

When the phone rang again, he slammed the bottle on the little table and snatched it up.

"Dave, you son of a bitch, I said I want the electric turned back *on*. Don't you fucking tell me you're working on it."

He waved the gun, and Phoebe heard Carter suck in his breath. She rubbed a hand over the point of his knee to keep him still, to keep him quiet.

As much store as Mama set by the little clock, she set a lot more by Carter. Reuben knew that, too. So hurting Carter was bound to be somewhere on Reuben's list of things to do.

"Don't you fucking tell me we're going to work this out. You're not in here sweating like a goddamn pig, using goddamn oil lamps. You get the air back on in here, and right quick, and the lights, or I'm going to hurt one of these kids. Essie, get your skinny, worthless ass over here and tell him I mean what I say. *Now!*"

Phoebe watched as her mother pushed out of the chair he'd ordered her to sit in. Her face looked haggard in the lamplight, her eyes stunned as a trapped rabbit. When she was close enough to take the phone, he hooked an arm around her throat, pressed the barrel of the gun to her temple.

Beside Phoebe, Carter braced to leap. Phoebe gripped his hand, hard, shook her head, to keep him on the couch. "Don't." She barely breathed the word. "He'll hurt her if you try."

"Tell him I mean what I say!"

Essie kept her eyes straight ahead. "He means what he says."

"Tell him what I'm doing now."

Tears slid down her cheeks, bumping into the dried blood from the cut his fist had ripped there earlier. "He's holding a gun to my head. My children are sitting together on the sofa. They're frightened. Please, do what he wants."

"You should've done what I wanted, Essie." He closed his hand over her breast, squeezed. "You should've kept doing what I wanted, then none of this would be happening. I told you you'd be sorry, didn't I?"

"Yes, Reuben, you told me."

"You hear that, Dave? It's her fault. Whatever happens in here, it's her fault. I was to put a bullet in her useless brain right now, it's her own damn fault."

"Mr. Reuben?" Phoebe heard her own voice, calm as a spring morning. It felt like it came from someone else, someone whose heart wasn't punching like fists into her throat. But Reuben's hard eyes tracked over and latched onto her.

"I ask you to talk, little bitch?"

"No, sir. I just thought maybe you were getting hungry. Maybe you want me to make you a sandwich. We've got some nice ham."

Phoebe didn't—couldn't—allow herself to look at her mother. She felt her mama's fear rising like a flood, and if she looked at it head-on she might drown in it.

"You figure if you fix me a sandwich, I won't shoot your whore of a mother in the head?"

"I don't know. But we got some nice ham, and some potato salad." She wasn't going to cry, Phoebe realized. It surprised her there weren't any tears pushing against that hammering heart. But there was fury in there, bubbling with the nerves in her belly. "I made the potato salad myself. It's good."

"Go on then, take that lamp with you. Don't think I can't see you in there. You try anything stupid, I'm going to shoot your baby brother in the balls."

"Yes, sir." She rose, lifted the little oil lamp. "Mr. Reuben? Can I use the bathroom first, please? I really have to go."

"Jesus Christ. Cross your legs and hold it."

"I've been holding it, Mr. Reuben. If I could just use the bathroom, real quick, I'd make you a nice plate of food." She cast her eyes down. "I could leave the door open. Please?"

"You better piss fast. I don't like how long you take, I'll start breaking your mama's fingers."

"I'll be fast." She hurried toward the bathroom right off the living room.

She put the lamp on the back of the toilet, then, yanking down her pants, prayed that nerves and simple embarrassment wouldn't clamp her bladder shut. She shot a quick glance at the window over the tub. Too small, she knew, for her to wiggle out of. Carter could probably make it. If she could convince Reuben to let Carter use the bathroom, she'd tell Carter to try to get out.

She hopped up, flushing with one hand, reaching up to ease open the medicine cabinet with the other. "Yes, sir!" she called back when Reuben shouted at her to hurry the hell up.

She grabbed the little bottle of her mother's Valium from the top shelf, stuffed it into her pocket.

When Phoebe came out, Reuben shoved her mother so that Essie went sprawling toward the sofa. "You there, Dave? I'm going to have me a little bite to eat. If the electric isn't on by the time I finish, I'm going to play eenie meenie miny mo and kill one of these kids. You go make that sandwich, Phoebe. And don't be stingy with the potato salad."

It was a shotgun house, and small with it. Phoebe made sure she stayed in his line of sight as she took the ham and the salad out of the refrigerator.

She could hear him talking to Dave, and struggled to keep her hands steady while she got out a plate and a saucer. A million dollars? Now he wanted a million dollars and a Cadillac, along with a free pass over the state line. Stupid as he was mean, Phoebe decided. Using the big blue bowl of potato salad as cover, she dumped pills on the saucer. Using her mother's pestle, she crushed them as best she could. She dumped a generous scoop of potato salad on the pills, mixed them together.

She slathered mustard on two pieces of bread, slapped some ham and slices of American cheese between them. Maybe if she could get a knife out of the drawer, maybe—

"What's taking so fucking long?"

Phoebe's head jerked up. He'd put down the phone—she hadn't been paying close enough attention—and with the gun jammed under Carter's chin, was halfway to the kitchen doorway.

"I'm sorry. I just have to get you a fork for the potato salad." Palming the pill bottle, she turned, yanked open the flatware drawer. She let the bottle drop in as she reached down for a fork. "You want some lemonade, Mr. Reuben? Mama made it fresh just—"

"Get that food out here, girl, and quick."

She snatched up the plate. It was easy to let the fear show, to let it mask everything else. Seeing the gun under Carter's jaw overwhelmed even her rage. Her hands shook so the plate bobbed up and down. When he smiled, she understood their fear was part of what he wanted. Giving it to him cost her nothing.

"Put that plate by the phone there, and go sit your skinny ass down on the sofa."

She did exactly as she was told, but before Phoebe could sit, Reuben lifted his leg to give Carter a solid boot on the ass that sent the boy pitching forward. Essie leaped up, stopping only when Phoebe blocked her way, shot her a fierce look.

Phoebe walked over to pull Carter up herself. "Hush, Carter! Mr. Reuben doesn't want to hear all that crying while he's trying to eat."

"Got some sense." With a nod, Reuben sat, laid the gun across his lap. He picked up the fork with one hand, the phone with the other. "Don't know where you came by it with that worthless whore who raised you. Where's that electric, Dave?" he said into the phone, and took a forkful of potato salad.

While Carter sniffled in their mother's arms, Phoebe watched Reuben eat. Had she put enough pills in? Enough to make him pass out? The liquor he washed down the food with would help, wouldn't it?

Maybe it would kill him. She'd read about things like that, pills and liquor. Maybe the son of a bitch would just die.

She leaned down, whispered into Carter's ear. Her brother shook his head, so she pinched him, hard. "You do just what I say, or I'll slap you stupid."

"Shut the hell up over there! Did I tell you to talk?"

"I'm sorry, Mr. Reuben. I was just telling him not to cry. He's gotta pee, too. Can he just go use the bathroom, Mr. Reuben? I'm sorry, Mr. Reuben, but it'll be an awful mess if he wets his pants. It'll only take him a minute."

"Christ's sake! G'wan, then."

Phoebe closed her hand over Carter's, squeezed viciously. "Go on, Carter. Do what you're told."

Knuckling his eyes, Carter pushed off the sofa and dragged his heels into the bathroom.

"Mr. Reuben?"

Mama hissed at her to stay quiet, but Phoebe ignored her. Carter could get out. If Reuben didn't think about him for a few minutes, Carter could get out.

"Do you think if I asked that man to turn on the electric, he would? It's so hot. Maybe if I asked him, if I told him we're all so hot, he'd turn it on?"

"Hear that, Dave?" Reuben kicked back in his chair and grinned. His glassy eyes drooped. "Got a kid wants to negotiate with you. Sure, what the fuck. Come on over here."

When Phoebe stood in front of him, Reuben passed her the phone. And pressed the gun to her belly. "Tell him what I'm doing first."

Sweat snaked a slow, fat line down her back. Why didn't the pills *work*? Had Carter wriggled out the window?

"Mister? He's got the gun at my stomach, and I'm awful scared. We're so hot. No, we're not hurt, but we're so hot it's going to make us *sick*. If we could just have the air-conditioning back on, maybe we could *sleep*, 'cept we're so scared I guess we'd need a bunch of sleeping pills or something. Please, mister, would you please turn on the electricity?

"And, sir?" She gripped the phone tighter when Reuben reached for it. When he shrugged, leaned back, the wave of relief was like giddiness. "Could you please give him the money and the car he wants? He's been real nice to us since I gave him the potato salad I made myself. He even let me go to the bathroom first. We're all just so tired we might just pass out any minute, you know?"

Reuben held out a hand for the phone, then gave her a nasty little poke with the gun to move her back. "Hear that, Dave? This girl here, she wants the electric back on. Wants me to have the money and that Caddy. Hell no, I didn't let them get anything to eat, and I won't till that electric's back on. Fact, I'm gonna go eenie meenie right now and . . . Where's that boy? Where is that little shit?"

"Mr. Reuben, he's right . . ." Phoebe shot out her arm as if to point and knocked over the bottle of Wild Turkey. "Oh, I'm sorry! I'm sorry. I'll clean it right up. I'll—"

She went down, pain searing over her face as the back of his hand slammed against her cheek. "Stupid bitch!" He lurched up, staggered. Phoebe looked straight into the barrel of the gun.

Like the wrath of God, Essie leaped off the couch and onto his back.

He bucked; she bit. Her nails scraped like razors down his face as they both screamed, both cursed. Phoebe scrambled back in a crab walk, barely avoiding a bullet as Reuben went down to his knees under Essie's assault.

"Help us! Help us now!" Phoebe shouted until her lungs burned. She grabbed the bottle, prepared to whale in, but Reuben went down, flat on his face. Weeping, screaming, Essie continued to pound him with her fists, even when the door burst open. Even when men rushed in with guns.

"Don't shoot us. Don't shoot us." Weeping, Phoebe crawled to her mother.

Things slowed down to a dream, it seemed like. And in the dream people walked her through water where voices echoed and the lights hurt her eyes. Once, she fell asleep, and did dream. But the dream was so scary she pushed herself awake again.

Mama had to have X-rays of her face to make sure her cheekbone wasn't broken, and stitches to close the gash. Phoebe sat in the little room in the hospital. She didn't want to lie down, didn't want to sleep again and fall back into the dream where the gun exploded, and the bullet—like a live thing—hunted her down and killed her.

Carter slept curled up in a ball on the narrow bed. His fists were clenched, and off and on his body twitched like a horse's did when flies landed on it.

Doctors and nurses and police came in and out, and asked questions. When they did, she wanted them to go away. When they went away, she wished they'd come back so she wasn't alone.

But there'd been water to drink, to wash the grit that had coated her throat. And then icy Coca-Cola, straight from the bottle.

She wanted her mother. She wanted Mama so bad it hurt worse than Reuben's hand across her face.

When a man came in with a big McDonald's takeout bag, the smell of burgers and fries had her stomach jittering with sudden and acute hunger.

He smiled at her, glanced at Carter, then came over to sit beside Phoebe on the bed. "Thought you might be hungry. Don't know about you, but I'd rather skip the hospital food. I'm Dave."

She knew she stared, knew it was rude. But she'd expected Dave to be old—older anyway. He looked barely older than the high school boys Phoebe liked to sigh over in secret. His hair was a light brown with a lot of curl to it, his eyes shades lighter and blue. He wore a dark blue shirt, open at the collar. And he smelled just a little sweaty.

He held out his hand, but when Phoebe offered hers, he didn't shake it. He held it, firm, just the way his eyes held hers. "I'm really happy to meet you, Phoebe. Really happy to see you."

"I'm glad to meet you, too."

Then she did what she hadn't done in all the hours inside the hot little house, in all the time she'd waited while her brother slept.

She cried.

Dave sat, held her hand. He didn't say a thing. At one point he got up, dug up a box of tissues and put them in her lap. When her tears slowed, he pulled the Quarter Pounders and fries out of the bag.

"My mama," Phoebe began.

"She's going to be fine. I checked on her, and I asked if I could have a little time with you before they took you and your brother to her, or brought her to you. Looks like he could use some sleep anyway."

"I guess."

"I know you were scared, but you were smart, too, and you were brave."

"I wasn't brave. I was mad." She picked up the burger, bit in. Her stomach clenched as if deciding whether or not it would accept the food. Then it relaxed again. "Carter was brave for climbing out the window."

"He said you told him to, that you said you'd slap him stupid if he didn't do it."

She flushed a little because she was forbidden to hit her brother. Even though there were occasions she judged he'd earned it enough for her to break the rule.

"I guess I did."

"Why?"

"Reuben would've hurt him. He'd've hurt him bad before he hurt me, or even Mama again. Because he's the baby, and Reuben knows Mama loves him more than anything."

"You'd already put the pills in the food before you told Carter to climb out the window."

"I should've put more in. I wasn't sure how many. You knew what I was trying to tell you, right away." She picked up a fry. "I felt better when I was talking to you."

"It was smart of you to find a way to tell me you put something in his food. It bought me just a little more time."

"How come you didn't turn the electric back on? He got so mad about that."

"Well, you know how you talked him into letting you go to the bathroom before you fixed his food? It's kind of like that. You try to get something back, like an exchange. Fact was, I was about to when we spotted Carter climbing out the window. I wanted to keep Reuben talking—or let you talk—while we got Carter to safety and figured out the new situation. Did you knock over the bottle to distract him, so he'd be mad at you and forget about Carter?"

"I figured he'd hit me, but I didn't know he'd get that mad. I think he'd have shot me if Mama hadn't jumped on him. I should've given him more pills, is what. Then it wouldn't have taken so long for him to pass out. Mama wouldn't've had the pills if it wasn't for him. That's irony." She smiled a little when Dave laughed. "I learned about irony in English class. She got the pills because he made her so upset and nervous. He pretended to be nice when he met her, when they started going out. But he started picking on her, and us, and pushing his weight around. He slapped her once, right across the face."

"She had a restraining order on him."

Phoebe nodded. "She told him she wouldn't see him anymore and to go away. But he kept coming around, or going to her work. Following her in his car. I think more than that, but she wouldn't tell me. He came to the house one night, too, drunk, and she called the police. They made him go away, but that's all they did."

"I'm sorry we didn't do more."

"They told her she could get that restraining order, so she did. I don't see how it helped her any."

"No. I'm sorry about that, too. It seems to me, Phoebe, your mother did everything right, everything she could do to protect herself and her family."

Phoebe stared down at the paper napkin balled in her fist. "Why didn't he just go away when she said she didn't want him?"

"I don't know."

It wasn't the answer she wanted, Phoebe decided. Worse, it was kin to a lie. She hated when grown-ups lied because they didn't think you could understand.

Phoebe ate more fries and shook her head. "Maybe you don't know exactly, but you sort of do. You just think I won't understand 'cause I'm only twelve—almost twelve. But I understand lots of things."

He studied her another moment, as if he could read something on her face like the words in a book. "Okay, I do sort of know, or I have an opinion. I think he's mean, he's a bully, and he didn't like the idea of anyone telling him what to do, or what he could have, especially a woman like your mother. So he tried to scare her and intimidate her, and he got madder and madder because it wasn't working the way he wanted. I think he wanted to hurt her, to show her he was the boss, and it got out of hand, even for him."

Phoebe ate another fry. "I think he's a son of a bitch."

"Yeah, that, too. Now he's going to be a son of a bitch in jail, for a long time."

She thought about this as she sucked on the Coke he'd brought her. "On TV, they usually shoot the bad guy. The SWAT team shoots him."

"I like it better when nobody gets shot. What you did in there? It helped it work out so nobody died. Dying's a short end, Phoebe. I know you're tired, and you want to see your mother." He stood, then pulled a card out of his pocket. "I want you to know you can call me anytime.

You need to talk about all this again, or ask questions, or you need help with anything, you just call me."

She took the card and read: Detective David McVee. "Carter, too? And Mama?"

"Absolutely. Anything, Phoebe, anytime."

"Okay, thanks. Thanks for the burger and fries."

"My pleasure, that's a fact." This time when he offered his hand, he shook hers. "You take care of yourself, and your family."

"I will."

When he left, Phoebe put his card in her pocket. She rolled up the takeout bag to help keep the food Dave had brought for Carter warm, shoved the trash in the waste bin.

She crossed to the window to look out. The sun had come up. She didn't know when dawn had broken or how long it had been light. But she knew the dark hours were over.

When the door opened and her mother stood there, her arms open wide, Phoebe all but flew into them.

"Mama, Mama, Mama."

"My sweet girl. My baby girl."

"Your face. Mama—"

"It's all right. I'm all right."

How could it be all right with that line of stitches running down her mother's lovely cheek, marring her soft, soft skin? When her sparkling blue eyes were dull and the bruising crawled out around them?

But Essie put her hands on Phoebe's shoulders. "It's nothing. We're safe, we're all safe. That's everything. Oh God, Phoebe, I'm so sorry."

"Not you. Not you." Tears spilled again as Essie brushed kisses over the bruise on Phoebe's jaw. "Mama, it wasn't your fault. Dave even said so."

"I let Reuben into our lives. I opened the door to him. That much, at least, is my fault." She stepped away to walk over, to lean over Carter and rest her cheek on his head. "God, God, if anything had happened to you, to either of you, I don't know what I'd do. You got him out," she murmured. "You got Carter out of the house. It's more than I did."

"No, Mama—"

"I'll never look at you quite the same way again, Phoebe." Essie straightened. "I'll always look at you and see my little girl, my own baby girl, but now, every time I look at you, I'll see a hero."

"You beat him down to the floor," Phoebe reminded her. "I guess you're a hero, too."

"Maybe at the end of it. Well, I hate to wake him up, but I don't want to stay in this hospital anymore."

"Can we go home now?"

Essie brushed a hand over Carter's hair, faced her daughter again. "We're never going back there. I never want to go inside that place again. I'm sorry. I'd never feel safe."

"But where can we go?"

"We're going to stay with Cousin Bess. I called her, and she said we're to come."

"To the big house?" The idea of it had Phoebe's eyes opening wide. "But you and Cousin Bess don't hardly speak. You don't even like her."

"This morning, she's my favorite person in the world, save you and Carter. And we're going to be grateful to her, Phoebe, for opening her home to us when we need it."

"She didn't open it to us when Daddy died, or when—"

"Now she is." Essie snapped out the words. "And we're grateful to her. It's what we have to do."

"For now?"

"It's what we have to do," Essie repeated.

They rode to Cousin Bess's in a police car while Carter wolfed down the cold burger and fries, gulped down the Coke. They circled the park with the fountain sparkling in the air. The grand old house was rosy brick and soft white trim; it was lush with green lawn and tended flowers and draping trees.

It was a world away from the tiny shotgun house where Phoebe had lived for more than eight of her twelve years.

She noted her mother's back was poker straight as they climbed up the stone steps to the front door, so she stiffened hers as well.

Mama rang the bell like company would, rather than family. The woman who answered the door was young and bright and beautiful. She made Phoebe think of a movie star with her golden fall of hair and slender build.

There was sympathy on her face as she held out her hands to Essie. "Mrs. MacNamara, I'm Ava Vestry, Ms. MacNamara's personal assistant. Come in, come in. Your rooms are all ready for you. You must be exhausted, so I'll take you right up. Or if you'd rather have some breakfast, or some tea?"

"They don't need anyone fussing over them."

Cousin Bess made the announcement from the curve of the grand stairs. She stood, dressed in a crow-black dress, her thin face pinched with disapproval. Her hair was as gray as a Brillo pad with odd wings of black at either temple.

Now, as always, the first glimpse of her father's cousin made Phoebe think of the mean Almira Gulch, come to stuff Toto in her basket.

Wicked old witch.

"Thank you for taking us in, Cousin Bess," Mama said in the same quiet voice she'd used when Reuben had a gun to her head.

"Doesn't surprise me you got yourself into a mess. The three of you are to wash, thoroughly, before you sit at my table or lie on my sheets."

"I'll see to it, Ms. MacNamara." Ava turned her beautiful, compassionate smile onto Phoebe, then Carter. "Maybe the children are hungry. Maybe after their bath, I could ask the cook to make pancakes or—"

Apparently the idea of more food after the horrors of the night, the burger, the fries, the ride in a police car, was too much for Carter's stomach. It tossed up the Quarter Pounder right there on Cousin Bess's antique Aubusson carpet.

Mortified, exhausted, Phoebe just closed her eyes. Maybe she hadn't been shot and killed, but she was sure her life was over.

Mama had tended Cousin Bess's house for twenty years now, scrubbing, polishing, arranging. She'd served that demanding old woman until the day she died.

Through those two decades, the house had become Essie's world—not just her home, or even her sanctuary. Her entire world. And what was outside it, her fears. It had been nearly a decade since Essie had gone beyond its terraces, its courtyard.

Reuben's death in prison hadn't broken those locks for her, Phoebe thought as she rose to put her gun in the lockbox on the top shelf of her closet. The bitter end to Cousin Bess's bitter life hadn't thrown the doors open for her.

In fact, it seemed to Phoebe those events had simply added more and stronger locks.

If Cousin Bess had done the right thing, the kind thing and—fat chance—passed the house to her mother instead of shackling Phoebe to it, would things have been different? Better? Would her mother be able to walk out of the house, stroll over to the park, pop in and visit a neighbor?

They'd never know.

Where would she herself be now if not for that night? Would she have married Roy? Would she have found a way to keep her marriage together, to give her daughter the father she deserved?

She'd never know that either.

So they'd have the lilies in the parlor, order pizza, and settle in together for a Friday night at home.

And Phoebe would go out to dinner Saturday—just this once. There was too much in her life already that needed tending without adding a man to it.

She'd cried when she spoke to Roy last, yes, she had. But those tears had mostly been anger. She'd shed most of the sorrow and disappointment long before, when Carly had been only a baby.

Too much that needed tending, Phoebe thought again as she changed.

She glanced at the blush pink lilies in the cobalt-blue vase on her dresser. Flowers were lovely. But blooms faded and died.

6

Still, flowers and an evening of girl movies smoothed out a lot of edges. At the end of the marathon, Phoebe carried her sleeping daughter to bed. Any-o'clock made it to just past midnight this time.

Twenty minutes later, Phoebe was as deeply asleep as her daughter.

The sound of the doorbell had her bolting straight up in bed. She rolled out, glancing at the bedside clock—three-fifteen—before snatching up her robe. She was already at the steps and starting down when Essie and Ava came out of their rooms.

"Was that the doorbell?" Essie clutched her robe closed at the neck, and her knuckles were white. "At this hour?"

"Probably just kids fooling around. You stay up here with Carly, okay? In case it woke her."

"Don't open the door. Don't—"

"Don't worry, Mama."

That twenty-year-old fear, Phoebe knew, was always waiting to push off from the bottom of the dark pool toward the surface.

"I'll go with you. Probably just a couple half-drunk teenagers play-ing pranks," Ava said before Phoebe could object.

No point in making it bigger than it was, Phoebe decided, and let Ava walk down with her. "She'll be upset the rest of the night," Phoebe murmured.

"I'll see she takes a sleeping pill if she needs it. Stupid kids."

Phoebe peered through the pattern of textured glass on the panel of the front door and saw nothing. They'd run off, she thought, likely laughing hysterically as kids would over waking up a household.

But when she rose to her toes to study the veranda more carefully, she saw it.

"Go on up, Ava, tell Mama it was nothing. Just kids being a nuisance."

"What is it?" Ava clutched at Phoebe's arm. "Is there something out there?"

"Go on up and tell Mama. I don't want her scared. Tell her I'm just getting a glass of water while I'm down here."

"What is it? I'll go up and get Steven's baseball bat. Don't you open that door until—"

"Ava, nobody's out there, but I need to open this door, and I can't until you go up and tell Mama everything's fine. She's working herself up into a state by now. You know she is."

"Damn it." Loyalty to Essie overrode the rest. "I'm coming right back."

Phoebe waited until Ava was up the stairs before she unlocked the door. She scanned the street—right, left, across—but her gut told her whoever had rung the bell was gone. She had only to crouch down to pick up what lay on the doorstep. Then she shut the door and relocked it before carrying it into the kitchen to set it on the table.

The doll had bright red hair. It had probably been long hair once but had been crudely hacked off. Whoever had done it had stripped it, bound its hands with clothesline, affixed a square of duct tape across its mouth. Red paint was splattered and smeared over the doll to simulate blood.

"Oh my God, Phoebe!"

Phoebe held up a hand, continued to study the doll. "Carly? Mama?"

"Carly slept through it. I told Essie it was nothing, and you were staying down just a little while in case those kids came back so you could give them a scare and a piece of your mind."

"Good."

"That horrible thing." Ava laid the ball bat she'd snatched out of her son's closet on the table beside it.

"Honey, why don't you get me the camera from the server drawer? I want to take some pictures for my files."

"But shouldn't you call the police?"

"Ava, you're always forgetting I *am* the police."

"But—"

"I'll be taking it in, but I want my own pictures. Don't worry, whoever did this isn't coming back tonight. He delivered the message. And don't tell Mama about this," Phoebe added as she went into the tool drawer for a measuring tape. "Not yet."

"Of course I won't tell her. Phoebe, I wish you'd call Dave. I wish you'd call Dave right now and tell him someone put this *thing* that's meant to be you right on the doorstep."

"I'm not going to wake Dave at this hour. There's nothing he can do." Phoebe rubbed a hand on Ava's arm as she walked back to the table. "But I'll talk to him about it, I promise. Get me that camera now, all right?"

She measured, took pictures, then double bagged the doll in plastic, tucked it into a shopping bag and stowed it in the foyer closet.

Essie called out softly as Phoebe passed her bedroom door. "Honey? Everything all right?"

"It's fine." Phoebe stopped in Essie's doorway. Her mother looked so young and vulnerable in the big old bed. "Excitement's over for the night. You going to be able to get back to sleep?"

"I think so. Kids pulling pranks. What are you going to do?"

"Don't let them know it bothered you. 'Night, Mama."

In her bedroom, Phoebe set the alarm for six. She'd take the doll into the precinct, file a report, be home again before anyone knew she'd gone out. She'd ask Sykes to look into it. He was solid and smart. If the doll could be traced, he'd trace it.

Nobody, nobody was going to upset her family.

As she lay sleepless in the dark, already knowing she wouldn't need the alarm, she wondered where Arnie Meeks had been at three-fifteen.

It had been enough to see the lights come on in her fancy house. Flash, flash, flash. Enough to see that before he'd bolted into the park, into the trees. Into the dark.

But it had been even better—a nice bonus—to see her open the door and pick up her little present. Worth the time, worth the trouble, yeah, to see her come out for his gift.

Just some foreplay, bitch, he thought as he drove home. Just a little tickle before the main event.

He wasn't nearly finished with Phoebe MacNamara.

She'd have canceled the date if it wouldn't have made the incident the night before too important. And if canceling wouldn't have meant answering a dozen questions from her mother, and even from Carly.

She'd already answered her share that morning as it had taken her longer than she'd hoped to deliver the evidence, make a report, get home again on the damn CAT. At least she'd had the foresight to wear sweats so she could use the excuse—simply lie, Phoebe admitted—and say she'd gone for an early run in the park.

Then, of course, Carly had walked her feet off during the afternoon. The battle of wills over the purchase of the "cutest" outfit had tried her patience so that she and her daughter were *not* on the best of terms when they'd returned home—Carly to sulk in her room and Phoebe to escape to the courtyard chaise with a broad-brimmed hat on her head.

Now she had to go out to dinner, she thought, as, after refusing all opinions, she pulled out her all-purpose black dress. If it was good enough for weddings, funerals and the occasional cocktail party, it was good enough for a dinner date.

The fashionista gene had skipped a generation, she decided with some irritation, along with the curls and dimples.

She started to put her hair up, but fiddling with it made her think of the rudely shorn hair on the doll. She left it down. And while she

knew her family would have preferred a little time to grill her date—
and for Phoebe to make an entrance down the stairs—she made sure she
was in the parlor well before seven.

And at the door first when the bell rang.

"Hello, Duncan."

"First let me say: Wow. Then, hello, Phoebe."

She stepped back, raised her eyebrows at the nosegay of pink rose-
buds he carried. "You already sent me flowers, which are gorgeous, by
the way."

"Glad you liked them. This isn't for you." He glanced around the
foyer. "I like your house."

"We do, too."

"Phoebe, aren't you going to invite the man past the foyer, introduce him?" Essie stepped out of the parlor, aimed a smile at Duncan.
"I'm Essie MacNamara, Phoebe's mother."

"Ma'am." He took the hand she offered. "It sounds like a line, but
has to be said anyway. I can see where Phoebe gets her impressive looks."

"Thank you. I'm pleased it had to be said. Come on into the parlor.
My son and his wife aren't here, but I'll introduce you to the rest of the
family. Ava, this is Phoebe's friend Duncan."

"I'm so pleased to meet you."

"Phoebe didn't mention so many beauties in the family. She did
mention you." He smiled over at Carly. "I went for pink." He held out
the flowers.

"Isn't that sweet!" Essie had already melted. "Carly, this is Mr.
Swift. And I believe those are your first roses from a gentleman caller."

The sulky child tumbled into a coy female. "They're mine?"

"Unless you hate pink."

"I like pink." She flushed nearly the color of the buds she took from
him. "Thank you. Gran, can I pick a vase for them myself? Can I?"

"Of course you can. Mr. Swift, can I offer you something to drink?"

"Duncan. I—"

"We should go," Phoebe interrupted. "The dazzle in here's getting
blinding." She picked up a jacket from the back of a chair. "I won't
be late."

"Ouch," Duncan said.

Ignoring him, Phoebe bent to kiss Carly's cheek. "Behave."

"You enjoy yourselves," Essie said. "And Duncan, you be sure to come back."

"Thanks. Next time I'll have to bring a meadow. Nice to meet you all."

Phoebe knew very well there were three faces plastered to the parlor window when Duncan opened the car door for her. She sent him a thoughtful look, then slipped inside.

She sent him the same look when he got behind the wheel. "Are you trying to clear the path by charming my daughter?"

"Absolutely. Now that I know about your mother and Ava, I'll work on them."

"Now I have to decide whether to appreciate your honesty or be insulted by it."

"Let me know when you make up your mind. Meanwhile, do you hate boats?"

"Why?"

"Because if you hate boats I need to make an adjustment. So, do you?"

"No, I don't hate boats."

"Good." He flipped out a cell phone, punched a number. "Duncan. We're on the way. Good. Great. Thanks." He clicked it closed. "Your daughter looks like your mother. The dimples missed you."

"To my great sadness."

"How's Ava related?"

"Not by blood, but she's still family."

He nodded in a way that told her he understood completely. "And you have an older brother."

"Younger. Carter's younger."

"Okay. Do he and his wife live in that great house with you, too?"

"No, they have their own place. What made you think to bring Carly roses?"

"Ah . . . Well, I don't know much about seven-year-old girls, and didn't know if this specific one went for dolls or footballs. There was also the possibility you're one of those sugar Nazis, so that eliminated the candy route. Figured I sent you flowers, and she'd probably get a kick out of getting some, too. Is there a problem?"

"No. No. I'm complicating it, and it was a sweet gesture. She'll never forget it. A girl doesn't forget the first time a man gives her flowers."

"I don't have to marry her or anything, do I?"

"Not for another twenty years."

After he'd parked, Phoebe assumed they were going to one of the restaurants along River Street. Something with a view, she supposed, even alfresco dining, which made her glad for the jacket.

Instead he led her to the pier, past a few boats, and to a graceful, gleaming white sailboat. There was a table on deck under a white cloth. Tea lights under a little dome in the center.

"This would be yours."

"If you hated boats, we were going for pizza, and this relationship would probably have ended with the last pepperoni."

"Fortunately for me I like boats. I had pizza last night."

She let him help her on board, adjusted to the sway. As first dates went, though she supposed technically this was their second, it had a lot of potential.

"Do you do a lot of sailing?"

"I live over on Whitfield Island."

"Ah." That answered that. She walked to the rail, looked across the river. "Did you always live on Whitfield?"

"No. Didn't plan to." He took a bottle of champagne from the ice bucket, began to work out the cork. "It just sort of happened and I got to like it."

"Like winning the lottery."

"More or less."

She turned at the sound of the cork popping.

"So this part?" he began. "It's the showing-off part. The boat, champagne, fancy food—which is under the table in a warming bin. But it's also because I thought it would be nice to eat out on the water, just you and me."

"The showing-off part's a bull's-eye. The just-you-and-me part is problematic. Not for dinner, but as a concept."

He poured the wine. "Because?"

She leaned back against the rail, wallowing in the breeze and the sway. "I have layers of complications."

"Single parent, complex career."

"Yes." She took the wine. "And more."

"Such as?"

"Long stories."

"So you said before. I'm not in any hurry."

"All right, let's just start this way. I loved my ex-husband when I married him."

He leaned back with her. "Always a good plan."

"I thought so. I loved him very much, even though I knew, I understood going in, we weren't on equal terms."

"I don't get it."

"He didn't love me very much. He couldn't. He just isn't built for it."

"Sounds like excuses."

"No. No. Easier if they were. He was never abusive, never—to my knowledge—unfaithful. But he couldn't put his whole self into the marriage. I was sure I could fix that, I could work with that. Then I got pregnant. He wasn't upset or angry. After Carly was born . . . There was just nothing," she said after a moment. "No connection, no bond, no curiosity. He coasted, we coasted for nearly a year that way. Then he told me he wanted out. He was sorry, but it just wasn't what he was looking for. He decided he wanted to travel. Roy's like that. Impulsive. He married me on impulse, agreed to start a family on one. Neither really satisfied him, so, on to the next."

He tucked her hair behind her ear again, just that casual swirl of finger around the curve. "Does Carly ever see him?"

"No. Really no. And actually handles the situation better than I do. That's only one complication."

"Okay, give me another."

"My mother's agoraphobic. She hasn't been out of that house in ten years. She can't."

"She didn't seem—"

"Crazy?" Phoebe interrupted. "She's not."

"I wasn't going to say crazy, hair-trigger. I was going to say nervous around strangers. Such as me."

"It's not the same thing. In the house, she's fine. She understands and feels safe inside the house."

"It must be rough on her." He ran the back of his hand down Phoebe's arm. "And you."

"We deal with it. She fought it a long time, about as long as she hasn't been able to fight it. She fought it for me and my brother. So now Carter and I—and Ava and Carly—deal with it."

"You've got some rough stuff." He turned, shifted so he was facing her, so his free hand rested on the rail by her elbow.

So she could feel him, the pull of him as their eyes met and held. "But I don't understand what it has to do with you and me as a concept."

Right that minute, she was trying to understand it herself. "My family and my work take nearly all my time, all my energy."

"You may be laboring under the mistaken impression I'm high-maintenance." He took her glass, moved back to the bottle. He topped hers off, then his own. When he went back to her, he leaned in first, laid his lips on hers. "Got a zing going there."

Oh, God, yeah. "Zings are easy."

"Have to start somewhere. I like here. Sexy redhead, beautiful night, bubbles in the wine. Hungry?"

"More than I like."

He smiled. "Why don't you sit down? There's supposed to be some sort of cold lobster deal in the cold box inside. I'll go get it. You can tell me some more long stories while we eat."

She wasn't going to tell him anything else about her life, her family. Keep it light, she decided. All on the surface. But he had a way, and somehow between the lobster salad and the medallions of beef, she let him in.

"I wonder how a girl from Savannah aims for the FBI and trains to talk people off ledges, for instance, then circles back to the local police. Did you play cops with your Barbies?"

"I didn't much like Barbies, really. All that blond hair, those big breasts."

"Which is why I loved them." He laughed when she only blinked at him. "What? You figure Malibu Barbie isn't going to start a ten-year-old boy thinking?"

"I do now. Unfortunately."

"So if it wasn't Barbies, what started you on the road? G.I. Joe?"

"Joe's a soldier. It was Dave McVee."

"Dave McVee? I must've missed him during my action-figure stage."

"He's a person and, though he's a hero, has never been a toy—that I'm aware of."

"Ah." He refilled their glasses and enjoyed the way the lights played over that porcelain skin, those clever cat's eyes. "High-school crush? First love?"

"Neither. Hero, first and last. He saved us."

When she said nothing more, Duncan shook his head. "You know you can't leave it there."

"No, I suppose I can't. My father was killed when my mother was pregnant with Carter. My younger brother."

"That's rough." He laid his hand over hers. "Seriously rough. How old were you?"

"Four, nearly five. I remember him, a little. But I remember more it broke something in Mama that took a long time to heal, and it never healed all the way. I know now, being a trained observer who's educated in psychology, that his death likely laid the groundwork for her agora-phobia. She had to go out to work, had to haul us around. No choice at all. But for years she kept mostly to herself."

"She had a choice," Duncan disagreed. "She chose to do what needed to be done to take care of her family."

"Yes, you're right. And she did take care. Then she met this man. She met Reuben. He'd come by, fix things for her. Little household things. I could see, being a girl of almost twelve, the flirt was on be-tween them. It was odd, but my father'd been gone a long time, and it was nice, too, to see her get all flushed and foolish."

"You wanted her to be happy."

"I did. He was nice to us, at first Reuben was awful nice to us. Play-ing catch with Carter out in the yard, bringing us candy, taking Mama out to the movies and such."

"But he didn't stay nice. I can hear it," Duncan said when she looked at him. "I can hear it in your voice."

"No, he didn't stay nice. They'd slept together. I'm not sure how I knew it, even then. But she opened herself up enough, after all those years, to be with him that way."

"And that's when it changed?"

"Yeah. He got possessive, proprietary, critical. He'd pick on us, all three of us really, but make it like a joke. Carter, especially Carter got the digs. Boy couldn't find his ass with both hands, ha ha ha. A man never grew balls reading books. And so on. He started coming over every night, expecting Mama to have dinner hot on the table, shoo us off so he could grope her. She wouldn't, and he'd get pissy. Started drinking a lot. I expect he always did, but he drank more at the house than he had at first.

"And this is terrible dinner conversation."

"I'd like to hear the rest. My father drank more than his share, so I know what it's like. Finish it off."

"All right. One day he came by when Mama was still at work. It was just Carter and me. He'd been drinking, and he popped open another beer, then a second one and pushed it at Carter. Told him it was time he learned to drink like a man. Carter didn't want it. God, he was only seven. Carter told him to go away, leave him alone, and Reuben smacked him, right in the face, for sass. Well, I sassed him then, you can believe it."

The old rage bubbled straight up. "I told him to get the hell out of our house, to keep his fat hands off my brother. Well, he smacked me, too. And that's when Mama came in. I'll tell you something, Duncan, up to that point I loved her. She worked so hard, she did her best. But I never thought she had any backbone. Not until she walked in and saw me and Carter on the floor and that son of a bitch standing over us taking off his belt."

She paused a moment, took a sip of wine. "He was going to use it on us, going to teach us a lesson. Mama lit into him like ball lightning. Of course, he was twice her size, and drunk, so he knocked her clear across the room. She was screaming at him to get out, to stay away from her babies, and I told Carter to run, to run to the neighbor's, call the police.

When I was sure he'd gotten far enough away, I started screaming, too, saying the police were coming. Reuben called me and Mama names I wasn't yet acquainted with, but he went."

"You kept your head." His hand gripped hers on the table now, a solid link. "You were smart."

"I was scared. I wanted the police because the police are supposed to help. They came, and they talked to my mother. I don't want to say they talked her out of filing charges, but they didn't encourage it. They took his name, said they'd go talk to him. They probably did. I don't know all that happened, just some. I know he went by her work, apologized to her. I know he came by the house with flowers, but she wouldn't let him in. I'd see him sitting outside in his car, just sitting there watching the house. And once, at least once that I saw, he grabbed her when she was outside, tried to pull her into his car. I called the police again then, and some of the neighbors came out, so he took off again. And Mama, she took out a restraining order. That's what they told her she should do."

"They didn't arrest him."

"I think they may have put him in holding for a few hours, and they gave him a stern talking-to. So a few nights later, he got liquored up, got his gun, and he broke into the house. He hit Mama so hard she still has a little scar here." Phoebe traced her fingers over her cheek. "He held the gun to her head, and he told me and Carter to go around, lock all the doors, the windows, close the curtains. We were all going to sit ourselves down, have a long talk.

"He kept us in there almost twelve hours. The police came, after a couple hours, I think. Reuben shot a few holes in the wall for sport, and the neighbors called the police. He yelled out he'd kill us all if they tried coming in. The brats first. Pretty soon, the police shut off the power. It was August, it was hot. Then Dave got him on the phone and kept him talking."

"He talked him into letting you go?"

"He kept him talking. That's the first rule. As long as Reuben was talking to Dave, he wasn't killing us. He would have; I could see it. Carter and me. Maybe not Mama because he'd gotten it into his head she belonged to him. But Dave got him talking about fishing. A long conversation about fishing, and kept us alive. But after a while, Reuben got himself worked up again. He was going to hurt Carter, I could feel it. So I distracted him, the way Dave had with the fishing. Between one thing and another, I got into the bathroom, unlocked the window in there, and I told Carter—bullied Carter—into going in first chance, getting out that way."

"You got your brother out," Duncan murmured.

"Reuben had a serious hard-on for Carter. He was going to hurt him."

She told him then about fixing the meal, the sleeping pills. And of sitting in the hospital while they stitched up her mother's face, talking to Dave.

"He kept my family alive."

"And you got them out. Twelve years old."

"I wouldn't have had a family to get out if it hadn't been for Dave. We moved into Cousin Bess's house after that, the house on Jones Street. Dave kept in touch. Lots of longer stories in all of that, but Dave talked to me about hostage and crisis negotiation. He thought I'd have a knack for it, and the perspective of what it's like on the other side. I wanted to please him, and it sounded exciting. So I trained, and I found out he was right. I have a knack for it."

She lifted her glass, half toast. "It's no lottery ticket, but it put me where I am."

"What happened to Reuben?"

"He died in prison. Pissed someone off enough for that someone to shove a shiv into him multiple times. As a moral woman, as an officer of the law, I'm obliged to deplore that sort of thing. I went out and bought a bottle of champagne, not quite up to these standards, but a very decent bottle. I enjoyed every drop of it."

"Glad to hear it." He gave her hand a quick squeeze. "You've had an interesting life, Phoebe."

"Interesting?"

"Well, you can't claim to have lived in the rut of routine."

She laughed. "No, I don't suppose I can."

"I've got some insight now on why I saw that purpose in you when you walked into Suicide Joe's apartment. And you have the sexiest green eyes."

She watched him with them as she sipped her champagne. "If you think because I've bared my soul, more or less, and have had several glasses of this lovely champagne, I'm going to slide down into the cabin and have wild sex with you, you're mistaken."

"Can we negotiate? Any other kind of sex a possibility?"

"I don't think so, but thanks all the same."

"How about a walk along the river where I can kiss you in the moonlight?"

"We can start with the walk."

He rose, took her hand. And as she came to her feet, he simply cupped the back of her neck to draw her mouth to his.

Warm lips and cool air, a hard body and a gentle touch. She gave in, gave up to the moment. Her fingers twined with his and curled tight as she leaned in for more.

He could feel the strength of her under the soft, soft skin. It was that, he knew, that had pulled at him from the first moment. Those contrasts, those complexities. There was nothing simple, nothing ordinary about her.

Yet he thought this could be simple—this one thing—this slowly building heat between them.

So the long, long kiss spun out, hinting of a spark that might flash at any moment, while the deck swayed gently under their feet, and the air blew soft over the water.

She brought her hand to his chest, kept it there a moment as his heart thumped beneath her palm. Then she used it to ease him back.

"Someone else has quite a knack," she commented.

"I've been practicing religiously since I was twelve." He brought the hand on his chest up, to rub his lips over the knuckles. "I've developed a few variations, if you'd like me to demonstrate."

"I think that was enough of a demonstration for right now. We discussed a walk."

"Probably best to save the variations. I'm not sure you're ready."

"Oh really? Don't think you can use that kind of maneuver on me. I'm a cop."

He stepped off, onto the pier, held out a hand for hers. "Variation Seven's been known to cause temporary unconsciousness."

"That's a straight dare." She stepped from boat to dock. "And I haven't taken a dare since I was seven. We're walking, Mr. Swift."

"Can't blame a guy for trying."

As they walked, she angled her head to study his face. "Variation Seven?"

"I'm required by law to give the previous warning before use. Now that you've been warned, I'm in the clear."

"I'll keep that in mind."

Her laugh floated over the water. And her face, bright with it, filled the field glasses.

He dug into the takeout bag for his fries as he watched her, watched them. And he considered how quick and easy it would be if he had that face of hers in the crosshairs of a rifle scope.

Bang!

Too quick, too easy.

But before much longer, she wouldn't be laughing.

7

At her desk Monday morning, Phoebe attacked paperwork, returned calls, then squeezed out time to go over her plans for the upcoming training session.

It might have been kicking Arnie Meeks when he was down—and absent—but she wanted to lay out the protocol, procedure and psychology of the first responder's actions.

Sets the tone, she thought. Arnie had sure as hell set the tone for the Gradey incident. What happened, why it happened, would be strong points made in training, and would illustrate, she hoped, why there were guidelines.

She added a copy of her own report to the day's packet, added it along with logs and tapes and transcripts from other incidents.

She got to her feet when Dave came into her office. "Captain."

"Need a minute."

"Sure, I've got a few before a training session. Want coffee?"

"No, thanks." When he shut the door behind him, the muscles between her shoulder blades tightened.

"Problem?"

"Could be. I got a call from Sergeant Meeks, Arnold Meeks's father. He's making noises about filing a complaint against you."

"For?"

"The unwarranted suspension of his son. Also there was some mention of a legal suit for slander, defamation. He wants a sit-down with you, me and his son's rep."

"I'm available for that, at any time. I instructed Arnie he was free to contact his delegate at the time of his suspension. And," she added, "that's on the record."

"You're going to stand by the thirty-day rip?"

"I am. He violated every guideline. He goaded Gradey, a hostage-taker, into suicide, and he's lucky Gradey didn't kill the hostages, too. You read the report, Captain, including the witness statements—civilian and law enforcement."

"Yeah, I did." Wearily, Dave rubbed the back of his neck. "He couldn't have screwed it up more if he'd set out to."

"I'm not sure he didn't. That's not colored by personal dislike," she continued when Dave frowned. "He's a power-tripper, and he's bigoted, sexist and rash. He shouldn't be a cop."

"Phoebe, that kind of stand, the bias in it, isn't going to help hold up your end of this."

"It's not bias, it's fact. And, I believe, the psych eval will bear me out. Dave, he put that mutilated doll outside my house."

Dave shoved his hands into his pockets, and inside the pockets they curled into fists. "I'm not going to contradict you on that, but you're going to want to be careful about making that accusation to anyone but me. You're going to need more to—"

"He called me a bitch to my face, that's not counting the number of times he's called me one behind my back. He stood just about where you're standing now and threatened me. He has no respect for my authority, and, in fact, only contempt for me."

"Do you think I don't want him out?" Dave tossed back, and for the first time he let some of the anger, some of the frustration show. "Out of this squad, out of the department? I've got no cause to put him off the job, not at this point. And, Phoebe, sitting behind that desk means you have to demand respect for your authority."

"And so I have," she said evenly. "Thirty days may give him time to consider that. Captain, he stood in this office and accused me of being behind this desk because I've performed sexual acts with you."

Dave stared at her a moment. "Son of a bitch. Son of a bitch." He sucked in a breath. "Were there any witnesses to those accusations?"

"No, and I'd turned off the recorder before he made them. But he made them. Very specifically. Which indicates he has as much contempt for you as for me. Moreover, I believe he was about to make a move on me—physically. Detective Sykes interrupted. I don't like playing it this way. I don't like spreading this kind of crap around, but the fact is, I think Arnold Meeks is dangerous. So ask Sykes about it."

"I'll do that. I'm going to schedule that sit-down for this afternoon. Make sure you're clear for it."

"Yes, sir."

"Do you want to file sexual harassment charges?"

"Not at this time. I'll stand with the insubordination."

He nodded, turned toward the door. "You may want to contact your own rep." He glanced back. "The Meekses have some muscle in the department, connections, history. Keep your ass covered, Phoebe, because even if we're able to take this asshole down, he could do some damage."

"I will. Dave? I'm sorry I had to pull you into it this way, this personal way."

"You didn't," Dave said shortly. "He did."

Trouble, she thought when she was alone again. Trouble was coming. Well, she'd dealt with trouble before. When the morning session was finished, she'd make some time to review Meeks's jacket, the statements from the Gradey incident and her own personal report of her altercation with Meeks in her office.

Through the glass wall of her office, she saw Dave was already gesturing Sykes toward the break room. A private talk. Her captain's protective instincts were up, and she was sorry, damn sorry, she'd had to incite them.

But she was damned if Meeks was going to endanger lives, threaten her, upset her family, then pull out his departmental pedigree as a shield.

She didn't care who his father was.

And right now, she reminded herself, she needed to put this aside and get downstairs. She swung by the PAA on the way through the squad room. "I'm in the conference room for the next ninety minutes."

"Oh, okay. Lieutenant?" Annie Utz, the squad's public administrative assistant, sent Phoebe a quick, nervous smile. "I, ah, may have to take a day off later in the week for some, um, personal business."

"All right. If you can let me know ahead of time, that'd be good. We'll see the desk is covered."

"Um . . . um . . . Lieutenant?" The smile wavered around the edges. "I know I'm still new and all. But I like working here. I hope I'm doing a good job."

"You're doing fine." Wouldn't hurt to tone down the makeup and buy the next size up in your shirt, Phoebe thought, but the work itself wasn't a problem.

"Um . . . I brought in pralines today. Homemade." She held up a covered paper plate. "Maybe you'd like one."

"After the session."

"You're taking the stairs, right? The way you run up and down those stairs instead of taking the elevator, sugar sure won't hurt you."

"My fondness for sugar is why I run up and down the stairs."

She hurried out before Annie could make her any later. With the opening of her lecture winding through her mind, she pushed through the door, started the jog down the stairway.

Her car *had* to be ready today, she remembered. Had to. She'd call the mechanic during the break and—

She barely saw the flash of movement, had no time to react much less reach her weapon as the attack slammed her against the stairwell wall. Pain burst along with an explosion of fear when her head rammed hard against the concrete. And her vision hazed with red.

Seconds, it took only the few seconds when her instincts were screaming *fight* and the stun from the blow buckled her knees for tape to slap over her mouth, for her arms to be wrenched back.

Struggling, dizzy from the blow, she tried to bring her heel down, missed the mark. Then she was blind from the hood yanked over her head. Her scream muffled to nothing against the tape as she pitched forward from a violent shove. Shock and pain radiated as her body hit the landing, rolled. She tasted blood, and through the thunder of her own gasps, heard her attacker laugh. Praying for a miracle, she kicked out. And when hands closed around her throat, she thrashed.

Not this way, she couldn't die this way. Unable to look into the eyes of who killed her. Who took her away from her baby.

Her body bucked, her legs pushed and kicked while her lungs wept for air. When the pressure released, she gasped and gulped it in only to fight to scream it out again when she felt a knife, the point of a knife, cutting through her clothes, and the quick, horrible sting of that point slicking carelessly into her flesh. Hands—gloved hands, part of her mind registered—squeezed her breasts.

It couldn't be happening. Attack and rape a cop in her own precinct? It was madness. But her kicks and struggles didn't stop his hands from tearing, from touching, from pushing roughly between her legs.

And she hated herself from the sobs and pleas that babbled behind the tape. Hated that they made him laugh, that they gave him power.

"Don't worry." He whispered it, the first words he'd spoken. "I don't fuck your kind."

Fresh pain erupted from the blow to her face. She teetered toward unconsciousness, almost welcomed it. Dimly she heard, thought she heard, footsteps.

Someone coming. Please, God. But no, no, leaving. He was leaving. Leaving her alive. She moaned. Everything wept, everything wept with pain. But survival, that primal need to survive, was stronger. She was afraid to roll, to try to get to her knees, to her feet. How close was she to the stairs, how close to a nasty, perhaps fatal, fall?

The cuffs he'd snapped on her bit brutally into her flesh, weighed down by her own body. The need to see—escape, survive—was greater than the need for relief. She hunched her shoulders, turned her head right and left, inching tortuously forward as she tested the ground with her feet. Slowly, keeping a vicious grip on panic, she worked the hood up her face until her chin was clear, her mouth, her nose. Then blessedly her eyes.

And those eyes wheeled around. She could see spots and smears of her own blood on the wall of the stairwell where her head had hit, just as she could taste it in her throat.

But she could see the door below. She had to reach that door, get down the short flight of steps to that door. To survival.

Now she rolled, and her gasp went to a keening as she pushed to her knees. Tattered strips of her shirt and skirt hung on her. The rags of the rest were scattered on the stairs.

He'd left her naked, humiliated, bound. But he'd left her alive.

She used the wall to brace herself, used her trembling legs to push, push, until she could stand, leaning back on the wall. Giddiness and nausea rolled through her, and she prayed she could hold off both until she reached help.

Even as the voice inside her head screamed to *hurry, hurry, he could come back,* she made herself step carefully down, back to the wall for safety. At the bottom, with her body quivering with fear and exhaustion, she had to find the strength to turn, to grip the door handle with her clammy hands and pull.

She fell through the doorway, into the corridor. Shuddering, she began to crawl.

Someone shouted. She heard it like some dim bell through a fog. And, spent, she collapsed.

She wasn't out long, the pain wouldn't allow it, but when she groped back, she was on her side and the rawness around her mouth told her someone had ripped the tape away.

"Get a blanket. Give me your damn jacket, and somebody get a key that'll open these cuffs. You're all right, Lieutenant. It's Liz Alberta. Do you hear me? You're going to be all right."

Liz? Phoebe stared into grim brown eyes. Detective Elizabeth Alberta. Yes, yes, she knew that name, she knew those eyes. "The stairwell." Her voice was a raw wheeze. "He got me in the stairwell."

"A couple of guys are already in there, checking it out. Don't worry. Paramedics are coming. Lieutenant." Liz leaned closer. "Were you raped?"

"No. No, he just . . ." Phoebe closed her eyes. "No. How bad am I hurt?"

"I don't know yet."

"My weapon." Phoebe's eyes flew open. "God, my weapon. I couldn't get to it in time. Did he get my piece?"

"I don't know yet."

"Hold on, Lieutenant. I'm going to get these cuffs off."

Phoebe didn't know who spoke from behind her, kept her eyes trained on Liz. "I need you to take my statement. I want you to take it."

"That's what I'm going to do."

Phoebe couldn't stop the sharp indrawn breath as the cuffs slipped off, or bite back the whimper when she moved her arms. "I don't think they're broken. I don't think anything's broken." She clutched the jacket to her breasts even as someone wrapped a blanket around her shoulders. "Can you help me sit up?"

"Maybe you should stay down until—"

There was a rush of footsteps, and a shout. Then Dave was kneeling beside her. "What happened? Who did this?"

"I didn't see him. He caught me in the stairwell. He put something over my head." Tears slid down her cheeks to sting the abraded skin. "I think he got my weapon."

"I'm going to get her statement, Captain, if that's clear with you. I'll go with the lieutenant to the hospital and get her statement."

"Yes." But he gripped Phoebe's hand as if he couldn't bear to let go.

"Don't call my family. Captain, please don't call them."

He gave her hand a squeeze, pushed to his feet. "I want this building searched, floor by floor. This is red status. Nobody comes in or out without a search. I want the whereabouts of every cop and civilian in this building accounted for."

"It wasn't a civilian, Captain." Phoebe spoke quietly as his furious face turned toward her. "It was one of us."

It all blurred, but Phoebe counted that as a blessing. The paramedics, the ambulance, the ER. There were a lot of voices, a lot of movement, more pain. Then less, blessedly less. She let herself drift while people poked and prodded, lifted. While cuts and scrapes were treated, she kept her eyes closed. When pieces of her were X-rayed, she shut down her mind.

There would be tears, she knew. There would probably be floods of them, but they could wait.

Liz stepped into the exam room. "They said you wanted to talk to me now."

"Yeah." Phoebe sat on the exam table. Her ribs ached, that rotted-tooth throb she already knew would give her trouble for days if not weeks. But the sling around her arm eased the pain in her shoulder.

"Mild concussion, bruised ribs, sprained shoulder."

Liz stepped closer. "Nasty cut on your forehead and a shiner coming on. Split lip. Your jaw's swollen. Son of a bitch did some work on you."

"He didn't kill me, there's that."

"Always a plus. Your captain was in. He left after the docs gave him your status. I'm to tell you he'll come back to take you home when you're ready."

"It's better if he stays at the house, finds . . . I don't know what there'll be to find. I was coming down from my office to the conference room for my training session. That's habitual. I use the stairs habitually."

"Claustrophobia?"

"No, vanity. I don't always have time to work out, so I go for the stairs instead of the elevator. He was waiting for me."

"You said you didn't see him."

"No." Cautiously, Phoebe touched her fingers to her face, just under her eye. She'd never had a black eye before, never appreciated how much it hurt. "I was going down pretty fast, and I caught just a blur of movement out of the corner of my eye—on the right. Thanks."

She took the ice bag Liz offered, laid it gently on the side of her face. "He had me before I could even turn my head, before I could reach for my weapon. He knew what he was doing. Disabled me immediately with the blow to the head. Rapped me face-first into the wall, stunned me. Taped my mouth and cuffed me quick. He's used cuffs before. Anticipated my defensive moves, such as they were, and had the hood on me, or whatever it was."

"Laundry bag. It's in evidence. You're thinking you should have been quicker, fought harder. Don't."

"I didn't get a single lick in. I realize, intellectually, that I was stunned, physically outmatched, and still . . . My weapon?"

"It hasn't been recovered."

The look between them held for a long moment. It was a hard blow when a cop was disarmed. It was a harder one when the cop was female.

"No one's going to blame you for that, Lieutenant. Not under these circumstances."

"Some will. You know it, I know it. He knows it. That's why he took it."

"Some are idiots. Did you get an idea of height? Build?"

"Not of height. He shoved me and I went down. But he was strong. He choked me at first . . ." Her fingers traced over the bruises on her throat, and she remembered the feel of those hands cutting off her air. "Choked me when I was down, put his hands around my throat and choked me. He had big hands. Big, strong hands. He wore gloves. I felt . . . I felt gloves—thin, probably latex—when he groped me. And a knife, maybe scissors, but I think a knife to cut through my clothes."

"He touched you."

"He . . ." Facts, Phoebe ordered herself. Think of them as facts. "He squeezed my breasts. He pulled my nipples, hard. He laughed. Just kind of a wheezing laugh, like he was real tickled and trying to hold it back. He pushed his hand— Shit. Oh shit."

Anticipating, Liz grabbed a bedpan, shoved it under Phoebe's face. Held it steady while Phoebe was sick.

Sheet white under the bruises, Phoebe leaned back. "God. God. Sorry."

"Just take a breath, take your time. Here." Picking up the plastic cup and straw on the table, Liz offered it. "Drink some water."

"Okay. Thanks. I'm okay. He put his fingers inside me. Rammed them in. It wasn't sexual. He just wanted to hurt me, humiliate me. Then, I think he leaned down because his voice was close to my ear. He whispered. 'Don't worry. I don't fuck your kind.' Then he hit me in the face. And he left me there."

"Do you have a gauge how long the attack went on?"

"It seemed like forever, but probably two, maybe three minutes. No more than that. He had his plan in place, and he executed it efficiently. It probably took me longer to get the hood off and get down to the door. Altogether, it was probably six or seven minutes."

"Okay. Did he say anything else? Anything at all?"

"No, he only spoke that one time."

"Did you notice anything else about him. A scent?"

"No. Wait." Phoebe closed her eyes again. "Baby powder. I smelled baby powder."

"How about his voice? Would you recognize it again?"

"I don't know. We're trained to pay attention to details, but I was so scared, and the blood was pounding in my head, and the hood. He was local," she said suddenly. "There was enough of an accent that he sounded like a local."

"Have you had trouble with anyone? Anyone you think would want to hurt you?"

"You know I have. We may not work the same division, but we work in the same house. You know I have."

"Do you think it was him? You think it was Arnie Meeks who attacked you?"

"Yes, I do. I can't prove it, but yes, I think it was. I reported an incident on Saturday morning."

"What incident?"

She told Liz about the doll.

"I'll touch base with Detective Sykes on that. And I'll make some discreet inquiries as to Meeks's whereabouts this morning."

"I appreciate it."

"You weren't raped, Lieutenant, but you were violated sexually. If you want to talk to a rape counselor, I know a good one."

"No, but thanks. You're good at what you do, Detective. I appreciate you being the one to take my statement, to be here."

"I'll be following up. I promise you."

"For now, can you steal me some scrubs so I can get out of here?"

"Why don't I call someone for you. If you don't want the captain, someone else. Have them bring you some clothes, take you home?"

Phoebe shook her head. "I don't want to go home until after I've had my breakdown, which is going to come along pretty soon now."

"Anyone else I can call for you?"

"Actually . . ." Phoebe touched her fingertips to the trio of butterfly bandages that closed the wound on her forehead. "There's a friend, if he's around."

The old building had potential. Of course its current owner was giving the deal what Duncan thought of as the pitch-and-wish. He let that play in one side of his brain while the other side played with the possibilities.

The warehouse was currently a dump, and no question about it. But it could be transformed into very decent apartments—close enough to the plants and the docks to fill up with blue-collar families. Reasonable space for a reasonable rent. Well off the tourist track, of course, well apart from the green elegance of the historic district. But toss maybe a bakery or a coffee shop on the first floor, a deli or a small family restaurant, and you'd get a return on your investment. Eventually.

Good thing he wasn't in a hurry for it.

The rank and file of the city needed good, safe housing as well as the rest. He should know. He'd been one of them most of his life.

Phin stood with the owner, shaking his head as Duncan wandered. That was Phin's fine skill, in Duncan's opinion. Just putting on that dour, disapproving look could lasso the pitch-and-wish and yank it back toward reality.

The guy wanted the moon for the dilapidation, figuring he had a bright gold fish on the line. Duncan didn't mind being thought of as a fish, especially since he'd already set his maximum offer at a couple of asteroids.

When his cell phone rang, he was studying a trio of broken windows. He kept studying them while he pulled it out. "Yeah, this is Duncan. What? When? How?"

He turned when Phin, obviously hearing the alarm in his tone, crossed the pocked concrete floor to him. "Where? Okay, all right," he said a moment later. "I'm on my way. I have to go." Already heading for the doors, Duncan shoved the phone into his pocket.

"Mr. Swift," the owner began.

"Personal emergency. Do what you do," he said to Phin and rushed outside to his car.

A dozen horrific images flashed and burned into his mind as he set the car racing toward the hospital. The woman who'd identified herself as Detective Alberta said Phoebe was being released, he reminded himself. She couldn't be that badly hurt if they were releasing her from the hospital.

Then again, the detective had been very brief. Coplike, Duncan thought in annoyance as he was forced to brake for a red light.

She hadn't said how; she hadn't said how bad. And when was this fucking light going to turn green?

Maybe she'd been shot. Jesus, Jesus.

He peeled out when the light changed. He threaded his way through traffic, then chewed his way through more. Years of hacking had taught him how to get from point to point fast—or how to get there round about and pad the fare.

He swung into the parking lot, cursing bitterly as he searched for a space. By the time he found one and was running for the ER doors, he'd worked himself up into a frantic mix of nerves and temper.

He'd have run right by her if not for the hair. The beacon of red caught his eye, had him stopping, spinning back around.

She sat with the other wounded and the sick in the waiting area. She wore pale blue scrubs. Her arm was in a sling, and her face—her fascinating face—was bruised and battered.

"Oh, Jesus, Phoebe." He crouched down in front of her, took her hand in both of his. "How bad are you hurt?"

"Ambulatory." She nearly managed to smile. "Not so bad. You just popped into my head as someone to call. I shouldn't have."

"Don't be stupid. What happened?"

"Duncan . . . Since I did call, and you did come, I need to go somewhere for a couple hours, so I can fall apart and put myself back together again before I go home. Can you just take me somewhere quiet for a couple of hours? Big favor, I know, but—"

"Sure I can. Are you sure you can walk?"

"Yeah." When she started to rise, he slid an arm around her waist, drew her up with the care of a man lifting a fragile work of art.

"Lean on me."

"I already did, calling you out here." And God, it was a relief to put a little weight on someone else. "I didn't even think you might be busy with something."

"Me? Idle rich." He dug out his sunglasses as she winced and turned her face away from the glare. "Put these on. That's a hell of a shiner you got coming up. What's the other guy look like?"

This time she couldn't manage the smile. "I wish I knew."

It could wait, he told himself. The questions could wait until he got her inside, got her settled. Got her tea or something. He helped her into the car, hooked her seat belt himself. "Let's put you back a little." He eased the seat back. "How's that?"

"It's good. It's fine."

"Did they give you anything for the pain?" he asked when he got behind the wheel, and she tapped the purse Liz had brought to the hospital with her.

"Good drugs. Got some in me right now. I'm just going to close my eyes if you don't mind."

"Go ahead. Try to relax, rest."

She didn't sleep. He could see her hand fist. It might relax for a moment or two, but then it would fist again as if she was determined to hold something tight inside it.

Bandages bound her wrists, and baffled him. If she'd been in an accident, why hadn't she contacted her family? And what sort of accident injured both wrists, bruised up the face and caused enough injury otherwise to have a woman walk as though her bones were brittle glass?

So it hadn't been an accident.

As other options began to circle in his mind, he shut them down. No point in speculating, not when speculation—where were her clothes?—sent him into a minefield of possibilities.

He gave her silence. He'd hauled enough passengers in his time to know what people wanted. Chat, debate, information, quiet.

Phoebe wanted silence.

She barely moved but for that restless hand-into-fist over that span of bridge from mainland to island, as he passed the marshes and creeks and drove through the green tunnels of arching trees.

Only when he slowed for the last turn, eased to a stop, did she stir and open her eyes.

He'd gone for grand with the house, leaning on traditional elegance and adding bits of quirk with the widow's walk that topped it like a crown. Oaks draped with moss fanned around it, strong accents for the soft blue with its delicate white trim. Gardens—azaleas just ready to pop and burst—flowed out and about in a casual way that turned the grand into charming.

Pots and baskets of mixed flowers decked veranda and terrace along with gliders and generous chairs that invited visitors to sit awhile, relax, have a cool drink.

"It's beautiful."

"Yeah, it's growing on me." He got out, came around to her. "Let me give you a hand."

"Thanks." She leaned into him. "Really. Thank you, Duncan."

"No problem." He led her to the steps, up to the veranda to the door with its Celtic knot in stained glass.

"How long have you lived here?"

"I guess about five years now. Mostly. I figured I'd sell it, but . . . long story." He gave her a quick smile as he unlocked and opened the door.

Golden light basked over rich colors, a wealth of space sweetened by curves from the elegant staircase, the wide archways. She moved beside him, stiffly, across the foyer into the parlor. There the atrium doors opened to a terrace, and beyond that more gardens danced, centered by an arbor where wisteria climbed and twined in a riot of beauty.

A piano angled to face the front windows, while chairs and divans in soft grays to offset the strong burgundy of the walls sat in groups. There was art on the walls, and she had an impression of marsh and river, Georgia dreamscapes along with a mix of antiques and the odd touch of a fat ceramic pig.

When he would have led her to a seat, she stepped away, crossed to the glass doors.

"I like your gardens."

"Me, too. I got into that kind of thing when I moved out here."

"I imagine so. It seems a lot of house for one man."

"Yeah. That's why I figured to sell it. But I actually use most of the place."

"Did you . . ." She rested her forehead against the glass, closed her eyes. "I'm sorry. I'm sorry. We're coming to the falling-apart portion of the program."

"It's all right." He laid a hand on her back and, feeling her shake, knew they'd hit the eye of the storm. "You go right ahead."

He gathered her in when she turned to him, gathered her up when she began to sob. He carried her to the divan, then sat with her cradled in his arms. And he held her there while the storm raged through.

8

Tears didn't shame her, not tears that needed to be shed. She was grateful as they poured out, as they washed the worst of the fear and sickness away, that he wasn't the kind of man who offered awkward pats and told a woman not to cry.

He only offered shelter and let her weep.

When the shaking eased and the tears slowed, he brushed a light kiss over her bruised temple. "Any better?"

"Yes." She drew a long breath, and when she let it out, felt her system steady. "God, yes."

"Here's what we're going to do. I'm going to go fix you something to drink, then you're going to tell me what happened." He lifted her face until their eyes met. "Then we'll figure out what comes next."

"Okay."

"I don't have a thing . . . a handkerchief."

"I've got tissues in my bag."

"Good, then . . ." He shifted her, sat her down beside him. "If you need, you know, the bathroom? There's one that way and to the right."

"Good idea."

When he left her, she sat for a moment, drawing back the reserves. She got achingly to her feet, picked up the purse he'd left on the coffee table, then made her way under graceful arches, over polished floors to the powder room.

The first glimpse of her face in the long oval mirror had her moaning as much in vanity as distress. Her eyes were puffy and red, with the right one sporting an ugly mottle of bruises, accented by the hard black smear of gathering blood under it.

Her jaw was another swollen cloudburst, her bottom lip about double in size and split. The butterfly bandages on her forehead closed the jagged gash, and stood out starkly against the raw, scraped skin.

"This isn't a beauty contest, Phoebe, so get over yourself. But God, *God,* could you look any worse?"

And when she took this face home, she was going to scare everyone half stupid.

Nothing to be done about that, nothing, she reminded herself, and carefully dabbed cold water over her face.

In short order, she discovered that even the elemental task of peeing with a bruised hip and an arm in a sling was an exercise in discomfort and frustration. That tidying herself up brought everything to a dull throb under the layer of medication.

And vanity or no vanity, she was already sick and tired of looking as if she'd run headlong into a brick wall.

Plus, she *hated* hobbling. As she hobbled her way back into the parlor, Duncan set a tray on the coffee table.

"I don't know what they gave you in the ER, so I figured alcohol was off the menu. You got tea—and my personal remedy for a black eye, and so on, a bag of frozen peas."

She stopped. "You made tea."

"You don't like tea?"

"Of course I do. You made tea, and in a pretty teapot, on a tray. And brought me frozen peas." She held up her good hand. "My emotions are all over the board yet. I'm getting weepy because somebody made me tea in a pot, and thought to offer me frozen peas."

"Good thing I didn't bake cookies."

She picked up the bag of peas, held it to the side of her face that suffered the most damage. "Can you?"

"I have no idea. Anyway, I wasn't sure if you'd be able to chew anything yet. How's that jaw?"

She walked, slowly, to the divan, sat again. "You want me stoic, or you want the truth?"

"I'll take the truth."

"It fucking hurts, that's how it is. I think there might be one square inch of my body that doesn't fucking hurt. And that makes you smile?"

He kept smiling. "That you're hurting, no. That you're pissed off about it, yes. Good to see your temper's in working order." He sat beside her, poured out the tea. "Tell me what happened, Phoebe."

"I got jumped in the stairwell at work."

"Jumped? Who?"

"I didn't see him, so I can't say for sure. He was waiting for me," she began, and told him.

He didn't interrupt, but when she spoke of her assailant tearing her clothes, Duncan pushed off the couch. As she had when she'd first entered the room, he walked to the doors, stared out.

And she stopped speaking.

"Go on," he said with his back to her. "I just can't sit right now."

He listened, and he stared through the glass. He didn't see the wild wisteria or the winding trails of the side garden. He saw a dim stairwell, he saw Phoebe hurt and helpless, struggling while some faceless bastard tore at her, pawed at her, terrorized her.

There had to be payment, Duncan thought. He believed strongly in payment.

"You know who it was," he said when she'd finished.

"I didn't see him."

Duncan turned now. His face was cool and blank so that the blue of his eyes burned all the stronger against it. "You know who it was."

"I have a strong suspicion. Suspicion isn't proof."

"That's the cop talking. What about the person?"

"I know who did it, and I'm going to find a way to prove it. Do you think I would *take* this? Do you think that's who I am?" She held up a hand as if stopping herself.

"No, go on. A good pissing rage is as healing as a good cry."

"He *hurt* me. That fucking bastard. He hurt and humiliated me. He made me think he'd kill me and leave my baby an orphan and my mother, my family grieving. He left me to crawl away naked, to crawl with most of my clothes torn away where I *work,* where I have to go every day and face the people who saw what he could do to me. And do you know why?"

"No. Why?"

"Because he couldn't stand taking orders from me. He couldn't stand having authority, female authority especially, disciplining him and setting out the consequences for his actions."

"Are you telling me another cop did this to you?"

Shocked that so much had spewed out of her, she pulled herself back. "I have strong suspicions."

"What's his name?"

The woman inside, the one who had been hurt and humiliated, warmed just a little at the tone. The tone that said, very clearly, I'll handle this. But she shook her head. "Don't get out the white charger, Duncan. This'll be dealt with. He'll be dealt with. It's now my mission in life to make sure of it. And having this time, this place to . . . well, to be, it's helped more than I can tell you."

"Well, that's fine and good for you, and glad to be of assistance. But that's not much help for me when I'm in the mood to pound somebody's face in like it was rotten wood, then twist his useless dick off and feed it to the dog I keep thinking about getting."

"No," Phoebe said after a long moment. "No, I don't guess it is. I'm going to confess that I find myself surprisingly comforted, and just a little aroused, by the sentiment."

"I don't know what this is yet, this you-and-me thing. I didn't figure I had to think about it all that much as yet. So putting that aside—whatever this is or isn't here, you should know my natural inclination, and you go right ahead and consider it sexist or outdated or whatever the hell you like—my natural inclination when some cowardly son of a bitch beats on a woman is to get out that goddamn white charger and kick some ass."

He could, she realized. She'd let that one slip by her. But looking at him now, with that hot rage burning straight through the cold fury, she understood there was a great deal more to him than charm and luck.

"Okay. I hear your natural inclination is to defend and to act, and you sound—"

"Don't pull that negotiator crap out on me."

"That would be my natural inclination," she returned. "My next is to say I don't need protection, but given the circumstances, that would be a stupid thing to say. Most of my life I've been the one protecting and defending, and that goes back long before I had a badge. I'm not quite sure how to react when someone wants to protect and defend me."

He walked over to her, hesitated, then leaned down. "I'm going to be careful about this, but you let me know if it hurts." And he laid his lips, very gently, on hers.

"It doesn't."

He kissed her again before straightening. "You've got a week."

"Sorry?"

"You got a week to complete your current mission in life. Then I get a name, and I help myself."

"If that's some sort of ultimatum—"

"It's not, not at all. It's just fact." Sitting on the coffee table across from her, he took the peas she'd lowered, turned the bag over, and put the cooler side against her swollen jaw. "I already know it was a cop, and one you had to slap back for something. I expect I could have a name inside an hour. But you have a week to do it your way."

"You think because you have money—"

"No, Phoebe, I *know* because I have money." Gently, he lifted her hands, in turn, touched his lips to her bandaged wrists, comforting even as he laid down the law. "It oils the wheels, and that's just another fact. You're smart, and you've got that purpose that just sets me off. I'm betting you'll have this bastard frying inside that week. If not, well, my turn."

"Your turn? This is a police matter, and it has nothing to do with turns. That's grade school."

He smiled at her, just enough to have the dimple flickering. "You know, you look like hell right now."

"Excuse me?"

"What I'm saying is, you look pretty damn awful, your face all banged up that way. Even with the *Grey's Anatomy* thing going with the scrubs, you look like hell. So, why it should be I can look at you right now and still be attracted right down to the soles of my feet is a goddamn puzzle. But I am."

Torn in a dozen directions, she dumped the frozen peas on the tea tray. "What the hell does that have to do with this?"

"Nothing. It just popped into my head. Want some more tea? And yeah," he added when she just stared at him, "that's a change of subject. Your mind's made up; mine is, too. So what's the point of arguing about it when neither of us is going to budge on the issue? And you can't be feeling your best, so I don't feel right fighting with you."

"No, I don't want any more tea, thanks. And you're right, I'm not feeling my best, but it's important that you understand there's a wide difference between retribution and the law."

"We'll have to debate that some other time, when you're back at full power. You want to take a whirlpool? Hot water, jets? It might help with some of the aches."

Another thing she'd let slip by, she thought, was the man had a head like a rock. "That's a nice offer, but no. I'm going to need to get home." And the thought of that had her looking down at herself. "God."

"Do you want to call them first? Prepare them?"

"No. No, then they'd just worry until I got there. I'm putting you out again, Duncan, having you drive me all the way back."

"So, you'll owe me."

He helped her out to the car. Even the short walk wore her out, so she just sat, out of breath, while he strapped her in.

Carly would be coming in from school any minute, she thought as he drove toward home. Mama would be finishing up taking her Internet orders for the day, or boxing up completed pieces to go out in the mail in the morning. Ava, likely home from errands, would be fussing around in the kitchen.

Just an easy Monday afternoon. And she was about to shatter it.

"Who plays the piano?"

"Nobody. I sort of do. Just by ear. I always thought a piano added class to a room."

"Cousin Bess insisted Carter and I take lessons. I got the mechanics of it; Carter got the heart." She let her head fall back. "I wish this part was over. The shocking them, the explaining it all again part. I wish it was over."

"I can explain what happened for you, if you want."

"I have to do it. Where's your family, Duncan?" It occurred to her that nowhere in the rooms she'd been in in the grand house had she seen any photos of family.

"Here and there."

"Long story?"

"Epic. We'll save it for another time."

Her cell phone rang, and with some effort she reached for her purse and pulled it out. "This is Phoebe. Yes, Dave, I'm all right, I'm better. No, I'm on my way home now. I've been with a friend. Could be worse."

She listened awhile. "I understand. I'll be in tomorrow to— Sir. Captain. Dave." She let out a frustrated breath. "Two days then. Three. Yes, sir, thank you. And I'd like the sit-down rescheduled for Thursday, if possible. I appreciate that. I will. Yes, I will. Bye."

"Okay?" Duncan asked.

"Not entirely, but better than it could've been. He was going to order me to take medical leave for two weeks."

"The bastard."

She let out a laugh, then sucked air as it pinged her ribs. "I'd go crazy sitting home having Mama and Ava fuss over me for two weeks. He knows that. I'll heal better if I'm working, and it makes a statement where a statement needs to be made. He knows that, too. He was probably after the three or four days all along. He's a sneaky son of a bitch."

"Sounds like somebody I'd like."

"Probably. He got away with my weapon."

"What? Captain Dave?"

"No. No, not the captain. Sorry, this whole thing's scrambled my brain so I can't seem to think in a straight line."

The cop who'd hurt her, Duncan realized. And since she was busy brooding over it, he gave her room.

Just as he gave her room to be agitated as they approached Jones Street. "Want a bourbon and a cigarette first?"

"Don't think I wouldn't. I'm about to take on multiple hysterical females." She prepared herself with deep breaths as he drove down the brick-paved street. "Oh God. That just caps it."

"What?" Duncan shot her a glance, saw her fit on a stoic smile. Then saw the man who'd been strolling along in the dappled sunlight break into a run.

"Phoebe! Phoebe, what happened?" The man wrenched the door open, reached down. "My God, what happened to you? Who are you?" He threw the words at Duncan like stones. "What the hell did you do to my sister?"

"Carter, stop! Stop. He didn't do a thing but help me."

"Who hurt you? Where is he?"

People strolled along Jones—residents and tourists—and now, Phoebe noted, any number of those strollers had stopped to stare at the beat-up woman and the two men on either side of a flashy white Porsche.

"You can stop shouting on a public street like a lunatic. Let's go inside."

"They're good questions." Duncan came around to the passenger seat. "I'd like the answers, too. I'm Duncan. She's got a lot of tender spots. We'll need to be careful—"

"I can take care of her."

"Carter, stop it. Do you want to add to the extremely crappy day I've had by being rude to a friend? I apologize for my ill-mannered brother, Duncan."

"No problem."

"Oh God, there's Miz Tiffany and that ridiculous dog heading over from the park. I can't deal with that. Carter, for the love of God, don't make me deal with that. Help me get inside."

"Easy does it," Duncan advised, and caught a glimpse of a woman, well past a certain age, with a blond bubble of hair, being led by a tiny, apparently hairless dog wearing a polka-dot tie. "She hasn't seen you yet. I'd be ill mannered, too, by the way, in your place," he told Carter as they got Phoebe to the sidewalk. "Still, under any circumstances, when I bring a woman home, I take her to the door."

Resigned to it, Phoebe allowed herself to be flanked, then all but carried up the steps. And with the overture complete, she thought, Here comes the show.

When the door opened, Essie was already on her way down the hall. "I thought I heard you shouting, Carter. I . . . Phoebe! Oh my God."

She went white as paste, swayed.

"Let me go," Phoebe murmured, then hurried forward. "Mama. I'm all right, Mama. Breathe for me. I'm all right, I'm home. Carter, go get her some water."

"No, no." Still ghostly pale, Essie lifted a hand to Phoebe's cheek. "Baby girl."

"I'm all right."

"Your face. Reuben—"

"Is dead, Mama. You know that."

"Yes. Yes. I'm sorry. I'm sorry. Oh, Phoebe. What happened? Your face, your arm. Ava!"

She'd snapped back, Phoebe noted. Still white as a sheet, but she'd snapped back.

Ava rushed out from the back of the house. And there was, for the next several minutes, a mass of confusion, voices, movement, tears. Duncan closed the front door, stood back. He'd always figured if you can't help, stay out of the way.

"All right, stop now."

He could hear Phoebe's voice, very calm, very firm, through the melee. She repeated the same order, once, then twice. And on the third, the words snapped out—a kind of verbal slap to the face—and shocked her family into silence.

"I'll explain everything, but right now I want everybody to just *stop* talking at once. I've been banged up, which is obvious, and all this badgering isn't helping. Now—"

"Mama."

As the verbal slap had shut down the hysteria, so did the single, quivering word stop what Duncan assumed might have been an irritated rant. Phoebe turned toward the little girl who stood holding a bright red ball.

"I'm all right, Carly. I know I don't look it, but I am. I will be. I got hurt, but I'm okay."

"Mama." The ball went bouncing away as Carly ran forward to grab Phoebe, to press her face against her mother's waist. From his vantage point, Duncan saw the ripple of pain, and the way it leached all color out of Phoebe's cheeks.

"Hey, sorry. I know this is a bad time, but, you know, I think Phoebe needs to lie down." He moved forward as he spoke and simply lifted Phoebe off her feet. "Carly, maybe you could show me where your mama's bedroom is."

"It's upstairs."

"I can walk. Duncan, I can walk."

"Sure, but hey, I already got you. Miz MacNamara? They gave Phoebe some medication. I think it might be time for her to take it, if she had some water."

"Of course, of course."

"I'll get it." Ava touched Essie's arm. "You go up with Phoebe. I'll get the water, and some ice. Carter, help me get some ice for Phoebe."

"I'm going up to fix the bed. I'm going right up to get it ready." Essie dashed up the stairs.

"Did you fall?" Carly's voice still shook as she walked up beside Duncan, with her fingers closed over the hem of the scrubs.

"That was part of it. I had a bad fall, and I had to go to the hospital. They fixed me up and let me come home. You know they don't let you go home if you're not fixed enough. Right?"

"Is your arm broken?"

"No. It's just hurt, so it's in this sling for a while so I don't bump it around."

"How come you didn't catch her when she fell?" Carly demanded of Duncan.

"I wish I could have. I wasn't there when she fell."

He carried Phoebe into the bedroom where Essie had already turned down the spread, fluffed the pillows. "Just lay her right on down. Thank you so much, Duncan. Phoebe, I'm sorry, I just lost my head."

"It's all right, Mama. Everything's going to be all right."

"Of course it is." Though her lips quivered visibly, Essie sent Carly a big smile. "We're going to take good care of your mama, aren't we? She needs some medicine now."

"It's in my purse. I—"

"Right here." Duncan set it on the bed.

"You're good with details," Phoebe commented.

"Wouldn't you like to go down and sit in the parlor, Duncan?" Essie began. "Carter, he'll fix you a drink. And . . ." She rubbed her fingers on her temple. "And you'll stay for dinner. You'll stay for dinner, of course."

"That's nice of you, but I'll leave y'all to tend to Phoebe. I hope I can have a rain check."

"You're welcome anytime. Anytime at all. I'll walk you down."

"You stay right here." He gave Essie's shoulder a pat before he looked down at Phoebe. "That goes for you, too."

"I think I'm going to do just that. Duncan—"

"We'll talk later."

As he left, Carter bounded up the stairs. Carter stopped, gripping a pair of ice bags. "Sorry about jumping on you out there."

"Forget it. Natural."

"Do you know who punched my sister in the face? I took enough fists in the face to know what the results look like," he said when Duncan lifted his brows.

"I don't know who hurt her, but I'm going to find out."

"When you do—if it's before I do—I want to know."

"Sure."

"Carter MacNamara." Carter shifted ice bags, held out a hand.

"Duncan Swift. See you around."

Duncan let himself out, glanced up toward the bedroom window as he walked to his car. Gorgeous house, he thought, and just full of problems. He had enough experience with problems to know they came in all flavors and varieties.

Just as he knew, without question, that whatever the problems, Phoebe was the glue that held the family together.

Gift or burden? he wondered. And decided it was probably a good chunk of both.

A smart man would drive away from the gorgeous house with its variety of problems. Drive away and keep on going. That's what a smart man would do.

Then again, Duncan thought, there were times it was more interesting, and certainly more rewarding, just to be dumb.

He ended up at a bar. The after-work crowd wouldn't flood into Slam Dunc for nearly an hour, so despite the multiple flat screens rolling out ESPN, and the scatter of customers playing pool or air hockey, Duncan figured it was quiet enough for a meeting.

Anyway, he wanted a beer, and felt after the afternoon he'd put in, he'd earned it. He kept an eye out for Phin, and when he saw his friend come in, Duncan signaled the bar.

"Already ordered you a Corona, and some nachos."

Phin slid into the booth. "Left me hanging today."

"I know, I'm sorry. Couldn't be helped. What do you figure?"

Phin puffed out his cheeks. "Jake, who you also left hanging as he got there two minutes after you split, did a walk-through. He's going to work up a detailed estimate of what it'll cost you to do what you want with the building. But his eyeball opinion? You're going to have to sink minimum of one-point-five into it, over and above the cost."

"Okay."

Phin leaned back as the nachos slid between them and the waiter set the Corona with its slice of lime on the table. "You ever look back, wonder how we got to be sitting here talking about a million and a half dollars like it was pocket change?"

"How much did that suit cost?"

Phin grinned, picked up his beer. "Fine-looking suit, isn't it?"

"Dude, you're my fashion god. Figure two for the overhaul; let's not be pikers. Add in what I'll pay that squirrel for the property."

"Does look like a squirrel," Phin commented.

"Maybe he'll take some of the buy money and spring for a decent toupee. Anyhow . . . Got a pen?"

Phin took a Mont Blanc out of his inside jacket pocket. "Why don't you ever have a damn pen?"

"Where am I going to put it? And you always have one." Duncan scribbled figures on a napkin.

And that said it all, Phin thought. The man might look like your average guy—the worn jeans, the untucked, rolled-up-at-the-sleeves shirt, the hair begging for a trim. He might come across to most as an extraordinarily lucky guy who happened to pick the right numbers at the right time. Appearances didn't mean dick when it came to Duncan Swift.

He'd use that borrowed pen and a napkin to figure out cost runs, overlay, buffer, outlay and potential income. He'd do it while eating nachos and drinking a beer, and by the time he was done, he'd have his projected cost and future returns figured as close to the mark as any fleet of accountants.

The man had a knack, Phin decided as he—with care—transferred some loaded nachos from platter to plate. "Where'd you take off to?"

"That's something I want to talk to you about. Or more specifically, with your lovely wife."

"Loo's in court."

Duncan glanced up, over, and smiled. "Not now, she's not."

She wore a conservative blue suit that managed to showcase her mile-long legs. Her sexy curls were tamed back into a clip so that her sharp cheekbones, deep brown eyes, wide mouth were subtly framed. Her skin was the color of rich caramel.

Duncan always wondered how any judge or jury could look at that face and not give her whatever she wanted.

Duncan slid out of the booth, wrapped his arms around her and spoke into her ear just loud enough for Phin to hear. "Dump him. I'll buy you Fiji."

She had a big, strong laugh, and let it rip. "Can I just keep him to play with when you're busy?"

"Give me back my wife."

"Not done with her." Taking his time with it, Duncan gave her a long, dramatic kiss. "That'll hold me. Thanks for coming, Loo."

"Thought you were in court."

"I was." She sat next to Phin, nuzzled her lips to his. "Prosecution asked for a recess. I've got them on the ropes. Now, which of you hand-some men is going to buy me a martini?"

"Being shaken even as we speak. One minute. Here's what we'll of-fer the squirrel and here's where we top off." Duncan pushed the napkin over to Phin. "Okay?"

Phin glanced at the figures, shrugged. "It's your money."

"Yeah. Isn't that a kick in the ass?" Duncan picked up his beer. He knew Phin and Loo would be holding hands under the table. They had the thing, the *it*, whatever that *it* was that locked people together and kept them damn happy about it.

"Y'all want something more than nachos?" Duncan asked them.

"Just that martini. As our gorgeous and brilliant offspring is spend-ing the night with her cousin, I'm going to have this fine-looking man take me out to dinner."

"Are you?"

"I am, but not until I've had that drink and am finished playing footsie with my lover here." Loo winked at Duncan. "So, baby doll, what can I do for you?"

Duncan said nothing for a moment, then grinned. "Sorry, my mind went in all sorts of interesting directions." He listened to that terrific laugh of hers again. "It's about something that happened to a friend of mine today, and my curiosity over what gets done to the guy who did it when he gets caught."

"Criminal or civil?"

"It's pretty fucking criminal."

Loo raised her eyebrows at the tone, then accepted the martini she was served. She took the first, slow sip. "Should this individual be charged and indicted, I take it you'd object if I or my firm repre-sent him."

"I can't tell you what to do, but I figured you'd know the ins and outs of what he might try to pull, legally, when they get him."

"Not if, but when." She broke off a minute corner of a chip. "Okay, tell me what this man allegedly did."

"Before I tell you what he did, I'd better tell you, he's a cop."

"Oh. Well. Shit." Loo blew out a breath, drank again. "Tell me."

Interesting. From his seat at the bar, he nursed a beer, ate some cheese fries and pretended to be interested in the reports on March Madness that dominated the near screen.

He had a perfect view of the booth where Phoebe's screw-buddy sat with the duded-up black couple. Interesting, damn interesting—and fortunate that he himself had been watching the house on Jones when the fancy car pulled up.

Phoebe hadn't been looking so good.

He had to smother a laugh he knew might draw attention his way. No sir, the redheaded bitch hadn't been looking her best.

She was going to be looking worse before it was over. But for now, he'd take a little time, a little trouble, to find who Mr. Fancy Car and his friends were.

You never knew who might be useful.

9

With one ear cocked toward Phoebe's room, Essie carefully folded the white-on-white bedspread with its stylized pattern of lovebirds. The intricate stitching had kept her mind calm, as it tended to. She often thought that being productive—and creative with it, if she could brag a bit—held a firm rein on her mind and refused to allow it to wander into those places where panic waited.

It was good work, she could think that, and the bride who received it as a wedding gift would have something unique and special, something that could be passed on for generations.

She arranged the dark silver tissue. Even that, the fussing with the finished product, the meticulous packaging of it, helped keep her hands busy and her mind steady.

Because she didn't want to be afraid every time Phoebe went out of the house, didn't want to whittle her family's world down to walls, as she'd whittled her own. She couldn't allow herself to let that fear in, to let it take over. It snuck up, she knew, inch by inch, stealing little spaces, little movements.

First it might set your heart thumping, it might shut your lungs down in the grocery store, right there in Produce while you're surrounded by tomatoes and snap beans and romaine lettuce with Muzak playing "Moon River" until you want to scream.

Until you had to run, just leave your cart there, half full of groceries, and run.

It might be the dry cleaner's next, or the bank where the teller knew you by name and always asked about your children. It might sneak up then, dropping rock after rock after rock on your chest until you were buried alive.

Your ears ringing, the sweat pouring.

You let it win all those little spaces, all those little movements, until it had them all. Until it owned everything outside the walls.

She could still go out on the terraces, into the courtyard, but that was getting harder and harder. If it wasn't for Carly, Essie didn't think she could push herself even that far. The day was coming, she could feel it sliding closer, when she wouldn't be able to sit on the veranda and read a book with her precious little girl.

And who was to say she was wrong? Essie thought as she put the pretty oval sticker with her initials on the folded tissue to close it in place.

Terrible things happened in the world outside the walls. Hard, frightening and terrible things happened every minute of every day, on the streets and the sidewalks, at the market and the dry cleaner's.

Part of her wanted to pull her family inside those walls, lock the doors, bar the windows. Inside, she wished she could keep them inside, where everyone would be safe, where nothing terrible could happen to any of them, ever.

And she knew that was her illness whispering, trying to sneak in a little closer.

She lay the card that detailed instructions for the care of the lovebird spread, then closed the bright silver box.

While she gift-wrapped the box as the customer had ordered, she was calmer. Her gaze strayed to the windows now and then, but that was just a check, just a peek at what might be out there. She was pleased it was raining. She loved rainy days when it seemed so cozy and snug and *right* to be inside the house, all tucked in like the lovebirds in the silver box.

By the time she had the gift cushioned in its shipping box, sealed and labeled, she was humming.

She carried it out, pausing to peek into Phoebe's room, and smiling when she saw her baby girl sleeping. Sleep and rest and quiet, that's what her baby needed to heal. When she woke from her nap, Essie decided she'd bring Phoebe up a tea tray, a nice little snack, and sit with her the way she had so many years ago when her daughter had been down with a cold or a touch of flu.

She was halfway down the steps with the big box when the doorbell rang. The jolt shot through her like a bullet, driving her right down, legs folding, heart slamming, to sit on the steps with her arms wrapped around the box as if it would shield her.

And she could have wept, could have dropped her head down on the box and wept at the instant and uncontrollable terror.

The door was locked, and could stay locked if she needed it to. No one in, no one out. All the pretty birds inside the silver box.

How could she explain to anyone, *anyone,* the grip of the sudden, strangling fear, the way it set the little white scar on her cheek throbbing like a fresh wound? But the bell would ring again if she didn't answer—hear that, it's ringing again. It would wake Phoebe, and she needed to sleep.

Who was going to protect her baby if she ran away and hid?

So she was not going to cower on the steps; she was not going to allow herself to fear opening the front door, even if she was unable to walk out of it.

She got up, made herself walk to the door, though she did continue to clutch the box in front of her. And the relief made her feel foolish, and a little ashamed, when she saw Duncan on the other side.

Such a nice boy, Essie thought as she took a moment, just one moment more, to get her breath back. A solid, well-mannered young man who'd carried her hurt baby girl up to bed.

There was nothing to be afraid of.

Shifting the box, Essie unlocked the door and beamed a smile.

"Duncan! How nice of you to come by. Look at you, all that rain and no umbrella! Come in the house."

"Let me take that for you."

"No, that's all right. I'm just going to set it down here." She turned as she did, hoped he couldn't see her hands still shaking. "I've got a pickup scheduled for it. How about some coffee?"

"Don't trouble. Hey." He took her hands, so she knew he had seen. "Are you all right?"

"I'm a little on edge, that's all. Foolish."

"Not foolish at all, not after what happened. I've been jumpy myself."

No, Essie thought, no, he hadn't. He wasn't the type to jolt at sounds and shadows. But it was sweet of him to say otherwise. "Don't tell Phoebe I said so, but it calms my nerves having a big, strong man in the house."

"Someone else here?" he said and made her laugh. "Secret's safe. I just stopped by to see how the patient's doing."

"She had a restless night." Essie took his arm, steered him into the parlor. "But she's sleeping now. Sit down and keep me company, won't you? Ava's at the flower shop. She works there a couple, three days a week when they can use her. My daughter-in-law's going to come by later. Josie's a nurse, a private-duty nurse. She took a look at Phoebe yesterday, and she's going to stop in later, with Carter, after his classes. And you know why I'm talking so much?"

"Are you?"

"Duncan, I'm so embarrassed by the way I acted yesterday."

"You shouldn't be. You had a shock."

"And I didn't handle it well."

"Essie, you ought to give yourself a break." He saw surprise cross over her face, as if she'd never thought of any such thing. "What've you been up to today?"

"Keeping busy, pestering Phoebe with food on trays until I imagine she wants to knock me over the head with them. I finished a project and made half a dozen lists I don't need."

Little tickled his interest more than the word *project*. Duncan stretched out his legs, prepared for a cozy chat. "What's the project?"

"Oh, I do needlework." Essie waved a hand toward the foyer, where the shipping box waited for pickup. "Finished up a bedspread—wedding gift—last night."

"Who's getting married?"

"Oh, a sometime customer of mine's goddaughter. I sell some of my pieces locally and over the Internet here and there."

"No kidding?" Enterprising projects doubled the interest. "You've got a cottage industry?"

"More like a sitting-room interest," she said with a laugh. "It's just a way to pay for my hobby, earn a little pin money."

While he sat, at ease, his mind calculated: handmade. Customized. One of a kind. "What kind of needlework?"

"I crochet. My mother taught me, her mother taught her. It was a keen disappointment I could never get Phoebe to sit still long enough to teach her. But Carly's getting a hand at it."

He scanned the room, homed in on the deep blue throw with its pattern of showy pink cabbage roses. Rising, he moved over to pick up an edge, study it.

Oh yeah, add in intricate and unique.

"Is this your work?"

"It is."

"It's nice. It's really nice. Looks like something maybe your grandma made over lots of quiet nights, then passed down to you."

Pleasure shone like sunshine on Essie's face. "Why, isn't that the best of compliments?"

"So, what, do you make specific pieces from, like, what, patterns, or tailor to clients?"

"Oh, it depends. Why don't I get you that coffee?"

"I've got to head out in a minute. Have you ever thought of . . . Hey."

It was the way his face lit up that had Essie pursing her lips, even before she turned and saw Phoebe in the parlor doorway.

"Now, what are you doing up and coming downstairs by yourself?" In full scold, Essie hurried over to her daughter's side. "Didn't I put that bell right on your nightstand so you could ring if you wanted anything?"

"I needed to get out of that bed. I'm not going to lie there Cousin Bessing it all damn day."

Duncan saw the look, the quick flash of maternal disapproval before Essie turned back to him. "You'll have to excuse her, Duncan. Feeling poorly brings out the sass in her. I'll go make us that coffee."

"Mama." Phoebe brushed a hand over Essie's arm. "Sorry. I didn't mean to snap at you."

"You get a pass on that, due to being hurt. Talk to Duncan awhile. He's come out on this rainy day just to see how you're feeling."

Phoebe only frowned at him as her mother left the room. "Yes, I know I look worse than I did yesterday."

"Then I don't have to mention it. Do you feel worse?"

"Some parts of me do. Including my temper." She glanced back toward the foyer, sighed. "Being fussed over makes me irritable."

"I'll try to restrain myself, then. And I should probably take these back." He picked up the shopping bag he'd brought in. "As it hits on two points—not wanting to lie around, and being fussed over. I assume bringing by a gift is fussing."

"Depends on the gift. Oh, sit down, Duncan. I'm irritating myself with my bad mood."

"I really have to go. I have a couple of things." He held up the bag, shook it lightly. "You want?"

"How do I know when I don't know what's in it?" She limped her way over, peered into the bag. "DVDs? God, there must be two dozen."

"I like to read or watch movies when I'm laid up. And I thought reading might be tough with the bum wing, so I went for movies. Chick flicks. I lean toward the oeuvre of *The Three Stooges,* but figured it would be wasted around here."

"You figured correctly."

"I don't know if you go for that type or if you like slasher films or watching stuff blow up, but I figured in a household of four women, this was the best bet."

"I like chick flicks, and slasher films and watching things blow up." Intrigued, she poked in the bag. "Since when is *The Blues Brothers* a chick flick?"

"It's not, I just happen to like it. It's the only one I picked out, actually. Marcie at the video store handled the rest. She assured me that they're all appropriate for a kid Carly's age, unless her mother's a real tight-ass. She didn't say tight-ass," he added, when Phoebe narrowed her eyes at him. "I inferred."

"It's very thoughtful of you. And Marcie. And when these help stave off screaming boredom, I'll think of you."

"That's the plan. I have to go. Tell your mother I said goodbye." He touched his lips to her forehead beside the bandages. "Take a dose of Jake and Elwood and call me in the morning."

"If I don't walk you to the door, I'll have to lie to my mother and say I did." She set the bag down to lead him out. "I appreciate the movies, and everything else you did—and didn't do. Such as comment on my bed hair and foul disposition."

"Good. Then when you're feeling up to it, you can pay me back and have dinner with me again."

"Are you bribing me with DVDs?"

"Sure. But I think my discretion over hair and mood earns even more points." Since it pleased him to see her lips curve up in a quick smile, he lowered his for a little taste. "I'll see you later."

He opened the door just as a woman jogged up the steps. "Hey," he said.

"Hey back. Lieutenant."

"Detective. Detective Liz Alberta, Duncan Swift."

"Oh yeah, we spoke on the phone." He held out a hand. "Nice to meet you, and I'll get out of your way. Talk to you later, Phoebe."

Liz turned, studied Duncan as he dashed out and through the rain. As she lowered her umbrella she raised her eyebrows at Phoebe. "Nice."

The tone, the look, told Phoebe that Liz referred to the exit view. "Oh yeah, it certainly is. Come in out of the wet."

"Thanks. I didn't think I'd find you up and around today."

"If I don't get back to work soon, I'm going to go straight out of my mind." She took Liz's umbrella, slid it into the porcelain umbrella stand.

"Bad patient?"

"The worst. Are you here for a follow-up?"

"If you can handle it."

"I can." Phoebe gestured toward the parlor. "Anything I should know?"

"Your weapon hasn't been recovered, but I did bring you this." She pulled an evidence bag out of her satchel. Inside was Phoebe's badge. "It was found at the base of the stairs, where we assume your attacker tossed it. No prints but yours."

"He wore gloves," Phoebe murmured.

"Yes, so you said."

Her badge would have been hooked to the waistband of her skirt, Phoebe thought. He'd cut her skirt to pieces, shoved his hand up under what he'd left of it to . . . She shook her head. No point, none, in putting herself back there. "Sorry. Please, sit down."

"How's the shoulder?"

"I tell myself it could be worse. It could. It could all be worse."

"Lieutenant—"

"Just make it Phoebe. This may be an official follow-up, but we're not in the house."

"Okay, Phoebe. You and I both know that sometimes the emotional injuries take a lot longer to heal than the physical ones."

Knowing and experiencing were two different things. "I'm working on that."

"All right."

"He set me up. Arnie Meeks set me up and he took me down."

Before Liz could respond, Essie wheeled in a cart. "Oh, I'm sorry. I didn't realize you had other company. Duncan?"

"He had to go. Mama, this is Detective Alberta. My mother, Essie MacNamara."

"You took care of my daughter when she was hurt yesterday. Thank you."

"You're welcome. It's good to meet you, Mrs. MacNamara."

"I hope you'll have coffee, and some of this cake." Essie set cups, saucers, plates on the coffee table as she spoke. "I just have a few things to see to in the kitchen." She lifted the tray holding the pot, the creamer, the sugar. "Y'all just let me know if you need anything else."

"Thank you, Mama."

"Detective Alberta, you don't mind pouring, do you?"

"No, ma'am." Falling in, Liz picked up the coffeepot, poured out the cups. She shot a glance over as Essie slipped out of the room. "I thought carts like that were just for movies and fancy hotels."

"Sometimes this house feels like a little of both. You're going to tell me that you're actively investigating, but don't have any solid evidence implicating Officer Arnold Meeks at this time."

"I am, and I don't. I spoke with him. He was in the building and was smart enough not to deny it. He claims he was getting a few items out of his locker at the time of the attack."

"This was payback, Liz."

She looked out the window as her mother had earlier, but instead of being comforted by the rain, felt trapped by it. Trapped inside when there were things to *do.*

"I've bumped up against a few other cops, that's just the way it is. But no one recently, and never anyone to the extent Meeks and I rammed heads. I slapped him back, I suspended him, I recommended a psych eval. He wanted to kick my ass then and there, and in fact considered drawing on me. I saw it in his eyes, in his body language. As did Sykes, who interrupted for that reason."

"Yeah, I spoke with Detective Sykes, and he concurs that he sensed trouble from Meeks that day in your office. 'Sensed' isn't going to be enough. I've got nothing that places him in that stairway. In the building, yes, with a grudge against you, yes. He's called in his delegate, and he's got his father's considerable weight behind him. If you can give me more, if you remember anything, any detail."

"I gave you everything."

"Let's go over it again. Not just from the attack, but from when you left the house that morning."

Phoebe knew how it worked. Every repetition of the story could add another detail, and another detail might turn the investigation.

She went through it. Heading out to catch the bus as her car was in for repairs. She'd borrowed the MP3 player Ava liked to use when she gardened, and had tried to convince herself the bus was more relaxing, maybe more efficient than driving herself.

She detoured for coffee before taking the to-go cup into work.

"Did you notice anything? Anyone? Get the sense you were followed?"

"No. I can't say I wasn't. I wasn't tuned for that, but I didn't have any sense of it either. I went straight up to my office, started paperwork."

She went through it, the officers and detectives she'd spoken with, the movements. Routine, routine, routine, she thought. Just another Monday morning.

"After my conversation with the captain, I started down."

"You always take the stairs."

"Yes. It's habitual."

"Did you stop, talk to anyone?"

"No . . . Yes. I stopped by my PAA's desk to tell her I was going down to the session. Wait." Phoebe set down her coffee, sat back, closed her eyes. She pulled it back into her head, the running image of herself striding out of her office, across the squad room.

"She held me up there for a minute, asked me some questions, nothing necessary—especially since she'd know I was running close to the clock. I didn't think anything about it at the time, except for being a little annoyed because I was cutting it close, and because she already knew—or should have—that I had the session waiting on me."

"Who's your PAA?" Liz asked as she pulled out her notebook.

"Annie Utz. I've only had her a few months. She stalled me." As she thought back, tried to bring it into focus, Phoebe closed her eyes. "I think she was stalling me, just a minute or two. Then she said something about how I'd be taking the stairs down, like always."

Phoebe opened her eyes, and now they were fierce with fury. "She was signaling him, by radio or phone. Son of a bitch, she was letting him know I was on my way."

"Do you know if Arnie Meeks and your PAA have a personal relationship?"

"No. She's new, like I said, only a couple of months on the desk. Sharp-looking, single, friendly. Maybe a little on the flirty side, but nothing over the line. She was nervous, a little nervous yesterday. I was in a hurry so I didn't pay attention. I didn't think of her, of that quick conversation again until now."

"I'll talk to her."

"No. No, we will. I'm going in with you."

"Lieutenant. Phoebe—"

"Put yourself in my place."

Liz drew a deep breath. "Do you need any help getting dressed?"

Phoebe was struggling, sweating and cursing her way into a shirt when Essie steamed into the room. "Just what do you think you're doing?"

"Trying to get into this goddamn shirt. I have to go with Detective Alberta."

"You're not to go anywhere but back to bed, Phoebe Katherine MacNamara."

"I should be back within an hour."

"Don't make me drag your stubborn self into that bed, Phoebe."

"Mama, for God's sake." Frustrated and starting to ache again, Phoebe dropped her arm. "Will you help me button this stupid shirt?"

"No. I said you're not going anywhere."

"And I said I am. There's a lead on my case, and I—"

"You are *not* a case. You're my child."

Out of breath, Phoebe cradled her bad arm. And through her own anger and annoyance saw the warning glints of panic in her mother's eyes. "Mama . . . All right, let's both calm down."

"I'll calm down when you get your beat-up self back into bed where you belong." Marching over, Essie flung back the bedclothes. "Right this minute! I'm not—"

"Mama, listen to me. My arm will heal, the rest of me will heal on the outside. We know how it is on the inside though, you and me. We know. So you understand when I tell you I'm not going to heal until the person who did this to me is held accountable."

"There are other people who can see that he's held accountable."

"I know you feel that way. I know you have to. Understand that I feel *this* way. That I have to. I can't live afraid, Mama, I just can't."

"That's not what I want, that's not what I'm asking you."

"But I am afraid. And I close my eyes and I'm back in that stairwell."

"Oh, baby." Tears swam as Essie hurried over to stroke her daughter's face.

"Part of me's going to stay afraid, and I'm going to keep finding myself trapped in that stairwell, until I do this. Help me with this shirt. Please."

Though her eyes were damp, Essie studied Phoebe's face and saw clearly enough. "I don't want you to live the way I do. I don't want you to be afraid."

"I know that."

Slowly, her eyes on Phoebe's, Essie buttoned the shirt. "Do you have to go so far the other way?"

"I guess I do. I'm sorry."

"Phoebe." Gently, Essie eased Phoebe's arm back into the sling. Then she brushed at Phoebe's hair with her fingertips. "When you get back, you're going straight to bed."

"Yes, ma'am."

"And you're going to eat all the dinner I bring up to you."

"Every bite." Phoebe kissed Essie's cheek where the little white scar rode under carefully applied makeup. "Thank you."

When Phoebe came back into the parlor with Essie at her side, Liz looked from one to the other. "Ah . . . your PAA called in sick this morning. I have her home address."

"We'll try her there."

"Detective? I don't care if she does outrank you, you take good care of my baby girl—and see she gets home."

"I'll do that, Mrs. MacNamara. Thank you for the coffee." Liz waited until they were outside to open her umbrella, and to speak again. "I don't care if you do outrank me, I take the lead on this."

"No argument. Friendly, flirty and efficient, that's how I'd describe her. Mid-twenties. I think she likes being around cops—likes the buzz. Thanks," she added when Liz opened the car door for her. "How bad do I look?" Phoebe asked when Liz got behind the wheel.

"Not quite bad enough to scare small children."

"Let her see me first. My gut says he didn't tell her he was going to hurt me. Scare me, maybe, or just plead his case." Despite the rainy day, Phoebe slipped on her sunglasses. "But I don't think she'd have gone along if she knew he intended to hurt me. She calls in sick the day after. She's probably scared, guilty, wondering what happened. The way cop shops work, she's heard a few variations. She sees me first, she's already going to start cracking."

Annie looked sick when she opened the door to her apartment. Against the cotton-candy pink of her pajamas, her face was white and drawn. Her eyes popped wide when she saw Phoebe. Stumbling back, she stuttered out Phoebe's name.

"Annie Utz? I'm Detective Alberta. Can we come in?"

"I—I—"

"Thanks." Liz pushed the door all the way open so Phoebe could walk in ahead of her. In the background a couple of soap opera actors argued bitterly over someone named Jasmine.

"Lieutenant MacNamara needs to sit down. She's hurt pretty bad."

"I . . . I have a head cold. I'm probably contagious."

"We'll risk it. You heard about what happened to Lieutenant Mac-Namara, didn't you?"

"Yes. I mean, I guess I did. I'm so sorry, Lieutenant. You should be home, resting."

"Annie . . . Mind if we turn this off?" Without waiting for permission, Liz picked up the remote and ended the threatening tirade of a shirtless blond hunk. "I'm looking into what happened to the lieutenant. You were the last one to speak to her before she was attacked."

"I . . . I don't know."

"You don't know that she stopped by your desk on her way out, on her way downstairs?"

"I mean, yes, sure. You said you were going downstairs for the training session." When she addressed Phoebe, Annie's gaze trained several inches over Phoebe's good shoulder.

"What time was that?"

"Just before ten. Just a few minutes before ten."

"You were aware the lieutenant intended to take the stairs down?"

"Everyone knows Lieutenant MacNamara uses the stairs." Annie tugged on a heart-shaped button on her pajamas. "I really don't feel well. I'm sorry."

"Lieutenant MacNamara doesn't feel very well either. Do you, Lieutenant?"

"No." Her sunglasses were back in her bag, where she'd tucked them on entering the building. Phoebe knew the bruised eyes, the scrapes, the bandages were a shocking and painful sight. Just as she knew how to wait, how to use the silence as a lever to pry Annie's eyes to hers. "He pushed me down, after he'd cuffed my hands behind me so I couldn't break my own fall."

Her gaze steady on Annie's tearful one, Phoebe lifted her hands to show her bandaged wrists. "After he'd taped my mouth, put a hood over my head." She brushed the hair back from her forehead so the livid bruises showed more clearly. "After he'd smashed my face into the wall."

Tears spilled, plump drops on pale cheeks. "I . . . I heard it was really just a bad accident. I heard that you fell. That you fell down the stairs."

"Was it an accident his fist rammed into her face?" Liz demanded. "That the cuffs snapped over her wrists?" She pulled up Phoebe's arm, gestured to the wrists. "Did her clothes accidentally rip off her body so she had to crawl, half naked, for help?"

"Things get exaggerated. I'm sorry, I'm sorry, I don't feel well. Can you go? Can you just go?"

"Did he tell you he just wanted to talk to me, Annie?" Phoebe kept her voice low, the tone even. "Just talk to me in private? Maybe scare me just a little, or push his point just a little, since I was being so unfair? I was being unfair to him, wasn't I? Did he tell you that when he asked you to signal him I was heading down?"

"I don't know what you mean. I didn't do anything. If you fell—"

"I didn't fall. Look at me, Annie!" Phoebe snapped the words out so that Annie jumped, then hunched her shoulders. "You know I didn't fall. That's why you're sitting here, sick, scared, trying to convince yourself it was an accident. He told you that. He told you it was an accident and I—what?—lied to save face? I made up the attack so I wouldn't be embarrassed about falling?"

"How long have you been sleeping with Officer Arnold Meeks, Annie?" Liz demanded.

"I didn't! We didn't. Not really. I didn't mean anything. I didn't do anything." As the dam broke, Annie snatched up tissues from a flowered box of Kleenex and buried her face in them. "He said it was an accident, that you were going to make things up, maybe to try to get him in trouble. He told me how you came on to him, and then—"

"Officer Meeks told you Lieutenant MacNamara approached him sexually?"

"He turned her down, and she's been trying to ruin his reputation ever since." Lowering the tissues, Annie turned a pleading face toward Liz. "He'd file sexual harassment charges, but he's embarrassed to, and his wife's not giving him any support at home. Plus she's sleeping with Captain McVee, so what good would it do?"

"He told you all this, and you swallowed it?" Liz shook her head from side to side. "Maybe that's excusable, maybe not. Maybe you thought, really thought, you were just doing Arnie a favor. Maybe you didn't want to believe he was lying to you, again and again and again, leading you on. But you know he lied to you now, don't you, Annie? You can't look at Lieutenant MacNamara and believe what he told you."

"I don't know. I don't know."

"How about some pictures?" Liz pulled some out of her satchel. "There's the lieutenant's blood in the stairwell. Oh, here, here's her clothes that *accidentally* tore off her body. How about the laundry bag he pulled over her head? Here's a good one, of her blood on the cuffs he snapped on her. That's some accident."

"Oh God." The tissue shield went up again. "Oh God."

"What kind of person does this, Annie? Maybe the kind of person who's thinking about doing it to you, or doing worse. Because you're the one who can tie him to it."

"I didn't know. I didn't know." Annie sobbed, yanked more tissues from the box. "I didn't do anything wrong. He just needed a few minutes to talk to her, to show he wasn't going to be intimidated. That's *all*. I only called his number, let the phone ring twice. That was the signal. It's all I did. I didn't know."

"But you know now. You're going to have to get dressed and come with me."

"Are you arresting me? Oh God, am I under arrest?"

"Not yet. If you get dressed and come in now, give a true statement—

tell the truth, Annie—I'll talk to the DA for you. He lied to you. I believe you when you said he lied."

"So do I." Phoebe kept her fury banked and spoke soothingly. "I believe you, Annie."

"I'm so sorry, Lieutenant. I'm really sorry."

"Yes, I'm sure you are."

Liz looked over at Phoebe. "I'll drop you back home and take it from here."

10

"**I want to be there.** I need to be there."

Dave leaned back in his desk chair, continued to scan Phoebe's face. "First, it's not my call. Second, this is Liz Alberta's case. You're the victim. If you have trouble remembering that, I can have a mirror brought in."

She knew how she looked. A couple of days meant some of the bruising was turning from black to sickly yellow and storm-cloud purple. Her jaw and eye were angry watercolors. Still, the worst of it was decently hidden under her clothes.

"The victim needs it. I need to sit in that room, look Arnold Meeks in the eye so he knows I'm not afraid of him."

"Aren't you?"

"Enough that I need to show him, and myself, that I'm not going to be. You and I know how the pathology works. How it is for someone who's held against their will, threatened or injured in a situation beyond their control."

"This isn't identifying an attacker in a lineup, Phoebe. Or facing the attacker in court."

"It's just more proactive. My mother faced Reuben in court. She got up on the stand to testify while he was only feet away from her, and I know that was nearly as terrifying for her as being trapped in that house with him all those hours. But she did it, and still she's trapped."

All the affection and understanding he felt was there to read on his face. "You're not your mother."

"No, but . . ." Phoebe fisted a hand on her heart. "I feel her fear, and I don't want it living inside me. How can I do what I need to do if it finds a place to live in me? So this victim needs it."

"Observation," he began, though they both knew he was losing ground.

"Isn't enough." She shook her head. "Face-to-face, and this time I know he won't be controlling the situation. The cop wants to be in that room with him because I may be able to help Liz get a confession out of him. I was there. Victim, witness, police officer. Makes me a triple threat."

"And still doesn't make it my call. It's up to Detective Alberta, her captain and the DA. The DA," Dave continued before she could speak, "who fishes with Arnie's daddy."

"Whoever he fishes with, Parnell's always struck me as solid. Do you really think he'll ease off an investigation of an attack on a police officer because he's buddied up with the father of a suspect?"

"It's a lot of who-you-know in Savannah, Phoebe, just like anywhere else. But I'll agree, Parnell's solid. Meeks is bringing his delegate and a lawyer in with him. Annie Utz is lawyered, too."

"All the more reason for me to give Liz—Detective Alberta—some backup—someone well invested who doesn't give a damn who Arnie's daddy drowns worms with. And I'll tell you something else. Having two women question him, put pressure on him?"

She wandered the office as she spoke now, because she could feel it, she could see it. She could all but taste it. "Oh, Arnie's not going to like that one little bit. He'll make a mistake. He'll end up leading with his ego, especially if I'm in there. Not your call, Captain, but you could make one. You could reach out to Detective Alberta's captain or her lieutenant, ask that I get a seat."

"I'll make a call, but I'm not making any promises."

"Any worthwhile negotiator's careful with his promises." She touched a hand to his shoulder. "The call's enough. Thank you."

"If you buy a ticket into the interrogation, have to deal with him that way, I might not have done you any favor. How's your family handling this?"

"It shook them up. My mother . . . you know how it is."

"I do. Would me coming by help things or add to them?"

"Mama always feels better after a visit from you. We all do. Why don't you come to Sunday dinner?"

He kicked back in his chair. "Would that mean sugar-glazed ham?"

"It could be arranged. Thanks for this."

"Phoebe . . ." Straightening again, he cleared his throat. "I want to say I regret there's been any speculation or gossip inside the department regarding an inappropriate relationship between us."

"Such as me giving you bj's in your office."

"Oh, Jesus." The tips of his ears went pink, as she knew they did when he was mortally embarrassed. "I'm old enough to be your father."

"First, you'd have been a very precocious fifteen to have pulled that one off. Second, since when does age factor into inappropriate sexual behavior? Neither of us is responsible for the speculation of small, ugly minds."

He picked up a ballpoint pen, clicked it a few times. "I opened you up for this when I asked you to take the desk in this department."

"You gave me an opportunity—which I grabbed—to do the work I'm good at. Am I qualified for the desk?"

"You know you are."

"There you are, then."

"Meeks, junior and/or senior, may push this into IAB."

"And we can both stand up to that, should that happen. Don't worry about me in this."

But he did. Even as he lifted the phone to put in the call she'd asked for, he worried.

Phoebe had a moment alone in Observation, studying Arnie Meeks through the two-way mirror. He looked careless, she decided. Carelessly confident. A kind of screw-you posture of a man who believes whatever he's done isn't going to stick to him.

He'd know he was being watched, or could be watched at any time. He didn't give a damn, Phoebe concluded.

And when she imagined his hands on her, his fingers inside her, her stomach rolled.

She gave too much of a damn.

"Lieutenant." Liz stepped in with a tall, reed-thin brunette. "ADA Monica Witt, Lieutenant Phoebe MacNamara."

"Lieutenant." Monica shook hands with Phoebe. "How are you feeling?"

"Better, thanks. I take it you'll be prosecuting the case."

"If you can make one. We have Annie Utz's statement, and her phone, which shows an outgoing call at nine fifty-eight. We can't tie that to Arnold Meeks. The number called was to a toss-away phone, un-traceable. We don't have any physical evidence linking Meeks to the attack."

"You have motive. You have opportunity, and a pattern of insubor-dinate and threatening behavior."

"My boss wants more than that to charge a police officer with assault and battery, with sexual assault on a fellow officer. Get me more, and I'll charge him."

Two men stepped in. Phoebe recognized Liz's lieutenant, nodded in acknowledgment. Just as she recognized, through the strong family re-semblance, Arnie Meeks's father.

He was thicker than his son through the chest, stronger along the jawline, harder in the eyes. But there was no mistaking the relation-ship. Just as there was no mistaking the insulted anger that pumped off him despite his ramrod posture.

"Lieutenant Anthony and Sergeant Meeks will also be observing."

"We'll get started." Liz walked to the door, held it open as Phoebe followed.

"When my boy's clear of this," Sergeant Meeks said as he shifted to block Phoebe's path, "and his suspension lifted, this won't be over for you, Lieutenant MacNamara."

"Sergeant, you're here as a courtesy." Anthony laid a hand on his arm. "Don't abuse that courtesy."

Phoebe moved around him to the door of the interrogation room. "Like father," she said under her breath.

"Shake it off," Liz advised. "I take the lead on this."

"We've been this round before."

"Just a friendly reminder." Opening the door, she walked in.

He didn't spare Liz so much as a look, Phoebe noted. His eyes aimed straight for her, held.

"Boys." Liz smiled easily, with a nod toward the trio at the table. She set the recorder, fed in the data, read Arnie his rights. "You understand all that, Officer Meeks?"

"I've given the Miranda enough times, I better."

"That's a yes?"

"Yeah, I understand my *rights*. Shouldn't you be in bed somewhere with an ice pack and some Darvon?" he asked Phoebe.

"Arnie."

Arnie shrugged off the quiet warning from his attorney.

"I'm surprised by your concern, Arnie," Liz began. "The way I hear it, you're not Lieutenant MacNamara's biggest fan."

"I don't think much of her as a cop. Then again, she's not much of one seeing as all she does is talk."

"We'll save your definition of 'much of a cop' for later, if it's all the same to you." Smooth as top cream, Liz kept an easy smile on her face. "The two of you—meaning you and Lieutenant MacNamara—have had a couple of set-tos recently. Is that true?"

"My client stipulates that he and Lieutenant MacNamara hold opposing viewpoints and professional styles. Those are hardly motives for a physical attack on her person. The lack of evidence—"

"We're talking here," Liz said. "Just getting things out on the table. Arnie, you don't much like Lieutenant MacNamara. Is that fair to say?"

Arnie kept his smirk aimed at Phoebe. "Yeah, that's fair."

"Did you have occasion to call Lieutenant MacNamara a bitch?"

"I call them as I see them."

"So, she's a bitch?" At Arnie's shrug, Liz nodded. "And you have no particular problem calling a superior officer a bitch? No problem threatening her when she took disciplinary action?"

"There's only Lieutenant MacNamara's word on this alleged threat," the lawyer interrupted.

"That, and . . ." Liz flipped through her file. "The statements of two detectives who observed your client in the lieutenant's office behaving in what they believed was a threatening manner."

"Their beliefs aren't fact."

"Arnie, do you remember why you were in Lieutenant MacNamara's office on Thursday last?"

"Sure I do. She was covering her ass after she screwed up a hostage negotiation by suspending me."

"Really?" Liz turned round eyes on Phoebe. "My goodness, if that was the case, who could blame you for calling her a bitch? Why don't we pull out a few statements and reports on that negotiation—at which you were the first responder—just to get the overview? Hmmm. FR did not call for backup. FR did not begin a log . . . Ah, here's a good one. FR antagonized the HT with threats. I like this one, too: Officer Meeks hampered and attempted to block Lieutenant MacNamara's contact with the HT."

Arnie rocked back in his chair, balanced on its back legs, rocked up again. "She can write anything she wants. Doesn't mean that's how it went down."

"Actually, all those examples are from witnesses—civilian and law enforcement. Well now, reading all this, it looks like you screwed things up there, Arnie."

"I had the situation under control until she pushed into it."

"So, you just needed a little more time to resolve the matter, and she didn't give it to you." Lips pursed, Liz nodded. "The guy blows his brains out, and you get the rap. Then, the bitch suspends you. I'd be pissed, too. Hard to blame you for wanting to pay her back."

Arnie smiled, shoved his hand at his lawyer before the lawyer could speak. "Just shut up. She's insulting me thinking she can bait me into saying something stupid. What about you?" he said to Phoebe. "Nothing to say for a change?"

"I was just sitting here wondering how your wife feels about all this. How she feels about you diddling with Annie Utz, for instance."

The smirk twisted his lips. "Annie's cute, and thick as a brick. I flirted, I admit it. Every guy in the squad did. But when she came on to me, when she wanted to take it past a wink, I set her straight. Got her feelings hurt, so I guess she figured to pay me back with this wild story. Or you pushed her to lie."

Phoebe looked over at Liz. "The man's surrounded by liars and bitches. It's a wonder he gets through the day."

"I don't know how he gets out of bed in the morning. So Annie's lying when she states you and she had a sexual relationship?"

He grinned widely, shook his finger. "I never had sex with that woman."

"Cute," Liz acknowledged. "And really adorable when you consider Annie states that relationship was limited to oral sex. A blurry line, I grant you. She 'came on' to you, that's what you said, and that's funny, too. In her statement she uses that same phrase. You told her Lieutenant MacNamara came on to you. And when you, being the moral, upstanding type, turned her down, she got her feelings hurt and looked for payback. My God, man, the women just make your life a living hell. I have to tell you, I'm actively restraining myself from coming on to you right now."

"Keep it up, Detective," the lawyer warned, "and this interview is over."

"Just going with what seems to be a pattern. You were in the building Monday morning between nine and ten A.M., Officer?"

"That's right. I had some things I wanted out of my locker."

"It took you an hour to get some things out of your locker?"

"I hung around. I'm a cop," he said with some irritation. "This is my house. I'm supposed to be here. I'm supposed to be doing the job. And I would be if it wasn't for her and the stick up her ass."

"Now she's a bitch with a stick up her ass who came on to you."

"I call them like I see them, remember?"

"But it was Annie who said Lieutenant MacNamara came on to you." Liz smiled pleasantly when annoyance crossed Arnie's face. "I think you're getting your excuses and lies mixed up here. But it's easy to see why. It's hard to tell one bitch from the other, isn't it? We're all pretty much the same. You didn't need to see Phoebe's face when you punched your fist into it. You didn't need to hear her scream or cry or curse you when you shoved her down, ripped her clothes to shreds. Of course, it didn't take any *balls* to do that, not when her hands were cuffed. I guess one man's payback is another man's cowardice."

"I'm man enough."

"Man enough to use one woman to ambush another." The sugary tone was a thing of the past now as Liz whipped out the words. "Man enough to lie in wait like a snake in the grass. And the only way you could put your hands on her was to cuff her, to knock her down. That's the only way you could get her naked and put hands on her."

"I was never in that stairway," Arnie shot back. "I never touched her. I got better things to do with my time. I sure got better things to do with my fingers." He flipped the middle one at Phoebe.

"She never said anything about fingers," Phoebe said quietly. "She said hands."

He sat back. "Hands, fingers. Same thing."

"It's really not." There was a hot ball jammed between her belly and her heart, hard and hot. She needed it to break apart and dissolve.

The victim needed it, she thought, to kill the fear.

"You rammed them inside me. You son of a bitch." She surged to her feet, ignoring the lawyer's objections as she leaned across the table. "You smelled like baby powder, just like you do now. Under the sweat. Because you're starting to sweat, Arnie. Do you remember what you said to me?"

"Can't remember something I didn't say. I wasn't there."

"You said you didn't fuck my kind. I figure you didn't use your dick because it's too small to make an impression. Your kind can't get it up half the time anyway."

"Too bad you didn't break your neck in the fall."

"This interview's over," the lawyer announced.

"You should've pushed me harder. Maybe if I'd broken something, you'd have gotten a decent boner."

"I should've kicked you down the damn stairs."

She eased back, nodded as that hard, hot ball began to dissolve. "Your mistake."

"I said, this interview is over."

"That's fine." Liz rose. "We'll just move right along, then. Officer Meeks, you're under arrest."

Phoebe went straight to her office, closed herself in, and did something she rarely did. She lowered and closed her blinds. Carefully, she sat behind her desk.

Everything seemed to be throbbing at once. Emotional upheaval, stress, she told herself. All of it pushing the physical discomfort up several notches. She couldn't take a pill, not here. They made her sleepy and fuzzy-headed, so she settled for four Motrin. And watched her hands shake on the bottle.

Yeah, the ball was dissolving, she thought, and there was a price to pay for it.

She didn't answer the knock on her door, and thought only, Go away. Give me five damn minutes.

But the door opened, and Liz stepped in. "Sorry. How you holding up?"

"Got the shakes."

"You didn't have them in there, when it counted."

"He looked at me, he looked me right in the eye. He was glad he hurt me. He only wished he'd hurt me more."

"And that's what did him," Liz pointed out. "I don't care how coached he is by his lawyer, it's going to show. He can't resist, he can't control it. When this goes to trial—"

"It's not going to trial, Liz. We both know that."

Liz walked around the desk, sat on the edge. "Okay, yeah. They'll make a deal. The department, the DA, nobody's going to want a public trial, and the publicity that goes with it. And even with what happened in interrogation, the case is a little shaky. Strong enough so Arnie's lawyer knows to take a deal when it's offered. He's going to lose his badge, Phoebe, and he's going to be disgraced. Is that going to be enough for you?"

"It'll have to be. I appreciate all you did."

"You pulled plenty of the weight."

"Hey," Phoebe said when Liz got up. "I know this nice bar—Irish pub on River Street. I'd like to buy you a drink. I need a few days' grace on it, until my vanity lets me go out in public."

"Sure, just let me know. Take care, Phoebe."

Down in Holding, Arnie paced his cell. They'd arrested him, booked him. Goddamn useless lawyer.

Goddamn bitches screwed it all up. Assault, battery, sexual mo-lestation. Railroading him, that's what they were doing, all because that *cunt* couldn't handle a few bruises she'd damn well earned.

It wouldn't stick. No possible way they could make it stick.

He whipped around when the door slid open, and bit back the words that wanted to spew out only because his father shook his head when he came in.

So Arnie held them in until the guard stepped away.

"They can't make this bullshit stick," Arnie began. "She's not going to get away with locking me up like this, with embarrassing me in front of my fellow officers. That bitch—"

"Sit down. Shut up."

Arnie sat, but he couldn't shut up. "You see how they put a girl ADA on it? Circle the fucking wagons. What's Chuck thinking, for God's sake?" Arnie demanded, speaking of the DA. "Why didn't he just kick this in the first place?"

"He's getting the arraignment pushed up, and he's going to recom-mend ROR."

"Well, Jesus, that's just great." In disgust Arnie threw his hands up. "I get charged for this bullshit, but released on my own recogni-

zance, and that makes it okay? Fuck that, Pa. I could lose my badge.
You need to reach out to IAB, get an investigation on MacNamara. You
know McVee's dipping his wick in that. You know that's why I'm
in here."

Mouth tight, Sergeant Meeks stared down at his son. "You're in here
because you couldn't keep your mouth shut, just like now. I'm going to
ask you one time. Just you and me. I'm going to ask this one time, and
I want the truth. You lie, I'll see it. I see it, and I walk out of here, and
that's the last I'll do for you."

Anger faded away into shock, and the first trickle of fear.
"Christ, Pa."

"Did you do this thing? You look at me, Arnie. Did you do this?"

"I—"

"Don't you fucking lie."

"She suspended me. She used me as a goat. You taught me to stand
up for myself, not to take shit off anyone. If you got to kick an ass, you
kick it."

Meeks stared. "Did I teach you to use your fists on a woman, boy?
Did I teach you that?"

"She wouldn't get off my back. She—" He broke off, eyes watering,
burning, when his father's hand slapped across his face.

"Did I teach you to jump a superior officer from behind, like a coward? I taught you to be a *man,* goddamn it, not to hide in some stairwell
and beat on a woman. You're a disgrace to me, to the family name, to
the job."

"They come at you, you come back harder. That's what you taught
me. That's what I did."

"You don't see the difference, there's nothing I can say." Wearily,
Meeks got to his feet. "I'll use what I've got to fix this for you, the best
I can. You're my son, so I'll do it for you, for your mother, for my grand-
son. But you're done on the job, Arnie. If I could fix that, I wouldn't.
You're done."

"Then how are you going to hold your head up, if you don't have
your son following you on the job?"

"I don't know. I'll get you out of this, the best I can. After that, I
don't know."

"I only did what I thought you'd do."

"If I believed that, I'd feel sicker than I do now." Meeks walked over to the cell door, set his jaw. "On the gate!" he called, then left his son.

By Sunday, Phoebe decided to ditch the sling. She was tired of it, tired of the meds, tired of the bruises.

And she had to admit she was tired of having to fight back the need to whine and complain so that she could ease her family back into routine.

Still, she felt better when she stepped out of the shower, especially if she avoided any glimpse of herself in the mirror. She managed to get her robe on without too much of a struggle, and decided she'd probably not only last through Sunday dinner, but maybe even make it until the crazy hour of ten o'clock that night before her energy just drained out like water from a sieve.

She walked into her bedroom just as her sister-in-law walked through the door. "Knock, knock," Josie said with a big smile. "How's the patient today?"

"I've crossed myself off the disabled list, thanks."

"I'll be the judge of that. Let her drop."

"Come on, Josie."

Josie's smile only widened. She was barely five-two, weighed in at maybe one-ten fully dressed, and behind that angelic smile was a hardass that would make Nurse Ratched tremble.

"Drop the robe, sweets, or I'll tell your mother."

"That's mean."

"I am mean."

"Don't I know. I'm going to run away to Atlanta, get myself an apartment and leave no forwarding address." But Phoebe dropped the robe.

Sympathy shone in Josie's big brown eyes, but her voice was brisk. "Bruising's fading. The hip looks a lot better. That shoulder has to be painful yet."

"It's coming along."

"How's the range of motion?"

"I'm still grateful I've got some front-hook bras, but it's improving."

Josie took Phoebe's hands, turned them over. If truth be told, those injuries hurt her heart more than the rest. "Wrist lacerations look pretty good."

"Bitching sore if you want the truth. Can I regain my modesty now?"

Josie picked up the robe, helped Phoebe into it. "Any trouble with your vision in that eye?"

"No, it's clear. And before you ask, the headaches are fewer and less intense. I can poke at my jaw without feeling like I've drilled a spike through it and into my brain. All in all, not too bad."

"You're healing well. Helps that you're young and in excellent physical shape."

"I knew those damn Pilates were good for something. You didn't have to come by to check on me, Jo."

"You get the bonus round because I came early so Ava can teach me to bake lemon meringue pie. Which you know she's making because it's Dave's favorite. Why doesn't she just jump that man and get the ball rolling?"

"I wish I knew." Phoebe moved to her dresser for underwear. "In all these years it's the first time they've both been free at the same time. His divorce has been final for almost two years now. But they're both still playing just friends."

"We could set them up on a blind date. You know, you tell him you've got somebody, and I tell her, and we don't tell either the some-bodies are each other. And then—"

"We both get our butts burned for meddling."

Josie pouted. "That's what Carter said when I tried the idea out on him. Well, I'm giving them six months more, then I'm risking my butt. Want me to help you get dressed?"

"I can handle it."

"Just between us now?" Josie watched Phoebe's range of motion as Phoebe eased into a shirt, and judged it improved. "How are you doing otherwise?"

"Okay. I know the symptoms of posttraumatic stress. I've had some unpleasant dreams. It's natural."

"It's also natural for stress to bottle up when you feel obligated to keep it inside and not upset the family."

"If I need to spew, I have my ways. Don't worry. I'm back on the job full-time next week. That helps me."

"Okay. Call if you need me."

To prove to herself as well as her family that things were approaching normal, Phoebe dressed with some care. The bold blue color of the shirt cheered her up enough to nudge her into taking some time with makeup. Then more time as she realized if she just kept blending, the bruises went from a shout to a murmur.

By the time she got downstairs, the kitchen was full of women cooking. It didn't hurt her feelings at all to be banished out to the courtyard and the sunshine with Carter and Carly.

"Mama!" Carly flew across the bricks. "I kicked Uncle Carter's *butt* at jacks."

"That's my girl."

"It's a sissy game."

"He says that when he loses," Carly announced. "Do you want to play the champ?"

"I don't think I'm up to sitting on the ground yet, baby. Give me another week, and we'll see whose butt gets kicked. You better practice."

"I'm going in for a drink, okay? Whipping Uncle Carter was thirsty work."

"Smart-mouth."

Carly grinned at her uncle and ran for the door. With a sigh, Phoebe sat on the circular bench around the courtyard's little fountain.

Here, she could not only see Ava's roses but smell them. She could hear the birds sing, and admire the tenacity of the thyme and chamomile that spread between the cracks of the pavers, the sweet faces of the violas that danced around a copper birdbath.

Here, with the brick walls and wrought-iron gates, Ava had created a personal sanctuary where shade dappled through moss onto benches and tea olives perfumed the air.

"God! It feels good to sit outside."

"Josie give you the thumbs-up?"

"Yeah, yeah."

He sat, slipped an arm around Phoebe's shoulders. "We get to worry about you. It's part of the package."

She leaned her head on his shoulder. "We all had a scare. It's over now."

"I remember how long it took me to get over being scared."

"Carter, you were just a little guy."

"That doesn't matter, and you know it. You looked after me. And you stood between me and Cousin Bess for years after."

"Old bitch. Which is mean and ungrateful, however true, when we're sitting here in her pretty courtyard while other people are baking pies and ham in the kitchen."

"It's Ava's courtyard," Carter said, and made Phoebe smile.

"Yes, it is. And really, even during the tyrant's reign, it was Ava's. Do you ever think how she was younger than we are now when she started working here? Barely twenty-two, wasn't she? And to have the spine to stick it out, to stand up to Cousin Bess."

"You had it at twelve," Carter reminded her. "And you're still look-ing after us. She knew you'd stay because Mama has to. She could've left Mama the house, after all Mama did for her, but she put it on you, with strings. Locked you in here."

There was no point in denying the truth, every word of truth. And still, it was too lovely a day for bitter old memories. "Locked me in this beautiful house, where my daughter thrives. It's not what we can call a sacrifice."

"It is. It always was. You let me walk away."

She took a firm grip on his hand. "Not very far. I don't think I could stand it if you went very far away."

He smiled, pressed his lips to her hair. "I'd miss you too much. But I'll tell you one thing, Phoebs, I never knew how much I needed to move out of this house until I did it. You never really had a chance."

"I had my time away." College, Quantico, my disaster of a marriage. "I'm happy to be back. I especially like being able to sit out here while three other women put Sunday dinner together."

"That's only because you're a lousy cook."

"Lousy's an exaggeration. I'm an unreliable cook."

"No, you're reliably lousy."

She laughed and poked him in the ribs. "You burn even the thought of food, so you're one to talk."

"That's why they invented takeout and delivery. You won't need to cook if you play your cards right with the rich guy. He's probably got a couple of chefs on staff."

"Listen to you." She gave him another, zestier poke. "Playing my cards. Plus, I don't think he actually has a staff." She frowned over that a moment. She didn't think he had one, but really, how would she know?

"I see he sent more flowers. Looked like a few thousand of them in the parlor."

"A couple dozen lilacs." That smelled so, so lovely. "He seems to be a man who likes to make gestures."

"I got the *look* from Josie when she saw them." Hissing out a breath, Carter narrowed his eyes at the kitchen windows. "Guys who make gestures make other guys make gestures, and now I'm going to have to remember to bring home flowers next week like I thought of it myself."

"You ought to think of it yourself. I have no sympathy for you."

"I brought her home her favorite panini and a cheap bottle of wine just a few days ago, and I ought to get credit for it. But I'm outdone by some forest of lilacs."

"You used the cheap wine to get lucky."

He grinned. "'Course I did. Well, megabucks aside, and having only met him once, I already like him more than I did Roy."

"You never liked Roy at all, so that's not saying much."

He shifted, pointed in that smug, brotherly way. "And who was right?"

She rolled her eyes. "You were. Shut up. Besides, I got the grand prize out of the bastard." She looked over as the door slammed open and Carly raced out.

"Mama! Uncle Dave's here!"

The minute he stepped out, the instant Phoebe saw his face, she knew. She kept her own blank as she pushed to her feet. "Carter, I want to talk to Dave just a minute. Can you take Carly in, keep her occupied?"

"Sure. Hey, Dave."

They didn't shake as many men did, or do the one-armed, back-slapping man hug as others did. They *hugged,* Phoebe thought; as always it made her smile. It was a good, strong embrace; it was father to son. "You'll have to excuse me and Carly. I have to reestablish my dominance and whoop her at WWE SmackDown."

"As if!" Hooting with challenge, Carly raced back inside the house.

"You look better," Dave began.

"So I'm told. Over and over. What happened?"

"They made a deal. I wanted to tell you in person. Phoebe, there was a lot of pressure from the brass on this, from the DA's office—"

"It doesn't matter." She sat again, needed to sit again. "What did they give him?"

"He's off the job, immediately. No benefits. He pleads guilty to simple assault—"

"Simple assault," she repeated. She'd prepared herself, and still she was stunned.

"It carries one-to-three, suspended. He'll get probation. He'll be required to take anger management and serve twenty hours' community service."

"Does he have to write on the blackboard a hundred times: 'I promise to be a good boy'?"

"I'm sorry, Phoebe." He crouched in front of her, laid a hand on her knee. "It's a bad deal. They want to put it away. You don't have to put it away. If you decide to file civil charges against him, I'll stand behind you on it. And I won't be the only one in the department who does."

"I can't put my family through that. Honestly, I don't know if I could put myself through it." She closed her eyes and reminded herself that not all deals were fair, not all deals settled the score. "He did what he did. Everyone who counts knows it." She let out a long breath before looking Dave in the eye again. "He can't be a cop anymore. The rest, it's not important. He's off the job, and that's what's right. That's what's needed. I'm okay with it."

"Then you're a better man than I, kid."

"No. I'm pissed. I'm seriously pissed, but I can live with it. We're going to eat sugar-glazed ham and lemon meringue pie. And Arnie Meeks? He's going to be eating disgrace for a very long time."

She nodded. "Yeah. I can live with that."

NEGOTIATION PHASE

Oh, to be torn 'twixt love an' duty.

—"HIGH NOON"

11

Even after a handful of years, Duncan found meetings weird. The whole business-suited, proposal/pitch/report, Danish-and-coffee and thanks-for-your-time elements of them. Then there were the politics, and the pecking orders.

Maybe that was why he didn't have an actual office. There was no escaping *the meeting* to his mind if a man had an office. Plus an office meant you had to staff it with people who had to be given particular assignments on a regular basis. If you happened to be the boss, that meant you had to come up with those assignments, and probably read reams of reports on the assignments before, during and afterward. And you'd damn well have to have more meetings regarding the assignments.

Vicious cycle.

An office involved desks, and giving people titles. Who actually decided on titles? What made, say, an executive assistant different from an administrative assistant? And should it be the Vice President of Marketing and Sales, or the Vice President of Sales and Marketing?

Things like that would keep him up at night.

Phineas nagged him off and on about the office thing, but so far he'd been able to slip and slide around it.

He liked meeting with people in one of the bars, or a restaurant. Or if it was absolutely necessary, in Phin's office, which was, in Duncan's opinion, meeting central. Going somewhere that wasn't essentially or absolutely his own place not only kept things looser, but he'd found those he met with tended to be more up-front and outspoken over a beer in a pub than they might be over glasses of spring water in a board-room.

He'd found, too, that it was often more interesting, certainly more telling, to go to the prospective meeter. Sitting in their homes, their place of business, their studio, whatever, generally made them more comfortable. It gave him a leg up on getting what he wanted or needed or hoped for if the other party was comfortable in their own space.

Following that philosophy, he'd buzzed from a breakfast meeting at a café downtown to a funky little theater in Southside, then wound his way to a sadly neglected house in the Victorian section.

In each case, he felt he'd gotten more accomplished, and had a bet-ter time of it, than if he'd summoned all the parties involved in all the prospective projects into some stuffy office where he'd be stuck behind a desk wanting to pull a Suicide Joe and jump out the window anyway.

As he made the turn onto Jones, he hoped the same would hold true for what he'd deemed his last meeting of the day.

He'd considered timing it differently, doing a kind of drop-by when Phoebe would be home. But that seemed just a little underhanded. Which was a valid strategy, true, but he figured she'd cop to it.

He parked, began the pretty stroll under arching trees.

He wanted to see her—and not just for the quick just-dropping-in-to-see-how-you're-doing visits he'd limited himself to for the last two weeks. Biding time, he mused. And maybe there was a little game-playing in there, too. She didn't know what to make of him, and he didn't mind that.

He didn't always know what to make of himself, and didn't mind that either.

One thing he did know was that she'd had a major trauma, and she was working her way through it. There wasn't any point in pushing her into a date, or rushing her into bed at a time when she was shaky on her pins.

He had plans. He liked to make plans, nearly as much as he liked adjusting, shifting and altogether changing them from conception to completion.

He had plans for Phoebe.

But right now, he had plans for something else altogether.

Before he turned up the walk to MacNamara House he spotted the woman with the strange little dog across the brick road. Today's doggy bow tie was red-and-white-striped, to match the wide-brimmed hat the lady had perched on her head. It set off, he supposed, her blindingly white suit and red sneakers.

The little dog currently sniffed happily, by all appearances, at the butt of a puffy pink poodle held on the end of a gold leash by an enormously fat black man in a blue seersucker suit.

The scrawny lady and the huge man chatted away under the shade of a live oak even as the hairless dog struggled mightily to hump the pink poodle.

God, Duncan thought, he loved Savannah.

He rang the bell, admired the pots and baskets of flowers on the veranda while he waited. It was Ava, he remembered, who had the gardening talent. He wondered if he could talk her into . . .

"Hey." He offered Essie a smile when she opened the door. "Got time for a bad penny?"

"You're no bad penny, and I've always got time for young handsome men."

They'd progressed over his occasional visits to cheek-kissing. He bussed hers now, caught the subtle scent of her perfume.

What was it like, he wondered, to get up every day, dress and groom, knowing you'd never go out the door?

"How'd you know I was baking cookies?" she asked him, so his smile spread to a grin.

"What kind?"

"Chocolate chip."

"Come on, really? All the way from scratch? Good thing I came by so you'd have a taste tester."

"Let's get you started on that. Phoebe won't be home for a couple hours yet," she added as she led the way back. "Ava, she's running errands. She'll be swinging by school to pick Carly up after play practice. Our Carly's one of the wicked stepsisters in *Cinderella*. She *loves* getting to be mean and bossy."

"I was a frog once. Not the turn-into-a-prince kind. Just a frog. I had to belch on cue. It was a shining moment in my life."

She laughed, shooed him toward the kitchen table. "I bet your mama was so proud."

He said nothing to that. What could he say? Instead he sniffed the air. "Smells like heaven in here."

"I got some still warm from the oven. You want coffee or milk with them?"

"Cookies and milk? I'd suffer through school again if I could come home after to you and cookies and milk."

Pleased, she pinked up. "You're a charmer, aren't you? What've you been out and about doing today?"

"Talking to people, mostly. And actually, I was hoping to finish up that part of the day talking to you. There's this property I was looking at. It's in the Victorian District, not far from a piece of the campus. Savannah College of Art and Design?"

"You don't say." She could barely remember what was outside the house and where it was set. All of that, the streets and buildings and open spaces, were a jumbled maze of squares and lines in her mind. "What kind of property?"

"Kind of a mess, actually. Like one of those Victorian ladies who fell on extremely hard times. You can still see the elegance under the neglect." He picked up a cookie, bit in. Then forgot everything in pure sensory pleasure.

"Oh God. Marry me."

She didn't laugh this time. She giggled. "If a woman can have you for a cookie, I'm surprised the bakeries all over the state of Georgia aren't working overtime." She reached across him, picked up one herself. And her eyes twinkled. "But they are damned good cookies."

"If I beg, will you give me some to take home? How can I settle for Chips Ahoy! now?"

"I believe we can spare some for you."

She moved to the stove to take out a tray, slide in the one she'd prepared.

"I lost my train of thought in cookie nirvana. This sad house off campus."

"Mmm-hmm. You're thinking of buying it and fixing it up."

He followed warm cookie with cold milk, and figured that was the sum total of heaven on earth. "That kind of depends on you."

Puzzlement lifted her eyebrows as she turned away from the stove. "On me?"

"I'm thinking of buying it and fixing it up, yeah. What I've got in mind is a shop. Now . . ." He gestured with the last bite of the first cookie before popping it into his mouth. "I know what you're thinking."

"You couldn't possibly. I'm too confused to be thinking anything."

"Okay, what some might think is, hell, Savannah's got a million shops already. It does, no doubt about it. But people love to shop. No doubt about that either. Right?"

"I . . . I do. I love browsing the Internet shops."

"Sure." He picked up another cookie. "So I'm thinking, location being near the campus, Art and Design. Why not art, crafts. Okay," he said before she could speak. "We've already got plenty of shops and galleries. Artsy, crafty."

"I . . . suppose."

"Even the style I'm thinking, which would be upscale, isn't new, particularly. Boutiquey. Boutiquesque? You know what I'm saying?"

"Almost." She shook her head, laughed again. "Duncan, if you're using me for a sounding board here, I'm flattered. But I don't know anything about real estate and location and boutiquey shops out there. I don't go out there."

"You know about art and craft." Okay, he was having a third cookie, even if it made him sick. "About creating it. About selling it."

"You mean my crocheting." She waved a hand at him. "That's just a paying hobby. It's just something I stumbled into."

"Okay. How about stumbling my way? I've got this idea. Don't you love getting ideas? I always got ideas, but I couldn't do anything with most of them. Now I can. It's a rush, let me tell you."

"So I can see."

"The idea is arts and crafts by Savannahians. Products created only in Savannah. Only Savannah," he repeated, narrowing his eyes. "Might be a good name for it. I should write that down. Savannah arts and crafts," he continued as he dug out his cell phone, cued up his memo function. "Created by Savannahians, displayed and sold in a gorgeous two-story wooden house that symbolizes Savannah. It's got this great porch, or it will be great. I know this guy who does amazing furniture. Tongue and groove. And this woman who does amazing things with wrought iron. So we could . . . getting ahead of myself," he said when he noted she was just staring at him.

"You want to carry some of my crocheting in your shop?"

"Essie, I want to carry buckets of it, trunkloads of it. I want to have it spread all through the place. What do you call them—doilies?—on tables, throws on the sofas. You said you did bedspreads, right? How about tablecloths, like that? And clothes. Sweaters, scarves."

"Well, yes, but . . ."

"See, we'd have rooms set up. Just like a home. Bedrooms, dining room, parlors. So we'd display your work that way. For sale, sure, but also part of the ambience, you know? Baby stuff in the nursery, scarves, sweaters in the wardrobes. You could keep doing your own Internet sales if you want. But we could take care of that for you, expand it."

"My head is actually spinning." She laid her hand on one side of it as if to keep it centered. "Why do you think I could do all that?"

"You are doing it. You'd just keep doing it—except for the boxing and shipping, depending on how you want to handle it. Here, come with me a minute." He grabbed her hand as he pushed back from the table, pulled her into the dining room.

"What do you call that?"

She frowned at the long runner she'd designed in soft pastels for the dining room table. "A runner."

"A runner. Got it. So, if you were to make one just like that and sell it, what would you charge?"

"Oh, well." She had to calculate. She'd made one very similar for a client once, and several shorter ones for others over the years. She gauged the price as best she could without a calculator.

Duncan nodded, did some rapid calculations of his own. "I could give you fifteen percent more than that, and still make a decent profit."

Her cheeks went white, then flushed warm pink. "Fifteen percent more?" She grabbed an end of the runner. "You want it now? I'll box it right up for you."

He grinned. "You keep that one, and start thinking about making more. And whatever else you've a mind to make. I'm going to need some time to get this up and running, but I guarantee we'll be rocking by the Christmas shopping season." He held out a hand. "Partner?"

Duncan considered it a really good day if by seven, regardless of what had come before, there was pizza and beer on the veranda.

He'd lit candles, as much to discourage the bugs as to add some light. His bare feet were propped on the padded wicker hassock. He'd left the TV on in the living room, angling himself so he could watch some basketball action through the window if he wanted. Or just listen to the play-by-play and stare off into the soft dark.

He'd had enough of people for the day. As sociable as he was, he hoarded his alone time. And he liked to listen to the sounds of the game, but he just simply loved the sounds of the night.

The quiet swooshing of air through the trees, the hum of insects, the incessant music of peepers entertained him. It was a good spot— veranda, chair and hassock—and the best time of day to figure things out. Or to let them go.

He'd been tempted to hang out in Essie's kitchen until Phoebe came in from work. So why hadn't he? Hang around too much, he decided, and become a fixture. Or an annoyance. It was all a matter of balance, to his way of thinking. And intriguing the woman in question so maybe she was just a little off hers.

Besides, every time he saw her, he wanted to grab her. Considering what she'd been through, he didn't think she was at the grabbing stage yet.

He finished off a slice of pizza, contemplated another. Then glanced over at the sound of a car. His brows lifted when he realized the car wasn't passing by but heading in.

He didn't recognize it, but he recognized the woman who stepped out of it. And this, he thought, was a better way to end the day than pizza and beer.

"Hey, Phoebe."

"Duncan." She pushed at her hair as she walked to the veranda. "I was at the bridge before it occurred to me you probably weren't here, and then it was too late not to keep going. But here you are anyway."

"I'm here a lot. I mostly live here."

"So you've said."

"Want some pizza? A beer?"

"No, and no. Thank you."

The formal tone had him lifting his eyebrows again. "How about a chair?"

"I'm fine, thanks. I want to ask what you're doing with my mother."

Okay. "Well, I asked her to marry me, but she avoided giving me an answer. I don't think she took me seriously so I settled for the cookies."

"I'm wondering how seriously you take her, or yourself."

"Why don't you tell me why you're pissed at me, and we'll go from there?"

"I'm not pissed. I'm concerned."

Bullshit, he thought. He knew a pissed-off woman when she was standing on his veranda ready to chew holes in him. "About?"

"My mother's bursting with excitement over this business you talked to her about."

"You don't want her to be excited?"

"I don't want her to be disappointed, or disillusioned or hurt."

His voice was as cool as his neglected beer. "Which would be the natural consequence of excitement over the project we discussed. Which, as I recall," he added, "doesn't involve you."

"My mother's state of mind very much involves me. You can't come in there talking about some store you're thinking of opening in some house you're thinking of buying, and how she's going to be a part of it. It's your business how you do business—"

"Thank you very much."

"But," Phoebe ground out. "You got her all worked up, making plans, making designs, talking about how she'll be able to help more with the expenses. What happens to all that if you change your mind, or it doesn't come through, or you just find something more interesting to play with?"

"Why would I change my mind?"

"Aren't you the one who opened a sports bar, then sold it?"

"Sold a piece of it," he corrected.

"Then a pub. And I don't know what else." Which was the crux of it. She didn't *know*, and he was taking her mother into territory she hadn't mapped out. "You bounce, and that's fine for you, Duncan, that's just fine. It's not fine for my mother. She doesn't bounce."

"Let me sort this out. In your opinion, I'm irresponsible and unreliable."

"No. No." She let out a sigh as the leading edge of her temper dulled down to the core of worry. "You're casual, Duncan, and it's part of your appeal. You can afford to be casual, and not just because of the money. No one depends on you, so you can do what you like, come and go as you please."

"Is that casual or careless?"

"I say what I mean, and I said casual. I don't think you're careless. But my mother's fragile, and—"

"Your mother's amazing. You know, I told her once she ought to give herself a break, but the fact is, you ought to give her one. Do you think because she can't go out of that house, she's less than amazing?"

"No. Damn it, no." Because the conversation, such as it was, had gotten out of her hands, Phoebe dragged them through her hair and tried to get back to center. "But she does. She's been hurt and pushed and shoved into the corner so many times."

"I'm not going to do any of those things to Essie."

"Not on purpose. I don't mean that. But what if, for whatever reason, you don't buy that house, then—"

"I bought it today."

That stopped her. That put a hitch in her stride, Duncan thought. He said nothing more, just picked up his beer, watched her as he tipped back the bottle.

"All right, you bought the house. But what if you find it isn't cost effective to fix it up? Or what if—"

"Jesus. What if the voices tell me to put on fairy wings and fly to Cuba? You can 'what if' till next Tuesday; it doesn't mean a damn. I finish what I start, goddamn it. I'm not stupid."

"You're not stupid. I never said or meant you were." But someone had, someone that mattered. "It's just that this all came out of the blue, and for my mother it's *huge*. I'm trying to point out the variables, and I'm trying to understand why you'd involve her in this. I can't understand what you're doing. I can't understand what you want. From her. From me."

"Tied those two together," he muttered, and pushed to his feet. "Must want something from you, so I use her. Let's answer this first. You want to know what I want from you?"

"Yes. Let's start there."

He grabbed her before the last word was all the way out. The hell with biding time. He was too pissed off to bide anything. He had his mouth on hers, showing her what he wanted, taking what he wanted with an impatient anger he rarely let free.

Hunger pushed and shoved at temper until his mouth ravaged hers.

Her back pressed back against the porch column, and her hands were trapped between his body and hers. Every muscle in her body quivered. But not in protest, not in fear. There was a difference between fear and thrill, and she understood it now.

When he broke off, there was such *heat* in his eyes.

"You got that now?" he demanded. "We're clear on that point?"

"Yes."

"Then—"

It was her move now. All hers. Her hands were free so she hooked one arm around his neck, yanked his mouth back to hers. She would have chained her arms around him if her injured shoulder had allowed. When he pressed her against the column again, she nipped at his lip, rocked her hips against his.

She let the pleasure flood her after months and months of sexual drought. The feel of his hands on her breasts, the feel of the night air on her skin when his busy fingers undid her shirt, unhooked her bra. The glorious sensation that rolled through her and escaped on a purring moan.

She went wet and needy, arching to his hands and his mouth, quivering, quivering when he tugged at the button of her waistband.

Here, standing right here, she wanted to be taken without thought, without care, without boundaries. Desperate, she reached for him. And the shock of pain in her shoulder had her crying out.

He jerked back as if she'd punched him. "Christ. Christ."

"It's all right. I moved wrong, that's all. Don't—"

But he held up a hand, turned away. He paced up, he paced down. Stopped and took a long, long gulp of his warming beer.

"You're hurt. You're still hurt. Jesus." And, setting the beer down again, he scrubbed his hands over his face.

"It's not that bad. Really."

"You're still hurt. And I'm not going to bang you against the post like . . . Okay, okay, another minute here."

He paced up and down again. "You pissed me off. No real excuse but I'm taking it."

"No excuses necessary as it was obviously mutual."

"Regardless. Anyway, that should answer the question, which I'm still trying to exactly remember as all the blood's drained out of my head. The second had to do with . . ." He'd turned to face her again, and just stared.

She stood, leaning back against the post, shirt open, hair tumbled, cheeks flushed.

"Wow. Seriously. Hold on," he said when she glanced down, then began to button up. "Would you not do that for just another minute. Maybe two? Since I'm not allowed to touch, it seems only fair I be able to look. You've got this really terrific body. It's all just . . . just exactly right. And the way you're standing there, and this light, and . . . Okay, yeah, you better close up shop there. That's about all I can handle."

"You're a strange man, Duncan."

"I've heard that. I want you, and it's keeping me up at night. I don't mind that so much, even though I like to sleep. But some things rate insomnia. You're one of them."

"Thank you. I think."

"But to get back to the rest. I think the point's just been made that

I don't need to use Essie to get to you. And you know what? You should think more of her than that. More of me, too, and more of yourself."

"You're right. You're absolutely right, and I'm absolutely wrong. I hate that. My excuse, since we're using them, is I love her so much."

"I get that. You're lucky to have her."

Phoebe raked a hand through her hair. He meant that, exactly that, she realized. He saw her mother, and saw the value of the woman she was.

"I know it. People, a lot of people, look at the situation and think she's some sort of burden. You don't. And I'm sorry for the way I handled this."

"I would be, too, except I got my hands on your breasts." She laughed. "Want that beer now?"

"Better not, I'm driving. Duncan, please don't take this the wrong way. I see the bars—you tended bar. And I could see if you bought a cab company, or a car service or some such thing. Maybe you have, I don't know, and that's part of it. I don't know how you do this sort of thing. And I don't know what you could possibly know about running a retail craft boutique."

"We'll find out, plus I wouldn't actually be running it. I've got somebody in mind for that. And you're thinking, hell, he can afford to lose a couple hundred thousand here or there."

"No, actually, I was thinking you'll probably find a way to make it work. I'm thinking I was scared because I came home to find my mother happy, bubbling with it."

"She was happy when she started with Reuben."

Now Phoebe pressed her fingers to her eyes. "Obviously I didn't connect those dots for myself before I came haring out here and laid into you."

"Hair trigger," he said, without heat.

"About some things, obviously. Now that I've connected those dots—or you have for me—I'm thinking if you hadn't had this idea I can't understand, exactly, my mother wouldn't have a chance to try something exciting."

"I wouldn't have made the offer if I didn't believe I could sell the sheer hell out of her work."

"Which, if I hadn't flown off, I'd have come around to on my own rather than driving out here to jump all over you. Which I don't regret because you got to get your hands on my breasts."

He smiled slowly. "How long before they think you'll be a hundred percent?"

She reached up with her good arm to touch his hair. She liked how it always looked as if he'd just taken a wild ride in that fancy car of his. "I'll get a note from my private duty nurse clearing me for physical activity."

"Works for me. Meanwhile, how about going out with me Sunday? Sunday-afternoon barbecue at a friend's. It'd be a chance to get to know each other, dynamics with others, before we lose ourselves in wild, sweaty sex."

"All right. Why not?"

"I'll pick you up about two."

"Two. I need to get home." She rose to her toes, kissed him, softly, slowly, on either cheek. "I hope I keep you up tonight."

He watched her walk away, flick a killer smile over her shoulder. And decided the odds were heavily in favor of insomnia.

As her car drove away, he went back to sit, to prop his feet on the padded hassock. Eating cold pizza, drinking warm beer, he thought it had been a hell of an interesting day.

12

The call came through at seven fifty-eight. The kid was smart, very smart. He hadn't panicked, hadn't tried to play the hero. He'd used his head, and his legs, dashing away from the bungalow in Gordonston, hopping fences between the pretty backyards back to his own house, to the phone. And to nine-one-one.

He'd given names, the address, the situation. En route to Savannah's east side, Phoebe listened to the replay of the emergency call and thought the boy had the makings of a good cop.

He's got them sitting around the kitchen table. Mr. Brinker does. Mrs. Brinker, Jessie, Aaron, even the baby. Um, Penny, in her high chair. He's got a gun. I think he's got two guns. Jessie's crying. Jesus, you gotta do something.

She had more information. It came rolling in as she and Sykes sped toward the pretty neighborhood. Stuart Brinker, age forty-three, associate professor. Father of three—Jessica, sixteen, Aaron, twelve, and Penelope, two. Recently separated from his wife of eighteen years, Katherine, thirty-nine, art teacher.

Twenty minutes after the nine-one-one, Phoebe walked through the barricade forming the outer perimeter. The media was already doing stand-ups outside the barricades. There were some shouts in her direction from reporters. Phoebe ignored them, signaled to one of the uniforms.

"Lieutenant MacNamara and Detective Sykes, negotiators. What's the situation?"

"Four hostages, three minor children. HT's got them in the living room now." He gestured toward the tidy white bungalow with azaleas blooming pink and white in the front yard. "Curtains closed on all the windows there. We can't get a visual. HT's got a couple of handguns. No shots fired. First responder's been talking to him off and on. The word I get is the guy's really polite, but isn't doing a lot of communicating at this point. Kid who called it in's over there with his mother."

Phoebe glanced over, saw the gangly teenage boy sitting on the ground, head in his hands. A woman sat beside him, her arm hooked firmly over his shoulder, her face pale as wax.

"Sykes?"

"Yeah, I've got him."

Phoebe moved on toward communications, and the edge of the inner perimeter, as Sykes walked to the boy. "Lieutenant MacNamara, negotiator."

Information came fast now. Tactical had the house surrounded, the near neighbors evacuated. Sharpshooters were moving into positions.

"He won't talk much," the first responder told her. "I've been trying to keep the line open with him. He sounds tired. Sad, not angry. He and the wife are separated—her idea, he says. Last time I got him to talk, he thanked me for calling before hanging up."

"Okay, stand by." She studied the log, the situation board, then pulled out her notebook as she picked up the phone. "Let's get him back on."

He answered on the third ring, and his voice was brutally weary. "Please, is this necessary? I want some time with my family. Some quiet, uninterrupted time."

"Mr. Brinker? This is Phoebe MacNamara. I'm a negotiator with the Savannah-Chatham Police Department. I'd like to help. How is everyone in there? Everybody okay?"

"We're fine, thank you. Now please, leave us alone."

"Mr. Brinker, I understand you want to be with your family. You sound as if you love them very much."

"Of course I do. I love my family. Families need to be together."

"You want your family to be together, I understand. Why don't you bring them out now? All of you together. I'd like you to put your weapons down now, Mr. Brinker, and come out with your family."

"I can't do that. I'm very sorry."

"Can you tell me why not?"

"This is my house. This is the only way we can be together. I thought about this carefully."

Planned out, not impulse, she thought as she made notes. Not anger but sorrow. "You sound tired."

"I am. I'm very tired. I've done my best, but it's never quite good enough. It's exhausting to never be quite good enough."

"I'm sure you've done your best. It's hard, don't you think, to make important decisions when you're tired and upset? You sound tired and upset. I'd like to help you, Mr. Brinker. I'd like to help you work this all out so you can make the right decision for your family."

"I painted this living room. Kate picked the color. I didn't like it— too yellow—and we argued. Remember, Kate? We fought over the yellow paint right there in the Home Depot, and she won. So I painted it. And she was right. It's sunny in here. She was right."

Living Room, Phoebe wrote on her pad, circling it. "You did the painting. I'm terrible at painting. Can't get the cutting-in part. Have you and your family lived here long?"

"Ten years. It's a good place to raise children. That's what we thought. Good neighborhood, good schools. We need a bigger house, but . . ."

"Your family's grown." Family, family, family, Phoebe told herself. Focus on family. "How many children do you have?"

"Three. We have three. We didn't plan on Penny. We couldn't really afford . . ."

"Penny's your youngest, then? How old is Penny?"

"Two, Penny's two."

Phoebe heard an excited child's voice call: "Daddy!"

"Is that her I hear?" Now she heard a choked sob from Brinker and kept talking. "She sounds very sweet. I have a little girl. She's seven, and I just wonder where the years went. I love her more than anything. She sure keeps me busy, though. I imagine your family keeps you very busy."

"I've done my best. I don't know why it's not enough. If I'd gotten the full professorship, we could afford a bigger house."

"You sound discouraged. It must be hard. You have an older daughter, is that right? Jessie, and then a boy in the middle, Aaron. Your wife, Kate, and you must be very proud. Still, it's a lot of work. I understand that. A lot of worry."

"I needed that professorship. I needed tenure. I needed Kate to understand."

The use of past tense, and the despair, set off alarms. "Tell me what you need Kate to understand, Mr. Brinker."

"That I can't do any more than I can do, or be more than I can be. But it's not enough. I'm the husband, I'm the father. I'm supposed to make it work. But things fall apart; the center cannot hold."

"That's Yeats, isn't it?" She closed her eyes, hoping she hadn't made a mistake.

There was a beat of silence. "Yes. You know Yeats?"

"Some. And I think sometimes that's true, things do fall apart, or seem to. The center can't always hold it all. But I also think things can be rebuilt, or reformed, and the center shored up again to hold it all differently. What do you think?"

"Once it falls, it's not the same."

"Not the same, but still there."

"My family's fallen apart."

"But they're still there, Mr. Brinker, and I hear how much you love them, every one of them. I don't believe you want to hurt them. Or that you want to hurt them by hurting yourself. You're the father."

"Weekend father. Perish instead of publish."

"I hear you're discouraged, and you're sad. But you're not ready to stop trying. You and Kate, eighteen years together, and those beautiful children you've made together. You don't want to stop trying. You love them too much."

"She doesn't want me anymore. What's the point? We made it all together. I thought we should end it all together. Here, in our home. The five of us, going together."

Thought we should. This time his use of past tense told her they might be turning a corner. "The five of you need to come out together, Mr. Brinker. Your children sound frightened. I can hear them crying now. You and your wife are their parents, you and your wife are responsible for keeping them safe and well."

"I don't know what to do anymore."

"Look at your children, Mr. Brinker, look at your wife. I don't believe anything's more precious to you. You don't want to hurt them. You can make the center hold. Look at the yellow walls. You gave them that sunny room, even when you weren't sure it would work. Put the guns down now, Mr. Brinker. Put them down, and bring your family out. You said you'd done your best. I believe you. Now, I believe you'll do your best again, and put the guns down. Bring your wife and your babies out."

"What's going to happen? I don't know what's going to happen."

"We're going to help you. You and your family. Will you come out with your family now? It's the right thing to do for them."

"I don't want to go into the black without them."

"You don't need to go into the black at all. Will you put the guns down, please?"

"I'm sorry. I'm so sorry."

"I know. Can you listen to me now, Mr. Brinker?"

"Yes. Yes."

"Put the guns down. Please put them down and step away from them. Will you do that?"

"Yes. All right. I'm sorry."

She wrote *Coming out. Surrendering.* Signaled that message to Tactical command. "It's going to be all right. Did you put the guns down?"

"Yes. I put them on the shelf. High, where Penny can't reach them."

"That was the right thing to do. I want you to come to the front door. You and your family. Don't be afraid. No one's going to hurt you. I need you to keep your hands up, just so everyone can see you did the right thing and put the guns down. There'll be police outside, but no one's going to hurt you. Do you understand?"

"I can't think."

"It's all right. Will you bring your family out, please?"

"I . . . I can't keep my hands up and talk on the phone."

Phoebe closed her eyes, took a breath. "That's fine. Why don't you give the phone to Kate now? And you can all come outside together."

"All right. Kate? You need to take this call."

"God. God." The woman's voice wrenched out the words. "We're coming out. He doesn't have a gun. Please, please, don't shoot. Don't hurt him. Don't hurt him."

"No one's going to hurt him. No one's going to get hurt today."

When they came out, what struck Phoebe right to the bone was the sound of the little girl crying for her daddy.

In what had become his workroom, he drank cold, sweet tea with a small sprig of fresh mint and watched the media coverage of the crisis in Gordonston.

He hoped they'd all die.

He didn't care about the Brinkers—they meant nothing to him one way or the other. But if that whining college guy put bullets in his family, then himself, Phoebe would take a hell of a hit.

That would be worth the airtime.

Then again, if she took too hard a hit, he might not get the chance to pay her back, his way.

Bitch would probably slide out of it anyway, even if she fucked up and the idiot put a bullet in the brain of the fat-cheeked toddler whose picture they'd shown on screen half a dozen times already.

She wouldn't take the blame for it, no matter how much she'd earned it.

With the tea, he sat down at his workbench. He'd heard the call come through on his police scanner while he was finishing up breakfast. It had given him a hell of a lift. Guy, wife, three kids. A bloodbath like that would get lots of attention.

He'd been right, and on his workroom TV, he watched while the local station preempted the *Today* show with live at-the-scene coverage.

And he'd seen Phoebe stride by the cameras, ignoring reporters in that superior, I'm-so-fucking-*important* way of hers.

He'd thought about putting a bullet in *her* brain. Oh, he'd thought about it, even dreamed about it, just the way he figured Mr. College Professor was thinking about putting one into his whole stupid family.

But that was too easy. That was too quick. Bang! And it's over.

He had a much better plan.

He kept the TV on while he worked. Usually, he had the spare scanner on down here, and maybe the radio. Television was too distracting when he was working. But he considered this an exception.

His lips thinned as the reporter on screen announced the Brinker family had come out, safe and sound, that the asshole surrendered peacefully.

"Pulled that one off, didn't you?" he muttered to himself as he turned screws. "Yeah, that one was easy. Didn't have to break a sweat, did you? Nice family, nice neighborhood. Just some stupid shit looking for some attention. You got them out just fine, didn't you? *Phoebe.*"

He had to stop, put his tools down, because the anger, the *rage,* made his hands shake. He wanted a cigarette. Actually yearned for one. But he'd made himself quit. It was a matter of willpower, and practicality.

He didn't need crutches. He couldn't afford to need crutches. He couldn't even afford the rage. Cold blood, he reminded himself. Cool head. When payback came, he'd need those, and a strong body, a clear purpose.

So he closed his eyes and willed everything inside him to slow, to still.

It was her voice that had his eyes opening again, had them burning toward the TV.

"Stuart Brinker surrendered peacefully. His wife and their children weren't harmed."

"Lieutenant MacNamara, as hostage negotiator, how did you convince Professor Brinker to surrender to the police?"

"I listened."

The glass flew across the room, shattered against the set before he realized it had left his hand. Amber rain dripped down over Phoebe's face.

Have to work on that, he told himself. Have to work on that control. Won't get the job done flying off the handle. No sir. But he smiled as the rivulets of tea slid down Phoebe's face. He imagined them red, long thin rivers of blood.

Because it pleased him, he was able to pick up his tools again with a steady hand.

He went back to work on the timer.

"It got to me. Some of them do, more than others."

After shift, Phoebe sat with Liz over a couple of glasses of wine in Swifty's. It was too early for music, so the booth was a quiet corner, an island to sink into and unwind.

"How so?"

Phoebe started to speak, then shook her head. "I didn't mean to talk shop. We should talk shoes or something."

"I bought this pair a couple weeks ago? Pumps, leopard-skin design. I don't know what I was thinking. Where am I going to wear leopard-skin pumps? Anyway, we'll get to that. Tell me about the incident. I know how it is," Liz went on. "I talk to a lot of rape victims, to a lot of kids who've been sexually abused. And sometimes it gets to you more than others. You get it out, or it roots. So?"

"The kids. You have to try not to think about them as kids. Just hostages. But . . ."

"They're kids."

"Yeah. And in this case, part of the key to talking him down. He loved them. You could hear it."

"And the question is, how do you hold what you love at gunpoint?"

"Because you're broken. Something was broken inside him. He wasn't mad, there wasn't any rage in him. It wasn't payback or punishment. It can be more volatile when it's not about payback. Maybe that's part of what got to me, too. I hear this guy, I hear him standing on the edge of an abyss. And he doesn't believe he can come back from it—that he deserves to."

"Why take the family, too?"

"He's nothing without them. They're essential to who he is. He doesn't want to die without them. So . . ." She lifted her wine. "Altogether now." She drank, blew out a breath. "He's been depressed for more than a year, and things have been slipping away from him. Career, marriage, both on pretty shaky ground. Wife wants a bigger house, oldest daughter wants a car of her own, he gets thumbs-down on the full professorship. Stuff you handle or fight about. But he just sank down, and kept sinking. The wife's so busy taking care of the kids and the house because he's barely able to get out of bed. She gets fed up, kicks him out. 'Things fall apart; the center cannot hold.' He couldn't hold it."

"You gave them a chance to try again."

"Yeah. Well. Nobody died. You listen good."

"Part of what we both do is listen." Liz tapped her glass to Phoebe's. "And we'd better be good."

"Did you always want to be a cop?"

"I wanted to be a rock-and-roll star."

"Who didn't?"

Liz laughed. "I was actually in a band for a couple of years when I was in college."

"No kidding? What did you do?"

"I got pipes, sister." Liz wagged her thumb at her throat. "And I was crazy in love with the lead guitar. We had plans. The kind you make at twenty and aren't ever going anywhere. Big, splashy plans. Which we made when we weren't screwing like bunnies."

"College." Phoebe sighed. "Those were the days. What happened to Lead Guitar?"

"He dumped me. No, that's not fair, or accurate. He backed away, rapidly. I got raped."

"I'm sorry."

"My turn to make the beer run. There was a place just a couple blocks from where we were living. Party time, all the time. You know?"

"Yeah, I know."

"I was in the parking lot when they jumped me. Two of them, laughing like loons. Seriously high. They dragged me into the back of a van, took turns with me while a third one drove. Then they switched off so he could have a go. I don't know how many times, because I zoned out after the first round. Then they just tossed me out on the side of the road. Cruiser picked me up. I was just stumbling along, clothes torn and bloody, in shock, hysterical. The whole ball. And the cops spotted me."

She drank to wet her throat. "Well. They got them, all three of them. I paid attention, until I had to go under. I paid attention. I had descriptions, and I made all three of those motherfuckers in lineup. Hardest thing I ever did, to stand there and look at them through that glass. And Lead Guitar? He couldn't handle it. Couldn't look at me, couldn't touch me, couldn't be with me. Too much for his head, he said. I didn't want to be a rock-and-roll star anymore."

"How long they get? The motherfuckers?"

"They're still in." Liz smiled for the first time. "Stupid bastards took me across the state line into South Carolina. Raped me in two states, had coke in the van, all three had sheets, two were on parole. Anyway, I gave up the band and turned to the glamorous world of law enforcement."

"Music's loss, our gain."

"Okay, shop's closed. Tell me about the guy with the great ass. You two an item?"

"We seem to be something, but I'm not sure what." Thoughtfully, Phoebe propped an elbow on the table, nested her chin in her palm. "I'm out of practice. Kid, job, raw spots from failed marriage. He's so damn cute."

"I noticed. How's the sex?"

Phoebe snorted out a surprised laugh. "You get right to it."

"Healthy sex is one of life's great entertainments. Take it from somebody who sees too much of the other kind. But if you don't want to share—"

"Actually." She hadn't made time for a female friend of her own age in too long. Now, Phoebe leaned forward, lowered her voice. "The other night . . ."

She gave a condensed version of her visit to Duncan's house.

"He stopped? You're about to go for the gold right out on the veranda—which, let me insert, is very sexy—and he stops?"

"Thirty seconds more, that's all it would've taken." Phoebe did a test roll of her bad shoulder. "If I hadn't moved the wrong way . . . what?"

"Romantic *and* sexy. I mean, God, how many guys are going to shut it down at that point?"

"I'm going to need a note from my sister-in-law to close the deal. Private duty nurse."

"Can I have him when you're done? No, seriously, Phoebe, when you two get that next thirty seconds, it's going to be memorable."

"I'm thinking. Listen, I've got to get home. My kid. But the next time, we'll explore your sex life."

"At the moment, we could do that over a bag of peanuts in the break room. Maybe Cute Guy has a friend."

"I'll ask."

"I'm available."

Phoebe got out of the car just as Lorelei Tiffany clipped up with her incredibly silly dog. Tonight's leash was candy pink, to coordinate with Mrs. Tiffany's ensemble—heels, pillbox hat, waist-cinching jacket and thigh-gripping capris.

"Evening, Miz Tiffany. How are you and Maximillian Dufree?"

"We're going to have ourselves a nice stroll in the park." Mrs. Tiffany tipped down her rhinestone-studded glasses to peer at Phoebe. "You just getting home?"

"Yes, ma'am. I'm running a little later than usual today."

"Got your car back, I see."

"I did. For now. I'm afraid I'm going to have to give it a decent burial soon."

"My uncle Lucius once buried an entire Cadillac DeVille, complete with passengers, in a soybean field outside of Macon. So they say."

"Hmmm, that must've been some job."

"That was Uncle Lucius for you. He never quibbled about getting his hands dirty. I saw you on TV today."

"Oh? There was some trouble over in Gordonston."

"Crazy man going to murder his whole family in a three-bedroom bungalow. I saw it. You're going to be on TV, honey, you need to dress for it. Bright colors do the trick, and more blusher. You don't want to look all washed-out and dull on the TV, now do you?"

Oddly, Phoebe felt washed-out and dull standing there on the wide sidewalk while Maximillian Dufree peed lavishly on the trunk of the near live oak. "I guess not, but I wasn't expecting to be on TV."

"Expect the unexpected." Mrs. Tiffany wagged her elaborately ringed index finger. "You remember that, and always carry your blusher, you'll do fine. You get yourself on TV like that, you might just catch yourself a husband. A man likes a woman with pink in her cheeks. And a nice, soft bosom."

"I'll keep that in mind. You and Maximillian Dufree have a nice walk now."

As Phoebe started up the walk to what she considered the relative sanity of home, she heard Mrs. Tiffany trill out with a "And good evening to *you!*"

She glanced back, saw the man strolling by. He tapped the brim of his ball cap toward Mrs. Tiffany. He wore a camera strapped crossways over his dark windbreaker and resting at his hip. A tourist, Phoebe thought idly, though there was something vaguely familiar about him.

Since he was a man, Mrs. Tiffany had to put her flirt on.

Amused, Phoebe continued up the steps. She didn't see him pivot, raise the camera, frame her in. When something tickled at the base of her spine, she glanced back. But he was strolling casually away. She could hear him whistle as he walked, something slow and sad and as vaguely familiar as he'd been himself.

She couldn't say why the sound of it gave her a chill.

13

She would not feel guilty because she was doing something outside the house and family on a Sunday evening. She would not feel guilty. It was a litany Phoebe repeated off and on through the day, starting when Carly bounced into her bed for Sunday Morning Snuggles.

Snuggle they did so Phoebe snuck kisses and sniffs of her daughter's soft curly hair, deliciously shampooed the night before. Cuddled up, she got the lowdown on Sherrilynn's brother Tear—so named because he always seemed to be on one—sawing off the heads of two of Sherrilynn's Barbies with his daddy's penknife before he was caught and suitably punished.

Heads on the same pillow, nose to nose, they expressed their mutual horror over the crime.

What had she ever done to earn such a perfect, precious child? Phoebe wondered. How could she not spend every free moment of every day with this incredible little girl?

Of course, later that morning when she and Carly bumped heads over Carly's desperate need for the purple butterfly sandals she'd seen in one of her grandmother's catalogues, Phoebe wondered how she could dare risk letting this pint-sized shoe hog out of her sight for ten minutes.

She would not feel guilty.

And wasn't Carly going off to a backyard picnic birthday party at her current best friend in the entire world Poppy's house? And wasn't Ava already set to drop her off, then pick her up, bookending her own trip to a flower show?

And Mama? Well, Mama was so busy designing new patterns, organizing her threads and yarns, she'd barely notice if Phoebe jetted off for a weekend trip to Antigua.

There was nothing to feel guilty about.

But she suffered twinges of it nonetheless as she brushed Carly's lovely bright hair, helped pick out the absolutely perfect hair clips. She fought against those twinges while she approved Carly's choice—after numerous rejections—of just the right outfit.

They tugged again while she stood on the front veranda, waving to Ava and her fashionable little girl as they drove off for their Sunday outings.

Inside, she hunted up her mother, only to find Essie on her sitting-room computer, laughing away as she clattered on the keyboard.

Chat room, Phoebe thought. The agoraphobic's constant friend. Still, Phoebe leaned against the doorjamb, watching as her mother's fingers flew and her eyes sparkled with humor.

This was one of her safe conduits to the outside world, after all. Neighbors still dropped by, or old friends paid calls. Now and then Essie would have a group of women over for tea, and God knew she always enjoyed it if she or Ava planned a cocktail or dinner party.

People came. Of course they came. The South loved their eccentrics, and to many in Savannah who knew the MacNamaras, Essie's condition was no more than a charming little eccentricity.

Essie MacNamara? they might say. *She was Essie Carter before she married Benedict MacNamara. Married up, too, and only to be widowed before she was thirty. Just a tragedy! She hasn't stepped one foot outside of MacNamara House on Jones in ten years or more, bless her heart. She comes out on the veranda sometimes, and she's still as pretty as a picture. And so slim.*

Of course, they'd never weathered one of Mama's panic attacks, or watched her struggle just to find the courage to step out on that veranda. They hadn't seen her weep with gratitude when her future daughter-in-law asked if she and Carter could have the wedding at the house.

God bless Josie, Phoebe thought. And hell, God bless the Internet while she was at it. If her mother couldn't go out into the world, at least the world could come to her through her computer.

"Hey, sweetie pie." Essie's fingers stilled as she spotted Phoebe. "You need something?"

"No. No, I was just poking in to let you know I'm going up to work out, then I'm going to get ready to go out."

Essie's dimples deepened with her smile. "With Duncan."

"To a barbecue at one of his friend's."

"You have a good time, and don't forget the flowers you put in the spare fridge now."

"I won't."

"And wear the green sundress," Essie called out as Phoebe turned. "Show off those nice shoulders. God knows you work hard enough on them."

Phoebe glanced back. "Should I wear more blush, too, so I can catch me a husband?"

"What's that?"

"Nothing. I'll check back with you before I go."

She escaped to her little gym, and a solid sweaty hour.

Later in the shower, she wondered if she'd been using exercise over the past months as a substitute for sex. She'd definitely kicked it up a few notches in the past six months.

Eight months, she corrected, rinsing shampoo out of her hair. Or was it ten?

Well, *Jesus,* had it actually been a year since she'd had sex? Shoving at her dripping hair, she began to obsessively backtrack and count.

Ava's son's friend's neighbor Wilson—Ava had arranged the date, pushed for it until Phoebe caved. He'd turned out to be very nice, Phoebe remembered. Kind of sweet with his shy smile and little goatee. He liked country music and football, and had been on the tail end of a divorce.

They'd enjoyed each other's company enough to date a few times, and she'd slept with him twice. It had been, she recalled, nice. The same way he'd been nice.

And then he'd reconciled with his wife. That was nice, too, really. She'd heard they'd had a baby since . . .

Wait a minute, wait one damn minute. She snapped off the shower, grabbed a towel. Wrapping it around her, she put the congenial, wish-you-all-the-best breakup with the very nice Wilson into the context of time, of season, of date.

Shortly after New Year's, she remembered. She'd slept with him on New Year's Eve, then again a few nights later. New Year's of *last* year, she realized with a jolt.

"My God! I haven't had sex in fifteen months." She stepped over to the mirror, wiped the fog away so she could stare at her own face. "I'm thirty-three years old and I haven't had sex in fifteen months. What's wrong with me?"

She pressed a hand on her belly. What if everything was rusted in there? It didn't matter if she knew better, intellectually, it was still a horrible and scary thought.

And what if she had sex with Duncan, and it was so good she started skipping the workouts (which surely were a substitute for sex)? She'd get out of shape, become flabby and lazy.

Then he probably wouldn't be attracted to her anymore. Hadn't he commented on her body? Hadn't he? So when her body went soft and flabby, he wouldn't want to have sex with her, which would send her back to Pilates with a vengeance.

It would cycle over and over, until she died with rusted plumbing and six-pack abs.

Jesus, she needed therapy.

Amused at herself, she wrapped her hair in a towel before she deliberately reached for her best, special-occasion-only body cream. Cycle or not, it was time to break the fifteen-month deadlock.

Not just with anyone, she reminded herself. She wasn't a slut—all too obviously. She avoided giving or receiving any signals from other cops, from criminalists, from prosecutors. Date or sleep with someone associated with the job, everyone on the job knew about it. That severely limited the field of play for her.

And it was true she'd been the one to make the first move toward bed with nice Wilson. But she'd liked him, enjoyed going out with him. Besides, before that New Year's Eve she hadn't been with a man for . . .

No, no, no. She wasn't going to count back again and make herself crazy.

She was picky, that's all—and good for her, right? She was picky about whom she dated, and a whole lot pickier about whom she slept with. She had pride, she had her values, and most important, she had a daughter to consider.

Yet here she was obsessing about sex while getting ready for a simple Sunday barbecue. Pitiful.

She took another long, searching look at herself in the mirror. Pitiful or not, she was going to use a little extra blush. And wear the damn green dress.

She took longer than usual to put herself together. Not as long as it took Carly, the Fashion Princess, to primp for a backyard picnic, but longer than her usual routine. Her first reward for the effort was the beaming smile her mother sent her when Phoebe stopped by Essie's sitting room.

Essie had switched from chat room to sketching, but stopped when Phoebe did a flourishing turn in the doorway. "Well?"

"Oh, Phoebe, you look a picture!"

"Not too much?"

"Honey, it's a simple dress, and just perfect for a Sunday barbecue. It's how it looks on you that snaps. You look all fresh and sexy at the same time."

"Exactly the combination I was shooting for. Duncan's going to be here in a few minutes, I expect. I'm going down to get those flowers. Anything you need before I leave?"

"Not a thing. You have a good time, now."

"I will. I'll be back before Carly's bedtime, but—"

"If you're not, I think Ava and I know how to tuck her up. I don't want you watching the clock."

She wouldn't, Phoebe promised herself. She'd just let it all unfold at its own time and pace. She'd enjoy herself, and enjoy knowing she looked fresh and sexy in a green sundress that showed off her arms and back. She'd worked hard enough on them.

She went down, and out to the summer kitchen. In Cousin Bess's day it had been used routinely. For the lavish parties she enjoyed throwing, for canning, for preparation of simple meals on hot nights. They used it more sporadically now, but the second refrigerator was handy for storing extra cold drinks. Phoebe took out the butter-yellow daisies she'd picked up as a hostess gift.

It was going to be a pretty evening, she decided, and turned to admire the flowers of the courtyard Ava had labored over.

"Well, my God!" She stared, openmouthed, at the dead rat at the bottom of the steps.

She had to bury revulsion to step down for a closer look. No doubt it was dead, but it didn't look mauled, as she'd expected. As she imagined it would if some cat had caught it, then gotten bored enough to dump it in the courtyard like some nasty neighbor's gift.

If she'd had to guess at cause of death, she'd have voted for the sharp spring of a trap, right across the neck. The idea made her shudder as she stepped back again.

Some kids, she thought, playing a particularly unpleasant prank, tossing a dead rat over the wall.

She went back inside, dug up a shoe box, got the broom. And, stomach rolling with disgust, managed to sweep and nudge the corpse inside. She wasn't ashamed to look away with her eyes half-closed as she put on the lid, or to hold the box at arm's length to carry it to the trash can.

Shuddering, shuddering, she backpedaled from the trash can, then turned to dash inside. She scrubbed her hands like a surgeon before an operation, all the while telling herself not to be an idiot. She hadn't touched the awful thing.

She had herself nearly settled down when the doorbell rang. The quick, appreciative grin on Duncan's face did the rest of the job.

"Hello, gorgeous."

"Hello back."

"Those for me?"

She tucked the flowers in the crook of her arm as she closed the door behind her. "They certainly are not. They're for our hostess. Or host. You never said which it was."

"Hostess. How's that shoulder?"

"It's coming right along, thank you." She sent him a knowing look. "I'm about ready to start arm wrestling again."

"I knew this guy when I was tending bar. Russian guy, arms looked like toothpicks. Nobody could take him down. I don't think he ever paid for a drink." He opened the car door for her. "You smell great, by the way."

"I really do." She laughed, slid in. When he got in, she shifted toward him. "Now tell me about this friend of yours who's going to be feeding me."

"Best person I know. She's great. You'll like her. Actually, she's the mother of my best friend, who also happens to be my lawyer."

"You're best friends with your lawyer? That's refreshing."

"I met Phin when I was driving a cab. Nobody hails a cab in Savannah, which you'd know since you live here. It was just one of those things. I was heading back to the line at the Hilton, just dropped off a fare. Raining cats that day. He spotted me, I spotted him. He waved me down. Heading to the courthouse, big hurry. Later, I found out he was this struggling young associate, and they'd called him to bring some papers down. Anyway, I get him there, and he pulls out his wallet. Which is empty."

"Uh-oh."

"He's mortified. Sometimes fares try to scam you that way, pull some sob story, whatever. But I've got a good gauge and this guy is seriously embarrassed. He's apologizing all over himself, scribbling down my name and the cab number from the license, swearing on his mother's life he's going to come down to the cab company with the fare and a big tip. Yeah, yeah, yeah."

"A likely story," Phoebe commented, enjoying herself.

"I spring him, figure I'll never see him again. No way is this guy going to haul down to the cab company over an eight-dollar fare."

"But?"

"Yeah, but. I'm clocking out that night, and he comes in. Gives me twenty. First, I'm floored he'd bother to come in, and second, twenty for an eight-dollar run's over the top. And I tell him, dude, ten's enough, thanks. But he won't back off the twenty. So I say fine, let's go have a couple of beers on the other ten. And we did."

"And you've been friends ever since."

"Yeah."

"I'd say that story shows a bit of what you're both made of." She glanced around as he began to drive through the pretty, residential streets of Midtown. "I grew up down this way—well, started growing up down this way. We had a nice little house on the other side of Columbus Drive."

"Good memories or bad?"

"Oh, both. But I've always liked the area, the mix of styles in the houses, kids everywhere."

He pulled into the already crowded drive of a lovely craftsman-style home, with its big front yard tidily mowed and edged with flower beds. "Me, too," he said.

He came around the car to take her hand. She heard the shouts and shrieks of children, the motorized thunder of a lawn mower. She smelled peonies, and meat cooking on someone's backyard grill.

She'd grown up like this, she thought, for the first little while. Then everything, everything had changed.

The screen door opened with a happy slam. The woman who stepped out onto the big front porch was hugely pregnant, with skin the color of semisweet chocolate and hair in a glossy profusion of dreads.

A boy dashed out behind her, scabs riding both knees. "Dunc, Dunc, Dunc!" He shouted it as he streaked like a little bullet down the walk. "Catch!" And flew.

Obviously an old hand at the game, Duncan caught the boy in midair, then flipped him upside down. "The strange creature you see below is Ellis."

"How do you do, Ellis?"

"Hi! Do it again, Dunc."

"Ellis Tyler, you let Duncan get in the house before you start jumping all over him."

The boy might've been upside down, but he managed a dramatic eye-roll. "Yes'm." When Duncan flipped him to his feet, he grinned.

"We got cherry pie. Come on in, Dunc. Come on! You can come, too, ma'am." With that he made his dash back into the house.

"My son likes to be the welcoming committee. You must be Phoebe. I'm Celia. I hope you came hungry." She tipped her face up for Duncan's kiss. "I know you did."

"How many cherry pies?" Duncan asked.

"Just you wait. Duncan's here!" she shouted as she scooted them inside.

There was an army of them, Phoebe realized, in all shapes and sizes. Babies, toddlers, gangly teens, and an ancient old man they called Uncle Walter, men, women, and all the noise that went with them.

Most were congregated in the backyard, sprawled in chairs, on the grass, chasing kids, pushing them on the bright red swing set. A couple of men stood by the grill, watching it smoke with all the pleasure and delight they might have shown were it a centerfold.

By Phoebe's estimate five generations were represented here, but the center of power, the magnetic north, was obviously the woman who stood supervising as younger family members hauled two picnic tables together to form one long space.

She was comfortably round in the way that made Phoebe imagine every child would want to crawl into her lap, would want to rest their head on her breast for comfort. Her handsome face with its deep-set eyes, strong nose and mouth, was capped off by a puffball of ebony curls.

Both hands fisted on her generous hips, and when a big yellow dog streaked by after the blur of a gray-striped cat, she threw back her head and laughed so her whole body shook with it.

Then she turned toward the ancient old man, her hands moving. It took Phoebe a moment to realize she wasn't merely gesturing but signing. The old man wheezed out a laugh, signed back.

Duncan's arm draped around Phoebe's shoulder, and when she glanced up to smile at him, she saw he was looking over at the laughing woman. On his face, deep in those soft blue eyes of his, was absolute and unconditional love.

It struck her suddenly, and with a little curl of terror, that this was a *moment*. Not just a backyard barbecue.

She had to fight the urge to streak away like the cat when Duncan led her forward. "Ma Bee."

Bee took hold of him first, her big arms going around him, pulling him into a hard, full hug. When she pulled him back, she patted his face with both hands. "You're still skinny, and you're still white."

"You're still the love of my life."

She gave that full-body laugh, but her eyes were tender on his face. Then they shifted, turning speculative, to Phoebe.

"Ma Bee, this is Phoebe MacNamara. Phoebe, Beatrice Hector."

"It's wonderful to meet you, Mrs. Hector. Thank you for having me today."

"Somebody's ma raised her right." She winked at Duncan. "You're welcome here," she told Phoebe. "You brought me daisies? I've got a fondness for daisies, thank you." She took them, cradled them. "They've got such happy faces. Tisha? You take these daisies in for me, and get that blue glass vase Arnette gave me last Mother's Day. It's in the right-side cupboard under the big server. That blue vase is just what these daisies want."

Bee made introductions as one of the teenage girls came over for the flowers. Phoebe got a polite if measuring look—Duncan a wistful one.

"Uncle Walter here's been deaf since he got hurt in the Korean War," Bee explained, and signed Phoebe's name for him. And snickered when he signed back. "Says you're prettier than the last one this skinny white boy brought by."

With a smile, Phoebe gave the sign for thanks. "It's one of the few I know," she said as Bee pursed her lips. "Hello, goodbye, thanks."

"You decide you need to converse with him, he can read lips if you talk straight to him, and slow. Mostly, he's going to sleep anyway. And this here's my daughter-in-law, my second boy Phin's wife. Loo—"

"I know you," Phoebe and Loo said together.

"Lieutenant MacNamara."

"Louise Hector, for the defense. Small world."

"Seems like, and previously we've been on opposite sides of it. Welcome to Ma's."

"Since you're acquainted, you get Phoebe what she drinks, and introduce her 'round the rest of the way." Bee lifted her chin toward the picnic tables. "We've got to get food out on the tables here."

Excellent, Phoebe thought, busywork. Just the thing to ease herself into the social. "Is there something I can do to help?"

"Guests don't haul out the dishes. That's for family. Duncan, we need some more chairs."

"Yes, ma'am. Get you ladies a drink first?"

"We'll take care of it," Loo told him, and led Phoebe away. "What do you drink?"

All right, alcohol, another way to ease into the social. "What's handy?"

Phoebe ended up with a plastic cup of chilled chardonnay, and so many names in her head she tried to alphabetize them to keep them straight.

"I didn't put the Phoebe Duncan talked about together with the lieutenant from the Hostage and Crisis Unit." Loo glanced over as they crossed the lawn edged with cheery flower beds and chunky shrubs. "I'm sorry to hear you were hurt a couple weeks ago."

"I'm doing fine now."

"Well, you look fine. Love the dress. Let me introduce you to the grill masters. Phoebe MacNamara, my brother-in-law Zachary, and my husband, Phineas. Phoebe's a cop, so watch yourselves."

"Off duty." Phoebe lifted the wine cup as she shifted to avoid the smoke billowing from the grill.

"Can you fix speeding tickets?" Zachary asked, and had Phin punching him in the arm.

"Pay him no mind."

"I'm not kidding. Tisha's had two since the first of the year." Zachary sent Phoebe a wide grin. "After you eat my chicken, we'll talk about it. You'll be softened up."

"Your chicken?"

"Boy, you couldn't boil the egg this chicken started out as. That right, Loo?"

"I take the Fifth."

"Couple a city lawyers," Zachary said to Phoebe, wagging his thumb between them.

"The lawyer with the empty wallet," Phoebe said.

"You will *never* live that down." Loo belted out a laugh, did a shoulder and hip wiggle as she wagged a finger at her husband. "Deadbeat."

"I thought the story illustrated his innate sense of honor," Phoebe put in, and had Phin flashing his teeth.

"I like her. Leave her here. You"—he pointed at his wife—"can go."

"Mom!" A girl sprinted over. Curly tails sprung out over both ears. "Hero won't come down out of the tree! Make him come down."

"He'll come down when he's ready. Say how do you do to Miz Mac-Namara, Livvy."

"How do you do."

"Just fine, and how about you?"

"The cat won't come down."

"They like being up high," Phoebe told her.

"Why?"

"So they can feel superior to the rest of us."

"But Willy said he was going to fall and break his neck."

"Oh now, Livvy, you know he just said that to get a rise out of you." Loo gave her daughter's pigtail a tug. "You wait till this chicken's on the table. That cat'll come down quick enough. You go on and wash up, 'cause it's almost time to eat."

"Are you sure he likes it up there?" the child asked Phoebe.

"Absolutely." She watched Livvy run off. "How old is she?"

"She'll be seven next June."

"I have a little girl, just seven."

"Boy!" Ma Bee's voice boomed over the yard. "You going to finish up that chicken anytime today?"

"It's coming, Ma," the men called back together, and began to heap it onto a platter.

There was potato salad and black-eyed peas, collards and red beans, corn bread and cole slaw. She lost track of the platters and bowls, and how many were passed to her. Arguments—mostly good-natured—and jokes jumped and jostled around the table as frequently as the food. Many went over her head—family history, which appeared in several cases to include Duncan. Kids whined or complained, mostly about one another. Babies were passed like the bowls and platters, from hand to hand.

Nothing like her family, Phoebe thought, the tidy number of them, the overwhelming female tone of even the most casual meal in Mac-Namara House. Poor Carter, she thought, forever unnumbered.

There'd never been an old man at one of their courtyard picnics to be fussed over until he dozed in his chair, or a couple of sparking-eyed little boys dueling with ears of corn.

A bit out of her depth, Phoebe chatted with Celia about her children—she already had two—and the one yet to come. She shared a smile with Livvy as the high-climbing feline inched his way down the tree to come beg at the table.

At one point Duncan and Phin debated heatedly about basketball, the sort that involved the jabbing of forks for emphasis and the slinging around of uncomplimentary names. As they insulted each other's brains, manhood, everyone else ignored them.

Not just friends, Phoebe realized as the insults reached the point of absurd. Brothers. Whatever their backgrounds, upbringings, skin color, they were brothers. Nobody ragged on each other that way unless they were siblings—of the blood, or of the heart.

She was having a Sunday barbecue with Duncan's family.

Not just a moment, Phoebe realized. A monumental moment.

"Are you kin to Miss Elizabeth MacNamara, lived on Jones Street?"

Phoebe jolted out of her thoughts to meet Bee's steady eyes. "Yes. She was my father's cousin. Did you know her?"

"I knew who she was."

Because the tone translated Bee's unfavorable opinion of Bess Mac-Namara, Phoebe's shoulders tensed. There were any number of people in Savannah who enjoyed painting all family members with the same sticky brush.

"I used to clean for Miz Tidebar on Jones," Bee continued, "until she passed, about, oh, a dozen years ago now."

"I didn't know Mrs. Tidebar, except by name."

"I wouldn't think. She and Miz MacNamara Did Not Speak." The phrase came out in capital letters.

"Yes, I recall a feud. Something about a garden club committee." Which was an old rift before she'd come to MacNamara House. As age had only ripened it, no one who lived under Cousin Bess's roof was permitted to speak or associate with the Tidebars.

"Miz Tiffany? She had her own people to clean, but I did for her now and then when she had a party or just needed another hand. She still living?"

"She is." And Phoebe relaxed again. The odd and delightful Mrs. Tiffany was much safer ground. "And as colorfully as ever."

"Was on her fourth husband when I did for her."

"She's had one more since, and I believe is currently on the prowl for number six."

"She always kept her name, didn't she? Tiffany, no matter how many she hooked down the aisle."

"Her second husband's name," Phoebe explained. "She stuck with that, however many came after, as she likes the sparkle of it. Or so she says."

Bee's lips twitched. "Your cousin, as I recall, didn't have much truck with Miz Tiffany."

"Cousin Bess didn't have much truck with anyone. She was a . . . difficult woman."

"We are what we are. I'd see your mama now and again, enough to say how do you do, when I did for Miz Tidebar. You favor her."

"Some. My daughter more. Carly's the image of her grandmother."

"She must be a pretty girl. You tell your mama Bee Hector sends her best."

"I will. I think she'll enjoy the connection. She's very fond of Duncan."

"We're fond of him around here, too." Bee leaned in a little while the men continued to argue. "What're you going to do with that boy?"

"Duncan?" Maybe it was the wine, the steady beam from Bee's eyes, but Phoebe said what first came to mind. "I'm still deciding what I'm going to let him do with me."

Bee's laugh was an explosion of mirth. Her thick finger tapped Phoebe's shoulder. "He's brought other pretty girls around here."

"I expect he has."

"But he hasn't brought any of them around for my approval before today."

"Oh." Phoebe decided she could use another sip of wine. "Did I pass the audition?"

Bee smiled easily, then she thumped her hands on the table. "Y'all want pie and ice cream, we have to clear this table." Under the general scramble, Bee looked back at Phoebe. "Why don't you grab some of these dishes, haul them into the kitchen."

And that, Phoebe decided, made her by way of family.

She ended the evening necking with Duncan at her own front door. "I can't ask you in." More brain cells fried when he changed the angle of the kiss, spun it out. "Which, mmm, is a euphemism for not being able to go up to my room and get each other naked."

"When?" His hands glided up her, torturing them both. "Where?"

"I . . . I don't know. I'm not being difficult or coy. I hate that word. Carly. My mother." She waved a hand toward the house. "It's all so complicated."

"Have dinner with me. My place."

Her bones turned to mush as his lips trailed down her neck. Dinner at his place, now that was definitely code for sex.

Thank God.

"You're going to cook?"

"No, I want you to live. I'm going to order pizza."

"I like pizza fine."

"When?"

"I . . . I can't tomorrow. I have to—" She should think it through, of course. Be practical, be cautious. "Tuesday. Tuesday night. I'll drive over after shift. As long as—"

"There isn't somebody on a ledge, or holding hostages. I get it. Tuesday." He leaned back. "What do you like on your pizza?"

"Surprise me."

"Planning to. Night, Phoebe."

"Okay. Wait." She threw her arms around his neck again, dove headlong into the kiss until the need inside her edged toward actual pain. "Okay."

She went straight inside before she did something insane like pull his clothes off, then almost dreamily wound her way upstairs. The man could kiss her into a steamy puddle of lust. And, she had to admit, though she was eager for Tuesday night, this anticipation, this not-quite-yet bumped up the pulse and warmed the belly.

If she'd felt this damn near giddy before over a man, she couldn't remember it—or him. That was saying something.

She heard the TV in the family room, and Carly's laughter. Not quite bedtime, she thought. And she wanted a moment, just a moment or two by herself before she took what must have been a dopey smile into the family room.

Because it was a pretty night, she opened her window. Soon enough, she thought, every window and door would be shut tight to hold in the air-conditioning and block out the steamy heat of Savannah in summer.

She decided to change out of the sundress into her sleep clothes before joining her girls.

She was stripped down to her underwear when she heard the whistling. It drifted through the open window, brought a quick chill to her skin.

That tune. That same tune. The man with the camera.

It came to her, the memory, the image of the man standing alone on River Street. But it couldn't be the same man, could it? Compelled, she grabbed her robe, pulled it on. By the time she got to the terrace doors, wrenched them open to go out to look, the whistling had stopped.

No one strolled down the wide white sidewalk of Jones Street.

14

Female voices—they always reminded Phoebe of happy birds—chirped and trilled out of the kitchen as she headed in for coffee. Since she could hear Carly's voice, a kind of quick piping, she marveled a bit. That wasn't the usual Monday morning routine.

The kid liked school, she really did, but she rarely liked it on Monday morning.

But when she stepped into the fashion show, Phoebe understood why her little girl was in the happiest of moods. Nothing like a new sweater—or a new article of *any* kind of clothing—to put a smile on Carly's face.

The one she was currently modeling like a finalist on Project Runway was a pale, almost fragile blue. It looked like it was made from clouds, Phoebe thought, the way it simply wisped over shoulders and arms, swirled at the waist.

Doing a practiced pivot, Carly spotted her mother.

"Look, Mama! Look what Gran made me!"

"It's gorgeous." Phoebe trailed a fingertip down one sleeve. It *felt* like a cloud. "You spoil her, Mama."

"My job to. But it's a sample. It's what I call market advertising. I'm going to do a few in adult sizes, but thought I'd start out small."

"Gran said she could make me a purse to match."

"Might as well surrender," Ava said under her breath as she handed Phoebe coffee. "You can't beat the two of them. How about a hot breakfast?"

"No, thanks. I'll just grab some toast."

"How about one of these instead?" Ava held out a basket filled with muffins. "I just made them this morning."

Phoebe took one, bit in. "And I talk about Carly getting spoiled. Carly, let's get some breakfast into you now. I'll drop you off at school on my way to work."

"We're supposed to drive Poppy and Sherrilynn today, too."

"Right. I knew that." Somewhere, in the back of her mind.

"I can haul them if it'd be easier for you," Ava offered.

"No, it's fine. Ah, listen, I was thinking about going out to dinner with Duncan tomorrow night, if that's not a problem."

Phoebe watched Ava and Essie exchange smug looks behind Carly's back as the girl dumped Frosted Flakes into a bowl.

"What?"

"Nothing." Essie offered the most innocent of smiles. "Of course it's not a problem. Not at all. Ava, I believe you owe me five dollars."

"You bet on . . ." Phoebe made herself zip it up because Carly's eyes were on her, and full of speculation.

"Is he your boyfriend now?"

"I'm too old for boyfriends."

"My third best friend Celene's mother has *two* boyfriends. Celene heard her say how she juggles them so the left hand isn't sure what the right hand's doing."

"Sooner or later your two hands get together and you end up with bruised knuckles. And that is *not* to be repeated," Phoebe added. "I'm just going out to dinner with a friend." And having sex, she thought. Probably a lot of really great sex.

Should she buy condoms? Surely he'd have condoms.

God, something else to worry about.

"I miss going out to dinner," Ava commented. "Just someone to sit across from for a couple hours, making conversation. You going fancy?"

"Ah, no." Should she buy new underwear? "Just pizza or something."

"That's nice. It's friendly."

"I like pizza." Carly piped up, with a look of anticipation.

Guilt, guilt, guilt. Great. Just let me get this horniness out of my system first and I'll make it up to you, baby. "Well . . ."

"We have our regularly scheduled pizza night," Essie reminded her. That smug smile stayed in place as Essie picked up the pitcher of juice, poured a little more into Carly's glass.

And just when Phoebe was thinking, Nice save, Mama, Essie threw a curve ball. "You ought to ask Duncan over to dinner one night soon, Phoebe."

"Oh . . . I—"

"A nice family dinner. From what you said when you got home last night, he took you to his family. Now, you should reciprocate. Why don't you ask him what night's good for him?"

"I guess I could." Complicated, complicated. Why did it have to be complicated? Couldn't a grown woman just have a simple affair?

The answer, of course, was no. Not with a daughter, a mother and an honorary older sister living in the same house.

"Finish that up now, Carly, we don't want to be late. Oh, I meant to ask. Does anyone know if someone new's moved into the neighborhood?"

"Lissette and Morgan Frye's daughter Mirri's come for a visit— which rumor has is a euphemism for leaving her no-good husband after she found out he was learning more from his mixed doubles partner at the club than a strong backhand." Ava topped off Phoebe's coffee. "Oh, and Delly Porter's hired herself a French au pair to run herd on those twins of hers. God help the mademoiselle."

"What's Delly going to do?" Essie wondered. "Is she going back to work?"

"She *says* having the au pair will give her children a cultural influence, and give *her* more time for her volunteer work. What she volunteers for, as everyone knows, is shopping five days out of six."

"No, I meant a man. Is there a new man in the neighborhood?"

"Looking to juggle after all?" Ava said with a laugh.

"I am not." Amused, Phoebe shook her head. "I thought I saw a new face around, that's all." But she hadn't really seen his face, Phoebe thought now. "A whistler—not wolf whistler, tune whistler. What *is* that tune? It keeps sticking in my head but I can't quite place it."

As soon as she started to hum, Essie broke in. "*High Noon.* You know how I love my old movies. That's the theme from *High Noon* with Gary Cooper and Grace Kelly. God, what a beauty she was. And him—now that was some handsome man. 'Do not forsake me, oh, my darlin',' " she sang in her light, pretty voice.

"Right, right. That's the one. Funny sort of song to whistle. Well." With at least that mystery solved, she shelved the rest. "Carly, get a move on now."

The minute they were in the car, Phoebe turned to Carly. "Does it bother you that I'm going out with Duncan? With anyone, really?"

"No. But if you're too old for boyfriends, why are you?"

That one bit you on the ass, didn't it? "I just mean boyfriend's kind of a silly term for a grown woman." A divorced woman with a child, Phoebe thought. "Just friend's more sensible, I guess."

"Celene's mother sort of brags about her boyfriends. She used to have three, but—"

"I'm not Celene's mother. And I don't know as I approve of her talking about her *boyfriends* so much around you."

"She mostly talks about them to her girlfriends, and Celene hears her. Then we talk about it."

"Oh." Phoebe blew out a breath as she began to drive. "Does it upset Celene that her mother goes out like that?"

"She likes the babysitter. Terri's fifteen and they do makeovers and watch TV. And the boyfriends sometimes bring Celene presents, and sometimes they take her places. Like one took her to Six Flags."

"I can *hear* your thinking," Phoebe said with a laugh. "You're such a little mercenary."

It wasn't the first time Carly had heard the word, so she grinned, too. "But if you don't ask for a present, and don't say would you please, please, take me to Six Flags, it's not mercenary. Is it? I mean, Gran always says when somebody gives you something, you should thank them and make them pleased they gave it. Even if you don't like it. That's manners."

"You're a tricky one, Carly Anne. Slippery as an eel. You make me proud."

Phoebe returned from a suicide threat that had amounted to a sad and pathetic bid for attention to find Sykes waving her away from the squad room.

"Just a heads-up, LT. You got the rat squad in your office."

"IAB's in my office?"

"One of them. Got here about five minutes ago."

"Thanks." She should have known it was coming. Had known, she corrected. But it didn't make it any less distasteful.

Lieutenant Blackman from IAB was a salt-and-pepper-headed fifty. He had a sloping belly, a ruddy complexion and thin, dry hands.

"I'm sorry, Lieutenant, to keep you waiting. Did we have an appointment for this afternoon?"

"You didn't keep me waiting. I thought we could have a conversation here rather than a formal interview, at this point. If you'd rather the latter, we can arrange that."

Like a fashionable suit, the Southern-woman polite slipped onto Phoebe. It generally served her well. "I don't know if I'd rather the latter until I have a better idea what conversation you'd like to have."

"Regarding statements and accusations made against you by Officer Arnold Meeks."

"Arnold Meeks is no longer a police officer, as you well know."

"He was when he made the statements and accusations, as you well know. I hope you're recovering from your injuries."

"I am, thank you. Lieutenant Blackman, if we're going to be having this informal conversation, would you like some coffee?"

"No, thanks. I'm fine. Prior to the attack on your person, you suspended Officer Arnold Meeks?"

"I did."

"And your reasons for taking this step?"

"Are outlined, perfectly clearly, in the file." She plastered a cooperative smile on her face. "Do you need a copy?"

"I have one."

Hard-ass, Phoebe thought, but kept the smile as she tipped her head. "Well then."

"Officer Meeks disputed your reasons for his suspension."

Phoebe leaned back, dropped the smile, sharpened her tone. "We both know he attacked me, that he lay in wait and assaulted me. We both know a deal was cut. And I suspect we both know Arnold Meeks has some significant problems with authority—particularly when it's female authority—anger management and control. Why are you pushing this?"

Blackman's dark eyes stayed pinned on hers. "He made serious accusations against you and the captain of this division."

Her temper wanted to leap and bite. And that, Phoebe knew, would only add fuel to a fire that needed to be stamped out quickly. "Yes, he did. He made some of them right here in this office, to my face."

"You have a personal relationship with Captain David McVee, do you not?"

"I certainly do. I have a personal and platonic relationship with the captain, whom I've known and respected for more than twenty years. If you've looked into this matter, into me, then you know the circumstances of how I came to know Captain McVee."

"You left the FBI to work in his division."

"I did, for a variety of reasons. None of which are unseemly or against departmental regulations. I've worked in this division for nearly seven years, without a single mark on my record. I believe my reputation and certainly the captain's are above reproach. Certainly from accusations made by a disgraced police officer whose answer to being disciplined was to beat the hell out of me."

Blackman puffed out his cheeks, the first sign Phoebe had seen that he felt anything at all. "I understand you'd find this conversation, the need for it, distasteful, Lieutenant."

"Distasteful? Lieutenant Blackman, as a police officer and as a woman, I find the *need* for this conversation deplorable."

"So noted. The officer in question also contends that you made inappropriate sexual advances to him, and used your authority over him to intimidate in a sexual context."

"So I've heard." And enough, Phoebe thought, was damn well enough. "I never made sexual advances of *any* kind toward Arnold Meeks. You can take his word or you can take mine. I wonder how much pressure the 'officer in question's' father and/or grandfather might be putting on IAB to pursue this matter."

"Complaints were filed against you, and Captain McVee."

"You ought to consider the source of those complaints. You ought to consider the fact that Captain McVee has served this department and this city for more than twenty-five years, and doesn't deserve even the hint of a smear on his record by the pointing finger of a son of a bitch like Arnold Meeks."

"Lieutenant—"

"I'm not finished. I want you to put that in your report of this conversation. I want you to put in your report that in my professional and personal opinion, Arnold Meeks is a lying son of a bitch who's trying to cover his disgraceful and criminal behavior by damaging the reputation of a good man, and a good cop."

She shoved to her feet. "Now I want you out of my office. I have work to do. If you want another conversation with me, it will be a formal one, and my delegate will be present."

"Up to you."

"Yes, it certainly is. Good afternoon, Lieutenant Blackman."

It took Phoebe only about forty-five seconds to admit she was just too pissed, too insulted to sit there doing paperwork. Even the pretense of doing paperwork wasn't possible.

She grabbed her purse, strode out of the office, through the speculative, and sympathetic, glances of the squad. "Lost time," she said to the new PAA. "I'll be an hour."

She had to walk. She knew herself and understood air and exercise were two vital components to cooling herself off. She walked fast, before she said or did anything she'd regret later, straight out of the building. Out of the cop, she thought to herself.

She could have chosen an easier career. Psychology, psychiatry.

Hadn't she considered both? But no, through all the years, all the schooling, all the choices, she'd kept circling back to this.

She knew it had given her mother more than anyone's share of sleepless nights. God knew it wasn't the best choice for a single mother with a child who needed her. It hadn't been the smart choice, really. She had a family to support, and could have done so with more style charging for fifty-minute hours instead of putting in countless nights on the job.

And for what? For *what?* To be accused by a man who brutalized her? To be questioned by her own over those accusations before the last bruises had completely faded?

She'd swallowed what in her heart was no more than a slap on the wrist of the man who'd used his fists on her. She'd accepted the politics of it, the face-saving, and to be honest had some small seed of relief inside her that she wouldn't be called on to sit in court and replay what he had done to her.

But this? She didn't know if she could swallow this.

And where were her choices now? Phoebe asked herself as she turned into the relative cool of Chippewa Square. She could give the department the finger, walk away. And toss away a dozen years of training and work—good work, she reminded herself.

She could demand a full and formal investigation, and blast the ugliness into the air for those who enjoyed such things to snatch at like ribbons on balloons. Or she could remember that sometimes pride was less important than doing what had to be done.

She dropped down on a bench—the one Forrest Gump had sat on, waiting for a bus.

"Box of chocolates, my ass," she muttered.

But she was calmer. It was good, she decided, that she'd said what she wanted to say to that rat-bastard Blackman when she hadn't been calm. Good that she'd stood up, showed him she wouldn't let herself be walked over by IAB, by politics, by any old-boy network or variation thereof.

Let him poke and prod around. She had nothing to hide.

She'd go back to work, because that's what she did. And really, it wasn't just the only choice she had. It was what she wanted.

But for the next five minutes, she was going to sit here—just like

Forrest—and watch the world go by. As screwed up as it was, it was still her world.

Phoebe glanced over as a woman sat on the bench beside her, then did a quick double take. A sassy white sun hat shaded the gorgeous curling auburn hair. Delicate, just ripened peach tinted the wide, expressive mouth. The long legs were set off in a filmy white sundress and given some jazz with the strappy high-heeled sandals.

Hollywood often came to Savannah, and still it wasn't a usual thing to have Julia Roberts cozy up on a park bench alongside you. Especially when Julia had a prominent Adam's apple and really big hands.

"I hope you don't mind me joining you." The voice was lazy, liquid Savannah, and on the contralto end of the scale. "These shoes are just killing me."

"Not at all. Fabulous shoes, by the way."

"Why, thank you so much!" The four-inch heels lifted, turned side to side, and showed off peach-tipped toes. "Saw them at Jezebel's, and I couldn't resist them. I know better than to go in that place, as I have such a weakness. But there they were, right in the window, and I couldn't live without them."

Phoebe had to smile, and think of Carly. Her daughter would understand the sentiment perfectly.

"But they are *not* made for walking more than five steps. I'm not her." Phoebe's companion tipped down fashionable sunglasses. "Lots of people mistake us, as Julia and I share certain qualities."

"You certainly do."

"And she is a married lady with those adorable children. While I am still on the market." With a wink, the woman extended her hand. "Marvella Starr."

"Phoebe MacNamara."

"I do believe I've seen you around here, Phoebe—that gorgeous hair of yours. I take a turn around the park most every day. It's near the police station, you know."

"Yes, I do."

"I do love a man in uniform. And the mounted unit, they patrol the park. A man in uniform on a horse." On a lusty sigh, Marvella leaned back, waved a hand over her heart. "I am helpless. I work at Chez Vous. You ever been to Chez Vous, honey?"

"I haven't."

"Oh, you should come on by some night, catch the show. Being in the theater, I do tend to sleep in most days, but I like to stroll on through the park in the afternoon, get my policeman fix." She dug into her peach-toned hobo bag, took out a lemon drop. "Candy?"

"Thanks."

Companionably, they sucked on lemon drops, and Phoebe felt better than she had all day.

"You live around here, too?" Marvella asked.

"No, actually, I work around here. At the police station. I'm a cop."

"Now you shut up!" Marvella poked her in the arm. "Is that the truth? I want to see your gun."

Amused, Phoebe folded back her jacket to expose the weapon and badge on her hip. And had Marvella whistling in delight.

"Pretty thing like you, I'd never have guessed it. But I guess we both know how appearances are deceiving—and it's what's inside the cover that counts."

"Yes, we both know that."

"You know any men in uniform who might be interested in a date with a woman of my particular style?"

"If they aren't it's their loss."

"Aren't you the sweet one!"

"If I come across any, I'll send them over to Chez Vous. I bet you can take it from there."

"Oh, that's a solid truth, Phoebe. That's a solid truth."

While she sat, he took pictures. It was such a bonus! He'd never expected to see her walking along, into the square, out again. But here she was, eyes shaded by sunglasses. He wished he could see them. But it was still a bonus. He'd only been scouting around, and lo and behold, here came Phoebe.

Walking fast—fast as a Yankee—legs striding, hips swinging. Hot under the collar, he was sure of it. And the idea of her anger, her upset, gave him a nice little thrill.

He wondered if she'd liked the little present he'd left for her. It was too bad, really too bad, he hadn't been able to stick around, to wait, to position himself to see how she reacted when she found the dead rat.

Still, they were going to have time, plenty of time to get to know each other again. To see each other. Eye to eye.

He didn't know what the hell she and the queer were blabbing on about, but the interlude gave him time for more pictures. And with her running her mouth, she wasn't going to make him.

When she rose, walked away, he blew a kiss at her back.

"See you soon, sweetheart."

Dave waited until it was nearly the end of shift to summon her. He was on the phone when she stepped into his office, and he held up a finger. "That was my take, yes. I appreciate it. I'll get back to you."

He hung up, swiveled a little right, a little left as he studied Phoebe's face. "This'll only take a minute. You probably want to get home."

"Monday night's homework session is often a study of temper and despair. By Friday, we have the hang of it again, only to fall victim to the tradition of two days of vacation. Is there a problem, Captain?"

"I know IAB's spoken with you."

"Yes."

"And I know you're pissed off."

"Yes."

"It's not going to go anywhere, Phoebe. It's got nowhere to go. But the Meekses have friends in the department, and at City Hall. It's important to them to save face to some extent."

"While your face and mine take the punch," she tossed back.

"I'm sorry that insult's been added to injury. I expect you'll handle it."

"I considered flipping them the bird and going into business as a therapist. Maybe marriage counseling." She watched his lips quirk. "But considering my own track record in that area, I rejected it and mused on the more entertaining notion of going to a voodoo practitioner and buying a curse. I'm still weighing the pros and cons of that."

"Let me know which way you decide. It's smoke, Phoebe. You know that."

"Smoke can leave stains and smears. And it kills. Haven't you been paying attention to the surgeon general?"

"Sergeant Meeks pulled some strings. He's got his son a job as a security guard. That's a hard comedown for a man like Arnie. It's a hard comedown for his father to see what I have no doubt he considered his legacy broken into very ugly bits. He's getting some of his own back."

He swiveled again when she said nothing. "As long as you hold your line, he won't even get that. Go on home, put this away. It's bad enough you're about to face the multiplication tables or the hell of long division."

No point in argument or debate, she thought, especially since he was right. All she had to do was hold the line. "Monday is, invariably, vocabulary. Carly has such a damn good one it annoys her to be told what words to learn. What are you going to do?"

"I'm going to finish up here, go home and have a beer with my Hungry-Man dinner."

"Come on to dinner. You—" She stopped, felt both temper and grief rise up when she saw the expression on his face. "Is that how it has to be? Because of this insulting stupidity? We can't be friends now?"

"Of course we're friends. Nothing changes that, and nothing ever could. But it's best, for the moment, that I stick with my Hungry-Man. Let the smoke clear, Phoebe. When it does, I promise you it's not going to leave a stain on either of us."

"I'm thinking more seriously about finding that voodoo queen."

He smiled at her, in that calm, patient way she loved, she depended on. "We do good work here. We're going to keep right on doing it. And speaking of that, you did good work at the college today."

"It was bogus. Report was the coed had barricaded herself in the dorm with a knife, a rifle and a bottle of pills. When I talked her out, what she had was manicure scissors, an unloaded twenty-two and a bottle of goddamn Tums."

"It could have been a loaded gun, a bowie knife and a bottle of barbs. You know that. You talked her out, that's what counts. Go on home."

Some days, she thought as she walked out to her car, it felt like it counted more than others.

It was odd, wasn't it, Ava decided, for the man her friend was seeing—was in fact having dinner with that very night—to ask to see her?

She wasn't sure why she'd agreed to meet him. Maybe it was curiosity, or manners, or that easy charm of his. Likely all of that, she admitted as she walked to Whitaker Street.

She'd decided not to drive. Parking could be such a nightmare, and besides, you couldn't window-shop in a car, could you? Or not safely in any case.

And she did love to window-shop. Between her and Essie, she supposed they'd completely corrupted Carly.

Anyway, it wasn't all that far. And Savannah was just gorgeous in April.

She loved Savannah. She loved MacNamara House—and deep in the core, it had been home more than anywhere else. Of course, she'd loved her pretty little house in West Chatham. Picture-perfect life, or so she'd thought. With a successful husband, a delightful little boy. Even the requisite golden retriever.

But there'd been nothing perfect about it, and what a hard blow that had been. Serial adultery wasn't pretty—especially for the blind wife who'd missed all the signals, all the signs until they slapped hard into her face.

So it had been back to MacNamara House. Minus the husband and the dog. She did miss the dog, she thought with some amusement. And she was grateful she'd had a place to go, a place where her son could thrive, where she could be useful.

And if she still wished, occasionally, that the cheating bastard would die in some fiery car wreck, she'd mellowed considerably from the days she'd actively prayed for him to be decapitated by a runaway train.

That was progress.

She was lost in her own thoughts and nearly walked right by the house.

"Hey! Ava!"

She stopped, glanced over, and there was Duncan coming down the steps of some poor old house left to ruin.

Talk about window-shopping, she thought with pure female appreciation. It was hardly a wonder Phoebe was taking a lot of looks at this particular piece of merchandise. Rangy build, tousled hair, killer smile.

Though she hadn't proven herself the best judge of men, she was betting this one lived up to his packaging.

"Sorry. I was daydreaming. Oh my. Is this the place you bought? The place you told Essie about?"

"Yeah." He looked back at it as a man might a beloved old aunt. "She needs some help."

"Yes, she certainly does."

Boards blinded half the windows while the front veranda sagged like an old pair of jowls. The paint—what was left of it—curled off the wood in a sickly yellow.

"You have your work cut out for you," she commented.

"That's half the fun. And I kind of wanted to talk to you about that."

"About what?"

"Come on up a little. The steps are fine." He took her hand, drew her up. "Structurally it's in pretty good shape. Some this, some that. But mostly it's cosmetic."

"It's going to take a lot of Max Factor, Duncan."

"Max . . . right, right. Got it. Yeah, it needs a lot of makeup, but I've got ideas about that. One of them's about curb appeal, you could say. Your place—MacNamara House?—it's got excellent curb appeal. I hear you do all the gardening around there."

"Most of it." She pulled a bottle of water out of her purse, offered it.

"You carry water in your purse?"

"I could open a small sundry shop with what I carry in my purse. I have no idea how you men get along with just pockets. Would you like it? I have two."

"No. Thanks. I'm good. Ah . . . gardening. Your gardening."

"Mmm." Taking a sip of water, Ava noted the tangled mess of the front lawn, and the viciously healthy bindweed that dominated. "Essie putters a little. Phoebe barely has time to do more than yank a few weeds now and then. I enjoy it most, so I do the most."

"I like to garden."

"Do you?" Now she looked at him with a smile.

"Found it out when I started fooling around with the house I—the house I live in. I'm not too bad. You're a whole lot better. So I thought maybe you might be able to help me out here."

"Here?"

"I'm thinking we'll have to start pretty much from scratch. Mostly what's here has gone woody, or it's dead, except for the weeds, of course. They need a good killing. We'd want some new foundation plants for sure and something splashy. Maybe a dwarf blooming something— little weeper maybe—on the side there. A trailing vine up the trellis."

Baffled, Ava studied the sorrowful house. "What trellis?"

"The one I think we should put up. Or an arbor. I got a fondness for arbors." Imagining, he jiggled the change in his pockets. "Then there's pots and window boxes. A lot of big—and let's go splashy again—pots and window boxes. And there's a space around the back? It's small, and I'm thinking a little patio with a pretty little table and chairs, that kind of thing. Needs a couple of beds to frame it in. Potted trees, so on so on. So, think you can help me out?"

"I'm confused. You want me to help you landscape this place?"

"I'm looking to hire you to landscape this place."

Because the breath stuck in her throat, Ava took a long drink to clear it. "Duncan . . . Why would you think I could take on a project like this? I'm not a landscaper. I just do some gardening."

He did a little gardening, Duncan thought. What Ava did was what Essie did with hook and yarn. She created art. "I don't want a landscaper here, exactly. Nothing against them, not a thing. I want something homey, but a little dramatic. Individual. I like what you've done to the Jones Street place. That's what I'm looking for here. I've got pictures."

He pulled a folder from a briefcase on the steps, pushed them at her. "Of the house, the grounds—such as they are, the verandas, so on. And I worked up some of the basic ideas I have in mind. Not set in stone, but ideas. And the budget I was thinking of."

Curiosity got the best of her, so she opened the folder, paged through until she got to the budget. "I'm going to sit down here on these steps."

"Okay." He sat down with her. He did love sitting on a step or a stoop in the city and just watching life go by. So he was content enough to do just that as she was silent for several moments.

"Duncan, I think you must be an awfully sweet man, but you may have a mental problem." When he laughed, she shook her head. "You don't offer a major project like this to someone who isn't proven."

"Well, major's relative. I have a major project elsewhere, which maybe we'll talk about some other time. I want this to look like a home." He wanted the life that went by to see it as one. "That's how I see what you've done. I know something about gardening, and—"

She snorted, jabbed a finger. "Tell me half a dozen of the plants you've seen at MacNamara house."

"Well, you've got that one urn thing on the veranda with heliotrope and that dark red phlox, with the lobelia and the sweet alyssum." He moved on to another pot, on to the shrubs and beds in the front.

She studied him now, her eyes narrowed behind shaded lenses. "Did you write all that down?"

"I notice things, especially if they interest me. You could think about it. I've got a couple weeks before I have to lock this in. Maybe you'll come up with some ideas, and we can kick them around. I could . . ." He glanced at his watch, winced. "But I've gotta get on. Phoebe's coming for dinner in a couple hours so I've got to . . ."

"Get on," Ava murmured. "I think I'll just sit here a bit longer, if that's all right with you."

"Sure, poke around." He rose, turned and studied the house again. "I'd really like to bring her back. Just give it some thought, all right?"

"I'll give it some thought."

She sat, after he'd gotten into his car and pulled away. She sat, thinking he must be a crazy man. Then she stood, studied the house, walked carefully around the sagging veranda.

She thought of the yard she'd had in that tidy subdivision in West Chatham. How she'd loved turning it into a showpiece. How she'd hauled soil, fertilizer, peat moss. How she'd dug, and planted, and sweated and weeded. Making her home, she remembered. Making it picture perfect, without a clue that there was a snake in her garden. Not a clue that she'd have to walk away from the dreamscape she'd imagined and worked so hard to create.

Wouldn't it be something if she could do this? If she could scrape away all the dead, all the ugly, and make something beautiful here? For no reason other than the beauty.

Yes, she decided. It was something to think about.

15

She'd nearly talked herself out of going to Duncan's. Which, of course, would be insane. She wanted to go. She really, *really* wanted to finish what they'd started on his veranda a few nights before.

But Sensible Phoebe elected to debate with Needy Phoebe—and damn her, had made some very valid points on the way home from work, during the change-for-date process and even now on the drive to the island portion of the evening.

They should get to know each other better. He was, no question, an appealing, interesting man. But what was the rush? Wouldn't it be more rational—read: safer—to have a few more dates in public venues before haring off to his house when and where the end result was inevitable?

She could argue with that, and did. She liked him, she enjoyed him, she was strongly attracted to him physically. She was thirty-three.

But really, what did she know about him—under the surface of things? For all she knew he might be the type who used that affability of his like a weapon and knocked susceptible females over on a weekly basis. He could be the male version of Celene's mother, busily juggling. Did she want to be one of his balls in the air?

What the hell difference did it make? Couldn't she date a man—couldn't she sleep with a man—without demanding or expecting absolute exclusivity? She deserved some fun and some companionship—and some goddamn sex—in her personal life.

So shut the hell up.

He meddled. At least it could be construed as meddling by someone with her twin antennae of cynicism and suspicion humming. An outlet for her mother's needlework, a gardening job for Ava. What was next? Would he offer to buy a shoe store for Carly?

Of course that was ridiculous. It was overreacting. It was overprotective. Certainly neither her mother nor Ava considered the opportunities offered meddling. And it wasn't as if they weren't particularly skilled at the arts and crafts he'd provided a channel for.

The problem was she could twist his actions, this relationship, the entire mass of it all into any of several forms. If she were going to be obsessive and picky about it. Instead of just taking a chance, enjoying the moment.

Besides, she was too close to his house now to turn back like some nervous idiot and bolt for home.

They'd talk, they'd simply talk about what was going on, about what this business with Ava was really about. They'd eat some pizza, maybe drink some wine, and have a mature, adult conversation about where—if anywhere—they might be going.

If Sensible Phoebe wasn't satisfied with that, she could get the hell out of the car and walk home.

It occurred to her as she turned into Duncan's drive that the first time she'd seen his house she'd been traumatized. The second time it had been after dusk. Seeing it now, in full light, with all her wits about her, was a different experience.

It was gorgeous, all those tall windows with the carved white trim against the pale, beachy blue of the wood. The sweep of terraces and verandas. And, of course, the sturdy elegance of the portico with its white columns. Where they'd very nearly taken an action that would have turned her recent debate to dust.

The charm of that widow's walk where she could easily imagine standing to look out at marsh and salt flat, at garden, at river.

And, of course, the gardens. The heaps and flows, the spikes and trails. She had to concede the man knew gardens, or hired a fleet of people who did. Which was one and the same, really. A man didn't have to dig and plant, to prune and weed, to appreciate the power of a lovely landscape.

The result was a gorgeous little slice of island living, sun and shade, bloom and fragrance, green and color all swirling around a house that managed to be grand and homey at the same time.

It took vision, she supposed, to pull that off.

She strolled along the walk, enjoying the dreamy, romantic sensation, and hoped they'd have that wine, that pizza and conversation, out on the veranda with the warm, moist air and those heady fragrances stirred up by the breeze.

He opened the door before she reached it, stood framed by that white trim, watching her walk toward him.

"I feel like I should be wearing a flowing white gown," she called out, "and a wide-brimmed hat—like this dead-ringer-for-Julia-Roberts transvestite I had a nice chat with yesterday. Only my hat should be trimmed with violets, I think—tucked into the band, and ribbons trailing."

"You look pretty perfect just the way you are, even if you aren't— far as I know—a transvestite."

"She might've been a transsexual. I didn't like to ask on so short an acquaintance."

"Either way. I like the dress."

"Thanks." It might have been something she often hauled out for PTA meetings, but at the moment the simple cotton felt pretty perfect. "You've had a busy day."

"It's all relative." He held out a hand to take hers, to bring her inside.

She didn't see it coming. So much, she'd think later, for instincts— cop or woman. But right at that moment, with her back up against the door and his mouth hot on hers, thinking wasn't part of the equation.

She might've put her hands on his shoulders in a gesture of whoa there, wait a minute pal, but they slid right up until her arms were locked around his neck.

And waiting was done.

His hands dove into her hair, skimmed over her shoulders, molded down her body with such purpose and skill that any idea of *whoa* went straight out the window, and kept on flying.

Sensible Phoebe didn't have a prayer.

He *smelled* so good, and felt even better—hard and tough and male. With her mouth under assault and her blood flashing from comfortably warm to desperately hot, her body ruled the moment.

He might have stopped—if she'd pulled out a gun and held it to his head, he might've stopped. But he heard, in some dim part of his brain, her purse hit the floor with a single hard thump.

Then she locked around him, those strong bare arms, and her teeth nipped and gnawed on his bottom lip. She moaned; she quivered. And her scent seemed to rise from light, teasing invitation to will-snapping opiate.

He slid her dress up, up, up those gorgeous legs, ran his hand over warm flesh, over the thin lacy bit that covered her. Under it.

Not warm here, but hot. Hot and wet and open. Her hips pumped, pressed, and she came on a low, feral groan that shot straight to his belly. Her fingers dug in, a hard bite on his shoulders.

Then they were pushing between their bodies, tugging at the button of his fly.

Now, now, now. Right this minute. Oh God! She didn't know if she said it out loud or just thought it. The sensations careening inside her flew too fast, too high for any kind of resistance, any hope of sanity. She wasn't entirely sure she could survive another ten seconds if he wasn't inside her.

And when he was, when he drove into her, she didn't give a damn about survival.

Fast, right on the edge of violent, thrust after thrust. It filled up places she'd forgotten had been empty, fired up places she'd forgotten had gone cool. It was an onslaught, and thank God for it.

Nothing strapped down now, nothing sensible. He had her arms over her head, wrists cuffed with his hand, her skirt hiked to her waist.

He battered her against the front door until the orgasm simply shredded her to pieces.

And with his own release his breath was ragged in her ear. He braced her against the door. She realized when her head cleared a little it was as much to keep his own balance as to hold her up.

"Thanks," she managed.

"It was at least fifty percent my pleasure."

When she wheezed out a laugh, he eased back, studying her face as he brushed her hair aside. "I had a different order of business in mind. Initially."

She could nearly focus again, and oh God, she loved the color of his eyes. "Order of business."

"You know, a couple of adult beverages on the veranda, or walking around the gardens. Some dinner with conversation. Then I realized I'd just be thinking about sex through all that, which would spoil my appetite."

He ran a hand up her leg as he spoke, had her quivering once more. And gently smoothed her skirts back into place. "That's one thing," he continued, "but I believed you might very well be in the same frame of mind. Here I'd be having you over for dinner and spoiling your appetite. That's no way to treat a guest."

"I see. So am I to understand we just had at each other against your front door because you didn't want to be rude?"

He grinned at her. "Absolutely. Only reason. Steady yet?"

"I think so."

He stepped back, glanced down. Bending he picked up her ripped panties. He said, "Oops."

She laughed. "I don't know why I bothered to put on good underwear."

"They were momentarily appreciated. I could lend you a pair of boxers."

"I'll pass on that, thanks all the same. I'll just use the bathroom for a minute."

"Yeah, sure. Listen, Phoebe . . ." Absently he stuffed the torn panties in his back pocket. "Included in that original order of business was my intention to suit up a bit more formally."

She stared at him, a quizzical smile on her face. Then it sank in, the smile dropped away to a look of stunned realization. "Oh. Oh, God."

"I stopped thinking," he began. "I'm—"

"It was mutual, as much me as you." Stunned, she rubbed the space between her breasts where her heart gave a couple of hard knocks. "I take the pill, but—"

"But," he said with a nod. "I can only tell you I'm habitually a hell of a lot more careful. We can exchange blood tests if you're worried. I can tell you, too, that's the first time that front door's been used in such an interesting manner. I may have it bronzed, but meanwhile, I'm sorry, and I'm willing to sacrifice a vial of blood if it gives you peace of mind."

"Let's just say we'll be more careful from this point."

"Okay."

She picked up the purse she'd dropped. "I'll be back in a minute."

She got a good look at herself in the bathroom mirror. Flushed, the sleepy cat-that-gulped-a pint-of-cream eyes, hair tumbled. All well and good, she thought. And God knew it *had* been good. But she wasn't allowed to be that reckless, and couldn't be again. Next date, she promised herself, there would be condoms in her purse.

When she came out he wasn't in the foyer, or the front parlor. She called out his name as she started to wander, then followed the answer to a room off the kitchen. Party room, she decided. A grand old bar, lots of cushy seating, framed posters of what she saw were reproductions of old magazine ads. All deco and stylized.

There was a card table that looked to be an antique like the bar, and display cabinets filled with this and that. Some of the this, she noted with amusement, were Pez dispensers.

"The gentlemen's club," she said.

"Sort of." He came around the bar with two glasses of wine. "Hungry?"

"I think you already took care of that."

His grin was quick and pleased. "That's good because I called in for the pizza, but I told them to bring it around in about an hour. Thought you might like to have a drink outside, maybe in the garden. Watch the sun go down."

"That's exactly what I'd like."

She went with him through a set of French doors onto the back veranda. And there, scanning, she took a sip of wine. "Nice—the wine," she qualified. "The rest? It's like a little piece of fairyland, isn't it?"

"Lots of secret places. I got carried away with it once I really started."

"So . . ." She stepped down, crossed the patio. "Why aren't you hiring whoever designed and created this to design and create the gardens you want at this shop you're planning?"

"You talked to Ava."

"She's terrified and thrilled in equal measure."

"Well, here's the thing. This? I sort of designed some of it. Not really designed, but fiddled around. I had help, and it's kind of evolved and shifted and changed its original layout."

"Whatever the original, this suits you." Phoebe turned a slow circle. "Fanciful, as I said, and its lack of formality enhances the charm."

He was looking at her now, only at her. "You standing in it enhances the charm."

She made a mock curtsy. "Aren't you gallant?"

"If I were, I'd have come up with something romantic about blooms or blossoms."

"You did fine. As to Ava?"

"Yeah, Ava, and the place. I don't think I'm going to have time to fiddle so much with that project, and I didn't really want the team sensibility. I wanted a woman's, a woman who understands a house like that one, an area like that one, and knows how to, well, lay the landscape, to put in the flourishes and the color so people walking or driving by will say, 'That's Savannah right there.' I like what she's done with the house on Jones."

He pushed through an ornate iron gate. Phoebe saw instantly what he'd meant about secrets. It was a little island on the island, one of tranquillity and whispers, with its little pool with floating lilies, its fanciful statue of a winged fairy.

She walked over to a small curved bench of white marble, sat. "Not just a good deed?"

"I don't mind good deeds or suspicious minds, as yours tends to be. But I don't mind profiting by being a good judge and picking people for projects they're suited for."

"Ever pick the wrong person?"

"A few times. I don't think Ava's one of them."

"She won't be. She had this house in West Chatham when she was married, and she created the most amazing gardens. She even got written up in *Southern Homes* . . . You knew that, didn't you?"

His dimple flicked on. "I might've come across something."

"Smarter than you look, and that's a pure compliment."

"You, too." He leaned over, kissed her breezily. "Want to walk around a bit, maybe down to the pier?"

"Yes, I'd like that."

Bricked paths, arbors and trellises, copper urns going soft and green, and pretty music as the evening breeze stirred hanging glass and wind chimes.

The sun was sinking, turning the marsh into shimmering colors. From the pier she could see other homes, other gardens, and what she thought was a young boy sitting on the edge of a pier with his line in the water.

"Do you ever do that? Fish off here?"

"I'm a crappy fisherman. Rather just sit here with a beer and let someone else drown the worms."

She turned around, noted how far they'd walked. "The grounds are more extensive than I realized." And there, she noted, were the sparkling waters of a swimming pool. "A lot to maintain. I'm still having a hard time seeing you as the country gentleman. How about that long story on how you ended up here?"

"It's not all that interesting."

"Not all that interesting to you, or potentially to me?"

"Probably either."

"Now, of course, my curiosity is piqued and, unquenched, will depend on imagination to satisfy. Such as you built it for a woman— unrequited love, heartbreak—who left you for another man."

"Not that far off."

She sobered instantly. "I'm sorry, bad joke. We should start back to the house, don't you think? I'd hate to miss the pizza boy. I'd love to eat on the veranda, or in the garden," she continued as they walked up the pier. "Wouldn't—"

"I built it for my mother."

"Oh." She heard the echoes of deep unhappiness in his voice, but said nothing else.

"I guess that's not the beginning of the story. My mother was seventeen when she had me. What we could call a very big oops. My father was barely older. For whatever reason they—or she—decided to go through with the pregnancy, get married. I'm grateful, obviously, about the first part of that decision, but the married part probably wasn't the smartest move on either of their parts. They fought all the time—the time they were together. He was lazy, she was a bitch, he drank too much, she kept a crappy house. Fun and games at the Swifts'."

"It's difficult for a child to grow up with that kind of friction."

"Yeah, well, the thing is they were both right. He was lazy and drank too much. She was a bitch and kept a crappy house. I was ten when he took off. He'd taken off a few times before—so had she. But this time he didn't come back."

"Are you saying you never saw him again?"

"Not for a lot of years. Man, she was pissed. Paid him back by going out a lot, doing what she wanted for a change. More than half the time I wondered if she even knew I was there. So to remind her I was, I got into as much trouble as possible. Fighting mostly. I was the neighborhood badass for five years running."

Saying nothing, she lifted her hand, traced a fingertip down the scar through his eyebrow.

"Yeah, battle scar. No big."

"It intrigued me when I first saw you. Scar here, little dimple right here." She tapped the corner of his mouth. "Opposite ends. You've got some opposite ends in you, Duncan. What happened in year six? How did you lose your title as neighborhood badass?"

"You're a smart one. I targeted this kid who was a lot tougher than he looked. He didn't kick my ass, but boy, did we kick each other's."

"And ended up the best of friends," Phoebe concluded. "Isn't that the manly cliché?"

"I hate being predictable, but close enough. While we're pounding each other bloody, and I'm wondering if my badass title is about to be stripped away, the kid's father comes along. Big guy, yanked us apart.

We're going to do that shit, we're going to put the gloves on and do it like men. Kid's father used to box for a living. No wonder Jake almost kicked my ass."

"And who won the title in the ring?"

"Neither. We never got around to the gloves. Jake's father dragged me to their place, cleaned us both up at the kitchen sink while his wife fixed me an ice bag and a glass of lemonade. Bored yet? I told you it was long."

"Not even close to bored."

"Well, you're going to need another glass of wine for the rest." He took her glass. Phoebe leaned back against the rail and waited until he came back with refills.

"Where was I?"

"At Jake's kitchen table drinking lemonade."

"And getting a whale of a talking-to. First time anybody—not including teachers, who didn't count in those days for me—ever gave me one. It occurred to me at this time that being the neighborhood badass was getting me punched in the face on a regular basis. And what was the point? She never said a damn thing about it when I came home bloody anyway. So I gave up the belt of my championship reign."

"You were what, about fifteen?"

"Thereabouts."

"Young for an epiphany, but I understand youthful epiphanies."

He shifted to look into her eyes. "Guess you would."

"So we have the common ground of that. I moved into MacNamara House after mine, which is another story for another day. What did you do after you retired from badassing?"

"I got a job, thinking that might be the way to please her—my mother—and it would be less painful than bare knuckles."

"A wise choice." But he'd never pleased her, Phoebe thought, she could hear it in his voice. "What kind of job?"

"I bused tables, gave her half of what I made every week. That was fine. Didn't change anything between us, but it was fine. I started to think that's just the way things were for people like us. Single parent, scraping by. She just didn't have time to pay attention."

He was quiet for a few moments while a whip-poor-will began its twilight call. "Of course, being a single parent, you know that's not the case."

"I know it shouldn't be."

"When I was eighteen she told me I had to get my own place, so I did. Time passed, and one day I picked up a fare whose wallet was empty. One thing led to another and I met his family. No father—he died when Phin was a kid—but the result was the same. There was no father there, but the mother, oh, you best believe she paid attention."

Phoebe thought of Ma Bee—big hands, steady eyes. "Even when you wished she didn't."

"Even. She had a brood of kids, but she paid attention. To me, too. So I saw it wasn't just the way it is. It was easier to believe that, or want to. But it was not the way it is.

"That'd be the pizza." He pushed off the rail. "I'll be a minute. If it's Teto, he likes to talk."

"All right."

She sipped her wine, looked out at the gardens now that the first stars were popping out. He'd thought the house, the gardens, the beauty here would make his mother, at last, pay attention. Phoebe already saw that, and that it hadn't worked.

Why did he stay? she wondered. Wasn't it painful?

He came back with a pizza box, a pair of plates riding the top, napkins tucked between.

"I'll set it up. Will you finish telling me?"

"I guess we can fast-forward to hitting the jackpot."

He lit candles as she set the plates and napkins on a wicker table. "Local boy makes way good, just because he bought a six-pack and a lottery ticket. Had a hell of a celebration. I think I was solid drunk for two days. First sober thing I did was go over to Ma Bee's. I bought this funny little brass bottle, like a genie bottle. I told her to rub it, to make three wishes. I was going to grant all three."

"Aren't you the cutest thing?" Phoebe said softly, then sat at the table.

"I thought I was pretty damn clever. She said that was all right, she'd make three wishes. The first was that I wouldn't piss this money away being an idiot and forgetting I had some brains. The second was that I take this opportunity, this gift, and make something of myself. I guess I looked like a balloon that had its air pricked out, because she laughed and laughed, and she gave me a slap on the arm. She told me if I needed to give her something, if I needed to do that to be happy, she'd like a pair of red shoes with heels and open toes. Size nine. Wouldn't she be some sight going to church Sundays in those red shoes?"

"You must love her beyond measure."

"I do. And mostly I tried to keep my word, too, all the wishes. The red shoes were easy. Not being an idiot's more problematic. People come out of the woodwork. That's the way it is, and passing out money, it can make you feel important. Until—like getting fists punched into your face—you start to realize it's just fucking stupid."

"And you're not. You're not the least bit stupid."

"I had my moments." He slid pizza onto her plate, then onto his. "I bought this land for my mother, had the house built. I used to hear her say, if she could just get out of the goddamn city. I could do that for her, and wouldn't that make me important to her? I gave her money in the meantime, of course. Got her out of that apartment and into a pretty little house while this one was being built. My old man turned up, as bad pennies do. I wasn't quite as gullible there. I gave him twenty-five thousand, all he was smart enough to ask for. But I had Phin draw up an agreement. He couldn't come at me for more. He wouldn't get it, and if he tried I could sue him for harassment, and other legal mumbo. It probably wouldn't hold up, but my father wasn't the brightest bulb in the chandelier, so he took the twenty-five and went away again."

"It must have hurt you."

"Should have," Duncan said after a moment. "It really didn't." He ate pizza, drank wine. "I brought my mother out here when the house was nearly finished, when it was easy to see what it was going to be. I told her it was for her. I'd furnish it any way she liked. She'd never have to work again.

"She walked around the empty rooms. She asked me why the hell I thought she'd ever live out here, in a house big as a barn. I said she just didn't see how it would be yet. I was going to get her a housekeeper, a cook, whatever she wanted. She turned around, looked at me. 'You want to give me what I want? Buy me a house in Vegas, and give me a stake of fifty thousand. That's what I want.'

"I didn't do it, not then. I kept thinking she'd change her mind, once she saw the house finished. I brought her out here again when it was—badgered her into it. The gardens were in, and I'd furnished a few of the rooms, so she'd get a real sense of it."

Gently, Phoebe touched his hand. "But it wasn't what she wanted."

"No, it wasn't. She wanted the house in Vegas and fifty K. I bargained. Live here for six months, and if you don't change your mind, I'll buy you a house wherever you want and give you a hundred thousand. She took the deal, and six months later called me out here. She was already packed. She had the number of a realtor she'd been working with, and had the house already picked out. I could take care of buying the house, and send her a check at Caesars in the meantime. I decided it was time to stop, metaphorically, taking that fist in the face. I had Phin draw up another agreement, then I went out to Vegas, did the deal, gave her the papers, which she signed without a blink. She took the check, and that was that."

"How long ago?"

"Going on five years now. She got a job serving drinks, ended up catching the eye of some high roller. He paid to track down the old man, get a legal divorce. They got married two years ago."

"And you live here."

"Seemed a shame to waste this place. Figured I'd sell it, but it kind of grew on me. And it was a point, too. Point being sometimes you don't get what you want, and it doesn't matter if it's fair or not. So you better find something else."

It was amazing, really, she realized. One evening had satisfied her sensible and her lustful parts. She'd not only had stupendous sex, not only gotten to know him better, but had come to understand him.

"I don't have to tell you she didn't deserve you."

"No. She might've deserved the badass in training, but she didn't deserve who I figured out to be—with a little help from my friends."

"Did you buy that house for Ma Bee, the one where we were on Sunday?"

"All the kids—which includes me—went together on that three years ago. She'd take it, you see, from all of us, from the family, but she wouldn't have taken it from any single one of us. If you see the difference."

"Yes, I do. And what about Jake? What happened to him?"

"He does the contracting, when I pick up a place. His father went into construction after he got out of the ring, a few years before my own fateful day with them. Jake went into the business. He's good at it."

"I bet he is." Obligingly, she plopped another slice of pizza on his plate. "You have a way of picking them."

"I do." He laid a hand over hers. "With a few disappointing exceptions, I have a hell of a way of picking them."

16

The air was full of sounds, the peeps, the clicks, the whirls of night, when Duncan walked her to her car. "So . . . what do you think about taking a sail some evening?"

"I think that would be very nice—some evening. It's a little hard for me to miss too many evenings at home. Added to that, you've been lucky so far that I haven't gotten called in before or during one of the evenings."

She turned, leaned back against the car. "You're complicating things for yourself, dating not only a cop but a single parent."

"Complications are interesting, especially when you figure out how to work them around the simple." He leaned down to kiss her. "Some evening."

"All right." She reached for the car door, turned back to follow impulse. "Why don't you come over for dinner this week? It wouldn't be without its complications, but my mother's already fallen for you."

"Yeah? Well, if I didn't get anywhere with you, I figured to hit on her next." He tucked Phoebe's hair behind her ear, gave the little gold hoop she wore a tap. "She makes a hell of a cookie."

"She certainly does. Thursday work? It would give them enough time to fuss appropriately for company, and not give them quite enough time to drive me crazy with the details of it."

"I can do Thursday."

She angled her head. "You don't have a book to check? Appointments to consider?"

"I can do Thursday," he repeated, and this time when he kissed her, he turned up the dial until heat balled in her belly.

"Well." She rubbed her lips together. "Well, I'd better go before I decide staying's an option. Because it isn't," she said, nudging him back when he started to speak. "Thursday. Six o'clock." She laughed as she slid into the car. "It's a school night."

"As long as I don't have to do any homework. You drive safe, Phoebe. And you should wait until you're home before you think about me. Otherwise you'll get all stirred up, maybe drive off the road."

She drove away laughing—just, she imagined—as he'd intended. Still, she'd just have to risk getting herself stirred up, because he'd given her plenty to think about.

He was fun, interesting and easy on the eyes. He was good in bed— or against the door. It occurred to her that while she couldn't claim a wide swath of sexual experience, hers wasn't narrow either. And she'd been married for a few years in there.

But she'd never had an experience to match the one Duncan had greeted her with that night.

He had an easygoing way, but he wasn't careless. Roy had been her experience with careless, and it was one she was determined never to repeat.

He hadn't flipped off his friends when he made his fortune. Phin was his lawyer, Jake his contractor. He remembered his friends. Loyalty was a vital element to her.

Easygoing and loyal he might be, but he wasn't what she thought of as a golden retriever kind of man. Too many layers, too much direction.

One of the layers was old hurts. How had he managed to bury that? She knew a lot about old hurts, and just how hard they were to keep down in the cellar of things. He didn't wear his wounds as a point of pride, and many did. He might brood over them from time to time, and she appreciated a good brood herself. But he didn't appear to let those old wounds, those old scars run his life.

On that score, he was probably doing better than she was.

Did the money help? Of course it did. Let's be serious. But she had a feeling he'd have gotten on well enough without it. She suspected the money had opened him to ambition. Or at least had made him realize he *had* ambitions and could start to act on them.

She'd always had ambitions, many of them very specific. And had made good on most. She doubted she could stay interested in a man for very long, regardless of how good he was against the door, if he didn't have goals and purposes.

But really, how much did she know about Duncan's goals and purposes? Bars, a shop in the planning stages. Considering the depth of the well, those were fairly small drops. What else did he do? What else did he want? Where else was he going?

And there she was, she thought with a sigh, picking things apart. Pinching folds of the cloth and trying to make it form into a shape she liked or could work with.

It was a quality that made her a good negotiator, she admitted, and one that probably had a lot to do with her crappy—until recently— love life.

So why not just go with it? Just let it flow instead of trying to direct the stream? Not the easiest thing for her to do, but she could work on it.

He'd come to dinner on Thursday. Maybe they'd take that evening sail sometime soon. They'd see each other, enjoy each other and, please, God, have more really good sex. And just see.

Just see.

When she pulled up in front of the house, she doubted she could feel much better. She'd peek in on Carly, who had *better* be fast asleep, then maybe she'd take a pitcher of tea upstairs and see if she could have a little girl time with her mother and Ava.

Humming, she locked the car, started across the sidewalk.

And nearly jumped out of her shoes. She barely managed to muffle her own squeal—and squeal was the only word for it. Cop or not, she was still a damn girl. Any girl might squeal when she saw a two-foot snake draped across her front steps.

Probably rubber, she told herself as she thumped a hand on her heart to get it going again. Probably one of the neighborhood boys playing a nasty boy prank on the houseful of females.

That smart-aleck Johnnie Porter around the corner on Abercorn— this was right up his alley. They were going to have words, she and Johnnie were. Some very stern words the first thing in . . .

Not rubber, she realized as she edged closer. Not some play snake from the toy shop. It was real, nearly as thick as her wrist, and though she wasn't in a position to take its pulse or call the coroner, it appeared to be very dead.

Maybe it was just sleeping.

Standing a foot back now, she dragged a hand through her hair, kept her eyes on the snake in case it moved. Dead or alive, she couldn't just leave it there. Dead it was, well, unsightly and just plain awful. Alive, it might wake up and slither off, anywhere. Even inside the house.

The very idea of that had her dashing back to her car. Her head swiveled back and forth between the snake and the trunk she popped. She actively wished she was wearing her weapon, though she wasn't entirely sure, should it make a slither for it, she was keen-eyed or steady-handed enough to hit it.

"Going to the firing range," she muttered as she grabbed her umbrella out of the trunk. "Going to the range, get some practice in. I've neglected that. Oh God, oh hell. I so seriously don't want to do this."

And what choice was there? Run to a neighbor, yank out her cell phone and call Carter. Come get the dead or sleeping snake off the front steps, would you? Thanks so much. God. God.

She kept swallowing as she inched forward, then with eyes squeezed half shut, poked at the snake with the tip of her umbrella.

The squeal almost got the better of her this time. She jumped back, heart cartwheeling. It lay still, the ugly black thing. After two more pokes, she officially pronounced it dead.

"All right, all right now. Just do it. Don't think about it. Just . . . Oh, oh, oh!"

She slipped the end of the umbrella under the body, fighting to keep her arms steady enough to balance the limp droop of it. She dropped it twice, cursing each time and dancing back as if she'd stepped on hot coals. Fireplace tongs would be better, she realized, but if she went into the house to get them, she might just stay there.

She managed to get it around to the side gate and through to the courtyard. By now she was queasy, and little bubbles of hysterical laughter kept rising in her throat. She dumped it all, snake and the nearly brand-new umbrella, into the trash. Slammed down the lid.

There was probably an ordinance against putting a dead reptile, uncovered, unsecured, in a trash can. But just screw that, she decided. She'd done all she was doing.

She'd call the waste management company. She'd bribe the trashman. She'd offer him sexual favors.

She backed away from the trash can. Her legs carried her as far as the steps of the back veranda, where she just let herself drop. Damn cat. She was going to find out whose damn cat was running loose, killing things and leaving their corpses on her property.

Though where some cat had flushed out a snake that size in the city of Savannah, she couldn't say. No, it was some idiot kid, that's what it was. Johnnie Porter or his ilk.

No longer in the mood for iced tea or girl talk, she rose, intending to go up and straight to bed.

She heard the whistling when she reached the door, and this time the chill arrowed straight to her belly.

He about busted a gut! He couldn't think of the last time anything had struck him so funny, until actual tears were streaming from his eyes. He'd had to wipe them more than once to keep his vision clear through the long night-vision lens of the camera.

God*damn*, the way she'd jumped! Had to damn near piss herself. His ribs ached from keeping the laughter down to a snickering, body-shaking snort instead of a belly-busting guffaw.

He'd expected her to take a wild leap over it, but hell, had to say she was made of sterner stuff. It only made it funnier and more interesting.

It had been a piece of good luck to come across that black snake, and to realize after giving its head a good solid smash with a shovel that he could use it. But, he could admit now, he hadn't known it would *tickle* him so to watch her deal with it.

He bet she didn't sleep half the night, and when she did, she'd dream of snakes.

Him? He was going home to print out the pictures, have himself another laugh. Then he was going to sleep like a baby.

She didn't sleep well. And there were enough scenarios and possibilities running around in her head that she gave it up shortly after dawn and called Carter.

When Josie answered, Phoebe launched into apologies, got a grunt in return. Then Carter's sleepy voice came on the line.

"I'm sorry. I'm so sorry. I should've waited until a decent hour to call."

"Too late."

"Well, I'm *sorry,* but I need you to come over here and look at something for me."

"What is it? A mermaid? A three-headed fish? The new Jaguar you bought me out of sisterly love and devotion? Because otherwise? Zzzzzzz."

"Don't you make snoring noises at me, Carter. I need you to get your ass out of that bed, put on some clothes and come over here. Right now. I don't want to wake up anyone else in the house, so you come around by the courtyard, you hear?"

"Yeah, yeah, yeah. Bossy and bitchy. There better be coffee."

He'd come. He'd grumble about it but he'd come. So she dressed quickly then tiptoed down to make coffee. She had two mugs in hand when she slipped outside to wait for him.

There'd been two thunderstorms in the night—she'd heard them both. The stones in the courtyard were still wet from the rain that had pounded down in those quick and violent intervals. There was a haze in the air, the pretty kind that would burn off within an hour or two and leave everything sparkling.

She sipped her coffee and watched drops of water drip, drip from the burgundy leaves of the little weeping peach Ava had planted the year before.

She heard Carter's feet on the path to the gate, and was opening the heavy cast iron before he reached it.

His hair was sleep-tossed, his eyes still heavy. He wore sweats and a Savannah U T-shirt with a pair of ancient running shoes. A knight in the shiniest of armor couldn't have looked better to her.

He scowled, grabbed the coffee. "Where's the damn body?" he demanded.

"In the trash can."

He choked on his first swallow of coffee. "What?"

"That one there." She pointed, keeping her distance.

"You kill somebody, Phoebs? Want me to help you bury him out here in Ava's garden?"

She just pointed again. With a shrug, he yanked off the lid. The coffee sloshed over the rim of his mug as he jolted, and that gave her some satisfaction. But then he just reached right in, even as she gargled out a sound of disgust, and pulled the dead snake out.

"Cool."

"Oh please, do you have to—" She yelped, pinwheeled back as he turned, grinning, to wag the snake at her. "Stop that! Damn it, Carter."

"Irresistible. Damn big guy to come sliding down Jones Street and into Ava's garden."

"I didn't find it in the garden. Would you stop *playing* with that thing? I found it on the front steps, already dead."

"Huh." He turned the snake's head around as if to converse with it. "What were doing there, big guy?"

"I thought maybe a cat killed it. There was a dead rat in the courtyard not long ago. A cat . . . But it's so damn big, I started thinking that it might be hard for a cat to take on a snake that big. Or maybe not. But why the hell would this damn cat be leaving dead things around the house? So then I thought—"

"Only way a cat killed this big boy is if the cat could swing a two-by-four." He wiggled the head of the snake at Phoebe. "Cat might chew it up some, but it sure couldn't crush the head flat as a pancake."

"Yeah." She let out a breath. "Yeah, I thought it might be more something like that." She kicked at the box she'd brought out. "Would you please put that ugly dead thing in there, then back in the can? And don't you touch me or anything until you wash your hands."

He dumped it into the box. "You said you found it on the steps out front?"

"Yeah." He wasn't grinning now. A little more satisfaction, she decided. "I got home about eleven last night, and—"

"From where?"

"I was on a date, if you have to know everything."

"With the lottery guy."

"His name is Duncan, and yes. In *any* case, that thing was draped right over the steps. Which means someone put it there."

"Some dumbass kid."

"Johnnie, you know Johnnie Porter around the corner? He's top of my list for that."

"You want me to talk to him?"

"No, I'll do that. I couldn't bring myself to go into that can and look at the damn thing again up close."

"That's what brothers are for." He dumped the box, closed the lid, then turned to her with evil in his smile. "Poor little Phoebe."

"Don't you dare touch me with your dead-snake hands. I mean it."

"I just want to pat my sister, to give her comfort in her time of—"

"You put one finger on me, your balls'll be tickling your tonsils." Defensively, she put up her dukes. "You know I can take you."

"Haven't put that to the test for a while. I've been working out."

"Oh, come in and wash up. You get points for riding to the rescue, and at this hour."

She led the way in, then leaned on the counter while he washed his hands at the sink. "Carter, there's this other possibility running in my brain. The one where it wasn't some dumbass kid like Johnnie Porter around the corner."

He glanced at her. "You're thinking asshole instead of dumbass."

"That's right. Just nasty pranks, nothing life-threatening, but still . . . And there was this other nasty business," she said, thinking of the doll. "I'll be talking to Johnnie, but I've got this . . . uncomfortable sensation, we'll call it. So I was wondering if you'd mind walking by the house, maybe after classes, just for a while. You don't have to come in, I know how that is. You stop by, that's it for a couple hours. But if you could just detour by here when I'm not around, I'd be easier."

"You know I will. Honey, if you're really worried—"

"Uncomfortable sensation," she corrected. "Not yet up to really worried. I guess I'm remembering . . ."

"The things Reuben used to do." Mouth tight now, Carter dried his hands. "Letting the air out of the tires on the car, spraying that poison on the flowers Mama planted outside the house."

Phoebe rubbed his arm. The remembering was always harder on Carter. "Yeah. Mean little things. If it is Arnie Meeks doing this, I expect he'll get tired of it soon enough."

"Or he'll escalate." He touched her now, a skim of fingertips under her eyes where the bruises had faded away. "He could come after you again, Phoebe."

"He's not the type for the direct approach, and believe me, Carter, he won't take me by surprise again. I'm not defenseless like Mama was."

"No, you made sure not to be, and still, this guy put you in the hospital."

"He won't do it again." Now she gave his arm a squeeze. "That's pure promise." She shook her head before he could say anything else. "Mama's coming. You went out for a run, all right? Just stopped by for coffee. If she hears about this she loses the courtyard."

Knowing she was right, he nodded, and made the effort to clear the grim from his face as his mother came into the kitchen.

"Well, look at this! Both my babies!"

The doll had been a dead end. The make and model had been discontinued three years earlier, and no shop in Savannah or the outlying malls carried it still. There was eBay, of course, flea markets, yard sales, all manner of other venues. And as it was hardly a matter of life and death, it didn't rate the time, effort and budget of the police department to try to track it down.

Johnnie Porter was unduly suspected as it turned out he was spending the entire week, along with the rest of his class, at outdoor school.

There were other young troublesome boys, certainly, but none
sprang to mind. And she couldn't think of any reason one—including
Johnnie—would target her house twice. Only her house, from what she
gathered by making casual inquiries among her neighbors.

So she made it a point to take a long walk around the square and
into the park after shift, to keep her ears pricked for anyone whistling a
mournful tune. That night she set up her own surveillance post inside
her terrace doors, in case anyone decided to drop off another gift.

She sat and rocked, field glasses in her lap, and felt a little like old
Mrs. Sampson on Gaston Street, who sat and rocked and watched everything and everyone from her front parlor window.

If the uncomfortable sensation bumped up a notch, she'd request a
radio car do a couple of drive-bys at night, maybe once or twice during
the day. The house had a good alarm system, something Cousin Bess
had insisted on. She was the one who usually armed it at night, making
that last round of the house when everyone was in bed.

Another thing Cousin Bess had insisted on.

People are no damn good, not a one of them. That had been Cousin Bess's
opinion. *But you're blood, so you'll have to do.*

Mama hadn't been good enough, of course, Phoebe remembered.
Except to fetch and carry and clean and slave in exchange for the roof
over her head, and the heads of her children.

Carter had been almost beneath Cousin Bess's contempt—almost.
His nightmares and night terrors in the months following Reuben was
a sign to Cousin Bess of weak and diluted blood—from Mama's side,
naturally. A true MacNamara would never blubber in his sleep, even at
the age of seven.

But Phoebe herself had been another matter. If she'd defended
Carter or hadn't been able to keep the sass from ripping off her tongue,
Cousin Bess had approved. *At least this one has a spine.*

So there'd been piano lessons she hadn't wanted and was a miserable
failure at, dance lessons she'd actually enjoyed. Art and music appreciation, trips to the right shops, the right salons, even an odd and daz-

zling week in Paris. Culminating in the dreaded and stupefyingly boring debutante ball.

She'd agreed to that only by bargaining with Cousin Bess over the guaranteed payment of Carter's college education when the time came. It had been worth one night of her life to secure four years of his.

Of course Cousin Bess had disapproved, vehemently, of Phoebe joining the FBI. Hadn't cared to have Phoebe train up north, so far out of her grip. But strangely enough had thoroughly approved of Roy.

And still, there'd been no mistaking that smirk of satisfaction when Phoebe came back to MacNamara House, with a baby and no husband.

"No surprise you couldn't hold onto a man like that when you're running after some career. A woman's got two choices: husband or career."

"That's nonsense. And my job had nothing to do with why my marriage is over."

She was dying. Phoebe could see it; she could smell it. In the weeks since she'd last visited, Cousin Bess had shrunk down to bone thinly covered by loose flesh. Only her eyes remained alive, and bitter.

"Married you for this house. Can't blame him for that. Marrying for property makes good sense."

"I don't want this house."

"You have it, or will. That's the way it's going to be. I put this house around you years ago. I put it around your crybaby brother and your weak-spirited mother."

"Be careful." Phoebe stepped closer to the bed. "Very careful how you speak about my family."

"Yours." Even poking a finger seemed to weaken her. "Not mine. You're my only blood at this point, and this house stays with my blood. I've made the arrangements."

"Fine."

Cousin Bess's dry lips twisted into a smile. It seemed to Phoebe her flesh was simply melting off the bone. That's how the Wicked Witch had met her end. Melting. Melting.

"You're thinking you can make yours, too. After I'm in the ground.

You're thinking that won't be long. You're right about the second part. I haven't got long."

"I'm sorry." Whatever their differences, Phoebe felt a pang. "I know you have pain. Is there anything I can do for you?"

"Still have that soft spot yet. Give it time and it'll harden up. The house comes to you. Don't think you can give it to your mother or your brother. I've fixed it so you can't. I've got the money put away for maintaining it. You'll get that from the lawyers. Held in trust, so don't think you can just be grabbing it with both hands. It's only for the house. That's made clear."

"I don't want your money either."

"Lucky for you then, because you won't get a dime. None of you. The house gets it all. On your death, it passes to your issue. If, only if, you abide by the terms. You'll live here now, miss, if you want your mother under this roof. You'll be in residence. There's no turning it into one of those bed-and-breakfasts or retail spaces or museums. It's a house, and it's where you'll live from here out."

Not a gun to her head, Phoebe thought, not a knife to her throat. No, no, Cousin Bess was too wily for those obvious weapons. Instead, she held those whom Phoebe loved over her heart.

"I don't need your house, your money or your approval. Understand me. I can and will support and house my child as I see fit. Not as you decree it."

"You will, or your mother goes today. Out of this house. Out of the house she hasn't been able to get the guts up to leave in years now. You think I don't *know*? I'll have her out within the hour, kicking, screaming. Imagine she'll need a padded room for a while, don't you?"

"Why would you do this to her? She's done nothing but tend to you. She's washed and bathed and emptied your slop for months now. Never once, in all of her life, has she caused you or anyone any harm."

"Might have been more respected if she had. I wouldn't be doing it. You would. The only way she stays in this house is if you do. You walk out of it, she's carried out of it. I took her in, took all of you in. I can put you out."

"So you always said."

"This time," Cousin Bess said with a thin smile, "it's permanent."

Phoebe woke with a quick jolt. Had she heard whistling? Had she heard it or imagined it?

She trained the field glasses on the street, toward the park, and saw nothing.

She rubbed her eyes, rubbed her neck.

Cousin Bess. How long had she lasted after that deathbed visit? Weeks more. Hard, miserable weeks, most of which she'd been delusional or drugged into sleep.

But long enough for Phoebe to learn—from the lawyers, from the trusts and wills and documents—that some things aren't negotiable.

She hadn't been able to have another lucid conversation with the old woman.

And here she was, years later, sitting in the house, looking out.

As it appeared she always would be.

17

Razz Johnson had something to prove. And he was gonna prove it today. The Lords figured they could come on his turf? Screw with his boys? They figured their way into the ground. They gonna come over to the west side, paint their shit right on his *doorstep?*

Uh-uh. They were gonna learn some respect.

Right now his brother was in the hospital, and maybe he'd die. They got the bullets out of his guts those motherfuckers put in him when his man led the force to Lords' turf for some goddamn retribution.

But T-Bone had ordered Razz to stay back, 'cause he hadn't reached the high level for warfare. Maybe, maybe if he'd been there, his brother wouldn't be lying in that hospital, maybe dying.

Razz knew what he had to do. Eye for an eye.

He drove along Hitch Street, enemy territory. He'd stolen the car, and he had his blue ball cap, part of his gang uniform, on the seat. If any of the Lords were hanging on the street, he didn't want them making him as Posse. Not yet. Not until he was ready.

He was fucking going covert.

He'd beaten his way into the gang. Even though his brother was high-ranking, he'd had to prove himself. He was a demon in a fight, fists and feet. He just didn't give up.

He had a talent for boosting cars, could be trusted on drug deals as he didn't care to use the shit. But so far he'd gotten shaky at the idea of guns and knives.

T-Bone said he couldn't shoot worth dick, and that was another why on leaving him back last night.

But there was a .45 semiautomatic, with the first round already racked, under the cap on the seat. And Razz wasn't shaking now.

He was going to put that round right between the eyes of the one who shot his brother. Anybody got in his way, well, he'd put a bullet in them, too. What they called collateral damage.

He was going in, in the daylight, and he was going in wearing his colors. And if he didn't come back out again, well, that's the way it was.

He was sixteen.

He pulled up across from the liquor store. He knew Clip used its back room for his "office." He hung out there, did some deals, talked his trash, got bj's from bitches trying to get raped into the gang.

He'd go 'round the back, that's what he'd do. Take out any guards if there were guards to take. Then through the door. Bullet between the bastard's eyeballs.

T-Bone was going to be proud. T-Bone was going to have the will to live when he heard he'd been avenged.

He put on his cap, proudly tipping it to the right. Under the long tail of his blue jersey he hitched the .45 in the waistband of his pants. It weighed like a cannon as he climbed out of the stolen car.

His high-tops were blue with yellow stripes. The bandanna hanging out of his back pocket was bright, bold yellow. The colors announced him as west side, as Posse, and such was his rage, his grief, his *righteousness,* he strutted in them across Hitch.

He was ready. He was so goddamn ready to do some damage. To do some death.

Maybe it showed on his face. He tried to make it show. His lips peeled back in a snarling grin, a surge of power, as he saw a group of women on a stoop glance his way, then rush inside.

Yeah, bitches. Better run. Better hide.

As he swaggered down the short alleyway around the liquor store, he drew the gun from his waistband. And he told himself the tremor in his hand was thrill, not fear. He put T-Bone's face, the way it had looked in the hospital, in his mind.

Already dead even if the machine was breathing for him. And their mama, sitting by the bed, holding her Bible and crying. Not saying nothing, not moving, just sitting with tears running down.

Those images pushed him around the corner, ripped a cry out of his throat as his finger quivered on the trigger.

But the back door was unguarded.

His heart thumped in his ears. It was all he could hear as he crossed the heat-softened tar and scrabbling weeds. He wiped the back of his hand over his mouth where sweat had beaded. For T-Bone, he thought, then kicked viciously at the door until it fell open.

The gun went off like a live thing jumping in his hand. He didn't feel his finger make the pull. It just seemed to explode on its own, blasting a hole in the wall a foot above the dented metal desk. There was no one behind it, no one to take that bullet between the eyes.

His arm shook as he lowered the gun, as he stared at the empty space, the empty room. They'd call him a fool now, and laugh. That would make T-Bone a fool, and that couldn't be.

He had to do something. Something big.

When the inner door opened and the man stepped up, he knew what it was he had to do.

"HT's name is Charles Johnson, street name Razz." Detective Ricks from the Gang Unit filled Phoebe in. "Shots were fired, no reported injuries. He's got four people in there."

"What does he want?"

"Blood. There was a gun battle last night—west side Posse—the HT's gang, and east side Lords. HT's older brother took three bullets. He's critical. This Razz wants us to find the guy he claims did it. One Jerome Clip Sagget. We send Sagget in, he'll send the hostages out."

"How old is he?"

"Sixteen. No violent knocks on his record. Petty shit up till now. Older brother's a different matter. Serious badass."

"Okay." Phoebe studied the board, the log. At the table of the diner set up for communications, she opened her kit. "He's been talking to you?"

"Playing the same tune, but yeah. He's in the first stage. Give me what I want or there'll be hell to pay. He set a deadline, it's coming up in twenty."

"All right." She picked up the phone. He answered on the first ring. "You got that motherfucker?"

"Razz, this is Phoebe MacNamara. I'm a negotiator with the police."

"Fuck you, bitch."

There was fury in the voice, but there was fear under it. "You sound angry. I understand that. I have a brother, too."

"You think I give rat shit about your brother? You best be bringing in the motherfucker shot him, or I'm doing one of these assholes in here."

"We're trying to work on that, Razz. For right now, can you tell me, is everyone all right in there? Does anyone need medical attention?"

"Gonna need it. Gonna need a goddamn body bag, is what." His voice pitched up and down with terror and rage.

"You haven't hurt anyone yet, Razz, is that right? So far we're trying to find a way to make this right for everyone."

"Not gonna be right until I put a bullet in that Clip's brain. When that's done, it's all done."

"I hear that you want to punish the person you believe hurt your brother."

"I know what he did. My family told me. You think my family's liars?"

"Are you saying your family saw what happened to T-Bone?"

"Fucking right. Two more of 'em shot up, but T-Bone, he's next to dead. And the fucker did it to him's gonna face me. You bring him here, you hear what I'm saying? You bring him here or somebody dies."

Family=Gang, she wrote on her pad. *Pride & revenge.* "You want us to find this man and bring him to you, so you can punish him yourself."

"How many times I got to say it?"

"I don't want to misunderstand you, Razz. I'm trying to understand what those people in there have to do with your brother being hurt. Do you think they were involved?"

"Don't mean a thing."

"They don't mean anything?"

"Collateral damage. I'll put a bullet in one right now, you don't think I mean what I say."

"I know you mean what you say, Razz. I need you to understand, Razz, that if you hurt anyone in there, we're not going to be able to work this out, not going to be able to try to get you what you want. I'm trying to contact the hospital, too. To contact the doctors who're taking care of your brother. I thought you might want to know how he's doing. Have you seen him today?"

She guided him into talking about his brother, through the first deadline. *Hero worship. Absolute loyalty.* When he spoke of his mother crying by his brother's bed, she nudged more out of him. *No other sibs, no father in the picture.*

Find the mother now! she scribbled on a piece of paper, and pushed it into Ricks's hand.

"Y'all getting hungry in there, Razz? I can send in some sandwiches."

"I got plenty of beer and chips. You think I'm stupid? You think I don't watch TV? Nobody comes in here, nobody but Clip."

"No one's coming in unless you okay it."

"Maybe I won't kill these assholes. Maybe I will. But they gonna be lying facedown in their own piss before long. I'm tired of talking to you. You got something else to say, you call back and tell me you've got that motherfucker."

When he broke the connection, Phoebe eased back. "Any progress locating this Clip?"

"He's gone under. We've got people on it."

"If we can tell the HT that Sagget's in custody, that he's being held, that may open a door. I want to know the minute he's found."

She glanced at the white-faced clock on the wall. Four forty-five.

Odds were she was going to be late for dinner.

Duncan was pretty pleased with himself when he rang the bell on Jones Street. He was even more pleased when Essie answered it and the big smile broke across her face.

"Oh my goodness! Who's back there?"

He spoke from behind an enormous basket of red poppies. "Three guesses. Any place special you want these?"

"Just set them down right here until we figure that out. Aren't they *beautiful!* Come right into the parlor. You're right on time. Wine, too?"

"I don't often get invited to have dinner with four beautiful women. It's an occasion for me."

"For us, too." She took the wine, gestured. "You haven't met my daughter-in-law, have you? Josie, this is Duncan Swift."

"Make that five beautiful women. Nice to meet you."

"Fifth one's spoken for," Carter said as he carried in a tray of canapés. Carly was right behind him with a second, smaller tray. "How's it going, Duncan?"

"Going good. Hey, Carly."

"Mama's going to be late. She's working."

"I guess that happens. Looks like enough food in here to hold me awhile. Oh, I got you something."

Her gaze arrowed straight to the little pink gift bag he held. "A present?"

"A token for one of my hostesses."

"Thank you very much," she said with formal politeness under her grandmother's eagle eye. Then squealed with delight when she pulled out the hair tie. It looked like a bouquet—purple and white violets with a filmy trail of white ribbons.

"It's beautiful! I love it. Thank you!" Formality forgotten, Carly threw her arms around Duncan's waist, then danced back. "Can I go put it on? Gran, *please,* can I go put it on right now?"

"Run on then."

Carly made the dash, stopping once to toss Duncan a big smile over her shoulder.

"Aren't you the clever one?" Essie commented.

"So they say."

By six-fifteen, Phoebe called home again and told Ava not to hold dinner on her account. Even if things resolved in the best possible way, there was no point in holding everyone else up while she dealt with the paperwork and debriefings.

She downed iced coffee, grateful someone had the foresight to make use of the diner's kitchen. Across from her sat Opal Johnson, Razz's mother. It had taken some time to track her down as she'd left her older son's bedside to sit on a bench outside the hospital and pray for his life.

Now she was here, in a diner filled with cops, struggling for her other child.

Progress had been made. Though he still refused to come out or release any hostages, Phoebe heard the changes in his voice, in his words. His resolve was weakening.

"He's going to jail, isn't he?"

"He'll be alive," Phoebe said. "He hasn't hurt anyone yet."

Opal stared blindly out the diner's window. She was stick thin, her dark face splotched from hours of weeping, her eyes exhausted from worry. "I did my best. I did all I knew. Work two jobs, made those boys go to school, to church. But my Franklin, he just goes his own way. And he took Charlie right along with him. Posse." She spat the word out. "I couldn't hold off against that."

"Mrs. Johnson, we're going to do everything we can to get your son out safe. To get everyone out safe, so he has another chance."

"They think it makes them men." Her hopeless eyes met Phoebe's. "The gangs, the drugs, the killing. They think it makes them men."

"I'm going to talk to him again now." Phoebe reached across the four-top, laid a hand briefly on Opal's. "All right?"

"You got any kids, miss?"

"Phoebe, and yes. I have a daughter. She's seven."

"Children rip the heart right out of you. And it lies there all bruised and battered, still beating for them. No matter what."

"Let's get him out safe." Phoebe started to make contact again, paused when Ricks rushed in.

"We've got Sagget in custody. Charges of possession—drugs and fire-arms. Took a gun from the apartment where he was hiding, matches the caliber of the weapon that shot Franklin Johnson. We'll run ballistics."

"Okay. This is good." Phoebe looked back into Opal's eyes. "This is very good. I'll need you to help me with this, Mrs. Johnson. The person who shot your son, who shot Charlie's brother, is under arrest. He's go-ing to be punished. We need to convince Charlie that it's enough, for now it's enough, and he should come out. All right, now."

She called the liquor store. There was more fatigue than defiance in his voice now. Another good sign. "Razz, I have some good news."

"My brother wake up?"

"Your bother's condition hasn't changed and that means he hasn't gotten worse. He's strong, isn't he?"

"Nobody stronger."

"So that's good. I want to tell you that Clip's been taken into custody."

"You got that rat bastard motherfucker?"

"Don't you use that language to this lady!" Opal snapped the words. "Don't you speak that filth, you hear me."

"He put bullets in T-Bone. I'll call him what he is, to anybody."

Phoebe held up a hand, easing it downward before Opal could speak again. "Your mother's very upset, Razz. She's worried about you *and* T-Bone now. But I think we have a way to make this all right, for every-one. The police have charged Clip, and he's in jail right now. He—"

"You bring that sumbitch to *me!*"

"I know you want to see him. I can arrange that. If you put the gun down and come out, I'm going to arrange to have you taken to where he's being held. So you can see him behind bars."

"I want to see him in the ground. Gonna put him there."

"You sound tired, Razz. It's been a long day, for everyone. I want to tell you that they found a gun with Clip, the same kind of gun that shot your brother. They're running tests right now. If the tests show it was the one used to hurt your brother, they'll be charging him with at-tempted murder. Do you know how long he could be behind those bars? For years and years. Maybe the rest of his life. If my brother'd been hurt like this, I'd want the person responsible to pay for a long time. A very long time."

"He'll burn in hell."

"I think Georgia State's a kind of hell, too. Razz, they told me he was hiding. Hiding. I wonder what his gang will think when they find out he was hiding away."

"You fucking with me?"

"I told you not to use that language! She's telling you the pure truth. I was right here, wasn't I right here when they came in and told her? That boy who shot your brother's in jail. Now come out of there, you hear?" Opal began to weep again. "Come out of there because I can't watch another boy of mine bleeding."

"Don't cry, Mama. I want to make him bleed, like T-Bone's bleeding."

"Prison's worse than bleeding," Phoebe said. "For a man like Clip? And now he's got no face left, no rep. Proved himself a coward. A coward who'll spend years paying for what he did. Your mother needs you, Razz. She needs you to put down the gun and come out. To show you're not a coward. You've got the balls to walk out of there."

"You'll take me to see that bastard? See him in the cage? That's a solid?"

"It is. My word on it."

"I'm going to jail, same as him. That's not right."

"Not the same as him, not the same at all. You haven't hurt anyone yet, Razz. Not a single soul. That makes all the difference. If you come out, just the way I tell you, that's going to make a difference, too."

"How do I come out?"

"You put the gun down." Phoebe gave the signal, making certain the surrender was relayed to Tactical. "You don't want to have a gun on you when you come out. All right?"

"You got guns out there?"

"Yeah, there are going to be guns out here. I don't want you to worry. You'll put your hands up, where everyone can see, and you walk straight out the front door. You come out by yourself, you're no coward, right? You come straight out the front, with your hands high in the air. Will you do that?"

"All right. I'm coming out. I'm hanging up."

"I'll see you outside, Razz."

Phoebe cut off the phone, stood. "Let's go get your boy." She took

Opal's arm and led her toward the door of the diner. "Listen now, they're going to have guns on him when he comes out. They're going to move on him, get him on the ground and cuff him. That has to be."

Phoebe scanned some of the windows and rooftops, spotted Tactical. Until Razz was out and in custody, she couldn't risk taking his mother too close to the inner perimeter. "I need you to wait here with this officer for just a few minutes. I'm going to come back and get you, and I'm going to see that you're taken to where Charlie will be."

"Thank you, for everything you did. Thank you."

Phoebe moved quickly, angling so she'd have a view of the front of the liquor store. When she saw the door open, saw the boy step forward, hands high, she let out a long breath of relief.

The gunfire was a stunning blast. For an instant she simply froze, simply stared as Charlie's body jerked, danced, fell. She heard herself screaming as she rushed forward, as dozens of cops dove for cover.

Someone shoved her down. With the breath knocked out of her she heard the screams from inside the store, and the shouts of: "Shots fired! Shots fired!" zinging around her.

It was *beautiful!* And so pathetically easy. All you had to do was slip and slide and know how to look like you belonged. Not so hard to find a good position, hold up, wait things out.

All that time she'd spent talking that asshole out. Wasted, wasn't it, bitch?

Stupid fucker deserved to die. Gangs were a blight on the city.

He could have put some bullets in her, too. Easy-peasy. But this was better. This *accomplished* something and kept it all rolling.

He hadn't known, really hadn't guessed, how much fun this would all be. Why end it too soon?

He'd left the gun, done some more slipping and sliding. Easy-peasy again, tucking the ID away, melting into the panicked crowd, then easing away in the confusion.

But not before he watched Phoebe scramble up, run toward the others at the door of the crap-shit liquor store and drop down beside the dead kid.

'Cause that kid was stone dead, and don't you mistake it.

Press was going to love this, he thought as he made his way west to where he'd left his car. Going to eat it up like Cheez Whiz on a cracker.

Lieutenant Bitch MacNamara had talked the asshole out all right. And straight into a hail of bullets.

He was going to pick himself up a six-pack and some takeout, go home. And watch the news.

When Phoebe got home she heard the voices in the parlor. Dinner long over, she thought. Dishes done and put away.

Coffee and brandy served in the parlor—the Wedgwood pot, the Baccarat decanter and snifters.

All on loan from the tight-fisted estate of Elizabeth MacNamara.

She wanted to go straight up the stairs, crawl into bed. Or under it. But it couldn't be done. Just one more thing that couldn't be done. So she walked to the doorway.

Carter was telling some story—she could tell by the way his hands were moving. He had such good stories. She knew he hoped to become a writer, and that he worked at it when he could. But teaching ate up most of his time.

Beside him Josie rolled her eyes, but she was laughing while she did. It was so sweet, the way they loved each other. Still so fresh and sweet.

There was Mama, looking so happy. Just peaceful and happy, her world full of people who made her so. And Ava perched on the arm of Mama's chair, sipping coffee from one of those lovely Wedgwood cups.

Her little girl, sitting on the sofa beside Duncan. And oh my goodness, what was that look on Carly's face when she smiled up at him? Her baby was having her first crush by the looks of things.

And didn't he seem just right at home, Mr. Duncan Swift, sprawled back, all relaxed and easy, sending her little girl winks like the two of them were in on a big secret.

How many blocks from here was Hitch Street?

How could that distance have an entire world between them?

It was Duncan who saw her first. A quick light in his eyes, then an equally quick fade into concern. Was she so transparent?

He rose, came to her. "Are you all right?"

"No. I'm not hurt, but I'm not all right. I'm sorry I missed dinner," she said in a voice that carried into the room.

"Mama, we had the best time! And Duncan said . . ." Carly's words faded away as she dashed over. Phoebe saw her bright blue eyes latch on to the blood on her pants.

She'd had a spare shirt in her locker, but she'd had to come home with the blood—Charles Johnson's blood—on her pants.

"It's not mine. I'm not hurt, not at all. But I need such a hug from you right now. I need such a big, enormous Carly hug right this minute." She crouched and squeezed tight as Carly wrapped around her.

She stayed crouched. She had her child tonight, right here, safe and sweet in her arms. Others didn't.

She leaned back, kissed both of Carly's cheeks. Then, straightening, she looked at her mother. Essie stood, face pale, hands linked tight.

"Nothing happened to me, that's first. Look at me, Mama. Nothing happened to me. Nothing. All right?"

"All right."

"Carter, pour Mama some of that lemonade there. You sit down, Mama. I'm going to say I know you think I share too much of what I do, what there is, with Carly. I'm sorry we don't agree on the boundaries of that. Well. I think I could use something stronger than lemonade right off."

"I'm going to get you some wine, and some food." Ava walked to her, squeezed her arm. "You ought to sit down, too."

"I ought to. I will. I want to change these pants first. I'm going to be right back," she said to Carly.

Duncan glanced over at Essie as Phoebe went out. "Essie, I hope you don't mind, but I'm going to go up with her."

He didn't wait for permission, but caught up to Phoebe on the steps.

"I'm just going to change my pants."

"I'm not looking to grab a quickie while you do. You look exhausted."

"It was a bad day. Very bad. I can't talk about it yet. I only want to talk about it once."

"I'm just going to be here, you don't have to talk."

In her room, she pulled out a pair of cotton pants. She stripped off the blood-smeared trousers, tossed them in the hamper. "Mama will likely perform some miracle of science and get that poor boy's blood out of those." She pressed her hand between her eyes as the grief swamped her. But before Duncan could take her into his arms, she stepped back, shook her head.

"No, no comforting hugs just yet. And no tears. If I have to cry, it'll wait until later. My mother's worried. She'll stay worried until I get back down."

"Let's go back, then."

He went down with her. Ava had already set a plate on a tray, had a glass of wine waiting.

"It'll be on the news," she began. "Probably has been. There was a situation over on Hitch Street. Gang-related. Hostages. The boy was sixteen. Just sixteen, grieving, so angry, so misguided. It took time to talk him down, but I did, I talked him down, and told him it would be all right. So he came out, just the way I told him. Unarmed, hands up high. And someone shot him. They shot him while he stood with his hands up, when he was surrendering. His mother was there, close enough I think she must have seen it happen."

"Is he going to be all right?" Carly asked.

"No, honey. He died." Before I got to him, Phoebe thought.

"But why did they shoot him?"

"I don't know." She stroked Carly's hair, then bent down to kiss it. "I just don't. We don't know why or who. Not yet. There'll be talk, on the TV about it. I wanted you—all of you—to know what happened."

"I wish it hadn't happened."

"Oh, baby, so do I."

Carly snuggled up. "You'll feel better if you eat. That's what you say."

"It is what I say." Deliberately she speared something on her plate. It didn't matter what, she couldn't taste it. But she ate it with a little flourish. "And as usual, I'm right. Now, everybody should stop worrying and tell me what you did for fun tonight."

"Uncle Carter and Duncan played a duelette."

"A duelette?"

"That's what Uncle Carter called it. On the piano. That was fun. And Aunt Josie told the joke about the chicken."

"Not *that* again."

"I liked it." Duncan worked up a smile. He saw what she was doing, needed to do. Get everyone back to normal.

"And Duncan said you and me could go on his sailboat on Saturday if you said we could. So can we? Please? I've never been on a sailboat before. Ever."

"You're obviously a neglected and abused child. I suppose we probably could do that."

"Yes!"

"But right now it seems to be somewhat past someone's bedtime."

"But we have company."

"And a polite, self-sacrificing child, too. How'd I get so lucky? Now, say good night, and I'll be up in a couple minutes."

Carly dragged her feet all around the room, stalled, looked beseechingly toward the other adults for intervention. She circled her way around to Duncan, sighed heavily. "I wish I didn't have to go to bed, but thank you for coming to dinner."

"Thank you for having me. We've got a date on Saturday, right?"

The sulks flew away. "Okay. 'Night."

The minute she was gone, Phoebe set down her fork.

"I'd better get on." Duncan rose.

There were polite protests, mutual thanks, cheek kisses and handshakes.

"I'll walk you out."

It felt so good to step outside, into the air. To take a breath of it. "I'm sorry I brought home something that tainted the evening."

"Don't think of it like that." He draped an arm around her shoulders as they walked down to his car. "Hard for you."

"It was awful." She indulged herself a moment, turning into him, holding on. "I don't know that I'll ever get it all the way out of my head. Maybe I shouldn't. I don't know how it could've happened. Some people are already saying it was us who did it. We're saying we suspect it was one of the members of the rival gang. We found the gun. AK-47. It wasn't one of ours. They *riddled* that boy. In seconds. One of the hostages inside was hit. He'll be okay, but . . ." She sucked in a breath, drew back. "That's not for here."

"It's for wherever you need it to be."

"I need to keep as much as I can away from here." She glanced back toward the house. "Whenever I can. So . . . about Saturday."

"I'll pick you and Carly up about ten. How's that?"

"It's nice of you to offer her such a treat. I don't want you to feel obliged to—"

"Don't." He tapped a finger to her lips. "Don't do that. And the fact is, you might as well know, if things don't work out with you and me, and Essie turns me down, I figure I can wait about, what, fifteen years, for the kid."

"Twenty. Minimum."

"Hard-ass." He tipped her face back. "Still, that oughta be some motivation for you, seeing I've got multiple choices here." He kissed her, long, very long, very soft.

"I'll see you Saturday."

"Saturday. I'll pack a few gallons of sunscreen for us redheads."

She waved him off, stood there a while. And after a while walked over and sat on the front steps. She needed to go in, of course, needed to go tuck Carly into bed, keep an eye on Mama, just in case. But she sat awhile longer.

Carter came out. Saying nothing, he sat beside her, took her hand.

Together, they sat awhile longer yet.

18

Phoebe wasn't wrong about the media storm. It raged across the television screens, the newspaper headlines, the Internet. In death, Charlie Johnson became a symbol of gang violence, racism, police corruption and incompetence—depending on which side you were on at any given time.

She fielded dozens of calls from reporters, and for the first time in her career received death threats.

And she once again found herself interviewed by IAB.

"How you holding up?" Dave studied her as she drew lines down the condensation of her glass of iced tea. He'd pulled her out for a quick lunch.

"I keep seeing him coming out, hands up. Just that one second when I thought: Good job, Phoebe. High five. Then the sound of the gun, the way his body jerked like a puppet. Just one more second, really, for it all to go to hell."

"You did a good job." He shook his head at her expression. "You did. Let's just get that on the table."

"Crisis negotiators are part of a team, Dave. Who taught me that? The team failed that boy, and the hostages. It failed everyone."

"Something broke down; we're still not sure what. Your end of it didn't. Regardless," he continued, "a boy died, a hostage was injured. No member of the tactical team fired their weapon. The weapon fired and discovered wasn't ours. And regardless," he repeated, "the failure's on us. Someone got through, or was overlooked, during the evac of the area."

"There was more violence on both the east and west sides last night," she pointed out. "More shootings. They're using that boy to justify killing. The media and the mouthpieces are using him, whittling it down or blowing it up—I'm not sure which applies—to race. To white against black. And I don't know that you can say race has nothing to do with it, because it's certainly one of the elements that play into gangs. But I don't believe Charles Johnson was shot because of his skin color. And I don't believe he deserves to have his death pushed into that."

She said nothing while the sandwiches they'd ordered were served. "Franklin Johnson died this morning."

"I know."

"Opal Johnson's lost both her sons. Her children are dead. The first, that's not on us, at least not on the surface. We found and arrested the man who killed him. Would we have done so as quickly, even at all, if Charlie hadn't gone into that liquor store yesterday? I don't know the answer. That troubles me."

"I don't know it either, but I do the best job I can. So do you. We save who we can, Phoebe, one crisis at a time."

"Maybe." She picked up one of the chips that came with her sandwich, broke it into pieces. "I told him it was going to be all right. If he came out, it would be all right."

"You didn't make a mistake. It *should* have been all right. He should be in custody now, with his public defender working to cut a deal with the prosecutor. The mistake was in Tactical, and we'll find it. Every minute of the incident is going to be investigated. Every move, every order. Meanwhile, there's the anger of the community, the public relations nightmare and the very real problem of keeping this from boiling over into riots and burning. You'll be giving a press conference this afternoon, along with the tactical commander. You'll each read a brief statement and answer questions. It'll be short, and it's necessary."

"And it provides a visual. I'm a white woman, the commander's a black man." She lifted a hand before he could speak. "I'm not discounting the fact that the visual doesn't matter nearly as much as the statements. I'll do my part. What time?"

"Three."

She nodded. "All right. That'll give me time to go over to Hitch. I want to see the crime scenes. Both of them."

She stood at the window where the shots had been fired, verified now by the crime-scene investigative team. It was a narrow window, casement style, on the second floor of a building diagonal from the liquor store.

According to the reports, the fifteen-unit apartment building had been evacuated, and SWAT team members stationed on the roof and on the third floor. As it was within the inner perimeter, no civilians should have been in or around the building.

But it wouldn't be the first time a perimeter had been compromised.

The sniper would have had a decent view and angle from there, Phoebe judged. Better on the roof, better on the third floor, but decent from here.

Especially if the intent was to take down an unarmed man who would step into clear view. Oh yeah, not so hard to hit the target when the target was standing still, hands in the air. All that body mass just open and waiting to be riddled.

"Tenant's a Reeanna Curtis, single." Detective Sykes spoke from behind her. "Two kids, boy age five, girl age three. No criminal. They were outside the barricade at the time of the shooting. Witnesses verify. Her boyfriend was at work at the time. Also verified."

Phoebe nodded. "I read her statement. She said a cop came to the door, ordered her out, hustled them along. Cops swarming through the building, according to her, and all over the place outside. She got out with her kids, straight to her sister's place a few blocks over.

"She doesn't remember if she locked the door. Can't clearly remember if she even *closed* the door. Said it all happened so fast, and she was scared."

"Somebody else is getting hustled out," Sykes speculated, "but doesn't want to miss the show. Dips in here."

"Armed?" Phoebe turned back. "Whoever came in, unless we suspect the single mother with two preschoolers kept an AK-47 in the broom closet, he came in loaded. And if it wasn't target specific, why not take out a big bunch of cops?"

"There are Lords members in the building, plenty more in this block. They'll all get a close look."

Didn't make Charlie any less dead, Phoebe thought. Then pulled herself in. It wasn't about that any longer, that was done. Now it was about fixing what had gone wrong.

"How did the shooter know Charles Johnson, specifically, was inside?" Phoebe wandered the cramped, cluttered apartment.

"Maybe not specific. Just a Posse was inside."

"All right, how did he know that? Did he see Charlie go in—he was wearing his colors. Timeline puts him inside for nearly ten minutes before the first response. And that came quick because one of the tenants in the building next door to the liquor store called in gunfire. She states she saw him crossing the street a few minutes before the first shot."

"Shooter sees him, or the word flies around. Gets the weapon, then gets lucky and finds a solid sniper spot."

"Let's find out if they've pulled the LUDs from this apartment—this building. See if any calls were made out of here after it was supposed to be cleared. Cell phones are more likely, but you never know."

She stepped to the window in a small bedroom obviously shared by the children. From that angle she could see the diner where she'd sat at a four-top, talking Charlie down, and out. "I wonder how many gang members could resist taking out cops. Resist until the specific target's out—or taken out, yeah, I can see that. But why not try to take a few cops out, too, once you open up? More blood, more confusion, more goddamn points, come to that. But the only other hit is a stray that injured one of the hostages inside. That's just odd, isn't it?"

He pursed his lips. "That's a puzzle. Any reason to think it wasn't gang retribution?"

"I'll let you know."

She did her own runs on the tenants of the building, and filled her briefcase with files for the trip home. She made certain she was home before dark.

Phoebe wanted all her family tucked inside before sundown, in case the rumblings in the city turned to a roar. In case those blocks between Jones and Hitch weren't enough to hold back the flood if it came.

She broke her own hard-and-fast rule, and though she put her weapon up on the high shelf in her closet, she kept it unlocked and loaded.

Once Carly was settled for the night, Phoebe checked the locks, the alarms, then settled at her own desk. She kept the TV on low, in case of a bulletin, and began reading through the logs, the reports, the witness statements.

When her cell phone rang, she answered it absently, her mind on the diagram of the apartment building on Hitch. "Phoebe MacNamara."

"Duncan Swift. Hiya, cutie."

The idea of being called "cutie" when she was surrounded by ballistics, diagrams and various crime-scene reports made her smile. "Hello, Duncan."

"Just checking to make sure I still have a crew for tomorrow."

"I think you'd best use the term 'crew' loosely, but yes, we're on for that. Carly would give me the silent treatment until her eighteenth birthday if I pulled out of this."

"Silent treatment's a formidable weapon. It makes me beg every time."

"Good to know."

"And stupid to admit. Anyway, I was meeting with Phin earlier today, and ended up asking his gang to come along tomorrow. That all right with you?"

"Absolutely. Carly'll be thrilled to have someone her age around. She loves me, but I will bore her after a bit." She leaned back from the work, rising to walk to the terrace windows. "It sounds more like a party. I could use a party, I think."

"Figured you had a rough one. I caught you on TV this afternoon. Is it shallow of me to say you looked hot?"

She laughed. "Yes, and thank you. It's a god-awful mess, Duncan. God-awful."

"Why don't I come over for a bit? I'll be shallow again, sneak up to your room and distract you with heroic sex."

She had one silly and delightful fantasy image of him scaling the wall to her terrace. "Oh God, that sounds amazing. But no. Are you home? On the island?"

"Yeah, I had some stuff, so I'm here. But I've dealt with a good chunk of the stuff, and the rest can wait. If heroic sex is out, we can just neck like teenagers in the parlor, or watch a bad movie."

"I'd love to do any of that. Possibly all of that. But I don't want you coming into the city, not tonight. Things are bubbling tonight. You're good where you are, should they boil over." She disengaged the alarm on her zone so she could step out onto her terrace. "It's warm tonight. Not hot but warm, and that's good. Heat can set these things off."

"How about if I tell you besides looking hot, you handled yourself really well in that press conference? Anybody looking at you during it who didn't see you cared had to be blind."

"A lot of this kind of thing is about blindness. And could I be any more depressing?"

"What are you wearing?" he asked after a beat.

"What?"

"I'm cheering you up with phone sex. What are you wearing?"

"Oh. Hmmm." She looked down at her cotton pants and tank. That would never do. "Oh, nothing much, just this little black slip I picked up in a vintage shop."

"Nice. Anything under it?"

"Just a few dabs of perfume . . . here and there."

"Very nice."

"How about you? What are you wearing?"

"Guess."

"Jeans. Just jeans, those washed-a-few-hundred-times Levi's. Riding low on the hips with the waistband button carelessly open."

"My God. You must be psychic."

With a sound of amusement, she sat down. For the first time in twenty-four hours her stomach wasn't knotted. "Oh my, these straps just keep falling off my shoulders. Those would be my delicately scented creamy white shoulders. I probably shouldn't be out here dressed like this, leaning over the railing. Why, my soft yet firm breasts might—oops—spill right out. What would the neighbors think?"

"You're a killer, Phoebe."

"Honey, I'm just getting started."

In the morning, it was easy to put the work away, to tuck it into a corner of her mind. Death and sadness, Phoebe supposed, had a way of making those who brushed up against them appreciate a blue-skied, sunny day, and the excited chatter of a child.

And Carly's first sight of the boat said it all.

"It's big! And it's pretty! This is going to be the best time ever."

"Then we better get started," Duncan decided.

"But where are the sails? You said it was a sailboat."

"They're rolled up right now. We'll hoist 'em once we're clear." He clambered on, then held out a hand for the girl. "Here you go. Welcome aboard."

"Can I look at stuff?"

"Sure."

"But don't touch," Phoebe called out as she came aboard. "It is big, and it is pretty. And I realized I should have asked if you really know how to handle this thing."

"I've only capsized her four times. Kidding. I always wanted to sail. Used to come down here and watch the boats. So when I decided to get a boat, I took lessons—and a course—as I didn't want to drown after achieving a lifelong dream. Still, the kids need to wear PFDs. Personal flotation devices. So will Biff."

"Who's Biff?"

"That would be Biff." Duncan pointed.

Phoebe spotted Phin, his wife and his little girl coming down the dock. Lumbering on a leash ahead of them was a stubby-legged, homely faced bulldog.

"Phin's dog. He figured a bulldog would lend an air of dignity. Which, you could say, he does if you discount the drool."

Obviously an old sea hand, Biff jumped aboard, then wiggled his butt until Duncan hunkered down to rub him all over.

"What a perfect day for this. I'm going to do as much of absolutely nothing as possible." Loo stretched. "Hi, Phoebe. I hope you'll be joining me."

"I'll be glad to. Hi, Phin. Hi, Livvy."

"Puppy!" Carly scrambled on deck from the cabin below and all but tackled Biff. "Oh, he's so cute! What's his name? Mama, can't we get a puppy?"

"She's painfully shy," Phoebe announced. "I hope you'll pardon her."

"He's Biff." Not quite as outgoing as Carly, Livvy clung to her mother's hand. "He likes his belly rubbed."

Carly beamed and obliged the now ecstatic Biff. "There're beds downstairs and tables, and a kitchen and a bathroom and everything. Do you want to see?"

"I've seen it before."

"Let's go see it again. With Biff."

Livvy looked up at her mother. "I guess so."

"Those are pretty shoes," Carly said as they started down. "Maybe I can try them on. You can try mine on, too."

It was an experience, Phoebe thought, to motor away from the dock, steam and slip through the water with the little girls fused together at the stern, and the not-so-dignified dog sitting on the starboard bench with his funny face lifted to the air.

But it was nothing to the moment when the white sails rose and filled with wind. Like the dog, Phoebe lifted her face.

"Mimosas," Loo announced, and offered a glass as she sat beside Phoebe.

"Oh God. This must be heaven. Are we going to have to jib or hoist or some other salty term?"

"Only if the spirit moves. Phin doesn't know what the hell he's doing unless Duncan tells him, but he likes to pretend he does." She smiled over at the men. "But he's game. Me, I tried to talk Dunc into a motorboat—cabin cruiser. But he just had to have sails." She drew in a long breath, stretched out incredibly long legs. "Hard to argue at times like this."

"You've known him a long time."

"Known him, been crazy about him. So if you screw with him, I'll find a way to hurt you. Other than that, we'll be fine."

"Do people often screw with him?"

"Not many, not often. He's got excellent radar. There was a woman a few years back cruised under that radar. Butter wouldn't melt." Loo sipped her mimosa. "I couldn't stand her. But Dunc, he was fond, and she was clever with her hard-luck stories. She got a few thousand out of him before she blipped for him."

"What did he do about her?"

Loo flicked her middle finger against her thumb. "He's an easygoing sort, but he has a low tolerance for lies."

"Are you warning me, Loo?"

"Irritated. Good. Makes me like you more, which I already do. And I like your little girl. I saw your press conference yesterday." Loo lifted her eyebrows as Phoebe's face went cool and blank. "Let me start off saying things aren't black and white for me. First, I'm a lawyer, so I live in the gray. Second, that man up there with mine is family—and I do believe he's white. And last, I thought you handled yourself very well in what's a very difficult, even delicate situation. That's all I wanted to say about that. Those are pretty shoes," Loo commented with a nod toward Phoebe's sandals. "Maybe I could try them on."

With a laugh, Phoebe relaxed and enjoyed the ride.

They had lunch on the lake, and splashed and swam in it. Carly was given the thrill of her life with a turn at the tiller.

"Having fun?" Duncan asked when Phoebe joined him at the bow.

"It's going down as the best day of my life in recent memory."

"We can extend it. Cruise over to my place. We can wear Carly out, tuck her up somewhere, tuck ourselves up somewhere else."

"What about Biff and company?"

"I'll just toss them all overboard." He leaned down to kiss her laughing mouth. "Say the word."

"The word is I like your friends too much to toss them."

"I was afraid of that."

"But I will be inviting you in for drinks in the courtyard when you escort us home."

"I'll be accepting. Listen . . ." He cupped his hand at the back of her neck and let his kiss shimmer out.

"What?" Phoebe managed.

"Not a thing."

"Why do people close their eyes when they kiss?" Carly demanded, and Phoebe turned to see her daughter studying her with considerable interest.

"I don't know." Duncan frowned thoughtfully. "Let's try it the other way." Eyes open and amused, he pulled Phoebe back for another kiss. "It's good that way, too."

"Mama says she's too old for boyfriends."

"Carly—"

"What do you think?" Duncan asked, interrupting Phoebe's protest.

"I think if you're going to be taking her on dates and kissing her all the time, you should be her boyfriend. And Ava told Grandma it's good Mama's getting some romance because—"

"Carly go get yourself one of those cookies, or something else to put in your mouth."

"You said I had enough cookies."

"I changed my mind."

"That's about enough snickering over there," Phoebe said, waving a hand toward Phin and Loo. And over here, too," she added to Duncan.

"Are we having some romance?" he asked her. He grabbed her, dropped her into a romance-novel dip. "Let's have some more."

Phin's wolf whistle joined the buzzing in her ears before she could struggle her way up again. "I think that's about all the romance I can handle in a public forum. I'm going to go have another cookie."

Romance, she thought after she'd given Duncan a final kiss good night. That was more complicated than an affair, no question about it. But it was foolish to pretend a romance wasn't what she was having. And enjoying.

So she wasn't going to pick it apart or second-guess it. She was just going to keep enjoying it for as long as it lasted.

She undressed, thinking how wonderful a shower would feel after a day on the water. When her phone rang, she half-expected it would be Duncan, calling her minutes after he left to tell her something to make her laugh.

The display on the Caller ID had her stomach sinking. "Hello, Roy."

Less than ten minutes later she was stalking downstairs and grabbing a half gallon of cookie dough ice cream from the freezer.

Essie walked in as Phoebe scooped it straight out of the carton and into her mouth. "Oh! You had a fight with Duncan."

"I didn't have a fight with Duncan. I didn't have a fight with anyone. I wanted some damn ice cream."

"Mind that tone," Essie warned with steel in her voice. "You only eat ice cream that way when you're upset. Duncan's barely out the door, so—"

"I said I didn't have a fight with Duncan. Duncan's not the center of my universe. I don't make men the center of my universe and I'm not about to . . ." She heard herself, could nearly see the nasty edge to the words slicing out like little shards of broken glass.

"I'm sorry. I am upset." She dropped down at the table, dug out more ice cream. "I haven't got enough of this in me yet to calm down or get good and sick, and not take it out on someone else."

Essie walked to the drawer, got out another spoon. She sat, spooned some ice cream out of the carton for herself. "What happened?"

"Roy called. He's getting married again."

"Oh." Essie took a second, bigger spoonful. "To anyone we know? So we know where to send our condolences?"

"Thanks, Mama. He's getting married to someone named Mizzy. Can you believe that? She's twenty-four."

"A bimbo, no doubt about it. Poor thing."

"The bimbo comes from money, and they're moving to Cannes, or maybe it was Marseilles. My ears started ringing by that point. Her family has *interests* there he's going to help run. And he tells me all this as he doesn't want my panties in a twist if the next couple child support checks are a bit late. Due to changing his location and banking and so on."

"He's always been timely with that anyway."

"Yes, because it's an automatic withdrawal from his account, so he doesn't even have to think of it. Of her." It wasn't rage anymore in her voice, on her face. It was grief. "He never even asked about her, Mama. He never asked how she was, never thought to suggest he might tell his daughter himself, or invite her to the wedding."

"She wouldn't go. And, baby girl, you wouldn't like it if she did."

"That's beside the point. It *is.* And I know I'm getting upset over something that isn't any different than it was, really. Except the son of a bitch is marrying someone almost ten years younger than me, named Mizzy, and his daughter isn't even an afterthought."

"What was it my grandmother used to say? A skunk doesn't change its stink. It's a little crude, but it fits. His life's about as deep as a puddle of spit—and that's crude, too. She won't care, Phoebe. Roy isn't so much as a bump against Carly's heart. You shouldn't let him be one against yours."

"You're right. I know you're right. She never had enough of him to miss any of it."

"But you did."

"I had the illusion." Phoebe scraped more ice cream from carton to spoon, studied it. Ate it. "Maybe that's worse. He can't help being what he is. Even if what he is is a goddamn skunk. Thanks."

Roy wasn't worth even her anger, Phoebe told herself as she went upstairs to shower. But the phone call had reminded her why romance was a slippery slope. Better, much better, to keep it all up front, keep it all simple. So no one got hurt.

It might be time to slow things down just a little with Duncan. She'd already made another date with him while the dream of the day had been on her. But that was fine. She'd just explain to him that she wasn't looking for anything more than friendship, companionship and sex.

What man could argue with that?

19

By her request, Phoebe received notification when Charles John-son's body was cleared for release. Noting the information, she con-tacted the funeral home regarding viewings.

Controversy and public debate aside, she needed to pay her respects. She could do so discreetly, and briefly. It meant canceling her date with Duncan, but that might be for the best.

A little cooling-off time there, she decided. A little stop-and-think-it-through.

She made the call, and though it was cowardly, felt a trickle of relief when she got his voice mail.

"Duncan, it's Phoebe. I have to cancel tonight, sorry. Something came . . ." Not fair, she reminded herself. He'd done nothing to de-serve the "something came up" brush-off. "Actually, they're holding a viewing for Charlie Johnson tonight, and I need to go. So I'll need a rain check. We'll talk later, all right? I'm just about on my way to a meeting."

Ass-covering was de rigueur, and Phoebe couldn't fault the department for going into circle-the-wagon mode. Or, she supposed, for looking for a reasonable scapegoat. She was fully prepared to defend her own actions and methods, if and when. She sat through the meeting with the crisis team, the chief and the representatives from IAB.

Questions were asked and answered. Her log was displayed, the situation tape replayed. She listened to her voice, to Commander Harrison's, to Charlie's and Opal's, to the relays between her or the second negotiator and command, from command to members of the tactical team.

"Lieutenant MacNamara clearly related the information that the HT agreed to surrender, was coming out unarmed. That information was received and acknowledged." The chief lifted his hands. "There was no breakdown in communications. The tactical commander did not give the go, and the shots were not fired by any authorized member of the department."

He paused. "The shots were fired from a weapon—recovered—not issued to any member of the crisis team, from a position where no member of said team was posted. Known members of the rival gang live in the building from where the shots issued, other known or suspected members reside inside the perimeter set during the crisis. These are facts. But there's another. The perimeter was breached. And from that fact come more questions. Who and how and when? The breech opens the department up to criticism and speculation, and potentially to civil suits."

"The who is being investigated," Harrison began. He was a tough-looking man of considerable presence, with a deep basso designed for giving orders. "Every known gang member of the Lords and the Posse is being interrogated. It's a long process, sir."

"The how?" The chief looked directly at the tactical commander.

"The building was cleared in a floor-by-floor sweep." Harrison got to his feet, stepped over to the diagram. "A three-man team entered the building here. Civilians were evacuated and moved outside the barricades. While this location wasn't optimum for coverage of the hostage scene, members were posted on the roof and at this third-floor post. Other members were posted in the building directly south, as this location afforded the best visual of the liquor store from the front. Others were posted here, to cover the back. Here, the sides.

"Each building was cleared, or thought to be cleared, and the perimeters set and posted. There were disturbances here and here during the negotiations. Heckling and threats from some onlookers. And here, a physical altercation between local residents."

He straightened stiffly as he turned. "It's possible that someone slipped through during the incendiary first stage. More likely, in my opinion, someone already inside the building slipped into the vacated apartment and set up his sniper's nest. The team's objective was to get civilians to safety quickly. It's not possible in these circumstances to spread the team thin enough to check every closet, under every bed. If someone was determined to evade detection, they could and would."

"Someone armed with an AK-47?"

Harrison's mouth tightened. "Yes, sir, as was the case."

"Chief." Phoebe caught Dave's frown when she interrupted. "You said the questions were how, who, when. Respectfully, I think a vital question is why. We can speculate, given the gang violence, the weapon used, the fact that its serial number was filed off, a member—or sympathizer—of the east side Lords is responsible. But I've been back to the scene, and I stood in the window where those shots were fired. I've looked at the diagrams, read the reports, replayed the coms."

"As have I," the chief reminded her.

"Then you're aware, sir, there were dozens of police officers and personnel outside at any given time during those hours. Officers and personnel in the open from the angle of the sniper's nest. Yet none of them was fired on. When Johnson was shot, not a single police officer was hit. Nearly every bullet went into Charles Johnson. I believe any of our tactical team would agree that's some damn fine shooting."

"Knew what he was doing," Harrison agreed, meeting Phoebe's questioning glance.

"As a negotiator, as someone who studies and deals with human behavior, I have to say it's also some superior control.

"Why kill Charles Johnson?" she continued. "He was low rung in the Posse."

"He'd made a stink on their turf," the chief pointed out. "He was demanding their captain be brought to him. It's disrespect."

"Agreed. Agreed. So maybe one or more of them would try to take him down, try to make an example of him. But if one of them was already in the building, or otherwise breached it—armed—it also strikes as solid forethought. Planning, sir, not just a lucky opportunity."

"A conspiracy theory, Lieutenant?"

She could hear the weariness in the chief's voice. He was more politician than cop, Phoebe knew—and politicians don't care for conspiracies. "Just speculation that there are other possibilities. Johnson may have been set up, goaded into going there. Someone outside either gang may have seen this incident as an opportunity to create chaos and dissent. Or—"

She broke off when the chief raised a hand. "Lieutenant, we're trying to defuse a powder keg, not add fuel. There are a lot of questions to be answered. For now, the most important apply to our own responsibility. The logs, transcripts, statements and coms show that you upheld yours. Now." He turned back to the crisis commander. "When the gunfire occurred . . ."

After the meeting, Phoebe went down to the firing range to work off some frustration. She set the target, put on her ear protectors and fired a clip.

Then could only sigh at her scores. She set again, fired again.

"You've always been a crappy shot."

Reviewing her grouping on the target, ear protectors lowered, Phoebe shrugged at Dave. "Extremely crappy. I don't practice enough."

"A good negotiator's rarely going to have to draw, much less discharge, a weapon. Not when she listens and talks as well as you do. Which is why—since you do—I wonder what you were doing up there in that meeting."

"Asking questions like someone taught me. Trying to make sure the focus isn't so narrow we miss what may be outside the blinders. I don't understand what happened out there, and I can't just swallow the easy solution."

"Has it occurred to you that you don't understand, and you can't swallow, because you did what you were supposed to do? You talked him down, talked him out. And you still lost him. You've been doing this long enough to know what an impact losing one has."

As he spoke, he set himself up with a fresh target. Once he'd fired his clip, he and Phoebe studied his results together. "You're a crappy shot, too."

"Yeah, but you're still crappier. How have you been sleeping?"

"Spotty. I know the signs, Dave. And yes, I have some of the classics—I feel let down, stressed, restless, irritable. But I *know* it, and I know why. What I don't know is why that boy's dead. That's the reason I spoke up in the meeting."

"Phoebe, the chief isn't what we'd call a creative thinker. He's more politician than cop—"

"I thought the same thing when we were up there. I guess we share more than crappy shooting."

He let out a half laugh, rubbed her shoulder. "Well, believe me, he's more concerned now with public relations and the possibility of civil liability than why a sixteen-year-old gangbanger's dead."

"You have ambitions for me." She loaded another clip. "I know that, too, Dave. I appreciate it."

"If I've got a legacy, it's you and Carter." Someone fired down the line, and the sound was harsh in contrast to his quiet voice. "When I'm ready to turn in my papers, I want to know you're taking my desk."

He'd wanted children; his wife hadn't. Though he'd never told her, Phoebe knew it because she knew him. So she and Carter were his. "You're worried if I speak up too often and don't say what the brass wants to hear, I'm shooting myself in the foot. Which is something I believe I could manage in the literal sense as it's fairly close range."

"The chief wants this put to bed. If he has to sacrifice Harrison in the public arena, he will. He'd sacrifice you, but there're no grounds. The simple fact is, Phoebe, logic and circumstances strongly support the idea that this was gang-related. A crime of opportunity and turf. That's the drum that's going to be beat."

"Maybe someone should listen to what's under the drum." She lifted her weapon again and fired.

Stupid, Phoebe thought later. Stupid to push and prod where the only result was going to be annoyance to all parties. Politics and public relations were going to play this out, she reminded herself as she changed into a gray suit—black seemed too presumptuous somehow.

She had nothing to add to the mix that wasn't already on record. Except for a few minutes before she'd taken over negotiations, and that horrible aftermath, she'd been inside the diner.

Nobody liked a Monday-morning quarterback, she told herself.

She would go to Charles Johnson's viewing, then she would have to put it away. No comment, she promised herself, unless the department directed otherwise. What more did she have to say, in any case?

She pinned her hair back. Nothing would sober the color, she mused, but the style seemed more respectful than loose.

She stepped into the family parlor. Her mother was crocheting in front of the TV, and Carly was sprawled on the floor paging through a picture book. Puppies, Phoebe realized with a little sink in the belly.

"I'm heading out now. I shouldn't be more than an hour."

"Mama! Wait, Mama, look! Aren't they cute?"

Carly scrambled up to hold out the book. The page was full of irresistible balls of fur and adorability. "They are, sweetie. They couldn't be cuter. But they also need to be fed and watered and walked, and cleaned up after, and trained, and—"

"But you said someday we could get a puppy."

"I said *maybe* someday." And only after she'd been worn down to a nub by pleading glances from those big blue eyes. "And I'm just not sure it's someday yet. I can't talk about it now because I have to go. And this isn't going to be just my decision. I'm at work all day and you're in school, so I need to discuss this with Gran and Ava before we get close to thinking about it. Where is Ava?"

"Book club." Essie gave Phoebe a puzzled look. "She mentioned it at dinner."

"Oh, of course she did. Slipped my mind." No, Phoebe admitted. She hadn't heard a word anyone had said at dinner. Apparently she hadn't just stopped active listening but listening at all. Time to pull it back together. "You be good for Gran." Phoebe bent to kiss the top of Carly's head. "I'll be back before long."

As she walked out she heard Carly using her slyest, most sugar-coated tone. "Gran, you like puppies, don't you?"

It should've been funny. She wished she could see it as funny. But all she could think about as she headed downstairs was that Carly was going to manipulate the other two adults in the house until they ended up with some shoe-chewing, puddle-making, middle-of-the-night-whimpering canine.

She *liked* dogs, damn it. But she just wasn't ready to take on another responsibility.

She knew Ava planned to take her son on a trip out West this summer. She deserved it, absolutely. And it meant ten days where there was no one around to run to the store, the bank, the dry cleaner's, to haul Carly, to *do* all the endless errands.

She already had an active seven-year-old and an agoraphobic to tend to. Phoebe didn't think it made her a heartless monster not to want to add a puppy to the mix.

But, of course, she felt like one, so when she opened the front door to go out, her scowl was already full-blown.

Duncan came up the last step to the portico. "That's timing."

"What are you doing here? You didn't get my message? I'm sorry, but—"

"No, I got it. I'm going with you."

"To the funeral home?" Shaking her head, she closed the door firmly behind her. "No, you're not. Why should you? You didn't know him."

"I know you, and you shouldn't go alone. Why should you?"

"I'm perfectly capable."

"A reason you could, but not why you should. If it irritates you so much to have me along, you'll just have to pretend I'm not there. You don't go into something like this by yourself. That's stupid, and you're not."

Phoebe yanked out her sunglasses, shoved them on. "Simple competence and responsibility aren't stupidity, thank you very much."

"Okay." Hair trigger, he thought again. Why did he like that about her? "Do you want to stand out here debating the issue, or do you want to go do this thing?"

"I'm not going to drive up to this poor boy's viewing in a Porsche and walk in with some rich guy in Armani."

"First." He stepped aside, gestured. There was a black sedan of some sort at the curb. "Second, this is Hugo Boss, or maybe Calvin Klein. I can't keep that sort of thing straight—so now that I think about it, it may be Armani. And I may be rich but I grew up not two spits from where that kid spent his short sixteen years. Not in a mansion on Jones. So don't call the pot, honey."

She stared a moment, then shook her head. "A few minutes ago something that should've made me laugh just couldn't. Now this just strikes me as funny. Or maybe it's just ridiculous."

She reached forward, flipped back the side of his jacket to find the label. "I was right about the designer. Never test the mother of a mini-fashionista."

"Points for you."

"No, for you." Irritable and let down, she thought. Yes, she knew the signs. "Thanks for coming to go with me. I was keeping the mad on the front burner so I wouldn't feel too much of the sad. And I neglected to remember one thing."

"Which one thing?"

"This isn't about me." She stepped down. "So, you've got a shiny black sedan. Sort of dignified."

"I thought about bringing the pickup, but that seemed wrong. And the SUV's just too big." He shrugged as he opened the car door. "I'm a guy. I have cars. It's what we do."

"As I have a car that is well on its way to becoming a heap, I appreciate being able to go in one of your manly fleet." She put a hand on his over the door handle. "I'm used to going alone, and I suppose that leads me to think I should. But I don't always want to, and I also appreciate you figuring that out before I did."

Because she looked as if she needed it, Duncan leaned down to touch his lips to hers. "I'm making a study of figuring you out."

The funeral home was small, the parking lot already crowded with cars and people. Phoebe saw reporters on the edge of the property. Some were doing interviews, others trying to hunt them up.

"Probably another way in," Duncan commented.

Avoiding the press was priority one, so she'd already prepared for it. "There's a side door, I checked. I thought I'd slip in and out that way. Five minutes. There'll be representatives from the department here. That's SOP on a homicide—and in this case, it's image, too. I'm not officially here."

"Got it." He found a place on the street, then glanced down at her heels. "Can you hike a block in those?"

"I'm a girl. It's what *we* do."

When they were on the sidewalk and he took her hand, she looked up at him. And for the second time since she'd met him, Phoebe thought, *Oh, well. Damn.*

"What?"

"Nothing. Nothing." She looked away again.

Hell of a time for her heart to start thumping, she decided, hell of a time for it to trip and fall. They were on their way to pay their respects to the mother of a dead boy. And she stumbled face-first into love.

It made no sense at all.

"Sure you want to do this?"

She knew she didn't. If she couldn't face the idea of training a puppy, how the hell was she supposed to deal with falling in love? But, of course, since he couldn't read her mind, he wasn't speaking of the big, long drop she'd just taken.

"I want to do it, for Charlie and his mother. And I guess part is about me. I need the ritual of it. I don't do well when I'm mad and sad, and I'm having a hard time putting either, or both, of those feelings away for very long."

Slipping into the side door was simple enough. But before Phoebe could congratulate herself on avoiding the gauntlet out front, she found herself faced with another inside.

A group of people clustered in and around a small parlor to the side of the main viewing room. The squeak of the door had heads turning. Conversations stopped instantly.

They weren't the only white faces, Phoebe noted. A few were scattered in. But her face had been on television. She saw recognition in some of the stares aimed her way, and resentment in others.

The crowd parted for a tall man, or maybe it parted for the anger pumping off him. "You got no place here. You get the hell out before—"

"You don't speak for me." Opal pushed forward. She looked a decade older than she had in the diner, with her eyes sunken dark in her face as if they'd never find light again. "You don't speak for my boy or for me."

"This here's for family. It's for neighborhood."

"You going to speak to me of family now, my brother? Where was my family when I needed them? You were up in Charlotte. You weren't here in the *neighborhood*. You don't speak for me." She drew herself up. "Lieutenant MacNamara."

"Mrs. Johnson, I'm sorry to intrude. I wanted to pay my respects to you and Charlie. I won't stay."

"Lieutenant MacNamara." Opal stepped forward and embraced Phoebe. "Thank you for coming here," she said quietly. "Thank you for not forgetting."

Emotion flooded Phoebe's throat, stung her eyes, ached in her heart. "I won't ever forget."

"Would you come with me, please?" Clutching Phoebe's hand, Opal turned. The man who'd spoken stood barring the way. "Don't you shame me. Don't you shame me so that this is the last time I look at your face."

"Your sons are dead, Opal."

"My sons are dead. And I have something to say." She walked through the crowd of mourners to the front door.

Her fingers twined in Phoebe's trembling ones. "Opal—"

"I've been afraid of so many things," Opal said. "Most all my life.

Maybe, I'd been braver things'd be different. I don't know, and it's hard not to question God's will. But I'm going to do this one thing, this one thing. And maybe, maybe, I won't be so afraid."

When she stepped out the front door with Phoebe, reporters shouted out, cameras whirled. Priority one, she thought, had been thoroughly breached. But there was a woman who'd lost her sons, who was clinging to her, who didn't give a damn about protocol.

"I got something to say." Opal's voice cracked, and her hand tightened like a vise on Phoebe's.

"Y'all been calling my home, and my mother's home. Calling where I work. I told you I wanted my privacy, but you won't give it. I got such sorrow in me, and I asked you to respect my grief. But you come 'round my house, my mama's, you call on the telephone. Say you want me to tell you what I got inside me, what I think, what I feel. And some of you? You offer me money to talk to you."

Questions boomed out. *Did you . . . Have you . . . How did you . . .* Opal's arm shook as if with a spasm as she turned those dark, sunken eyes on Phoebe. "Lieutenant MacNamara."

"Let's go back inside, Opal," Phoebe murmured. "I'll take you back inside, to your family."

"Stand here with me, please. Would you stand here with me so I can do this?"

Opal closed her eyes, then lifted her voice over the storm. "I've got something to say here, something to say for free, and you'll just *hush* if you want to hear it. My sons are dead."

In the silence that followed, Phoebe heard Opal's indrawn sob. "My boys are dead. Both killed. Guns and bullets took their bodies, but it was something else took 'em before that. They had no hope. They had a fever of anger and hate and blame, but no hope to cool it. I wish I could've given them that, but I couldn't get it into them.

"You want me to blame somebody. You want to see me point my finger, to scream and cry and curse. You won't. You want me to blame the gangs? They got part of it. The police? They got part. Then so do I got part, and my own dead babies, they got part. There's plenty of blame to spread around. I don't care for that. Doesn't matter about that."

She pulled a tissue from her pocket to mop her tears. "I know this woman standing beside me talked to my boy, and listened to my boy. For hours. And when that terrible thing happened that took my boy away so I can't ever have him again? She ran toward him. Didn't matter to her who was to *blame*. She ran to him to try to help. And when I could see again, when I could see, what I saw was her holding my son. And that's what matters.

"Now I got nothing more to say."

Ignoring the hurled questions, Opal turned for the door. Her body shook lightly as Phoebe put a protective arm around her shoulders.

"I'm going to take you to see my Charlie now."

"Okay, Opal." Taking Opal's weight, Phoebe walked toward the viewing room. "Let's go see Charlie."

Phoebe's knees felt a little weak by the time she returned to the car. It was funny, she thought, how joints often took the brunt of emotional upheavals.

Duncan merely ran a hand down her arm, then started the ignition.

"I need to make a call," she said, and pulled out her phone. Impulse again, she reminded herself. She seemed to be doing a lot on impulse these days. "Mama? I'm going to be going out awhile if you don't need me back. Yes, all right. Tell Carly I'll come in and kiss her good night when I get home. I will. Bye."

She drew in a deep breath. "All right?"

"Sure. Where do you want to go?"

"I think your place would be just fine. Then you can fix me a nice cold drink of an alcoholic nature. And after we've had a nice cold drink, you can take me up to bed."

"That fits pretty well into my schedule."

"That's good, because it seems to be just the thing that was missing in mine." She leaned back, flipped through issues that were on her mind. "Duncan, what do you think of a man who decides to marry a woman named Mizzy who's a dozen years younger than he is?"

"How big are her breasts?"

Phoebe's lips twitched as she stared up through the sunroof. "I don't have that information."

"It's pretty relevant. Who's marrying Mizzy?"

"Carly's father."

"Oh."

Sympathy and speculation, Phoebe thought, in a single syllable. "I know I shouldn't care, but of course I do. I know I'll get over that—which is comforting. He's moving with her to Europe, which infuriates me, and which I won't get over even though I know it's stupid. It doesn't matter if he's around the corner or thousands of miles away, he's not going to love that sweet child, or pretend he does."

"But if he's around the corner, so to speak, you can keep hoping he might eventually."

"That's right." That, she realized, was exactly, perfectly right. "Opal Johnson couldn't push hope into her sons, and they needed it. I can't—or haven't—let go of mine when it's a useless weight."

"How does Carly feel?"

"Carly doesn't care." They soared over the water, where boats skimmed below the span of bridge. "She's healthier about it than I am."

"She has you. A kid knows she's loved, absolutely, she's got a healthy base."

He hadn't had that absolute love, she remembered, but had built his own base. "I haven't told her about the wedding yet. I will, when I'm not so mad. I don't think he'd have bothered to tell me about all this except the child support checks will be delayed while he changes banks. Changes his damn dollars to Euros and back again. Whatever."

"So you're pissed he's moving to Europe."

"Oh, I'm just pissed altogether." And suddenly just a little amused at the entire business. "I don't care who she is, no woman likes being traded in on the Mizzy model. Especially when the trade-in has a lot higher mileage."

"I bet the Mizzy model is high maintenance and can't handle the curves nearly as well."

"Hopeful thought. I'm telling you all this because it factors into my overall mood, which is restless and conflicted, and a little aggressive." The faintest smile curved her lips as she tilted her head to study his profile. "I'm wondering how you feel about aggressive women."

"Am I going to find out?"

"I believe you are."

"Oh boy."

When they were inside his house, she decided the cold drink could wait. They'd both probably need a gallon of cold liquid after they were done. Since he'd been considerate enough to wear a tie, she grabbed it and, strolling toward the stairs, pulled him behind her.

"Bedroom's up here, I assume? We didn't get that far last time."

"To the right, all the way down. Last on the left."

When she glanced over her shoulder, her eyes sparked on his. "I bet the view's lovely. We won't be paying much mind to that for a while, but I bet it's lovely."

She tugged him inside. She got the impression of space, of strong colors, tall windows. And best of all, a big iron bed.

"Now." She turned, tugged the knot on his tie loose. "This may hurt a little."

"My tolerance for pain is rising as we speak."

Laughing, she yanked his jacket off, flung it aside. Then backed him toward the bed, where she gave him a little shove until he sat. With slow, deliberate movements, she straddled him so the skirt of the sober business suit hiked high on her thighs.

"Now, gimme that mouth."

She used her teeth on it, her tongue, and all those wildly veering emotions coalesced into one hard, hot ball of lust. Her fingers got busy with his shirt, flipping open button after button until she could run her hands over flesh, scrape her nails over him. The quickening of his breath, the urgent way his hands streaked over her, made her feel invincible.

She let him peel her jacket off, tug the tank over her head. And, arching back, invited his lips and hands to feast and to take. The way he took, the way he feasted, electrified.

She was clamped around him, arms and legs. The most seductive of traps. A careless rake of his fingers and her hair came spilling down, fragrant red rain. A quick flick and her breasts, white satin, filled his hands.

Energized silk, he thought. Everything about her was smooth, soft, everything inside her so avid with purpose.

She let out a gasping laugh when he flipped her onto her back. Then a low purr of pleasure as his hands, his lips began to roam over her. Slowly now, he slid the skirt down her hips, her legs, following the movement with his mouth. The inside of her thigh, so firm and warm. The back of her knee, sensitive enough to cause quivers.

And when he retraced the route, and found her center, she went from quiver to quake.

Pleasure, dark and deep, swamped her. Sensation powered into sensation in a roaring, raging river. She tumbled into it, drowned in it until he dragged her gasping to the surface only to plunge her down again.

She rolled with him, hands slipping, sliding over flesh damp with sweat; her mouth, frantic, greedy, seeking his. Until at last, at last, she straddled him again, took him in. Deep, deep as hearts thundered. Their bodies locked.

She rode him hard and long. His hands gripped her hips as she bowed forward or back. The sheer beauty of that shape, that silhouette, shimmered in his mind while the stunning drive of need ruled his body.

And all of it was her. There was nothing but her when he shot blindly over that last jagged edge.

When she collapsed on him, simply fell limb by limb, he managed one final groan.

"I forgot—" She had to stop to wheeze in another breath.

"I didn't—I remembered that time. One suit off, another suit on."

She let out a weak laugh. "No, not that—good memory, by the way. I was going to say I forgot how much I like sex."

He rested his forehead on her shoulder and hoped that, eventually, his brain would find its way back home. "Happy to remind you, as often as possible."

"Oh God, Duncan, I'd give almost anything for a glass of water. A half glass. One swallow."

"Okay, okay, don't beg. It's embarrassing." He rolled her over, and she kept going until she was splayed on her belly.

"You're my hero," she mumbled into the pillow, and drifted off. A faint smile curved her lips as she heard him walking back into the bedroom.

Then she leaped in shock as the ice water hit the center of her back. *"Duncan!"*

"What?" He stood, an innocent smile on his face, the glass in his hand. "You said you wanted water. You didn't say where you wanted it."

Eyes narrowed, she got to her knees, held out a hand. She took a long sip. Then, with a half laugh, reached out to tug his hair. "Very funny." She tugged him again until his lips met hers.

Then poured the rest of the water over his head.

20

Phoebe leaned over after Duncan stopped the car. "Thank you for going with me." She kissed him lightly. "Thank you for the sex. And thank you for the ride home."

"You're welcome. And on the second part? Pretty much anytime."

"An additional thank-you." She brushed his lips one more time. "For understanding I have to get myself home earlier than Cinderella most of the time."

He trailed a finger around her ear. "If I buy you some glass slippers, do you think we could arrange a sleepover?"

With a laugh, she got out of the car. "You know, I was talking myself into backing off this—whatever this is—with you."

"Oh?" He got out so they stood for a moment, studying each other on opposite sides of the car. "Why is that?"

"I'm trying to remember. I had my reasons. Duncan, I'm resistant to being swept away."

"I'll leave the broom in the closet."

Too late, she thought. Much too late. "You're better at this than I am."

"At what?"

"At whatever this is."

Lights sparkled over in Forsythe Park, and there were soft pools of shadows along the street. Ava's flowers perfumed the air that threatened to turn sultry. Through the open windows of a passing car Delta Blues throbbed like a broken heart.

Here she stood, Phoebe thought, looking over at a man who excited her so she noticed those small details she often overlooked. So that those details were like colorful backdrops in Act Three of her personal play.

And she was fretting over it because she wasn't absolutely certain how the play would end.

"Did you ever get your heart broken? No, don't answer that now," she said quickly. "That may be one of those long stories, and I have to get inside."

"Go out with me tomorrow night, and I'll tell you all about the many shattered pieces of my abused heart."

"How much of it will you be making up?"

"You'll have to go out with me to find out."

"You're just a little too appealing for my own good." She let out a sigh, glanced back at the house. "I can't tomorrow—shouldn't. I don't like to spend too many evenings away."

"Pick a night."

"Don't you know about playing hard to get?"

He walked around to her. "I'm not playing."

Her heart took a hard bump. "No, you're not. I . . . well." Flustered, she glanced back at the house again. "This week is a little difficult. Carly's school play is Thursday night, and there's a school holiday on Friday, so—"

"Can I go?" He eased a little closer and touched her. Just fingertips sliding down her arms until she wanted to shiver and sigh. "To the play."

She managed a laugh. "Oh, trust me, you don't want to sacrifice yourself on the altar of an elementary school play."

"Sounds like fun." Sensing nerves, he smiled. Wasn't she the most *interesting,* contradictory woman? *"Cinderella,* right? Wicked stepsister."

"How do you know that?"

"Essie told me. Thursday night. What time?"

"Seven, but—"

"Seven's curtain? Should I meet you there, or come by and pick y'all up? Plenty of room for you and Carly, Ava and . . . Essie can't go," he realized, and his easy humor faded. "That must be hard, must be hard for her."

"Yes, it is. Very hard. We're getting it videotaped, but it's not the same. Duncan, if you really want to go—and that's very sweet—you should just meet us. I have to get Carly there an hour ahead, for costumes and such. I'll get you a ticket, leave it out front for you. But you don't have to feel obligated."

Don't feel obligated, he thought, intrigued when she backed up a step. He decided on the spot that wild horses wouldn't keep him from a Thursday night date with Cinderella. "I don't think I've ever been to a kiddie school play."

"You must've been in one."

"I was once a belching frog. And I have a vague recollection of being a turnip once, or maybe it was a radish. But it was so traumatic, I've blocked it out. Y'all got any plans for the weekend?"

"Ah, we're working out a Saturday playdate with Carly's current best friend. Details are not finalized."

"Great. Maybe they can do me a favor. Family fun center. Playworld? Heard of it?"

"Been there, yes."

"Did Carly like it? Hate it? See I'm thinking about investing, but I haven't decided whether to go into an established place like that or maybe do something new. Fresh. We could go on Saturday. Kid-test it."

She stared at him as if he'd sprouted a second head. "You want to spend your Saturday in an amusement center with a couple of little girls?"

"You make that sound just a little perverted. Actually, more than a couple of little girls would be better. I've been tugging on Phin to bring Livvy into it, and maybe some of the others. You up for that?"

"I imagine Carly would be delighted. Why an amusement center?" she asked as she turned toward the house.

"Ah, well, fun would be the primary factor. If you're going to— Hold it." He grabbed her arm, pulled her back.

Over the top step in the wash of the house light, the carcass of a dead rabbit drooped. The ruff around its neck was matted with dried blood that shone black against the brown fur.

"Oh, God, not again. I need to— Don't just *touch* it," Phoebe snapped out, "with your hands."

"I use my hands instead of my feet for touching. Just a quirk." He lifted it by its hind legs. "What do you mean, not again?"

Because her stomach pitched, Phoebe gave herself permission to look away. "Let me get something. A bag, a box. Jesus. Take it around to the courtyard, would you? I'll be right there."

She dashed into the house while Duncan frowned at the rabbit. Wasn't mauled, he mused as he studied it. It sure as hell didn't strike him as roadkill. He'd given up hunting after his first and only foray into that area on a trip with a couple of friends as a teenager.

He'd liked the gun—the feel, the sound, even the jolt—but he hadn't much cared for what it could do when the target was flesh and blood.

If he had to guess, the rabbit had been shot, small caliber. But why anyone would shoot a rabbit and toss it on Phoebe's steps was a mystery.

He carried it through the courtyard gate just as she rushed out with a plastic grocery bag. "We need to put it in here."

"You want to tell me why Bugs ended up dead on your steps?"

"I don't know, but I'm going to have to build a damn graveyard if this keeps up. This is joining the rat I found out here a couple weeks ago, and the snake on the steps a few days ago."

"You had any altercations with any of the neighborhood boys?"

"No. I ran that one down already. I don't think the local hellions are responsible. Put that thing down, will you?"

As he heard distress as well as disgust, Duncan eased the corpse into the bag. "I think you're going to want to take this one in—to forensics or whatever. I'm pretty sure it's got a bullet in it."

She let out a long breath. "I'll deal with it in the morning. Come inside, wash your hands."

He'd go inside, Duncan thought, but washing a little dead rabbit off his fingers wasn't primary.

He followed her in, stepped to the kitchen sink. "Got any beer?" he asked.

"No. Yes. I don't know."

After drying his hands, he simply walked to the refrigerator, opened it. Mostly girl food, as he thought of it. Lots of fruit, fresh vegetables, cartons of yogurt, skim milk. Why did anyone want to skim milk? A question for another time.

He didn't find any beer, but pulled out an open bottle of California chardonnay. "Glasses?"

"Oh." She pushed at her hair as she turned to a cabinet. It was manners that had her reaching for glasses, he thought. She'd have been happier if he'd dried his hands and said good night. So she could think, and so she could handle whatever was going on herself.

Tough for her, he decided. He wasn't built that way.

He poured the wine himself, sat at the little table. Which, he knew, left her trapped by those manners into sitting down with him.

"I appreciate you dealing with that," she began. "I hate knowing I'm squeamish enough to balk at doing it myself."

"Who dealt with the rat?"

"Well, I did—with a lot of embarrassing squealing and shuddering. I called Carter about the snake. That, apparently, went over my level."

"Have you reported this?"

She puffed out her cheeks. "I assumed that some cat dumped the rodent out in the courtyard. I didn't think about it. I initially thought the same about the snake, until Carter said its head was crushed, which is when I had a talk with the mother of the leader of the neighborhood hellions. But it wasn't him. Neither was this. So, yes, I'll take that thing in tomorrow, and I'll report it and have it checked out."

"Anyone got any reason to hassle you other than Meeks?"

She took a sip of wine. "You're quick."

"Not a big leap, Phoebe. Sounds like this Arnie needs a talking-to."

Not just quick, she realized. Furious. Quietly, coldly and absolutely furious. "A talking-to isn't what you mean, and it isn't for you. It isn't," she said firmly. "I find the sentiment . . . Well, to be honest, I don't quite know how I find the sentiment, but we'll come back to that sometime. The point is, if indeed Arnie Meeks needs a talking-to, it's best done in an unofficially official way. If you go getting in his face as my . . ."

"We're going to have to come up with a term," Duncan said dryly, "as you object to 'boyfriend.'"

"Anyway, it'd put his back up and it makes me look weak. If he's doing this, I can't afford to look weak, I can't give him the satisfaction of believing it's given me any particular bad moments."

"But it has."

"I wish I could say otherwise. I think . . ."

"Think what?"

She drank again. She wasn't used to talking to anyone about her own business. Not difficult business. The priority was to keep the house a safe zone. "I think there might've been someone watching the house. I caught a glimpse a couple of times, or more heard. He whistles."

"Sorry? He whistles?"

"I know, it sounds odd and off. But I think someone's been around the neighborhood a few times, walking by the house, whistling this same tune. If it's Meeks—and I didn't get a close enough look to say, either way—he's taking a huge chance for more payback. He might've put a friend up to it, or paid someone. But it's a big and foolish risk."

"He got a big kick in the ass. Could be worth it to him. These things can escalate, can't they?"

"They can, of course." She glanced up, seeing in her mind's eye her family tucked safe away for the night. "I'm not discounting the possibility. I'll talk to the people I need to, first thing in the morning."

"I can bunk here. Spare room, spare couch."

"That's a nice offer. But if you do, I'd have to explain it in the morning. At this point, I don't want to give anyone, especially my mother, something more to worry about. She's holding. My getting hurt, and then the shooting, those were hard knocks for her. I don't think she's been out in the courtyard for the last few days. I can't stand to think she'll lose that, too."

Duncan studied his glass, had another long sip of wine. "I believe I've had too much to drink. I don't think I should drive. As a duly authorized officer of the law, and as my current hostess, you should discourage me from doing so."

Those soft blue eyes, those clear and sober eyes, met hers. "It's as simple as that, Phoebe, if you let it be."

"I don't know why men think women can't defend themselves or their home."

He only smiled. "Do I need to explain the power of the penis to you—so soon after you've experienced its wonder?"

She tapped her fingers on the table. "You can have Steve's—Ava's son's—room for the night. But if it's all the same to you, we won't use your drunken behavior as the reason. It just got late, and seemed easier for you to stay than to drive all the way back to the island."

"Fine. We'll save my drunken behavior for another occasion. Can I ask something that's none of my business?"

"As long as the answer can be that's none of your business, sure you can."

"Is Essie getting any therapy?"

"She was," Phoebe said on a long sigh. "As it's difficult, even with agoraphobia, to get a therapist who'll make house calls, most of it was by phone. There were regular weekly phone sessions for a while, and she tried medications. We thought she was making progress."

"But?"

"Her therapist encouraged her to go out. Just ten minutes, outside the house, to somewhere familiar. They picked Forsythe Park. She'd just walk over to the fountain and back home. She made it over, she got over, and then had a major panic attack. One of the fears is being caught in public, or embarrassed in public, or trapped. She couldn't get her breath, couldn't find her way back. I'd gone after her. I watched her walk over, and went out behind her when she was nearly out of sight. So it took me a while to get to her once she panicked."

She could see it, still see it perfectly. Her mother terrified and disoriented, and her own heart banging in her chest as she sprinted over pavement and grass, pushed aside stunned tourists to reach her.

"She was gasping for air, and running. She fell. It was terrible for

her. People were trying to help her, but it scared her so much, humiliated her so much."

"I'm sorry."

"I got her back. Held on tight, had her close her eyes, and I walked
her back. She hasn't been beyond the courtyard since. That was four
years ago. She wouldn't go back into therapy afterward. Gets testy
about it," Phoebe added with a little smile. "She's fine in the house.
She's happy in the house. Why can't we leave her alone? So we do. I
don't know if it's the right thing, but we do."

"It's right enough. Sometimes the right thing changes, so you have
to do what's right for now."

She thought about that after she showed him where he could sleep, after digging up a spare toothbrush and making sure the towels were
fresh and plentiful.

The right thing changed, that was true. And sometimes what you
thought was right ended up being a wrong turn but a necessary one.
She wasn't sure if Duncan was the right thing or a wrong turn, but
she'd fallen in love with him.

Had probably stubbed her toe on that the first time she'd seen him,
then tripped a little when she'd sat in the pub, laughing with him and
enjoying the music. Another little stumble here, a loss of balance there,
and the fall was inevitable.

Now, she supposed, she had to figure out what the right thing was,
and how to do it. For now.

A big perk to waking up the lone guy in a household of women, Duncan decided, was the big, home-cooked breakfast. It didn't suck to be
fussed over, either, like the newly crowned prince of Femaleland while
he enjoyed coffee and freshly squeezed orange juice.

Ava managed the morning stove, and by his gauge that was the general routine. But due to manly company, Essie set out what he figured
were the good dishes, with coordinating linen napkins.

Essie fussed, filling a fancy sugar bowl and creamer, pouring freshly

squeezed juice into a sparkling pitcher, rounding up a little squat bottle of zinnias. He could only assume, as the tasks had her all but bouncing around the kitchen, she was having as good a time as he was.

"Now don't pester Duncan, Carly. He hasn't even finished his first
cup of coffee yet."

"Great coffee," Duncan said.

"How come I'm not having cereal?" Carly wanted to know.

"Because Ava's making omelets. But you can have cereal if that's
what you want."

"I don't care."

Duncan gave Carly a poke in the ribs. Despite the pout, she looked
pretty as a picture in a ruffly yellow shirt and blue pants. "Hard day at
the office coming up?"

She rolled her eyes in his direction. "I go to *school*. And we have to
take an arithmetic test today. I don't see why we have to multiply and
divide all the time. It's just numbers. They don't *do* anything."

"You don't like numbers? I love numbers. Numbers are a thing of
beauty."

Carly sniffed. "I don't need numbers. I'm going to be an actress. Or
a personal shopper."

"Well, if you're an actress how are you going to count your lines?"

Duncan considered earning a second eye roll a badge of honor.

"Anybody can count."

"Only with the beauty of numbers. Then you have to figure out how
much you're going to make—so you can buy that house in Malibu—
after you pay your agent her percentage, and pay your bodyguards so
the paparazzi don't hound you. You got to have yourself an entourage,
kid, and do the math so you can call up that personal shopper when it's
time for the Oscars."

Carly considered. "Maybe I'll just *be* the personal shopper. Then I
only have to know about clothes. I *know* about clothes already."

"What's your commission?"

This time he got a frown instead of an eye roll. "I don't know what
that is."

"It's how much you make when you sell Jennifer Aniston that vintage Chanel gown. You get a cut of what it costs. So say it costs five thousand, and you get ten percent. Plus, she needs shoes, and a purse thing. So what's your commission? Gotta do the math."

Her eyes narrowed now. "I get something every time they buy something? I get money, every time?"

"Pretty sure that's how it works."

Interest lit her face and banished the pout. "I don't know how to do percent."

"I do. Got paper?"

When Phoebe walked in, her family was circled around the table. Creamy omelets, fancy strips of Ava's masterful French toast, crisp bacon invited healthy appetites to tuck right in.

Duncan ate with his left hand while Carly, her chair scooted up beside his, leaned over his rapidly scribbling right.

"She needs earrings! She has to have earrings, too."

"Okay. How much for the ear dangles?"

"A million dollars!"

"You're the Satan of personal shoppers." He flicked a glance up, smiled. "Morning."

"Mama! We're doing percent, so I can figure out how much I'll make when I'm a personal shopper. I already made six thousand dollars on commission."

"Jennifer Aniston's up for an Oscar," Ava explained. "She needs to be outfitted, of course."

"Of course."

"And needs ensembles for various appearances."

Phoebe walked around to read the list Duncan had going. "Jen's on quite the spree."

"Numbers are fun."

Phoebe gaped at her daughter. "I think I've walked into a parallel universe, one where numbers are fun and there's omelets on Tuesday mornings."

"Sit right down," Essie told her. "We've kept yours warm in the oven."

Phoebe checked her watch. "I guess I've got time to force down a few bites. Numbers are fun," she repeated as she sat on the other side of her daughter. "How come they weren't fun when I made little bunnies and kittens out of them to show you how they multiplied?"

"Numbers are more fun when they're money."

Phoebe picked up her coffee, shook her head. "Mind yourself with this one, Duncan. She's a gold digger."

"She picks up a couple more clients like Jen here, she's going to be supporting me. Look how pretty you are in the morning. Even prettier than Ava's omelets—which is going some. I expect there isn't a man in Savannah with a better view than I've got here in this kitchen."

Phoebe's brows winged up. "What did you put in his omelet, Ava?"

"Whatever it was, I'll make sure it goes in every time."

He ate cold cereal straight out of the box and washed it down with bitter black coffee. He hadn't shaved that morning. He hadn't showered. He knew he was standing on the slippery edge of a bout of depression.

He wanted the anger back. The anger and the purpose. They could get lost in that blue pit of depression, he knew. He'd lost them before.

There was medication, duly prescribed. But he preferred the speed he'd bought from a friend of a friend. Still, he knew the uppers were a bad choice. He could do the rash and the reckless with that heady juice rushing through him.

He'd already done the reckless, hadn't he? Plugging that idiot rabbit was one thing. But he should've saved it—a few days in the freezer, then he could've dumped it on Phoebe anytime in the dead of night.

He'd nearly gotten caught by rushing it. But he'd been so pissed off! She wasn't taking the heat for Johnson. Not from the department, not from the press, not from the public. The stupid fucker's mother had made Phoebe her new best friend. And that maudlin, that *pitiful* statement outside the funeral home played over and over on the news, on the talk shows.

Made that fumbling bitch look like Mother fucking Teresa instead of the ambitious, grasping, stumbling cunt she was.

He'd let the anger take over—always a mistake. He'd let it rule so he'd driven straight to her house, tossed the corpse up. He'd meant it to land on the veranda but his hand had been shaking with rage, and his aim was short.

He'd nearly gone after it, had started to, when light spilled out of the house next door.

He could see himself—humiliated even now—hiding in the bushes while that crazy bitch walked out with her ugly excuse for a dog.

And he knew, he *knew* she walked that dog right at dusk, every single night. He knew, but he hadn't used the knowledge. He'd only used the anger.

And what if that crazy woman or her ugly excuse for a dog had seen him? It wasn't time for that yet.

He'd actually imagined killing them both. Snapping necks like celery stalks and leaving *them* on Phoebe's front steps.

But it wasn't the time.

He had a plan. A plan and a purpose. An *agenda.*

Now the rage was gone, and the purpose was blurred with a damning sense of failure. He'd wasted his time on that Posse asshole. Taken a stupid risk and wasted bullets.

It meant nothing.

He looked around his workshop and nearly wept with despair. None of it meant anything. He'd lost what mattered, and she'd lost nothing.

Now he was reduced to leaving dead animals on her doorstep.

He should've killed the crazy old woman and her dog, he decided. Coulda, shoulda. That would've made a statement.

He took out one of the little black pills, studied it. Just one, he thought. Just one to give him back some juice.

Because it was time to make a statement. Time to stop screwing around and kick it all up a notch.

Johnson hadn't put a hitch in her step. Something else—or somebody else—would.

"Twenty-two caliber." The criminalist, a skinny guy named Ottis, held the slug up with gloved fingers. "You gonna kill da wabbit, this is plenty hot enough."

"Single shot?"

"Yeah." Ottis frowned at Phoebe. "Do you want me to run it through ballistics? Ah, do any trace on the . . . vic?"

"Actually, I would. If someone's playing a prank, I'm not laughing. And I think it's more than that. So anything you can tell me about the bunny or the bullet would be helpful."

"Sure, no problem. I'll get back to you."

She went back to her office and wrote up an official incident report. Then she took a copy out to Sykes's desk, filled him in.

"Do you want me to go have a conversation with Arnie?"

"No, at least not yet. I'd like you to pull a few lines, if you can. Find out how he's handling the security job, get a sense of his routine. See if you can find out if he's been spending any time in my neighborhood. He's got a mouth," Phoebe added. "If he's messing with me, he's probably bragged about it to someone. Someone he drinks with or works with."

"I'll poke around."

"Thanks. Thank you, Bull."

Best she could do, Phoebe decided. But not all she could do.

Back in her office, she wrote up a log, listing the times and dates, the incidents she believed were connected. To these she added her own speculations.

Rat—symbol—snitch, turncoat, deserting sinking ship.

Snake—symbol—evil, sneaky, bringer of ruin to Paradise.

Rabbit—symbol—cowardly, running away.

Might be taking it all too far, psychologically, she mused, but it was better to err on the side of caution than to just err.

Whistling keeps the voice disguised, anonymous. What does the song mean? Do not forsake me. Who was forsaken? Who did or might do the forsaking?

High Noon. One man standing up against corruption and cowardice (rabbit as cowardice?). Rat as desertion of townspeople. Snake as corruption. Cooper as sheriff (wasn't he? Rent the damn movie), standing alone in the final showdown.

Was it about the movie or just the song? she wondered. She did a search, found the lyrics and printed them out for the file she would make.

High noon was a kind of deadline, wasn't it? Do this by this time or pay the price.

She sat back. And if it was Arnie Meeks harassing her, he wouldn't be thinking about symbols and hidden meanings. It just wasn't his style.

Still, she'd make up the file. And on the way home, she'd hunt up a copy of *High Noon*.

TERMINATION
PHASE

I do not know what fate awaits me.

—"HIGH NOON"

21

Screaming kids and the lightning-flash mood swings of little girls didn't appear to ruffle Duncan's feathers. In fact, his easy slide through kid world had Phoebe wondering if the man had any feathers to ruffle.

What he did, she noted, was play like a maniac. Whatever it was—video arcade, miniature golf, whack-a-mole, he was *into* it. She liked games as much as the next person, and God knew she'd done her stints at fun centers. But she'd never come out of one, in her memory, without a vague headache, a stomach uneasy from strange combinations of food, and feet that ached like a tooth headed for a root canal.

She had a touch of all three results, and sat herself down on a bench while Duncan took on all challengers in what he called the Champion Round of mini-golf.

Carly was having the time of her life, and the other kids who'd packed along were flocked around him like he was the Pied Piper. And how, Phoebe wondered, did spending hours racing virtual cars or hitting a red ball through the rotating fans of a plastic windmill equal researching an investment possibility?

Loo dropped down beside her. "I should've gotten a manicure. These places wear me out and I *knew* that man would talk me into coming."

"Phin's looking a little worn himself."

"Not Phin." Loo sucked diet soda through a straw. "I know all his tricks by now. Duncan. I know all his, too, but damn that man always gets around me."

From her vantage point, Phoebe studied him. He'd sat through an elementary school production of *Cinderella* with every appearance of being thoroughly entertained. And had capped that off by insisting on buying the redheaded stepsister an ice cream cone.

Naturally, Carly was crazy about him.

And now he was giving every appearance of being thoroughly entertained by playing mini-golf with a platoon of overexcited children.

"Duncan doesn't look worn at all," Phoebe observed.

"Probably live here if he could." Loo slipped her own aching feet out of her sandals. "Look at him, crouched down on that old green carpet eyeballing the hole like he's Tiger Woods in the Playland Open. Kids eating it right up like ice cream sundaes, which I warn you, he'll insist on after this is over."

Phoebe pressed a hand to her stomach. "Oh God."

"Won't play real golf. Phin's dragged him out several times, and tells me Duncan says stuff like: 'Where's the windmill?' or 'When do we get to the troll bridge?'" She let out her big laugh. "Bruises our Phin's dignity, which is exactly Dunc's purpose."

Because she could hear Duncan say it, Phoebe smiled. "So he just wanted to come out and play. This investment business is a ruse."

"Oh no, he's given it serious thought. He'll be working out the pros and cons now."

Lips pursed, Phoebe studied Duncan as he argued the count of strokes on a hole with Phin. "Yes, I can see that."

"I mean it." Loo gave Phoebe a poke. "He's going to have a good ballpark idea how many kids and adults came through the turnstiles today, which areas got the most play, which didn't. You can bet he's asked the kids we brought, and those of complete strangers, what they like. He'll have himself a baseline before we're sick off ice cream sundaes, then he'll go—or won't go—from there."

"I can't quite fit him into the businessman mold."

Loo's smile was lit with affection. "He's his own mold."

"Apparently."

"Got a nice ass on him, too."

"Unquestionably."

"He's got what my mother calls the calf's eyes for you."

"Does he? It's hard for me to see clearly with all these hearts circling in front of mine. I just wanted a hot affair." She shifted toward Loo, kept her voice low. "I figured, hell, I deserve one."

"Who doesn't?" Loo shifted in turn. "How about some salient details?"

"Maybe some other time. The thing is, I don't know if I can manage what's going on in here." She pressed a hand to her heart. "I don't know if I have the tools or the room or—"

"Why? You're—"

"Wait." Phoebe turned her hand palm out now. "You're married, and happily by every sign. You have a pretty little girl and an ugly dog. You have a big family, dual careers that complement each other and exceptional taste in shoes."

"I do." Loo pursed her lips at the stacked-heel, copper-toned sandals. "The shoes are the kicker."

"I'm divorced with a career that pulls me in conflicting directions constantly, and a family I love, but that does the same. My foundation is shaky at best, and what I've built on it takes a lot of time and effort to tend. It's never been just me for a lot of reasons. It can never be just me."

"You're thinking Duncan can't handle the complications of your life?"

"I'm not sure he'd want to, or why he would. Right now, he's infatuated and intrigued. And the sex, like the shoes, is quite the kicker. But I'm a lot to deal with on a daily basis. And there are things I can't change or adjust. I'm just not in a position to."

Loo sucked through her straw, considered. "Do you always analyze everything into tiny pieces, and pick out the harder points?"

"Yes. Occupational hazard, I guess. Tough fit, I'd think, for a man who appears to take in the big picture quickly and find the shiny nuggets. I keep trying to . . . I'd say talk myself down from all this. Step back from the ledge, Phoebe. Your life's good enough, full enough as it is, so accept that. Take that last step, there's no coming back from it, not without a world of hurt."

"Love as suicide?"

"Maybe it is. Or it's walking out with your hands up in surrender, to take the consequences."

"Or it's coming out free, instead of staying a hostage."

"That's a point. I know what I'm doing, have to know what I'm doing just about all the time. It's annoying, and damn disconcerting, not to know what I'm doing with him."

"Can't tell you. But I think it'd be fun finding out."

Fun was exhausting. Carly gave in to it and sprawled sleeping in the back of Duncan's car on the way home.

"In case she's too zonked to thank you, I can tell you she had a big, bright, red-letter day."

"Me, too."

"I noticed. Boys and toys. She's got a whopping crush on you."

"It's mutual."

"I noticed that, too. Duncan, I have one favor to ask, and I hope you'll understand why I need to."

"Sure. You had too many hot dogs and want me to stop for Pepto."

"I had *one* hot dog, and I have Tums at home. Duncan, seriously. I'm saying—asking, really—that if things between us take a slide, or we get pissed off and each decide the other is the spawn of Satan, if you'll ease away from Carly. Give her time to adjust. This is a crappy thing to bring up after you've given us such a good day, but—"

"You've got—what's his name?—Ralph stuck in your head."

"Roy," she corrected. "And, yes, that's part of it. I can't think of anyone less like him than you are."

"If that's true, you should already know it's a favor you don't have to ask. I know what it's like to be shut out and shut down."

"You do." She touched a hand to his arm. "I'm a worrying, overprotective mother."

"She's lucky to have one." He aimed a look at her. "Even if you turn out to be the spawn of Satan."

She wiggled her tired toes as he turned toward the house. "How about coming in, having a cool glass of wine in the courtyard?"

"Exactly what I had in mind."

A week later, Phoebe sat in Duncan's garden. Carly was having a sleepover at her new second best friend Livvy's house, which meant her mama could have the adult version of a sleepover.

They'd had a swim, and made love. They'd had dinner, and made love. Now it was nearly midnight—and it didn't matter!—with her sitting out in a lush garden smelling night-blooming jasmine, a glass of wine in her hand. She wore a flimsy excuse for a robe she'd paid entirely too much money for.

But if a woman couldn't splurge for such an occasion, when could she?

The night hummed, the breeze just balmy enough to cut back the heat while a fat old moon sailed over a sky dashed with stars and smeared with filmy clouds. He'd turned music on so that Bonnie Raitt's Delta-rich voice oozed out of the garden speakers.

Phoebe sipped wine and gave some lazy thought to making love again.

"I feel like I'm on vacation," she told Duncan.

"I should've put little umbrellas in the drinks." His voice was as lazy as she felt. "Something with steel drums on the stereo. Except I don't have little umbrellas or any steel-drum CD. No, Jimmy Buffett. It should've been Jimmy Buffett and margaritas."

"This is fine. This is perfect. I may never move from this exact spot." She turned her head to smile at him. "You'll have to start charging me rent."

"I'll take it out in trade."

"I'm so glad you didn't want to go anywhere tonight. Clubs, bars, movies. It's so nice to just be."

"Clubs, bars, movies, they're not going anywhere. It's nice to just kick back."

"You had a busy week."

"Ava's a slave driver. Beneath that pretty face is the heart of Simon Legree. I think I looked at every tree and shrub for sale in greater Savannah yesterday. And all those drawings and layouts. Sod. Fountains. Statuary. Birdbaths, feeders, houses. What-all. She doesn't care for the concept of 'do whatever you like.'"

"She mentioned you took her by an old warehouse the other day. That you're converting it into apartments and shops."

"Yeah. Thought she'd get some ideas going on that and be too busy to drag me to another nursery. How about we take a sail in the morning? In fact, we can sail over to Savannah."

"That sounds perfect. Everything's just about perfect."

"Give me a couple minutes." He shifted toward her on the wide chaise, then slid a finger down to open the thin robe. "And I'll make it absolutely perfect."

She didn't have a doubt in the world, not when his mouth found hers, when his hands began to cruise. She reached out blindly until her glass clinked against the table. With her hands free, she tangled her fingers in his hair.

The breeze played along her skin; the music thrummed just under it. When her head fell back so he could run his lips down her throat, there was the white ball of moon overhead.

She moved under him, opened for him so when their mouths met again he slipped inside her. Slow and easy now, loose and lazy. Her eyes stayed open so that she could see herself in his. She felt herself rising and falling, rising and falling, in long, liquid waves of arousal and pleasure. When she spilled over the crest, she was still there, trapped in the blue of his eyes.

Why, she wondered, would she want to be anywhere else?

"One more." He murmured it, then captured her mouth again, sumptuously. Her heartbeat thickened, her bones softened.

I love you. The words rose in her throat, ached to be said.

They were good words, Phoebe told herself. Good, strong words that deserved to be said. But perhaps saying them for the first time when still coupled with the man on his garden chaise wasn't the best choice of time and place.

Instead, she framed his face with her hands. "You were right. You made it perfect."

"Being with you . . ." He turned his head so his mouth pressed to her palm.

The gesture had her heart taking another stumble. Something fluttered inside her belly. "Being with me?"

His gaze leveled on hers. "Phoebe—"

Her cell phone rang.

"I jinxed it!" She struggled up. "I should *never* have said perfect." She thought of Carly, her mother, her brother. Snatched up the phone. "Phoebe MacNamara." The sound of Dave's voice didn't loosen the knots in her gut until she was certain it wasn't her family.

"Bonaventure? Where?" Without pen, paper or much of anything else, Phoebe took mental notes. "Yes. For me, specifically? I'm on Whitfield Island, at a friend's. I'll be there as soon as I can. All right. Yes, all right. I'll be headed out in five minutes."

In fact she was already up and hurrying toward the house as she spoke. "Tell him I'm en route. No, no, don't." She glanced at Duncan as he pushed the door open for her. "I have access to a very fast car, but I'll need a kit. I'll call you back when I'm on the road."

She clicked off.

"I need to borrow your Porsche."

"No problem, but it comes with me at the wheel."

"I can't take you where I'm going."

"Yes, you can," he corrected as they ran up the stairs.

"Duncan." She tossed off her robe as she rushed into his bedroom. "There's a man chained to a grave at Bonaventure Cemetery." She grabbed clothes. "All he's wearing, apparently, is a vest of explosives."

"If he's going to blow himself up, I hope he's already got a reservation. Bonaventure's pretty full up."

"He's the hostage," she snapped back as she pulled on clothes. "He's claiming to be, and he claims whoever strapped the bomb on him ordered him to call nine-one-one at a specific time, and ask for me by name. If I'm not there by one, whoever's holding the trigger pushes it, and he goes up."

"Only another reason I'll be driving. You don't know the car, I do— and I know the roads better. I'll get you where you need to be. When's the last time you drove a six-speed?" he demanded when he saw the argument in her eyes.

Phoebe dragged on her shoes, nodded. "You're right. Let's go."

It made more sense to have him driving the Porsche like a hellhound over the island roads toward the bridge. She had her hands and mind free to contact Dave, to take notes.

"He claims he can't give his name, not until you get here," Dave told her. "He's saying he's wired for sound as well as the bomb, and the person behind it can hear everything. He's wearing an ear bud and a mike."

"Is he lying?"

"I don't think so. I'll be there inside five minutes myself, but from the sound of it, my professional assessment would be he's scared shitless. On-scene reports there are a lot of fresh bruises on his face, his torso, arms and legs. So far, he hasn't told us who did it, how, when, why. He can't, he says. He can only tell you."

"The way we're moving, I'll be there inside fifteen. What grave is he chained to?"

"Jocelyn Ambuceau, 1898 to 1916."

"Unlikely that's random. It or she means something."

"Having it run."

"Tell me more about the unidentified man."

"White, mid-thirties, brown and brown. Solid build. Accent sounds local. No jewelry, no tats. Arms and legs in shackles, shackles hammered into the ground with posts. He's in his boxers, barefoot. He's broken down twice since officers arrived. Just cried like a baby. He's begging us not to let him die. Begging us to get you here. Get Phoebe."

"My first name? He calls me by my first name, like he knows me?"

"That's my take, yeah."

"Tell him I'm nearly there." As they roared around a turn, she braced a hand against the dash. "Make sure if anyone is listening, they can hear I'm nearly there." She looked at her watch. "I know it's nearly deadline, but we'll make it. Make sure they know I'm coming in. Ten minutes, Captain."

"I'm turning in now. I'll hold things until you get here."

She clicked off, looked at Duncan.

"You'll make it." His eyes stayed on the road as he took the car down the little two-lane road at a hundred and ten. "Have you ever dealt with something like this before?"

"No. Not like this." She spotted the lights up ahead, got Dave back on the phone. "I see the radio cars. Let them know we're not stopping at the gate. Have one lead us in."

The Porsche fishtailed on the turn, grabbed road and lunged forward again. It was a blur of moss-draped trees, ornate statuary that gleamed under the moon. Heat put a shimmer on the air, on the thin spit of ground fog. Then there were lights up ahead, through dripping arches of trees. The Porsche slammed to a halt behind the radio car, and Phoebe jumped out.

"You have to stay back," she shouted at Duncan as she dashed through gravestones and winged angels.

Dave moved toward her quickly, gripped her arm. "The bomb squad's marked off the minimum safe distance. Nobody goes beyond it. Not negotiable."

"All right, okay. Situation changes?"

"I just got here two minutes ago."

"Let me get started."

She went forward slowly now. Even with the lights there were pockets of dark. Someone handed her a vest, and she shrugged it on as she studied the weeping man sitting on the grave.

An angel looked out over him, her face serene, her wings spread wide. There was a lute clutched against her breasts.

Below, the man hunched with his face pressed to his updrawn knees, the sound of his weeping raw and harsh against the insect buzz. Pink roses—fresh to her eye—were scattered around him. "I'm Phoebe Mac-Namara," she began, and his head jerked up.

She froze, stopped in her tracks well before reaching the tape strung out by the bomb detail. Everything in her turned to ice, then thawed again in a sudden gush of hot panic.

"Roy."

"Jesus." Beside her Dave clamped a hand on her wrist. "I didn't see his face. I didn't recognize him." Wasn't entirely sure he would have. "Phoebe, you can't approach," Dave said over Roy's wild shouts. "You cannot approach."

"Understood. Understood." But panic sweat sprang onto her skin. "Roy, be quiet now. You have to calm down. Take a breath and calm down. I'm here now." While she spoke, she wrote quickly on her pad. *Check on my family! Cop on the door. Carly here.* She dashed down Phin's address. "We're going to be all right."

"He's going to kill me. He's going to kill me."

"Who?"

"I don't know. Oh God, I don't know. Why is this happening?"

"Can he hear us, Roy?"

"He says he can hear. Yes, he can hear. You . . . you fucking bitch. I have to say what he tells me or he'll blow it up."

"It's all right. If he can hear me, can he tell you what he wants?"

"I . . . I want you to shove some of this C-4 up your twat, you useless cunt."

"Do we know each other?"

"You cost me," Roy said with tears running down his cheeks. "Now I cost you."

"What did I cost you?"

"You're going to remember. Phoebe, help me, for God's sake, help me."

"All right, Roy. All right. Let me keep talking to him. You must be angry with me. Will you tell me why?"

"Not . . . not time yet."

"You called me out here, and I came. There must be something you want from me, something you want to tell me. If you'll explain to me why—"

"Fuck you," Roy said on a hitching sob.

"I feel as though you don't want to talk to me yet. Is it all right if I talk to Roy? Can I ask Roy questions?"

"He's laughing. He's laughing. He . . . Go ahead, have a nice chat. I need a beer."

"Roy, how did you get here?"

"He . . . drove." Eyes swollen from weeping and blows darted around the graveyard. "I think. In my car."

"What kind of car do you have?"

"M-Mercedes. E55. I just got it a few weeks ago. I just . . ."

"All right." She scribbled down the make of the car. *Find,* she wrote. "He drove your car from Hilton Head?"

"I was in the trunk of my car. I couldn't see. Blindfold, gag. Coming home, driving into the garage. In the garage. Gun to the back of my head." He pressed his battered face to his knees again. "Came up behind me. Then, I don't remember. I don't know until I woke up and I couldn't see or talk. Hard to breathe. In the trunk, tape over my mouth. Couldn't find air."

She took one relieved breath when Dave stepped back and wrote *All safe. Cop on doors.* "How long ago?"

"I don't *know.*"

"Okay, it's okay. How did you get here, where you are now?"

"Heard the trunk open." He lifted his head again, shivering. Phoebe could see the insects feasting on him. "Something over my face—got dizzy, tried to fight. Hit me, hit me in the face. I woke up, and I was here, like this. He was talking in my head. In my head. I screamed and I shouted, but nobody came. He talked in my head, told me what to do. My phone, he left me my phone, told me to call nine-one-one, what to say. Only that one call, he said, only say what he told me to say, or he'd push the button."

"You never saw him," Phoebe said as she scribbled down Roy's full name, address, telephone number, and wrote *How long missing?* under it, circled it twice before passing it to Dave.

"Roy . . ."

But he was sobbing now. "I didn't do anything. Why is this happening?"

"That's not helping, Roy. Roy!" She sharpened her voice enough to get through. "You need to try to stay calm. The important thing is for us to work together so we can resolve this. I'd like to talk to him again, if he's ready. I wonder if he could give me a name—it doesn't have to be his name, just any name he's comfortable with. So I'd have a way to address him."

"I feel sick. I feel . . . No! No! Don't! Please, don't!" Roy's eyes wheeled as he strained against the shackles. "Please, God . . . Okay . . . Okay. I . . . I'm—I'm tired of listening to you whine, you worthless piece of shit. Keep it up and—and I'll blow you to hell and be done with it."

"If you do that, I won't know why you wanted me out here tonight. Why you're angry. Will you give me a name to call you?"

"He—" Roy's teeth chattered. "S-sure, Phoebe. You can call me Cooper."

Though her throat tightened, she wrote the name clearly on the pad, followed it up with *High Noon.* "All right, Cooper. Since I can't talk to you directly, I can't hear how you feel. Can you tell me how you feel?"

"Powerful. In fucking charge."

"Is being in charge important to you?"

"Damn right."

"Wouldn't it be more direct, more in charge, if you and I talked face-to-face?"

"Not time."

She stared into Roy's flooded eyes, listened to Roy's tortured voice, and fought to get inside the head of a man she couldn't see, couldn't hear.

"Can you tell me how we know each other, Cooper? Where we know each other from?"

"You tell me something."

"All right. What do you want me to tell you?"

"Do you care about this . . . worthless son of a bitch?"

Tricky, she thought. Care too much or care too little, either could incite. "Do you mean Roy?"

"You know I mean fucking Roy asshole Squire."

"He's my ex-husband. I don't want to see him or anyone else hurt. You haven't really hurt anyone yet, Cooper. We can resolve this without—"

"Tell that to Charles Johnson. You see—you see— God, okay— Did you see how surprised he looked when those bullets hit him?"

"Are you telling me you're responsible for the death of Charles Johnson?"

"Can't you fucking understand fucking English, bitch? I put him in the ground. Not the first time you helped somebody into the ground, is it? Is it? Won't be the last, and that's a promise. Please," Roy wheezed. "Please, please, please." And he shuddered under the spreading wings of the angel.

"Did you know Charles Johnson?"

"Just another worthless gangbanger. But you got him to come out, didn't you? Got him to come out without doing any hostages. Nobody inside that place worth crap, but you saved them, didn't you?"

"Who didn't I save, Cooper? Are the roses for her? Who is it you cared about I didn't save?"

"Figure that out, Phoebe, figure it out and beg for forgiveness. Maybe you'll save yourself."

"I'll beg for forgiveness now. If I wasn't good enough or smart enough to save someone, I'll beg for forgiveness now. Tell me what you want me to say, and I will."

"Better get started. Say . . . what? No, no, no!" Roy tried to stand, could only kneel. "Please. Okay, okay. Say time's up. Goodbye, Phoebe."

"Cooper, if you—"

The blast lifted her off her feet, shot her back through a hot burst of air. She landed in a heap, across a stranger's grave.

She knew what was whizzing overhead, thudding into the ground. Pieces of an angel, pieces of dirt. Pieces of Roy.

Images flashed through her mind, fast, disjointed. The first time she'd met him, at a party, and the big megawatt smile he dazzled her with. Making love with him on the big bed in the hotel suite where he'd surprised her with a weekend, and roses, and champagne. The instant before their lips met the first time as husband and wife. Dancing. Lights.

Then blank dark.

Someone was shouting for her.

Phoebe pushed up to her elbows. She caught a blur of movement as Duncan dove. And he was over her, holding her down. Through a tunnel she heard more shouts, pounding feet, the crackle of radio static.

She didn't struggle; there was nothing to struggle for.

"What have I done?" she whispered. "Oh my God, what have I done?"

22

She'd told him to go home. It pissed him off. What the hell did she take him for?

Duncan paced the area outside her squad room. He couldn't sit; he couldn't settle, and he wished to God he couldn't think. Unfortunately, he could, and his mind kept sneaking back to that moment, that ohmyjesusgod moment when what had been a man had become . . . nothing.

Bits and pieces of meat and bone, and something like a horrible red fog.

He couldn't remember, not exactly, moving. He remembered feeling something—like a quick punch of air, and the sounds, whizzing and shouting, thunks—thunks of statuary and earth and God knew hitting trees and ground, other stones and statuary.

He knew he'd seen a piece of what had been Roy hanging in the lacy webs of Spanish moss. He thought he'd seen the stone angel's disembodied head fly, her face splattered with red, her smile peaceful and serene. But he might've imagined it.

He didn't remember running, walking, jumping toward Phoebe.

Just being there, he remembered just being there on top of her while the chaos boomed around them. He remembered hearing her say: *What have I done?* She said it over and over until someone—Dave, he thought, the captain—had pushed at him, pulled at them.

Are you hurt? Are you hit? That's what he'd asked first, Duncan was nearly sure of that. His face had been as white as the flying angel's.

It blurred some after that. Lots of movement, lots of sound, more sirens.

And she'd told him to go. She'd stood in the middle of that nightmare and told him to go. Fuck that.

She was in with the captain, that's what they'd told him. In with Captain McVee and some others. So he'd wait. He'd goddamn wait.

He wanted a drink. He wanted to be sick. He wanted to touch her just to assure himself one more time they'd both come through it whole.

But all he could do was wait.

"Dunc."

He turned, and his stomach did one hard shudder when he saw Phin striding from the elevator. For reasons he couldn't explain, seeing his friend had his legs going weak enough to have him sinking down onto a bench.

"Jesus. Oh Christ."

"You're okay?" Phin took a hard grip on Duncan's arm as he sat beside him. "You're bleeding. Are you okay?"

Dully, Duncan looked down at his shirt. "It's not my blood." Just a little souvenir from Bonaventure, a little memento of Roy. "But I think I've got a ways to go before I get within shouting distance of okay. Jesus, Phin. Fucking Christ Jesus."

"What the hell happened? Do they know what the hell happened?"

"He blew up. He just . . . It's not like the movies. Man, it's not like that." He pushed a hand through his hair. "Loo? The kids?"

"Fine. Kids are sleeping. We got cops around the house. This was Carly's father?"

"Roy. Roy Squire. Had him chained to the ground on a grave, strapped with explosives. Poor son of a bitch. Something about being grabbed out of his own garage, beaten up some, maybe drugged. Phoebe

was talking to the guy who did it through Roy—the ex. He had, ah . . ."
Duncan made a helpless gesture at his ear.

"Okay, I get it." Studying his friend's face, Phin pulled a flask out of
his hip pocket. "Take a slug, brother."

"I'd kiss you for this, but I'm not feeling romantic." Grateful,
Duncan took the flask and swallowed straight whiskey. "He was—
Roy—he was crying, begging. The guy . . . Cooper," Duncan remem-
bered. "He told Phoebe to call him Cooper. He wouldn't say what he
wanted, he wouldn't say why. Then he must've told Roy to say goodbye.
And he pushed the button, he set off the bomb. He blew apart, Phin.
Fuck, he just blew apart."

"Duncan, did you set the security before you left your house?"

"What? No." Had he? No. "We were out of there too fast."

"Okay, here's what I'm going to do. I'm going to make some calls,
get some people over there to do a sweep and to secure the place."

Duncan let his head fall back. "Because he went after Phoebe's ex, he
may come after me."

"No point in being sloppy, is there?"

"No, no point."

In the office, Phoebe sat ramrod straight. Her family was safe, and their
homes under guard. She could put that worry out of her mind. Roy was
dead; she couldn't change that. She had to block that guilt out of her
mind, her heart, her belly.

"Hilton Head PD is investigating. They've got a crime-scene unit
going over the house and garage. We're looking for the victim's car."

"The grave has to be symbolic of something or someone."

"We're getting the information."

"I need my family protected, not just for tonight—"

"Phoebe." Dave spoke quietly. "They will be."

"All right. He was engaged. I only know her first name—Mizzy. I
don't know if they were living together or—"

"It'll be taken care of."

Of course, yes, of course it would. "A personal attack of this nature has to stem from a personal grudge. Who have I pissed off, hurt, threatened?"

"We'll need to speak to Arnold Meeks."

"Yes." She drew a deep breath. "He needs to be interviewed and his whereabouts confirmed. But this wasn't his doing. He was a bad cop, he's no doubt a violent man, and a complete asshole. But he's not a killer. If what this Cooper told me tonight is fact, he's killed at least twice now. In cold blood. Meeks acts in rage, short-term planning, without factoring in the consequences."

"Someone acting on his behest. With or without his knowledge."

"Maybe. But I think it's more personal yet. You hurt me, I'll hurt you, and a whole lot worse. Something I did or didn't do. Someone I didn't save."

When she closed her eyes, pressed her fingers against her lids, all she could see was Roy. She dropped her hands into her lap. "A failure, a professional failure that was personal to him. Who did I lose, Dave? When? How? I need to go back over my case files, all the way back. Any hostage or hostage-takers, any cop or bystander, anyone who was injured or killed during an incident where I was negotiator.

"I think it's going to be a woman," she added.

"Why?"

"Because he's Gary Cooper. Because Roy was chained to a woman's grave. We can't discount anyone, but I think it's going to be a woman. He knows, or he's learned how to handle, weapons and explosives. Maybe he was trained in the military or law enforcement. Or maybe he trained himself. Because he planned this. Roy wasn't impulse, not spur of the moment."

She pounded her fisted hand on her thigh. "I couldn't *hear*. How could I listen and know how to respond, know how to bring him down when I couldn't hear his voice, the inflection, the emotion?"

"Phoebe, you're not responsible for this."

"Then why did he set it off? Did I ask the wrong question, choose the wrong tack? All the time, trouble, the risk he took to get Roy where he wanted him, to get me there, then he ends it? I have to listen to the tape, I have to figure out what I said—or didn't say—what pushed him to end it."

He swiveled his chair until they were knee-to-knee, face-to-face. "You know better than that."

"Under normal circumstances, we all try to know better than that. But this wasn't normal circumstances. It was about me this time."

"What you said or didn't may not be the answer."

"No. He's killed two people, because of their connection to me. I have to know why. We have to find the answer, Dave, because he has no reason to stop at two. He's been outside my house." She closed her eyes again. "He may try for someone I love next."

"He won't get near them."

"He can't once we identify him, find him, stop him. I . . . I need to contact Roy's fiancée. And I have to tell Carly. I have to find a way to tell Carly."

"What you have to do right now is go home, get some sleep. Take a little time, Phoebe. It might be a good idea for you to talk to the counselor about this."

"The best cure for guilt and misplaced responsibility in the negotiator is work, study and training." She managed a ghost of a smile. "Someone wise has been known to say that, often."

"Maybe I have, but in this case, you need sleep first. We'll talk about the rest of it later."

When she walked out of Dave's office, she went straight into the women's room and finally let herself be sick. Viciously, violently sick.

Emptied out, skin clammy, eyes running, she sat back against the stall door until she got her breath back. She didn't weep. This had gone far beyond anything as simple and cleansing as tears. She simply sat on the floor, back braced, until she was sure she wouldn't be sick again.

Then, after rising, she walked to the sink to wash her face, to rinse out her mouth with cupped handfuls of cold water. He'd been looking into her eyes, she thought as she lifted her head to look into her own now. He'd been looking straight into her eyes, his full of fear and pleas, this man she'd once loved. This man she'd made a child with.

Then he was gone. Gone, she thought, because she once loved him and made a child with him. Not for his own sins, but because she met him one night at a party, and let herself love.

So she'd find the answers. She'd search until she found them.

After drying her face, shoving her dampened hair away from it, she started toward her office. She'd go home—Dave was right about that. But she'd take some files with her. The odds of getting any real sleep were slim, so she could work off the hours, and maybe find some answers.

She didn't see Duncan until he was pushing to his feet and walking toward her.

"You should've gone home."

"Don't even start that crap with me, okay?"

"What?"

"Goddamn it, Phoebe." He took her arms. Then he just jerked her against him. "Okay, fight later. Let's just do this for a minute."

"I'm sorry. I'm sorry you had to go through that."

"Yeah, me, too, and back at you." He eased her back to take a good study of her face. Her eyes were reddened, shadowed, exhausted. "I'll take you on home now."

No car, she remembered. She didn't have her car. "I have to get a few things out of my office first."

"I'll wait."

"Duncan—" She broke off when she saw Phin coming toward them, clicking his cell phone closed.

"Carly."

"She's fine. She's fine." Phin kept walking, opened his arms and took Phoebe in. "She's sound asleep. Got a patrol car out in front of the house, another couple cops out the back, and my fierce wife and lovely dog inside."

It surprised a muffled laugh out of her. "Thank you. I should go by and get her, bring her home."

"Honey, it's four in the morning. Since it was damn near midnight before the giggling stopped, I bet those girls are going to be sleeping a few hours yet. Why don't Loo and I bring her home after she's up and around? We'll call you first, then bring her home. How's that?"

"Good. That's good. No point in waking her up to . . . No point. I'm grateful, Phin, grateful to you and Loo, and I'm sorry."

"No need to be either about this."

"I need to get a few things. I'll only be a minute."

Phin watched her go. "She holds up pretty good."

"She's got that strong spine. Something that appealed to me right off. Everything okay on the home front?"

"Taken care of. I'm going to go on. You get some sleep, you hear. We'll talk about all this later."

Duncan gave him a bump on the shoulder. "Thanks."

When Phoebe came back, Duncan stepped over to take her overloaded briefcase. "Good idea. You're going to work from home for a while."

"Not instead of, in addition to."

"Only so many hours in the day, Phoebe."

"So I need to make good use of as many as I can. This is police business, Duncan."

"Oh, don't pull that crap on me either."

She remained silent a moment, ordered herself not to respond. But her willpower snapped when they stepped off the elevator. "I seem to be pulling quite a bit of crap on you tonight."

"Yeah, and I can't say I care for it."

"Then you ought to just go on. I can get my own way home."

"In about one more minute, I'm going to take this shovel I'm using to pitch away this crap and hit you over the head with it. I've had a bad night, too, Phoebe, so watch where you push."

"I told you to go home, didn't I? I said—"

She didn't say a thing more as the breath whooshed right out of her when he whipped her around and pushed her back against his car. She'd seen him irked a time or two, even seen him on the edge of nasty temper. But this was the first time she saw the full-blown affair.

His eyes had the hard, hot look of a man who could and would kick any number of asses, then gesture for more to come on.

"We found out I like aggressive women—thanks for that. I like strong women, and smart women. I like women who can handle themselves. I like, apparently, a woman who knows where the hell she's going and how she wants to get there. You getting this?"

"You're hurting my arms, Duncan."

He eased his hold a fraction. "What I don't like is being told what to do, or how I should feel or what I should think. I don't like being fucking dismissed when—"

"I didn't mean—"

"Shut up, Phoebe. I'm not finished. I don't like being dismissed when a smart, strong, knows-how-to-handle-herself woman figures she doesn't need me anymore. I don't like, and I won't tolerate, being told it's none of my non–police ass's business when I stood out there tonight and saw that poor bastard blown to pieces. So go ahead, Phoebe, tell me one more time to go on home."

Her breath shuddered out once before she controlled it. "I didn't think I could face you again tonight."

"What? Why?"

"I wasn't sure . . . I thought I might break down if I did, or worse, that you'd look at me differently. I don't know. It's not rational, it's emotional, all right? I've got plenty of goddamn emotions."

"I'll say. Phoebe, first, if you'd broken down—"

"I said it wasn't logical." The shove she gave him to push him back had a little heat along with it. "Don't stand there trying to make it logical."

"Good point." He considered a minute, then reached into his back pocket for the flask Phin had given him.

"Oh God. Thank you." She took a short sip, then a long drink. "Oh Jesus." She leaned back against the car. "Oh Jesus, Duncan."

"I never . . ." He took back the flask for another quick pull. "It's not like I ever imagined. What happens to a person."

"The bomb guys call it pink mist."

He capped the flask, opened the car door for her. "You've been through it before?"

"Not like this." She waited until he was behind the wheel. "I've been on teams, a few times, when we weren't there soon enough, or something went wrong. I've never seen . . . nothing like this. I was so mad at him, I was so *angry*. About him getting married again and moving to Europe without giving Carly a thought." She rubbed the heels of her hands on her eyes. "I think it's worse, it's worse having those feelings in me for him than if we'd managed to be friends, or at least friendly. But that's what I had in me for him."

"That's not what I saw out there at Bonaventure. You weren't thinking about how mad you were. You were thinking about saving his life."

"Didn't think hard enough. And that's destructive," she said before he could speak. "I know it. It's indulgent and egotistical. Duncan, are you going to consider it more crap if I tell you it's best if we don't see each other for a while? If I tell you because the man who killed Roy may decide it's more fun to go after someone current in my life, it's best if there's some distance between us."

"Plenty of distance between you and Roy."

"Yes, but—"

"I'd consider it crap. And if I give you the respect of admiring the fact you can handle yourself, I'd appreciate the quid pro quo."

She said nothing, just pulled out her badge as they approached her house. "Let me ID us to the radio car first." She stepped out, crossed over.

He waited by the car while she had a brief conversation. She'd have noticed, he assumed, that there were lights on inside the house. No one, it seemed, was getting a good night's sleep.

"I'm not telling you to go home," she began, "because I don't want to get beaned with that shovel. I'm just going to tell you that you don't have to stay."

In answer he simply took her hand. Ava opened the door as they stepped onto the veranda. "I'm so glad you're home!" She dashed out barefoot to wrap her arms around Phoebe. "They said you weren't hurt."

"I'm not. Mama?"

"I'm here." Her face gray, Essie stood a foot back from the open door. "Phoebe. Phoebe."

So the veranda was lost to her, for now, Phoebe thought, and moved into the house quickly to take her mother into her arms. "I'm fine. I promise."

"They said there was trouble, something bad. Carly—"

"Is fine. You know she's fine. She's sleeping."

"And . . . and Carter and—"

"Mama. Mama. You need to breathe. You need to keep breathing. Look at me now, and you listen. Everyone is fine. Carter and Josie and

Carly. You and Ava. I'm right here, too. Duncan's here. He brought me home."

Even as she spoke, Phoebe could see her mother was falling into a panic attack. Her breath was short and choppy—quick, strained indrawn gasps. The shakes had started. Sweat beaded on Essie's face.

"Ava."

Together, Phoebe and Ava eased Essie down to the floor before her legs buckled.

"Mama. I'm right here, Mama. Feel my hand?" She glanced up as Duncan draped the throw from the back of the parlor sofa over Essie's shaking shoulders. "Feel my hands, Mama? Rubbing your arms? Hear my voice? Take a nice breath now."

It eased, bit by stingy bit, minute by endless minute.

"All right now, all right." Phoebe drew Essie close, stroking her hair. "Nice deep breaths now. There you are."

"I couldn't stop it. I'm so sorry, Phoebe."

"Ssh. Ssh. It's all over now."

"Here, Essie, why don't you drink a little water?"

Essie looked over as Duncan crouched to offer a glass. "Oh, Duncan. I'm so embarrassed."

"Sip a little water. I'm going to go make y'all some tea."

"Oh, but—"

"You're not going to make me feel like company, are you, Essie?"

A tear dripped down her cheek as she shook her head. "Phoebe, I'm so sorry. I'm so sorry. You shouldn't have to come home and worry like this about me. You look so tired."

"We're all tired. Come on now, Ava and I are going to get you up and get you to the sofa."

"Ava, you should go in and make that tea. That poor man. What must he think of this household?"

"Don't worry about Duncan." Ava helped Essie to the sofa. "Are you cold?"

"No, I'm fine now. I—" She passed a hand over her face and grimaced at the sweat. "Look at me! Like I had the mother of all hot flashes."

"I'm going to get you a cool cloth."

"I couldn't stop it," Essie told Phoebe when they were alone.

"I know."

"You wish I'd take the medicine, but most of the time I'm fine the way things are. I was just so worried. We were both so worried. Then wouldn't you know when you're home and I know you're safe, I have a spell like that."

She reached out, touched Phoebe's face. "Something very bad happened."

"Yes, something very bad. Mama, I've got some of the pills. You could take one. I don't want you upset."

"I'm all right now. You said Carly and Carter and Josie weren't hurt. Or Dave?"

"Dave's fine."

"Okay. Okay. I'll be all right with anything else."

Ava came back with a small white basin and a damp cloth.

"You better sit down, Ava."

She told them about Roy. Though Essie's face went sheet white again, she didn't have another attack. She and Ava sat together on the couch, gripping hands. Duncan said nothing when he came in, just passed around the tea, then sat while Phoebe finished.

It was Essie who rose to sit on the arm of Phoebe's chair. She put her arm around her daughter's shoulders, eased Phoebe's head against her and stroked.

"Oh, Mama."

"I'm sorry, baby. I'm so sorry. What a terrible thing. Poor Roy. Poor Roy. The man was useless as tits on a bull, but he didn't deserve to die like that."

"Mama!"

"People who say not to speak ill of the dead are hypocrites, because you can take it to the bank they're thinking ill."

Essie looked over, saw Duncan struggling against a grin. "And look at you, just worn out, too, aren't you? But the house is all locked up. Locked up tight and we're safe inside it. You need to rest awhile."

"Yes, we all need to rest." Phoebe took Essie's hand. "I'd never let anyone hurt you."

"We'll all go rest. Duncan, you're going to stay. It's safe in the house, so you'll stay. Come on, baby girl. Duncan's going to stay in with you so you're not alone. You'll sleep better."

When Phoebe lifted her eyebrows, Essie just shook her head and continued to walk her out of the parlor. "As if I had no idea the two of you haven't found your way into bed together already. Sun's going to be up before long. We'll all get some rest. We'll have a late breakfast."

Ava nodded at Phoebe over Essie's head, then slid an arm around Essie's waist. "Eggs Benedict? Won't that be fine, Essie? And fresh berries."

Phoebe sighed as Ava walked her mother down the hall to Essie's bedroom. "She's closed the worst of it out of her mind for a while. It's too big right off, so she keeps it out."

"Sounds like a healthy idea to me."

Phoebe turned into her bedroom. "If she can keep her mind on something else like eggs Benedict, she won't panic. But eventually, it'll claw its way in."

"Phoebe."

She sat on the edge of the bed, looking up wearily as she pulled off her shoes.

"I'd say what happened tonight, and the overall threat of what could happen? That earns a good dose of panic."

"Hard to argue. God. I'm too tired to get undressed." She simply lay down on top of the spread, curled on her side.

Duncan slid in behind her, spooned her. "Didn't expect our first overnight would end up with us both fully dressed."

"Duncan? I want to say that I appreciate the fact that you shovel away the crap when I get into one of those get-away-and-let-me-do-this-all-by-myself spells."

He smiled into her hair. "I'm going to buy a couple of spare shovels tomorrow."

"That sounds like a good idea." She took his hand in hers, pressed it between her breasts.

And within moments, Essie proved right. Phoebe did sleep better with him there.

23

With Carly curled in her lap, Phoebe rocked and stroked as she used to when Carly was a baby. She knew what it was like to lose a father, to be told he was gone and never coming back. The hitch and jolt of it, the impossibility of the concept of death and forever to a child.

But she didn't know, couldn't know, what it was to lose a father she'd never really had. Or to lose anyone to such sudden and stunning violence.

No matter how she'd softened or edited the details, it was still horrible. And those details would eke through, like fetid water through a crack in a wall—widening little by little from the whispers of neighbors, the blasts on television, the questions from other children at school.

There was no shoring it all up, blocking it all out. So it was best, always best, to be as honest as possible.

"Did it hurt?" Carly asked her.

"I don't know. I just don't know. I hope not."

"How come he had to die here when he didn't live here?"

"I'm not sure. I'm going to try to find out."

Carly nestled in closer. "Is it bad I didn't love him?"

"No, baby." Phoebe could only hold tighter. "No."

"I didn't love him, but I didn't wish he would die."

"I know. Me, too. I know."

"Poppy's granddad died, and she went to the funeral, where he was dead in a big box. Do I have to go to the funeral?"

"No. I don't know if there's going to be one, or where or when. We weren't . . . it's not up to us. If I find out and you want to go—"

"I don't. Is that okay? Please, I don't want to."

"That's fine." The quick fear in Carly's voice had Phoebe rocking again. "You're not to worry about that, sweetie."

"What if he hurts you? The man who hurt Roy, what if—"

"I'm not going to let that happen. Carly—"

"The other man hurt you. He hurt your face and your arm." Tears trembled now as Carly rubbed her hands on Phoebe's cheeks. "What if he comes back and hurts you again, or he kills you like Roy got killed? Mama."

"He's not going to come back and hurt me. The police are going to make sure he doesn't. Isn't that what I do, Carly? You have to trust me to take care of you and Gran and Ava, and myself. Even Carter and Josie. We're going to be careful. Don't cry now, listen to me. Listen, okay? We're going to be so careful," Phoebe said gently. "We're going to have police right outside the house for a while, even inside if it makes you feel safer."

"If he comes into the house, will they shoot him with their guns? Will you?"

Oh, well, God. "He won't get into the house. But if he did, we'd do whatever we had to do to be safe. I promise you. We're all going to be careful, right? So you'll remember everything I told you about talking to strangers, and getting into someone's car—even going near the car. No matter what they say to you, no matter what they tell you. What do you do instead of going near the car?"

"I yell *no* as loud as I can and I run away."

"That's exactly right. We're all going to be fine, baby, because I'm going to find out who did this to Roy. Then he's going to go to prison. And he'll never get out again."

"Will you find out soon?"

"I'm going to try. And Uncle Dave's going to try. All the police I work with? They're all going to try."

Satisfied, comforted, Carly laid her head back on Phoebe's breast. "Are you sad, Mama?"

"I am. I am sad."

"Are you scared?"

Truth, Phoebe thought—but simple truth. "I'm scared enough to be careful, and to work really hard to find out why this happened. You know what happens when I work really hard?"

The smallest hint of a smile curved Carly's lips. "You get the job done."

"That's exactly right." She gathered Carly close, spoke almost to herself. "That's exactly right."

She got the call, and had to go. It was difficult, more difficult than she'd prepared herself for to leave her family. Cops on the door, she reminded herself. But none of those cops was her. She'd consider the control issue some other time, Phoebe told herself. But right at the moment, she wished that she could split herself into two parts, and that one of them could stand watch over the house and everyone in it.

She hated, too, that she'd had to ask Carter and Josie to move in temporarily. It was safer, and more efficient to have the people she considered most at risk under one roof.

But it was still a hell of a thing to ask a couple who were basically still on their honeymoon.

Yet they'd come. There was little, she knew, Carter wouldn't do for her. And less yet, Phoebe thought, he wouldn't do to make sure his wife was safe and sound.

And still, come morning, they'd all have to go on—to some extent—with their lives. To work, to the market, to the bank. She'd keep Carly home from school—just a day or two of indulgence there—until she was confident her daughter could be protected outside the house.

For now, she went downstairs to tell her family she had to leave.

And was surprised to see Duncan huddled in the parlor with Carter and Josie. She'd assumed he went home after she took Carly upstairs to tell her about her father.

They stopped talking when she stepped in, and every eye turned to her.

"Plots, plans?" she said, in a halfhearted attempt to keep it light. "Duncan, I didn't realize you were still here."

"Thought I'd hang around awhile. How's the kid?"

"She's a tough little bird. She'll be okay. She went down the back way to see my mother in the kitchen. Carter, Jo . . . Lousy situation, that's about all I can say. I have a number I'd like both of you to log into your cell phones. Direct line to the precinct, and a situation room set up for your protection. Anything, anything at all strikes you as off, you call it. Duncan, I'd appreciate it if you'd log in the number, too."

"Do you really think this lunatic would try to hurt one of us?" Josie asked her.

"I'm not going to take the chance." Stress, Phoebe noted, around Josie's usually cheerful eyes. Death threats weren't the norm for a hospice nurse who marries a schoolteacher. "You're on a case now, right?"

"Yeah. I'm taking the seven-to-four shift, cancer patient. Private home on Bull Street."

"Good, close to my cop shop. If you could write down all the particulars, all the names—the other nurses, the people in the house, your routine, it'll be helpful. Same for you, Carter—your class schedule, meetings, everything. Duncan—"

"I'm probably a little less structured, schedule-wise."

"Have you considered private security? Just temporarily."

"I'm not having some hulk walking two steps behind me. My house is covered; I've taken care of it. You've got enough to worry about. I'll worry about me."

"I'm not egotistic enough to say this is happening because of me. It's not. But I'm pissed enough—and I'm good enough—to say I'm going to find out who's trying to get to me through the people in my life. And doing that is one of the reasons I have to go."

"You're going out?" Carter moved forward immediately to take her arm. "Phoebe, the point is he's trying to get to *you*. Herding us up eliminates his being able to hurt any of us. And gives him more reason to go straight at you."

"If and when, I'll be ready. Carter, I've got a child who needs me. I don't intend to be careless or stupid. Dave's coming by to pick me up, and I'm going into the station house, where I'll be surrounded by other cops."

"Being surrounded by cops didn't stop one of them from sending you to the hospital," Josie pointed out.

"No, and I won't be that easy a mark again. Arnie Meeks is the reason I need to go in. He's being brought in for questioning. I need to be there. I need you to stay here, to keep everything as calm and normal as possible." She touched Carter's cheek. "Roy wasn't prepared. Why should he have been? But we are. And we're going to get through this. It's what we do, isn't it? Get through."

"Mama's scared to death."

"I know." Nothing could be done about it. "I'm counting on you. And I'm resting easier on that count having a nurse in residence. You're taking a lot of weight off me, Josie."

"We'll be fine," Josie assured her. "We were just talking about what we could do to keep things as normal as possible. Food, games, music. Business," she added with a quick smile at Duncan.

"I thought Essie and I could come up with a business plan."

"Good. That's good. Keep them busy, will you? And when they ask, tell them I'm with Dave. I'll be back soon. Duncan, maybe you could walk me out."

"Sure."

She waited until they were on the veranda. "It has to be said," she began. "You'd be smarter, safer and certainly saner if you went home, kept your distance. Not only from me, but from my family."

He nodded as he studied the lovely tree-lined street. "Didn't help Roy much, did it?"

"No." Blunt help, she discovered. Straight to the point. "You have the resources to go anywhere, and for any length of time. You could get out of Savannah for a while, and those resources would also ensure no one outside your inner circle had to know where you are."

"Cut and run."

"It's not running, and you'll still have your balls in Tahiti or wherever."

"Easy to say when you don't have any balls—so to speak—in the first place. I'm not going to Tahiti. Savannah's my home, and I have projects in the works I'm not prepared—okay, not willing—to put on hold. And I'm not ditching the redheads to go drink mai tais. But you knew that."

"Deduced that," she corrected. "Still, it had to be said. I also have every confidence you'll take care of yourself, but that doesn't mean I won't worry—and you knew that. So I need to ask you to check in, every two hours. A quick call, a text message, I don't care how you check in, but I need you to do it."

"I can agree to that, if it's reciprocal."

She lifted her eyebrows. "You want me to check in with you?" Brows still lifted, she flipped back her jacket where her badge was clipped to her waistband.

"Yeah, real pretty. I call you, two hours later you call me, two hours later, back to me. That's how it works."

She tapped her fingers on her badge as she studied him. "You might be good in my line of work. That's agreed. Here." She handed him a piece of paper. "Emergency number's on there. If you could make sure everyone inside has it on both cells and the house line, I'd appreciate it."

She turned, scanned the street, the trees, the cars, over to the park. "He could be watching the house. He could be anywhere."

"Let's give him something to look at." He pulled her close, covered her mouth with his.

As he started to ease her back, she wrapped her arms tight for one hard embrace. "Don't take any chances. Zero chances. If it even seems like it might somehow be related to taking a chance, don't."

"Yoo-hoo!"

Phoebe's nerves were stretched tightly enough that even recognizing Lorelei Tiffany's voice, she laid a hand on the butt of her weapon. But her tone was easy when she turned and waved. "Hey there, Miz Tiffany."

"Don't you two make a picture! That's a handsome man you got there, Phoebe. Few years ago, I'd've stolen him right out from under you."

Decked in daffodil yellow, with little Maximillian Dufree coordinating with leash, collar and bow tie, Mrs. Tiffany sent Duncan a flirtatious smile.

"Ma'am. When the woman's as delicious as you, I'd be the one doing the stealing."

Mrs. Tiffany let loose a girlish giggle. "Oh, you! Better keep a hold of that one, Phoebe. Maximillian Dufree and I are about to take a turn in the park, if y'all like to join us."

"I wish we could."

"Don't blame you. I'd find something more energetic than dog-walking to do if I had a handsome man like that around. Bye now."

"Normal," Phoebe murmured when the pair clipped off. "There's still a lot of normal in the world."

"Savannah's a world where a dog in a yellow bow tie's pretty normal. I saw that hairless dog humping a pink toy poodle across the way a while back. I guess that's normal, too."

"For Maximillian Dufree, it is. The pink poodle would be Lady Delovely, who carelessly seduces Maximillian Dufree—despite his lack of essential equipment—and all the other dogs—including several females of her acquaintance—with wanton regularity."

She watched Mrs. Tiffany, in bright yellow glory, breeze into the park. "I wish we could do something as nice and normal as walk in the park and watch a couple of silly-looking dogs."

Duncan ran a hand down Phoebe's arm when Dave's car pulled in. "You take care, Phoebe. We'll get down to some normal of our own real soon."

"Counting on it." She took one last look at him, one last look at the house, and walked down to Dave's car.

"Everybody okay?" Dave asked her.

"Holding."

"Mr. Lucky appears to be sticking."

She glanced back, saw Duncan still standing on the veranda. "He does. I think that's one of the things he's good at. He's good at sticking. So are you," she added. "You stuck by my whole family, all these years. Which makes you a target, Dave. You're as close to me as any of my family, a hell of a lot closer to me than Roy was."

"I'm taking precautions." He took one hand off the wheel to pat hers.

"Be sure." She shifted toward him. "You've been my father since I was twelve. The one I looked up to, depended on and, in a lot of ways, the one I've tried to emulate. If he knows me, and he must, he knows that."

This time his hand squeezed hers. "I've been proud of you since before I ever met you face-to-face. Fact is, I love you like my own. I'm not going to let him use me to hurt you. All right?"

"Yes. Yes. All right." She took in a breath, let it go. "Why did they bring Arnie in? I thought they were going to question him informally at home."

"They did, or attempted to, then hauled him in when he took a swing at one of the detectives. Little bastard put his own ass in the sling."

"Short fuse," Phoebe replied. "The man who killed Roy has a long one. Long and cold. Arnie Meeks doesn't fit the profile, Dave."

"Maybe not. Could be he has a friend or family member who does. Let's put it through the process, Phoebe. One step, then the next."

He hadn't asked for a lawyer. That was to prove he was a hard-ass, Phoebe concluded as she studied Arnie through the one-way glass. It was also monumentally stupid. He'd been a cop long enough to know better, but he wanted to show that he could tough it out, this was no big deal.

He wore a gray T-shirt and jeans, scuffed Nike low-tops and a surly expression. He hadn't shaved, so there was a rough stubble on his face that suited the look in his eye. The screw-you-all look.

He'd hurt and humiliated her, laid in wait for her and violated her. She understood the knot squeezed in her sternum was a normal, natural reaction to that, to standing here looking at the man who'd bound and beaten and stripped her.

But she couldn't loosen it.

"You don't have to do this." Dave put a hand on her shoulder, gave it a quick squeeze.

"Yes, I do."

"You've already faced him down once, Phoebe. There's nothing to prove."

"I have to do this. I have to see him while they question him." *Look in his eyes, listen to his voice.* "It's the only way I'll know, that I can be sure, if he's the one who killed Roy. Or if he knows who did."

"I'm going to say what has to be said. You don't owe Roy anything."

"Maybe not. But I owe it to Carly. I'll be fine."

Fine might have been an exaggeration, but she got through and that was good enough. She watched Sykes and Liz double-team him, work him around, and poke and prod at Arnie's non-answers. All three knew how to play the game, she thought. But Arnie was outnumbered, out-matched.

"Can't deny you've got it in for Lieutenant MacNamara," Sykes said casually.

"Old news."

"A man pounds on a woman that way, it never gets old. The kind of man who does that?" Sykes stopped, shook his head. "On my gauge he's low enough to do anything."

"Oughta have your gauge checked."

"Tell you what mine says, *Arnie.*" Liz circled around to speak from behind him. "It says you're a fucking coward. The kind of sick son-of-a-bitching coward who'd blow some helpless bastard to pieces. Did it make you feel big? Make you feel *important* to take him out?"

"I didn't even know the asshole. I told you. I never touched the bas-tard. Why would I? Seems to me he had the good sense to dump that know-it-all bitch. I'da bought him a drink if I'd met him."

"He was nothing to you, right?" Liz leaned in. "Nothing but a tool you could use to fuck with the lieutenant."

"I don't need to fuck with her. Like I said, old news."

"How do you like playing rent-a-cop for a bunch of yuppies in Calvin Klein suits, tourists in flip-flops, Arnie? Bet that never gets old."

Arnie's face darkened—anger, Phoebe thought, and more. Embar-rassment.

"It's temporary."

"Oh yeah? You think your daddy's going to get you back on the job?" Drumming the flats of his hands on his own belly, Sykes let out a hoot. "Pig's eye, Arnie, and you know it. You're done, broke the family chain. Some bitch cost me my badge, I'd sure as hell want payback. Why don't you tell us where you were last night, Arnie? Where you were from ten to three in the morning?"

"I *told* you. I was home, with my wife."

"Stupid to lie, don't you think? Doesn't show a bright light." Sykes tapped his temple. "Especially when the wife's not too happy with you to begin with." Sykes pushed through the file in front of him. "Her statement says she doesn't know when you got home, but you weren't there when she went to bed at eleven."

"She's wrong." After a shrug, Arnie tipped his head back to study the ceiling. "I was down in the den, fell asleep watching TV."

"She locked up, Arnie. She did the walk-through before she went up to bed. If you were there, snoozing in front of the tube, where was your car?"

"She didn't see it. She's pissed at me, sure. Just giving me a hard time."

"He's lying," Phoebe stated. "He's lying about being home. And he's nervous."

"She can't place you on the day of the Johnson shooting either. Too bad."

"It was my day off, goddamn it." Anger punched through the shaky nonchalance. "I was running errands. I had things to do."

"Yeah, things to do," Liz agreed. "Like set yourself up in an apartment window and shoot an unarmed man, a surrendering teenager."

"Fuck that. Fuck this. Fuck you. I'm not getting screwed on this because that bitch MacNamara wants more blood. She's got you bowing and scraping and doing whatever she wants. I wanted to kill anybody, you can bet your ass it'd be her."

"Killing her ex in front of her, that's a handy way to shove it in her face. Killing Johnson after she'd spent hours talking him down, that's rubbing it in." Sykes shot out his index finger like the barrel of a gun. "You've got a twenty-two pistol, Arnie. You shouldn't have left the slug in that dumb rabbit."

"What? What rabbit? What the fuck are you talking about?"

"He's not lying about that." Phoebe shook her head. "He doesn't know what they're talking about."

"Once we match the bullet and the gun, we'll have ourselves stalking and harassment charges. Breaks your probation. You'll do time. You'll go inside. No way your daddy's going to be able to dig you out this time."

"Leave my father out of this."

"You won't," Liz tossed back. "You'll be calling Daddy for help any minute. We'll match the bullets from the rabbit. Then there's the dead snake, the dead rat. Upped it from the doll you mutilated and left for her. I'm betting you upped it from wildlife to Roy Squire."

"I don't know anything about any damn dead rabbit."

"The doll," Phoebe said quietly, even as Sykes narrowed his eyes.

"You know something about the doll, don't you? You got sweatier over the doll."

"I don't know what you're talking about."

"Messed up the doll like you'd planned to mess up the lieutenant," Sykes continued. "Rang her bell one night and left it outside her door. Then the dead rat, then right up to Roy Squire. Yeah, smells like pattern to me."

"That's bullshit. Maybe I tossed a doll by her house, so what? That was weeks ago, and I haven't gone near her place since. I haven't gone near MacNamara since . . ."

"Since you beat her in the stairwell?" Sykes finished. "Since you put a fucking bag over her head and stripped her down? You don't have any friends here, Arnie. Nobody wants to help you, so you keep lying. Makes me warm inside. You keep right on lying your way into a cage, and this time there's going to be a hotshot on the other side. There's a needle waiting for you, you sack of shit."

"You're out of your goddamn mind." Arnie was sheet white now, and running sweat. "I didn't kill anybody. I didn't shoot any damn rabbit either."

"We got motive, means, opportunity. Yeah, keep lying, fuckhead. You know how the DA loves it when a coward killer whines and lies. He'll go for the needle, no question."

"I didn't *know* the son of a bitch. I haven't been to Hilton Head where you said he lives. You can't put me there."

"Give us time. I was never happy, were you, Liz, with the way this asshole skated after messing with the lieutenant?"

"Me, I wanted to see him get some serious tuning on that. This time . . ."

"She's behind it." Arnie swiped the back of his hand over his mouth. "You know damn well. Trying to set me up, that's what she's doing. I saw the damn doll at a yard sale, just used it to give her something to think about. I didn't kill anyone, I haven't been to goddamn Hilton Head. She's trying to fuck me over. She can go to hell. I wasn't anywhere near Bonaventure last night."

"Where were you, Arnie? Prove it, and make this go away."

"I got me a girlfriend, okay? My wife's not giving me any support, or any sex, or anything else. So I've got someone who will. I was with her last night at her place. And I was banging her until after two in the morning."

"Name." Liz shoved a notebook across the table. "Address. We'll ask her how much she got banged."

"She's got a husband, okay? He was up at Myrtle Beach playing golf for a few days, so we used her place. You've got to let me talk to her first, tell her this is serious shit so she won't blow it off. Her husband finds out, he'll knock her around. She has to know you're not going to use her name."

"Let you talk to her first, prime her?" Sykes snorted out derision. "Not going to happen, Arnie. You're telling the truth, we'll keep her out of it. Sounds like you deserve each other."

"My wife's already talking divorce, and all because MacNamara—"

"Oh yeah, all this is MacNamara's fault. Sure. She tricked you into busting her up just so you'd get tossed off the job. Write the name down, Arnie."

"She's an exec at Terrance, Inc. You go see her there, not at her place. You go talk to her at her office. You have to give me the courtesy of being discreet."

Sykes's eyes were hard as stone. "You lost the right to courtesy from anyone here when you jumped Lieutenant MacNamara in that stairwell.

You remember that, asshole. Ain't nobody on your side. You want to save yourself, you write down the name. Otherwise, you're going in on assaulting an officer and you're staying in until we put all these ducks in a row."

As he wrote, Phoebe turned to Dave.

"It wasn't him. He's a pig, and he's stupid with it. He didn't kill Charles Johnson or Roy. He hasn't got the stones or the smarts." She turned back to the glass. "He'd really like to hurt me. He'd still like to make me pay. But he wouldn't understand that killing that boy, that killing Roy, hurts me, that it makes me pay. He doesn't understand me at all. Whoever did those things does."

"We'll check out the woman, see if the alibi holds."

"Yeah. I'm going home. I'll start going through the files. He'll be in there. He's in there somewhere."

As Phoebe stepped out of observation, Liz slipped out of the interview room. "I was just coming back to talk to you. Got a minute?"

"Sure."

"Let's, ah . . ." Liz glanced over, gestured toward the women's room. "Take it in here."

When they were inside, Liz leaned back on a sink. "Hard for you, watching that. Watching him. The glass isn't much of a barrier."

"Yeah, it was, and no, it's not. But it had to be done."

"He's not the guy, Phoebe."

"No, he's not the guy. You and Bull did good in there. His alibi's going to check out, and we'll be able to eliminate that avenue."

"How are you holding up?"

"Truth? I have no idea." Phoebe ran her hands over her face, back into her hair. "I've got my family holed up inside the house like a group of hostages. No choice. Whoever did this to Roy has made us all hostages, and I don't know the terms. I don't know what he wants or why. I can't negotiate their safety if I don't know the terms."

"You want to go grab some coffee?" As she asked, Liz tipped back her watch to check the time. "I can take thirty while Bull wraps up."

"I look that bad?"

"You look like you could use a cup of coffee and a friend."

"I could, but I need to get home. Pull out the linchpin, the wheel slips off. Right now, for my family, I'd be the linchpin. Could you let me know if and when his alibi's confirmed?"

"No problem."

Phoebe opened the door, shut it again. "I wish it was him. Wish it was that son of a bitch. Roy's dead, can't change that. Part of me wishes it was Meeks so it would be over and done, and I'd know my family's safe. But there's another part, Liz, just as active, just as sharp, that wishes it was him so he'd go down. All the way down. And not for Roy, not in the guts, you know? So he'd go down for every minute inside that stairwell. I thought I'd come to terms with the way all that shook out, with the payment made. But standing in there, looking at him? I haven't come to terms with it."

"Understandable."

"Is it?"

"Scales are only balanced when your gut tells you they are. You may have to accept the payment. You don't have to like it."

"I don't." Something loosened in her chest because she'd been able to say it, to spew it out to someone who understood. "I don't like it one damn bit. He should do a little time helpless and terrified, then maybe . . ." Phoebe shook her head. "Problem for another day. I think I have enough others to fill the plate for now."

"You should give some thought to talking to the counselor."

"I will. Really. I need to get through this first." She managed a smile. "That was better than coffee. Thanks for the ear, Liz."

"I got two when you need another."

24

She put it away, locked up the turmoil that seeing, hearing, watching Arnie Meeks had made swirl inside her. No time, no place for it now. It would come back, she knew, spurting up to twist her belly into knots. When it did, she'd just have to find a way to uncoil them until there was time, until there was a place.

She had a whole checklist of priorities ahead of that one.

On Jones, she parked, got out of the car. Why, she wondered, did the house seem to *loom* sometimes? She could go weeks, even months, without thinking of it as anything but home—a beautiful, graceful place to raise her child, to house her mother, her friend. A place to eat, sleep, live, even entertain occasionally.

What did it matter that she hadn't chosen to live there, to *be* there? In the end, it was only a house. Only brick and glass. Cousin Bess's ghost had long since moved on.

Lack of choice, she thought. It was all about choice, and not having options.

Despite the fact she was needed inside, Phoebe walked around to the courtyard gate. Away from the police car, away from that looming face of brick and glass.

Here, at least, there'd been choices, even if she'd left them almost entirely up to Ava. Gardens and paths and shady nooks, graceful tables, whimsical statuary.

She sat on the steps of the veranda, looked out, and imagined that lovely courtyard somewhere else. New Orleans maybe, or just another street in Savannah. Could be Atlanta or Charlotte.

And what difference, really, at the base of things?

All the difference, she admitted. All the difference in the world.

She heard the door open but didn't turn. So much, she thought, for solo brooding time.

Carter sat beside her, put a glass of wine in her hand. And said nothing at all.

She took the first sip in silence, with only the elegant music of the fountain trickling through. "I'm having a sulk."

"Hence the wine. Want me to go back in?"

"No. I decided to pick at an old scab. Cousin Bess, this house and the locks she put on the door I can't open. Nothing to do about it, so it's a good one to sulk about as I don't have to find the solution."

"Which in every other instance you do."

She looked at him. "It's what I do, isn't it?"

"It's what you've taken on, almost as long as I can remember. Reuben was the big demarcation, but there was stuff before that. In the blurry before time."

She leaned her head against his shoulder a moment. "Everything changed when Daddy died. For me, before *that's* the blurry time. She could've helped us then, you know. Cousin Bitch. There might not've been a Reuben if she'd done the right thing by Mama then. But she didn't, and there's no point speculating on what might've been."

She sat silent awhile, drinking wine, studying the fountain. "Mama came through for us, every day."

"I know it."

"It must've been so hard. When I think about it, I can't fully imagine what it was like for her. The worry, the work, the grief. The fear. But she always came through for us. Then, she takes a chance on someone who makes her think she's special, and who starts off treating her so well. And it nearly kills her and her children. Hardly a wonder she started closing doors."

"I never blamed her for that."

"No, no, you never have, and sometimes I do. God, it shames me that sometimes I do. It doesn't matter what I know, sometimes it just pisses me off she won't walk outside, go down to the market, go to the damn movies. Anything. It doesn't matter I know she can't. Sometimes . . ."

She shook her head, took another sip of wine. "I think about now, this situation, and how I can't send her and Carly away somewhere. I wouldn't have to worry so much if I could put them on a plane to anywhere else until this is over."

"We need to talk to her about therapy again. Not now," he said before Phoebe could answer. "Not when she's already tied up. But later, when . . . like you said, this is over. Josie and I could move in. Not just temporarily."

"You wouldn't be happy."

"Phoebe—"

"You wouldn't. And I am happy here, most of the time. I'm just having a champion pissy spell. I got all these wires crossed in me right now. Arnold Meeks is clear on Roy. I knew that before I went down there to observe. But observing got me twisted up and mad and scared all over again. I'd rather be pissed than scared, so I'm out here concentrating on that part."

"Doing a good job."

"That's the important thing."

Across the courtyard a hummingbird, bright as a jewel, flirted with the riot of morning glories climbing the iron trellis against the wall. Free to choose any blossom, Phoebe thought, free to fly on.

People weren't birds.

"How's Mama?"

"Crocheting. Before he left, Duncan had her working on ideas for stock and cost analysis. God knows. Just the right thing to keep her mind off all this. He's good at that. Working people."

She lifted her eyebrows. "Compliment or complaint?"

"I like him. He got Carly in on the discussion about stock. Fashion consultant. She was completely into it."

"As a future personal shopper should be."

"Knowing what buttons to push, well, that's a talent, and he's got it in spades. How and when and where you push them shows what you're made of, to my way of thinking. So yeah, Phoebs, I like him just fine."

"I more than like him fine."

"Oh. Really?" Eyes narrowed now, Carter took a long look at her face. "And that worries you because?"

"I didn't say I was worried."

He rolled his eyes, then tapped a finger on the faint line dug in between her brows. "Right there says you are."

She shrugged, then rubbed the line away. "Come on, Carter. Crappy track record."

"Roy was a jerk. Everyone's entitled to screw up with a jerk once. And I'm sorry I said that, sort of, because I just remembered he's dead. Still."

"A jerk, dead or alive. True. Crappy track record," she repeated. "Demanding career that often messes up personal plans."

"A guy's dating a cop, he's got to figure on that already. I don't buy either worry. Sorry. Try again."

"A seven-year-old daughter. I'm not saying she's a problem or a worry. She happens to be the love of my life. But she's a factor. Her happiness is first. And forging a serious, lasting relationship with someone when they have to accept someone else's child as part of the package is tricky."

Carter flicked that away with his fingers. "People do it every day. Several times a day. I could do a Google search and get you stats."

"They do, but those people aren't me, or Carly, or Duncan for that matter. Add in this house. He has this fabulous place out on Whitfield Island. He built it. I couldn't—say if things went to a much higher level—ever live there. I can't move. And there's Mama. Take me on, take her on, too.

"Now, maybe one of those factors isn't such a deal, just one thin string. But add them all up, that's a big, messy ball of sticky twine. And tying it all up? I don't know if he more than likes me fine."

"Could ask him."

"Yeah, easy for you to say. You man you." She blew out a breath. "Well, I've succeeded in depressing myself on that score, which has nicely distracted me from my brood, which distracted me from this horrible situation. Now it's time to leapfrog back to horrible situation." She got to her feet. "I need to work awhile." She leaned down, kissed Carter's cheek. "Thanks for the wine, and the rest."

"It was your wine but the rest is always available."

It could have been worse, Phoebe thought. With Ava and Josie huddled in the kitchen and her mother and her daughter closeted with designs and yarns, Phoebe had a solid chunk of time to work undisturbed.

For a house under siege, she decided, theirs was clicking along at a remarkably normal pace.

In the morning, she thought, she'd contact the FBI, relay the situation and request copies of files where she was a part of a crisis team.

Long time gone, she mused as she opened more current files. But she'd take no chances.

Every case file she read took her flying back. Amazing, she realized, how every detail popped clear. Four years, five, it didn't matter how long ago. Once the log was in front of her, she remembered.

Suicides, domestic disputes, robberies gone wrong, custody battles, embittered employees, revenge, financial gain, grief, mental or emotional instability. Any and all could and did arrow toward hostages.

And sometimes, no matter what was done, negotiations failed. She failed.

She organized by year, and started with the first year she joined the Savannah police.

By the end of that year she'd lost three. One suicide, one hostage and one hostage-taker. It didn't matter that there'd been dozens more she'd talked down, or talked out. She'd lost three, and now each was fresh in her mind.

So fresh she began second-guessing the steps she'd taken, the words she'd spoken, the tone used. Too long a pause—not enough of one.

Fruitless to do so, she knew. Even dangerous.

Still, three lives had slipped out of her hands. Was Roy dead because of one of them?

She started a fresh file with the names of the dead, the year, the place, the nature of the crisis. Then began to chart the names of those connected to them personally, professionally. And added the names of team members.

She was halfway through the second year when Ava gave her door-jamb a knuckle rap. "You've got to come up for air. And a meal."

"I'm fine, Ava. Promise."

"You're not. None of us are. But we need to breathe and eat and sleep." She crossed to the desk. "Your mother and your daughter need to see you doing those things, even if it's only for a bit here and there."

"All right, I'll come down. Ava, I know you're planning to take a couple weeks with Steven out West later in the summer. I was thinking you ought to bump that up. The semester's over in just a few days any-way. You could head on out, hook up with him early, then—"

"Be out of harm's way, if by any chance I'm in it? Seeing as we're all stuck in this house for however long that might be, it's pretty short-sighted of you to make me mad on day one."

"I'm not trying to make you mad, Ava. I'm trying to give myself one less person—two, actually, as Steven'll be coming home—to worry about. You'd be doing me a favor if you and Steven take your vaca-tion now."

Ava tilted her head. "I'm not doing you any favors, Phoebe. I'm not leaving Essie or Carly, and that's all there is to it. If it was just you, I'd go, because a more self-sufficient woman I've never known. To the point of being annoying at times. Such as now."

Phoebe shifted in her chair. "You shouldn't make me mad on day one either."

"Then I'll hope to avoid that and tell you I've already talked to Steven and told him he should go on up to Bar Harbor with the family of his college roommate as they've hit it off so well. He won't be com-ing home until June. And if we're not back to normal by then . . ." Ava scooped a hand through her swing of hair. "I'll think of another way to keep him from coming home."

"Which tells me you didn't tell *him* why you're so easy about him going to Maine."

"He's my baby same as Carly's yours, no matter how old he is. I'm not letting him come into this. Essie needs me, and while Carly has some of your self-sufficiency, she's just a little girl, and she needs me, too. And so, damn it, Phoebe, do you. So you can just forget tossing me off like I was more weight than value."

"If I didn't value you, I wouldn't want you to go. You could take Carly and . . ." Phoebe dropped her head in her hands. "I know that won't work. I *know* it, but it doesn't stop me from wanting it. If I sent Carly away, she'd be upset and scared, probably more than she is now. Mama'd be frantic. I *know* it, Ava. Just as I know I can't leave Mama on her own day after day after day in the house. I need you here, but I love you, and I wish you could go."

"There, I'm not mad at you anymore." She skirted the desk and chair to wrap her arms around Phoebe from behind, press cheek to cheek. "We're all on edge."

"It's what he wants," Phoebe said quietly. "Whoever he is, that's what he wants first."

"Then sitting down to a nice meal is like flipping him the bird, if you ask me. We got us a nice roasted chicken, and I taught Josie how to make scalloped potatoes."

"Which means I'll give him the finger a second time when I have to go up and work out to make up for eating two helpings of those damn potatoes."

"Better keep it to one and save room for strawberry shortcake."

"Oh God, why do you torture me?"

"When I'm upset, I cook." Ava eased back. "I cooked a hell of a lot today."

It had been beautiful. He couldn't believe how perfect and powerful it had been. Every minute, every breath, from the moment he'd tossed that worthless fuck Roy into the trunk of his overpriced status car until the instant he'd blown him to hell had been an e-ticket ride.

Better, by far, than shooting the gangbanger. That had been so quick, and so much less dramatic.

Still, he wished he could have seen Phoebe's face when Roy went boom. That would've been the icing.

He looked at it now, the face tacked to the wall of his workshop. A face among many faces. All hers. Phoebe MacNamara. Coming home from a hard day of screwing with other people's lives. Standing around talking to one of her idiot neighbors. Walking her spoiled brat to the park, or along River Street. Swapping spit with that rich bastard she was screwing now.

Since he was still celebrating his recent success, he popped the top on another beer and toasted the many faces of Phoebe.

"Sweating now, aren't you, bitch? Oh yeah, you're sweating now. And you'll shed buckets before I'm done."

Trying to figure it out, he thought. She'd be racking her brains on this one. Who would kill poor Roy? Who'd do such a cruel thing? Boo hoo!

Hearing her voice in his head, he laughed so hard he had to sit down.

Too bad she hadn't started fucking the rich bastard a couple months sooner. With more time, more research, more legwork, he might've been able to target the new playmate instead of the ex-husband.

Still, might be able to work something out. Just needed to think, to plan, to consider. Maybe take an opportunity, or make one.

"See what we see when we see it there," he muttered. "Got us a time-table, Phoebe." He lifted the beer again. "Counting down now. Tick, tick, tick. The last tick, and it all goes up in blood and smoke."

Like she had, he thought, as another face swam into his mind. And with that image burning behind his eyes, he wept.

After dinner, after her daughter was safely tucked into bed, after the last call from her captain, Phoebe sat staring at the files.

There was a hollow place in the center of her now, as if something vital had just been carelessly scooped out.

She needed to work through it, or around it. If she could get her focus back, she could concentrate on the names, on the cases, on the reason. But that hollow place sat there, and threatened to pull the rest of her inside it.

She picked up the phone and called Duncan's number without asking herself why she reached for him. Or why when he answered the rim around that hollow place began to shake.

"I . . . Duncan."

"Phoebe. I was just talking to myself about you. Whether I should call you, or leave you alone for a while. Are you home?"

"Yes." The hand holding her cell phone wanted to shake, too. "I'm home. Are you?"

"Yeah. Checking up on me?"

"I didn't mean to . . ." To what? "To hover."

"Let's back up. I'd ask what's wrong, but answer's obvious. Is there something else?"

"I just talked to Dave. Everyone here's as settled as they can be, considering. I didn't want to say anything, to tell them now when . . . Jesus. So, I call you and babble. Sorry. I should . . . something else."

"What did Dave tell you that you don't want to tell them?"

"Quick trigger on the brain. I like that about you. I'll probably find it annoying eventually. If it comes to eventually. He called to tell me—I needed to know—that they found . . . one minute." She lowered the phone, got her breathing back in order. "There was a timer on the explosives. Roy. There was a timer set. The remote, that was backup, I guess. Or in case he wanted to go early. There was a timer, Duncan, set for one thirty-five. He was never going to let Roy live. No matter what I did or said, no matter what was done, it was always going to end the way it ended."

There was a pause, and she could hear Duncan let out a long breath. "He gave it enough time to make sure you'd get there. Built in some time so he could play with you. He wanted you to see it. He wanted you on the spot. You know that, Phoebe."

"He wanted me to bargain and wheedle and beg. And he wanted me to know, after it was done, that none of it mattered. Nothing I do will matter, because everything's already set. Clock's ticking down."

"He's got the last part wrong, because what you do will matter."

"He's got me scared to death. Just where he wants me."

"You called the wrong guy if you expect me to tell you not to be scared. What are you going to do about it?"

"What am I going to do about being scared?"

"No, what are you going to do about finding him so you don't have to be scared anymore."

"I'm reading files and looking for any . . . You're not going to tell me to be strong and brave?"

"I've seen you in action, I know you're both. But there are limits. Why don't I come over? I can read files."

She swiveled from her desk so she could look at the dark pressing on the windows. "You're offering to come over so I don't have to feel strong and brave." The empty spot inside her began to close. "That's done the job."

"Give me half an hour and—"

"No, no, I don't need you to come. I guess I just needed you to say you would. I just needed to hear that . . . that I had an option," she realized. "Let me ask you one question, and remember, I'm an active listener, so I'll know if you're lying. Considering the situation, are you sorry you asked me out for that drink?"

"Considering any situation, I figure it was the best move I ever made."

She could smile. "Maybe second best, after deciding to buy a six-pack and a lottery ticket."

"Might be running neck and neck. Phoebe, why don't you pack it in for the night? Get some sleep."

"Yeah, maybe I'll do that."

"I don't know if I'm an active listener, but I know a lie when I hear one."

"Maybe I'll do that in a couple hours. Thanks for saying what I needed to hear."

"I'll be around if you need to hear something else."

"Good night, Duncan."

After a short, restless night, Phoebe considered working from home. Which would mean, she knew, little work at all, as she'd decided to keep Carly out of school for at least a few days.

Even if she could convince Carly to occupy herself elsewhere, Phoebe knew she'd be distracted—and she'd feel guilty being at home and barricading herself from her daughter. And her mother.

Better to go in, stay busy, be productive. There were cops on the house, no need to worry. Unless he got past the cops, she thought as she tried to work a miracle with makeup. Which he wouldn't, but if he did, there was the security alarm.

And someone who could rig a bomb with remote and timer could probably bypass an alarm.

But he wouldn't, she told herself.

He wouldn't.

She gave up on any attempt to style her hair and simply yanked it back in a tail.

All her efforts were going to focus on identifying Roy's killer, finding him and arresting him. Until then paperwork would wait, the scheduled training sessions would be postponed.

Lack of sleep meant she had a solid list of names. She'd start knocking on doors that morning, asking questions, gauging ground. It could be over by end of shift, she told herself as she gathered her files. And if it wasn't, she'd keep right on until it was over.

As she started out of her room, she calculated it was early enough for her to slip downstairs, make coffee, leave a note and be out before anyone stirred.

She stopped by Carly's door, peeked in.

Her daughter was sprawled across the bed, covers kicked off. The worn-eared bear Carly chose most often for a sleeping companion dozed at the tips of her fingers.

Satisfied, Phoebe backed away. If she caved and crept in to cover Carly, give her a quick kiss, that would be that. The kid was a light morning sleeper. Blue eyes would pop right open, and the questions would begin.

Instead, Phoebe continued downstairs. Coffee, she thought again, and maybe a quick carton of the low-fat yogurt she constantly tried to convince herself she actually liked. Leave a note on the fridge, check with the cop on duty, and she'd be gone.

As she stepped into the kitchen, Essie turned from the stove. Both women gasped and stumbled back.

"I thought you were upstairs asleep," Phoebe said.

"I thought you were." Essie gave her heart two quick pats. "Though you might as well shoot me as scare me to death, I'd as soon you didn't. Shoot me," she said with a nod toward the hand Phoebe had on the butt of her weapon.

"Sorry." Phoebe let her hand slide away. "It's barely six in the morning, Mama. Why aren't you upstairs sleeping?" And at her mother's quiet stare, Phoebe shook her head, then moved over. "Mama." With her arms around Essie, she rocked. "What a goddamn mess."

"You're dressed for work."

Phoebe kept holding, kept rocking, but the eyes she'd closed opened again. "I need to go in."

"I wish you didn't. I wish you wouldn't. I wish . . . No, don't pull back to pat and placate me." Essie's voice sharpened as she tightened her hold on Phoebe. "You're still my little girl, and I wish I could keep you safe in this house. My whole family's under this roof now, and I wish— I know it's sick and it's selfish but, my God, I wish I could keep all of you here."

It was Essie who stepped back. "And I know I can't. I'll get your coffee."

Phoebe started to say she'd get it herself, then stopped. Busy hands, she knew, helped her mother's worried mind. "I know you're scared, Mama."

"'Course I'm scared. I'd be stupid not to be. Roy's worthless ass is blown to hell." She glanced back as she got out a mug. "I keep thinking I should feel bad saying that kind of thing, but I don't. You never blamed him nearly enough, to my way of thinking. Didn't matter, because I blamed him plenty for both of us. But I'm scared for you, baby. For all of us."

She poured coffee, added the cream and sugar exactly as Phoebe preferred. "I know you're worried I've gotten worse."

"I worry," Phoebe agreed. "I'm still your little girl, right? Well, you'll always be my mama."

"Sit down, baby. I'm going to fix you some breakfast."

"I don't have time. I'm just going to grab a carton of yogurt."

"You hate that stuff."

"I know. But I'm trying to acquire a taste." Determined, Phoebe opened the fridge, grabbed a carton at random. Once she'd opened it, gotten a spoon, she leaned back against the counter. "I know that with what happened, with being smart enough to be scared, you'd be cautious about going out in the courtyard, or onto the front veranda, but—"

"I've been having trouble with that for a while now." Idly, Essie picked up a dishcloth to wipe the already spotless counter. "The veranda, the bedroom terrace especially. Palpitations," she said. "Knowing it's in my head doesn't make my heart beat any easier. But what you've never really understood is, I'm content inside this house. I don't need what's out there."

Phoebe ate some yogurt. It tasted sour, just like her thoughts. "The world?"

"I've got a nice world inside this house most days, and if I need to know anything more about the outside one, I've got my computer. Honey, let me fix you some eggs."

"This is fine." She picked up her coffee to wash the taste away. "Have you been having panic attacks when I'm not here?"

"Not full-blown ones. Tickles now and then. Phoebe, there's only one reason I wish I could walk out that door. That's so you could, if that's what you wanted. So you could walk away from this house. If I could, is that what you'd do?"

"Mama, I don't have time to talk about this now."

"It's not yet six-thirty in the morning, and if you're in a hurry, then you can answer quick and be done with it."

Phoebe opened a cabinet, tossed the half-eaten yogurt in the trash. "I don't know. Some days, I'd say yes. I'd walk away from this house just to spite Cousin Bess. She had no right, no *right* to work you like a dog and give you nothing."

"She gave me a place to take my children when I was desperate."

"And made you pay and pay and pay, every single day."

"Do you think that mattered?" The little white scar stood out sharply when Essie's cheeks flushed with emotion. "Do you think that ever mattered to me?"

"It should have."

"That's you, Phoebe. You've got a tough mind in there, and you tend to draw hard lines with it."

"Mama—"

"Maybe you've had to have one, and maybe you need those lines. And still, my darling girl, what wouldn't you do to be sure your Carly is safe and well? Did you leave Roy, when God knows you hate to give up on anything, hate to lose? Did you walk away from the FBI for yourself, or because you believed it was better for her if you took the position with the local police? For her, and for me—and don't think I haven't always known that. Did you count the cost?"

"It's not the same, Mama. She treated you like dirt, and Carter little better."

"And I've always felt there was a special place in hell with her name on it for the times she pinched and poked at that poor little boy. But he had a home, and food, and he had you and me. He had Ava, God love her, for good measure."

"The house should've been yours, free and clear."

"It's mine close enough, not free and clear, but mine all the same. Do you hate it so, Phoebe?"

"No." She sighed. "No. Some days I hate the idea of it, I hate the strings she pulls even from that reserved table in hell. She knew I would, and it burns my ass, Mama, to prove her right. But the fact is, Carly loves this house. She loves the courtyard and her room, she loves the neighborhood and the park. So, no, I don't count the cost. Or only when I'm feeling pissy. So I don't know, Mama, if you could walk out the door, if I would, too."

She drained her coffee. "I have to get to work."

"I know you do."

Essie stayed where she was, listening to Phoebe walk down the hall, across the foyer. She heard the door open, close. And she moved to the window, to look out at the courtyard with its lovely flowers and shrubs, its elegant fountain and pretty pockets of shade.

And she saw a bottomless black pit.

25

She got in early enough to push through more files, to add to her list. The feds could've made her jump through hoops, but Phoebe knew enough people in the local bureau to slip through several tangles of red tape.

More than ten years, she thought, between her time with the Bureau and with the SCPD. Almost a third of her life. More than a third of her life if she counted the time in college, in the academy.

But a decade at the work, on the job.

She'd lost fourteen people.

Her mother was right, Phoebe admitted. She hated to lose, and she'd lost fourteen in a bit under eleven years.

It didn't matter that three of those had died of injuries sustained before she'd been called on scene. And if it didn't matter to her, she was damn sure it didn't matter to Roy's killer.

So, all those losses would have to be reexamined.

She pushed back from her desk, prepared to go into the field, and Sykes tapped on her doorjamb. "Lieutenant?"

"Come on in. Ah, Arnie Meeks. His alibi hold?"

"Yeah. Story matches." Sykes's face twisted into a sour expression, as if he'd swallowed something that didn't sit quite right. "More, the woman he's cheating with has one of those nosy neighbors. She saw Arnie go in the alibi's house just before ten Sunday night. Knows his car, too, as she's seen him there before. He'd parked up the block, but she spotted it when she took her dog Lulu out for a walk around midnight."

"Right."

"Had to take the pooch out again right before sunrise. You ever wonder why people have a dog if they're going to have to drag their butt out of bed before dawn so it can water the petunias?"

"Yes, actually. I've been giving that specific arrangement a good deal of thought lately."

Amusement glimmered. "Kid wants a puppy?"

"You're an ace detective, Bull. Yes, she does."

"Well. This particular dog's doing what she needs to do, and that's when Lulu's mommy reports she saw Arnie . . ." Sykes flipped open his book, thumbed pages. " 'Strutting out of Mayleen Hathaway's front door like the top rooster on the dunghill.' "

"Well, that clears him on this."

"Too damn bad. But I could tell you he's going to deserve this Mayleen, who has the breasts of a goddess, the brains of a peanut and the wrath of a wounded pitbull." His smile was hard and brief. "I do believe she's going to make his life a living hell for some time. Add his wife making it the same at home, and he's not in a cozy spot right at the moment."

"I'm feeling small enough, between you and me, to tell you that's nice to hear."

"I'm going to check with CS, see if they've got anything more on the victim's car. Bastard shed a hair, they're going to find it, Lieutenant."

"Maybe you can do that on the way. I've got some avenues I'd like to explore. I could use you. Legwork first, then we'll deal with the rest of the interviews and follow-ups by phone from here. I'll explain on the way to the first."

She picked up her bag, then set it back down when she spotted Sergeant Meeks striding into the squad room. "Give me a few minutes here first, will you, Detective?"

He glanced around, and his face hardened. "I'm happy to stand right here, wait till you're ready to go."

"No need. Just give me a minute."

The look on his face said he'd do that, and he'd be watching the office while he did. Sykes and Meeks faced each other in the doorway like, Phoebe thought, a couple of tough mongrel dogs. Not so different in build, she noted, or in sensibility, she supposed, when it came to protecting their territories.

But so much different in approach.

Sykes spoke without taking his eyes off Meeks. "I'll be right out at my desk, Lieutenant, when you're ready."

"Thank you, Detective. Sergeant?"

"Lieutenant."

She kept the neutral expression on her face as Sergeant Meeks firmly shut her office door.

"Something I can do for you this morning?"

"You got hurt," he began, "and my son lost his badge over it. His wife and his own son are upset and embarrassed."

"I regret your daughter-in-law and grandson are troubled by the fact that your son put me in the hospital, Sergeant Meeks." Her voice was Southern cream over cold steel. "My own family was, and is, considerably troubled by that event, too. Particularly my seven-year-old daughter."

"The circumstances of your injuries aside, when you take on the badge, you take on the risks. A woman with a young child should consider that before going into law enforcement."

"I see. And I see where your son picked up his opinion of women on the job. Was there something else, Sergeant, because regardless of your opinion of my choice of career, I have work to do."

Nothing, not a flicker of the rage she knew had to be burning inside him, crossed his face. And there, Phoebe thought, was the control his son sadly lacked.

"You're going to want to watch how you play this."

"Is that another opinion, or is that a threat?"

"I don't make threats," Meeks said evenly. "You got some bruises, and they look healed up to me. But my son doesn't have his badge or his reputation."

"He's not in jail either."

"Is that what you want? Is that why you sent a man to his workplace to question him? You sent men to take him out of his house and haul him in for questioning in front of his family, his neighbors. You questioned his wife."

"What I want is not relevant. His prior actions earned him the questioning, and he wouldn't have been hauled out of his home in front of his family and his neighbors if he hadn't taken a swing at Detective Sykes. Or didn't you receive that portion of the report?" She angled her head. "Should I have a copy sent to you?"

"If he was provoked—"

"You make excuses for him all you like, as his father. But when you come into this office in uniform, you also represent this department. That's something *you* better remember. I notice you're not complaining that I also sent a man to question your son's married lover in order to verify his alibi for the time in question. Or wasn't she on your list?"

She saw it hit, that one instant of surprise and disappointment. Then his eyes went flat. "The deal was struck, Lieutenant MacNamara. If you keep harassing my son, I'll take my complaints to the DA, to the chief of police and to the mayor."

"You're free to take your complaints to whomever you like, Sergeant." The edge of her anger was a hot blade carving up her spine. "Before you do, I'm going to point out that rather than answer questions in his own home, or requesting that said questioning be done elsewhere, your son verbally harassed and threatened two of my officers, and assaulted one of them. I could see that his probation is rescinded and he do the time at Georgia State."

She let that hang, let it steep. Then, placing the palms of her hands on her desk, leaned forward.

"And, oh yes, Sergeant Meeks, we'll be honest. I can't think of many things I'd like more. But for now? I'm going to suggest that instead of you coming in here and throwing your weight around my office, or try-

ing to make me shiver with tossing around your fishing and golf bud-
dies, you consider getting your son some professional help. Because you
know what? That anger management? It doesn't seem to be doing him
much good."

"If you think you're going to lay this murder charge on him—"

"I do not think any such thing. He's cleared of that. And by clearing him—a person known, without question, to have an unhealthy dislike of me—we can now focus on other leads and avenues in the matter
of the murder of Roy Squire. Now if you'll excuse me, I'm on my way
to do just that."

"You didn't have to drag him out of his own home in cuffs."

He sounded tired now, she noted. She felt the same damn way.
Anger was energizing, but when it started to drip away with fatigue, it
could easily form into bitterness.

"No, and he wouldn't have been if he hadn't called Detective Alberta a fucking cunt among other pleasantries, and taken a swing at Detective Sykes while threatening to beat him bloody. He swung at
Alberta, too, and those officers were forced to subdue him.

"I believe your son is twenty-seven years old? I hope to God in
twenty years' time my daughter's woman enough to stand up for herself, and doesn't need her mama to do it for her."

Phoebe wrenched open the door. "Don't you come around here anymore to rattle your saber at me. You go right on to IAB, or the chief,
the mayor or the damn governor of Georgia. But don't you come here
again to push your face into mine over your pathetic offspring."

She swung out into the squad room. "Detective Sykes? Would you
come with me now?"

"Yes, ma'am." Sykes pushed back from his desk, didn't bother to
disguise the snarky grin as he looked over at Sergeant Meeks. Then he
strolled out in Phoebe's wake.

She started with the oldest case first. She'd been Special Agent Mac-
Namara then. Still fresh from Quantico. She wouldn't meet Roy for another few weeks, she remembered.

A pretty day, late fall, a breeze stirring the air.

Her hair had been longer then, hadn't it? Yes, past her shoulders in those days, and she'd habitually pulled it back into a twist or knot because she'd thought it looked more official. More professional.

And because it made her feel sexy at the end of the day to pull out the pins and let it fall free.

Ava was still in the suburbs. Carter in high school and gangly with a growth spurt. And Mama's world shrunk down to a square of about six blocks, but no one talked about it then.

"Botched kidnapping. Woman walked out of a hospital nursery down in Biloxi with a newborn baby girl. Posed as a nurse. She brought the baby here, to Savannah, to pass it off as her own. This was a surprise to her husband, who believed she'd gone south to visit her sister for a few days. She told him that she'd found the baby, abandoned, that it was a sign from God, as she hadn't been able to conceive in their eight years of marriage, despite spending several thousand dollars on fertility treatments."

"He buy that?"

"He did not. But he loved her."

She sat at a light. Over the hum of the car's AC, she heard the clip-clop as a mounted cop turned into the park.

"He'd also seen the news reports on this stolen baby girl, and put it together. He tried to talk to his wife—Brenda Anne Falk, age thirty-four. She wouldn't listen. Couldn't he see how that baby had her eyes? He called her sister, whom she had never seen on that trip south, and her parents, who were frightened and concerned. Then, not knowing what else to do, he tried to take the baby away from her."

Phoebe stopped in front of a tidy office building. And continued when Sykes joined her on the sidewalk. "She got her husband's thirty-two revolver, pointed it at his head and told him to put her baby down, that it was time for her nap."

"Off the tracks."

"Well off." Inside the building, Phoebe pushed the button on the elevator. "He was afraid the baby could be hurt, so he put her down, tried to reason with his wife, who proceeded to shoot him."

"Off the tracks and over the cliff."

"Yes. Fortunately, she hit the meat of his bicep for a through-and-through. She locked herself in with the baby, shoved the dresser in front of the door. He called the hotline number he'd seen on the TV bulletins. And shortly thereafter, I came on as negotiator."

"The baby make it through?"

"Yes, the baby came out fine. Screaming—hungry by that time—but right as rain." She could hear it, Phoebe realized, she could hear that baby crying in her head. "Brenda Anne Falk, however, did not make it through. After over two hours of negotiations, of believing I was getting through to her, she told me that she thought it was time she gave up after all. And by giving up, she meant putting that thirty-two to her temple and pulling the trigger."

She stepped off the elevator, checked the names on the doors along the corridor, then opened the one marked COMPASS TRAVEL.

It was a small operation with two desks on opposite sides of the room and a long counter at the back. Stands held a bounty of brochures, while the walls were decorated with large posters of exotic locales.

She recognized Falk immediately, though his hair had thinned some, and there were glasses perched on the tip of his nose. He tapped keys on a computer, but Phoebe shook her head at the woman at the counter and stepped over to Falk's desk.

"Excuse me, Mr. Falk?"

"That's right. I'm happy to help you if you don't mind waiting. Or Charlotte can help you now."

"I'm sorry, Mr. Falk, but I need to speak with you." Phoebe palmed her badge so he could see it.

"Oh. Well, what . . ."

She saw it come, carving slowly through the puzzlement, that recognition, and the shock. And the shadow of old grief.

"I know you," he said. "You were . . . you were talking to Brenda when she—"

"Yes, I was. I was with the FBI at that time. I'm Phoebe MacNamara, Mr. Falk. I'm with the Savannah-Chatham Police Department. This is Detective Sykes."

"What do you want?"

"I'm sorry, Mr. Falk, is there somewhere private we can talk?"

He took his glasses off, set them on the desk. "Charlotte? Would you put the 'Closed' sign up and lock the door? Charlotte and I are engaged. I don't need to be private from her. She knows everything about what happened with Brenda."

Charlotte locked up, came immediately to Falk's side. She was a pretty, sturdy-looking woman, and Phoebe judged her to be in her early forties. Her hand, with its simple, round-cut diamond ring, lay supportively on Falk's shoulder.

"What's this about?" she demanded.

"You're getting married?"

"Two weeks from Friday."

"Congratulations. Mr. Falk, I know you went through a very, very difficult time. You did the right thing, and I wasn't able to help you."

"I did the right thing?" His hand came up to squeeze Charlotte's. "No, I didn't."

"Pete—"

"No, I didn't," he repeated. "I didn't get help for Brenda. I knew how much she wanted a baby . . . I thought I knew," he corrected. "But I didn't get help for her. I didn't see, didn't want to see, didn't look. We had a good life, didn't we? That's what I kept telling her. I bought her a kitten, like that was a substitute."

"Oh, Pete, don't—"

But he shook his head. "We were married eight years, and together nearly two before that, and I didn't know what was inside her. That awful need. I didn't see that what was inside her snapped. Going to her sister's for a few days, well, hallelujah. That's what I thought. She'd stop moping around one minute and rushing around the next. Shouldn't I have seen something was broken in her?"

"I can't tell you that, Mr. Falk."

"Something was broken in her, and I never tried to fix it. She couldn't live that way, couldn't live with what was broken, knowing you were going to take the baby away."

"Rough," Sykes commented when they stepped out into the thick air.

"It's a crappy thing to do, taking him back through that."

"It's a crappy thing to do, blowing some poor bastard to juice." Sykes winced. "Sorry, Lieutenant, I forgot for a minute."

"It's all right. What's your take on Falk?"

"He didn't make you when you walked up to him, and our guy would. Maybe he's a good actor, but it didn't play for me. He's got a nice woman, a decent business, what I'd say was a decent life. I don't see him screwing it all for revenge."

"Agreed." She dug out her sunglasses. "Next on my list, geographically, is a casualty from a bank robbery. A spree—three men hit a couple of banks heading down from Atlanta, then tried for one here, where they ran into trouble. Radio car made their plates from an APB, called it in. There was gunplay in the initial phase, and a woman was hit. A few hours into negotiations I managed to talk them into letting us take her out. But it was too late. She was DOA before she made it to the hospital."

"How's that on you?"

"She died, and that's enough." She dug into her bag again when her phone rang. And frowned at the Unknown Caller display. "Phoebe MacNamara."

"Hi there, Phoebe."

She signaled Sykes, who quickly stepped off to use his own phone to call in for a triangulation. "Who is this?"

"Your secret admirer, sweetheart. It sure was nice of Roy to have your cell phone logged into his. I wanted to check in, see how you were feeling. You looked upset when you left the station house this morning."

Cupping the phone between her ear and shoulder, she dug in her bag for her notebook. "Aren't you the bold one, coming around all those cops."

Georgia cadence. Sounds satisfied, sarcastic.

"That doesn't worry me. You know, Roy said you were a hell of a good lay."

"You call me just to talk dirty, or do you have something to say?"

Sweetheart. Good lay. Intimidating the female.

"Just passing the time. Oh, you don't want to waste yours trying to trace this. Isn't it something, this age we live in, when you can walk into a place and buy some toss-away phone already loaded up with minutes? Didn't see that pretty little girl of yours go into school this morning. Hope she's not sick."

Her pad shook in her hand, dropped onto the sidewalk. She had to bite back the rage, the absolutely blinding red flash of it. "Spying on little girls? That seems low for a clever man like you."

Fighting to keep her voice cool, she squatted to pick up her book, and crouched there, continued writing notes.

Watching the house, the family. Wants me to know.

"Why don't you and I get together and have a real conversation? Get down to the nitty."

"We will, I promise you. We'll have us a nice, long talk. You won't know when or how or why until it happens."

"Who was she? Did you love her? How'd she die?"

"We'll talk about all that. You know, I could've taken out your boyfriend that night you had your romantic dinner on his boat. I had the shot. Maybe I'll take it next time. Maybe I'll give myself the green light on that. Bye, Phoebe."

"He's off," Phoebe said to Sykes.

"Keep yours open, they're going to try to triangulate off your signal."

"Unregistered cell. He'll have been moving while he was on with me. I could hear traffic. And he'll have tossed the phone. He's too smart not to ditch it."

She looked around, down the street, across at a little strip of shops. He could be anywhere. He could've been driving right by while she was talking to him. How would she know?

Slowly, she straightened, then skimmed her notes. "I think he's a cop."

"What?"

"He's smart, but he's puffed up, too."

"Smart and puffed up equals cop?"

"He needs to show he's smarter and better." She tapped her pen on her notebook. "He said he could've killed Duncan, taken him out, was how he put it, when we were having dinner on Duncan's boat. I could've taken the shot, he said. And that he might give himself the green light next time."

"How does that— Hold on." Sykes angled away, listening to his own phone. "They had him on River Street," he told Phoebe. "Moving west on River, and lost him."

"He threw it in the water, that's what he did. Small investment in a phone, big results. But he had to give me that one last needle. He didn't say I could've shot your boyfriend, but I could've taken the shot. That's cop speak, or military."

She held up a hand before Sykes could answer, walked a few paces down the sidewalk and back while she thought it through. "And yeah, anyone who watches TV could pick up the jargon, but it was natural. I don't think he planned to say it, he just had to push my buttons a little harder, so it came out. Green-light the shot. It's not the usual term for a civilian to use. He's a cop or military, or he was."

"Arnie's clear."

"It goes back further than Arnie Meeks. And it goes deeper than just being a misogynistic asshole. It's in those files. He's in there, somewhere. I need to contact Duncan, make sure he's covered. Then, goddamn son of a bitch, we're going to find this bastard."

Sykes watched her stride back to the car, punching viciously at her phone. It was tough not to appreciate a redheaded woman in full temper, he thought, so he only said, "Yes, ma'am." And followed her.

Duncan walked into Ma Bee's house without knocking. He'd never had to knock on that particular door. He called out for her, but since neither the TV nor the radio was on, he kept going through the house.

If she was inside, she'd have what she called her company on. She wasn't much for silence. He moved through the house as casually as he would his own, and spotted her out the kitchen window.

She knelt in front of one of her flower beds, a big straw hat with a band of wildly colored flowers on her head and neon-pink gardening gloves on her wide and generous hands.

Love was a quick, warm spurt right through the heart.

She'd given him a mother when he'd already been a man, a family he'd never hoped to be a part of, and a home he'd never found anywhere else.

He knew there'd be a pitcher of tea in the refrigerator, and cookies in the grinning-cow cookie jar. He got out a couple of glasses, filled them with ice, a plate for the cookies. He carted everything out to the little table shaded by a red umbrella before crossing the yard to her.

She sang in her tumbled gravel voice. He recognized "The Dock of the Bay" and, spying the MP3 player clipped to her shirt, figured she was dueting with Otis.

He started to reach down, touch her shoulder, hoping not to startle her. Then he jumped when she spoke.

"Boy, why aren't you working at something?"

"Didn't think you heard me."

"Didn't." She switched off the music as he squatted down. "But you still cast a shadow." She gave him what he thought of as the hairy eyeball. "You a man of leisure today, Duncan?"

"I had a meeting on the warehouse project this morning, and I've got some things going on later. But if a man can't take a little time out of the day to flirt with the love of his life, what's living for?"

She flashed him a grin, gave him a poke. "Fancy talk. Well, flirt while you yank some of these cursed weeds."

The hat might have shaded her face, but there were beads of sweat along her temples. Enough gardening in this heat for now, Duncan thought. "I'll weed for you after we flirt over a couple glasses of tea and some cookies."

Lips pursed, she looked over in the direction of the table. "That looks appealing. Help me up, then."

When they were settled at the table, Ma's pink gloves tucked into her gardening apron, she took a long drink of tea. "Close today," she commented. "Going to be heavy by afternoon. Hope those couple of things you got going are inside."

"Some are, some aren't. Why don't you let me send you on that cruise this summer, Ma Bee? Or anywhere else you'd like to go."

"I like where I'm sitting well enough. What's on your mind? You're not here just to flirt with me. Worried about your redheaded girl? Phineas told me what happened to her ex-husband. Said you were right there when it did."

"It was . . . I don't have a word for what it was." He drank deep.

"It's evil's what it is. People toss that word off so it loses the darkness of it. But that's what it is. Are you having trouble sleeping? I can make you up some herb tea would help some."

"No, I'm all right. It's bad business, Ma. This guy, he says he killed that kid. The one over on the east side who had those people in the liquor store. Shot him after Phoebe talked him into surrendering. So yeah, I'm worried about her. She knows what she's doing, but . . ."

"When somebody matters, you've got to worry."

"She's got her family pretty much locked up in her house on Jones while she's out there knowing what she's doing. Her mother . . . Well, she's had some hard knocks."

He began to tell her, found himself going through all of it. What he knew, what he'd deduced, what he'd observed.

"Girl's got a lot on her plate. 'Course any woman raising a child without its father's got an extra serving right there. And her mother having that condition." Thoughtful, Ma looked out over her yard. "I don't know what I'd do if I couldn't go where I wanted when I wanted. Walk down to the neighbor's, or drive to the market. Fear's a hard burden to carry. Responsibility's a heavy one. That's a complicated business, Duncan, even without this awful, ugly business heaped on it."

"They seem to have a system, and it mostly works for them. But Phoebe—she's the glue, you know? She knows what to do. That's what I saw in her the minute she walked into Suicide Joe's apartment that day. It's . . . magnetic."

"You got the moon on for her, do you?"

He smiled a little as he lifted his glass. "I guess I do. Bad timing, as it turns out. Hard to romance a woman under these particular circumstances." He shrugged. "That can wait. Finding the son of a bitch who's after her, that can't."

"It's her job to find him." Fanning her face with her hat, she studied him. "Hard for you to sit back and let her do her job."

"Yeah. Okay, yeah. In this particular situation anyway. I mean Jesus—sorry—jeez," he corrected when she narrowed her eyes. "This guy wants her dead. More, he wants her to suffer first. If somebody matters, are you supposed to sit back while somebody else wants to hurt them?"

Ma broke a cookie in half, passed a share to him. "Is that what you're here for? You want me to tell you what to do?"

"No. Not exactly. She's a lot like you. She does what has to be done, she takes care of her family. And she sure as hell doesn't like to be told what to do—or what she can't do. I guess I'm trying to work out a way to help her without putting her back up—got a temper on her—so she gives me the boot out of pride or mad."

"Mmm-hmm. Like you coming here, and thinking: Ma Bee's probably been out in the sun long enough for now. She should sit down and have a cold drink. So you fix that all up so you don't have to tell me to stop and sit, and don't get an argument."

He grinned as he bit into his cookie. "Something like that."

"You've got a sly mind in there, boy. I always admired it. You'll figure it out. Now, go yank those weeds while I have another glass of tea."

"Yes'm."

His phone signaled as he rose. "It's Phoebe," he said as he read the display. "Hey. I was just . . ."

As she poured more tea, Ma watched Duncan's face. She knew her boy and saw the flash of irritation in his eyes. Phoebe, she thought, wasn't the only one with a temper.

"I've got a couple things going today. No, I'm not rescheduling. For . . . Phoebe, stop. Hold it. Let's remember, first off, you don't outrank me because I don't work for you. No, *you* be quiet for a damn minute. I'm not rescheduling because some psycho *might* try to track me down somewhere in the city of Savannah and then decide *maybe* to try to do me some harm, and I'm sure as hell not running home to lock myself in like some hysterical girl. In case you failed to notice, I've got a pair."

Ma lowered her head, shook it and sighed.

"Sexist, my ass. Protective custody? *Your* ass. You go ahead and try it and yeah, you're right. We'll see who's got the biggest pair. You want to talk about this, we damn well will. Face-to-face. Later. Right now, Lieutenant MacNamara, I'm busy. I'll see you later."

He shut the phone, shoved it into his pocket. "Wants me to shut everything down, go home and hide like some dickless coward. Threatens to sic cops on me to haul me in, for my own safety. Screw that."

"Who're you calling?" Ma demanded when he yanked the phone out again.

"Your son, my lawyer. We'll just see how she likes—"

"Hang that up, you fool. Just close that up. You go yank those weeds till you cool off a little."

"I'm not having—"

"You're not having, she's not having. Fine, fine, fine. Talk about it later, in person, like you said. Meanwhile, there's no use stinking up the pot by calling lawyers. You find cops on your doorstep, that's the time to call Phineas. Right now, that bed needs weeding."

Children, Ma thought as Duncan strode grumbling over to do what he was told. People in love were like squabbling children half the time.

She sure missed that part of having a man.

26

In the squad room, Phoebe used a large whiteboard to create a chart. As she built the diagrams, added names, she struggled to keep her conversation with Duncan from playing back in her head.

Stubborn, macho idiot. Going off on a tangent about his precious balls because she expected him to take proper and reasonable precautions.

She'd never have thought it of him. It just went to show how wrong you could be about someone.

If he got his head, or his damn balls, blown off, it was his own fault.

She had to stop, shut her eyes and order herself to calm down.

That wasn't going to happen. If she didn't know just where to find Duncan, how the hell would Roy's killer? And why would he waste his time and energy cruising around the city looking for Duncan, and then risk exposure by trying something stupid?

He was too smart for that.

He had a plan, of that she was certain. And he wouldn't have tipped his hand to her if Duncan was his primary and immediate target. Duncan might very well be one, but there was time.

She'd let herself panic, and she knew better.

Calm, rational thinking was the way to find the answers.

She'd pulled another detective and an experienced uniformed officer into the case.

"We believe," she began as she continued to write on the board, "that the UNSUB is connected to one of the female victims of a previous hostage situation, suicide or crisis in which I sat as negotiator. What we know is he targeted, abducted and killed Roy Squire, specifically because of the victim's connection to me. We know he has knowledge of explosives. We know he traveled to Hilton Head, and returned to Savannah with Roy in Roy's car, which was found abandoned and wiped clean in the long-term lot at the airport, where we can assume he had his own car parked or took a cab. We do not know, yet, how he got to Hilton Head."

She turned around. "Detective Peters, I need you to check on one-way car rentals that were picked up in Savannah, dropped off in Hilton Head. One-way railway and bus tickets, air tickets. Or any round-trips purchased that were used only one way. He may have chartered private. We don't know how deep his pockets are. Find out what you can from private planes, destination Hilton Head, within the last week."

"Why didn't he use his own car, coming and going?" Sykes wondered. "If he has one. Drive's not that far from here to there. Why use the victim's to transport?"

"We don't know that either. It's possible he doesn't own a car."

"Or," the new team member, Nably, began, "the one he owns, or has access to, isn't geared for hauling a full-grown man, bound and gagged, forty, fifty miles."

"Too small," Phoebe mused.

"Or a hatchback SUV with no trunk, no place to conceal the abductee." Nably pulled on his prominent bottom lip. "Or maybe he just likes the idea of having us puzzle on it, and spend the time finding out."

"Very possible." She paused to drink from her bottle of water. "It's also possible, and I believe probable, that the subject has had police or military training. He knows how we work, so yes, he might have done things this way to add to the legwork. He's had training. He was able to slip through the perimeter on the Johnson situation, dispatch his target and slip back out without a ripple."

"Maybe he was in uniform," Sykes suggested. "Or had ID."

"Yes. He got through the posts, into the building and into Reeanna Curtis's apartment. It had been cleared, and she rushed out with her children—doesn't remember if she locked the door or not. Either way, he got in. He chose that apartment, that window. Why?"

"Because he knew enough to know it wasn't optimum angle, and SWAT wouldn't use it."

"I agree." She turned back. "The pink roses on the grave—which we have not been able to trace—indicate the UNSUB's attachment to a woman, most likely a dead woman. These are the names of all female casualties in any negotiations in which I took part, both for this department and previously for the FBI.

"Brenda Anne Falk, suicide. Her husband is clear on this. She had a brother and a father, both of whom have been verified as in Mississippi during the time frame of Roy's abduction and murder. At this time, we have no leads on anyone else connected to her who has either motive or opportunity. Linked here are the other law enforcement personnel who are listed in the file on that incident. There is no known personal connection between any of them and Brenda Falk."

"Maybe he doesn't have connections to any of them," Sykes put in. "Maybe it's a cop or a fed who just went south. Picked up on any of those," he continued with a nod toward the board. "And/or you, Lieutenant, because the voices said so."

"Then it'll be a lot harder to find him. Victim two, chronologically, is Vendi, Christina. She was part of an organization called Sundown, a small, extreme fringe terrorist group. Poorly organized, poorly funded, and still they managed to invade the home of Gulfstream Aerospace's CEO during a dinner party, taking fifteen people hostage."

"I remember that." Nably pointed a finger. "You were on that."

"I was. The demands were as radical and extreme as the group, and as poorly thought out. After twelve hours of negotiation, during which time it was known that at least one of the hostages was seriously injured if not dead, it was determined by tactical command to move in."

"You talked them into letting the kids out, and a pregnant woman. I remember this."

"They did agree to release the CEO's two minor children and a female guest who was seven months pregnant, taking the hostages down to twelve. Two members of Tactical were able to gain entry through a second-story window, and took out two of the hostage-takers. Vendi opened fire on law enforcement and was terminated. The single remaining terrorist was taken into custody. He's still inside."

She could remember how horrible it was. The screams, the gunfire.

"Vendi's father was career army until his recent retirement. He has, always, disavowed her actions, and cannot be placed in Savannah nor in Hilton Head during the time frame. However, there would be any number of military connections there, and further connections to Vendi from any remaining members of the disbanded Sundown organization."

She pushed at her hair. "I've asked the FBI to look into this angle. I know," she said, reading the expressions. "This is our case. But the Bureau's resources for this kind of investigation are wider and deeper than ours."

"Next is Delray, Phillipa, who was killed during a carjacking. Her five-year-old daughter was in the car, and was then taken by the two carjackers as hostage. They were pursued to a garage on the west side, managed to get inside. Negotiations were successful, the child released and the two men surrendered. Delray's brother was in the army, serving in Germany at the time of his sister's death. He now lives in Savannah, as does Delray's husband. Delray's brother, Ricardo Sanchez, is with the mounted patrol."

"I know him." The uniformed officer held up a hand. "I know Rick Sanchez. He's a good guy."

"I hope you're right, but he'll have to be interviewed."

Didn't sit well, she could see that, just didn't sit well for cops to poke at another cop. "I'll be speaking to him myself," she decided on the spot. "We then have Brentine, Angela, killed during an attempted bank robbery. Her injuries were received during the initial phase, and initial attempts to secure medical attention for her were refused. She succumbed on the way to the hospital during hour four of negotiations, when we were able to secure her release. Her husband, Brentine, Joshua, was in New York on business. He remarried nineteen months after his first wife's death, since divorced. He has never served in the military or in any law enforcement capacity. Angela Brentine has no living male relations."

"There was a lot of press on that one," Sykes remembered. "Not only the bank-robbing spree that ended here, but Brentine's wife. He's old Savannah, money and status. Rumors floated around, as I recall, that her dying saved him a messy divorce."

"I'll be talking to Brentine very soon. Officer Landow? I'd like you to re-interview Reeanna Curtis, from the Hitch Street incident. Any details she remembers before, during, after she was evacuated. Talk to neighboring apartments as well. Take another officer of your choosing. I'll authorize it. Detective Sykes, I'd like you to reach out to members of the tactical team on that same incident. I believe they'll be more . . . relaxed with you than with me. I'm not looking to cause trouble for any of them. I want to know if anyone caught so much as a glimpse of another officer—uniformed or just badged—that they might not have recognized right off. If anyone is reluctant to speak about this, I'd suggest you show them a couple of the crime-scene photos of Bonaventure. After Roy Squire was blown to pieces."

"I'll take care of it, Lieutenant."

"Thank you." She nodded because she saw Dave step in. "Let's get started."

When Dave gestured to her office, she walked into it ahead of him.

"You've got a lot laid out in a short time, Phoebe. Get any sleep in there?"

"Some. Truth? It kept coming back when I drifted off. Roy chained on that grave, the explosion. I was better off awake and doing. I'm not so scared when I'm doing as I am when I stop."

"Your family?"

"I don't know. How long can I keep them shut up in that house? Fine for my mother," she said with a tired laugh that wanted to turn bitter. "But the rest? I just don't know. I'm going to go out, start talking to witnesses, connections to those four female victims. Something's going to break out of it. I know it will."

"Take one of the men with you."

"I don't have anyone to spare. We're already spread thin with the details on my house, the ones taking Josie and Carter to work and sitting on them."

It made her sick to think of it, sick in mind, in heart, in the belly. "And I know that can't go on much longer either. I know we don't have the manpower or the budget for unlimited babysitting."

"They're there today, so we think about today. How's Ava . . . everyone handling it?"

"Everyone, including Ava, is handling it as best they can. You might call her, or go by. It might ease her mind."

"Well. Hmm." He slipped his hands into his pockets. "About the interviews, I'd go with you myself, but I've got a meeting at City Hall. If you could pick someone out of the hat, not just the squad, who would it be?"

Maybe, *maybe* either he or Ava would make a move before they were both collecting Social Security, but she wasn't putting money on it. "Sykes is solid, and that's why I want him tugging on the tactical team. Liz Alberta. She's SV, I know, but she's got a good ear. But I don't know what her case load is, or—"

"I'll find out, see if it can be worked. Take ten minutes, call home. You'll feel better, clearer in your mind."

"You're right. You take five, call yourself, it would do the same for you."

They met Sanchez in Forsythe Park, and stood in the shade with his wise-eyed horse. The thick air of the morning had turned oppressive, so the rich brown hide of the horse gleamed damp.

Close to MacNamara House, Phoebe thought. Close enough that in uniform, mounted on his pretty horse, he could watch her home without anyone noticing.

Sanchez stood about five-feet-eight by Phoebe's gauge, with a tough, scrapper's build. There was a little hook-shaped scar under the corner of his left eye, and a hard, stubborn line to his jaw.

Was the man in the ball cap, the whistler, taller? She thought by an inch or two. But had she paid enough attention to be certain?

"She didn't care about the car," Sanchez said, speaking of his sister.

"She just wanted to get Marissa out. She fought them because she wouldn't leave her baby, so they put a knife in her and left her bleeding to death on the street."

"You were in Germany when it happened?"

He nodded at Liz. "They gave me hardship leave, let me come home for her funeral. My mother, I thought it would kill her, too. And my brother-in-law, he was like a dead man for days."

"You were only nineteen when it happened. You were training as a weapons specialist."

"I thought I'd make the army a career. See the world, fight the fight. But after Philli . . . I finished my tour and came home."

"And joined the mounted unit about two years after."

"That's right." His eyes narrowed. "What's this about, Lieutenant MacNamara? The one who put that knife in her, he's still in. Have you come to tell me he's getting out?"

"No. Can you tell me where you were last night, Officer Sanchez? Between eleven and three?"

"I could," he said evenly. "I'd want to know why. I'd want to know why you're asking me where I was around the time a man was blown up in Bonaventure."

"I'm asking you because a man was blown up in Bonaventure."

"What does it have to do with me?"

"Let me ask you this first. You didn't say how your niece was spared that day while your sister was killed."

"I told you, the bastards killed Philli because she fought them. Cops caught up with them at a garage; they'd locked themselves in with Marissa. Cops surrounded the place, got them to let the baby go and surrender."

"Who got them to surrender?" Phoebe asked him.

"The cops." His horse tossed its head at the impatience in Sanchez's voice, and automatically he stroked a hand over its cheek to soothe. "The cops saved her life. Men like that? Men who'd kill a mother trying to protect her baby? What's to stop them from doing the same to a little girl? Cops saved Marissa. It's why I'm a cop."

No possible way this is the guy, Phoebe thought, and when she exchanged a look with Liz, saw they were in agreement. "I was the hostage negotiator in the crisis situation with your niece."

"You?" Some of his color drained, then poured back again, deeper, darker. "I didn't know there was a negotiation." His voice had thickened.

"You didn't ask for details?"

"I . . . when I got here . . . everyone was in shock, in mourning. It was like a blur. Then I had to go back, finish my tour. When I was discharged and came home, I didn't want to know. I didn't want to look back at that. I wanted—I wanted—"

"To be one of the ones who saved lives, who helped people in trouble."

"Yes, ma'am," he managed after a moment, and nodded to Liz. "You asked where I was last night. I stayed the night at my girlfriend's apartment. Here." He took out his pad, his pencil. "Here's her name, her number, the address. Is there anything else you need to know?"

"This is fine. Thank you, Officer Sanchez."

When she took the paper, he reached into his pocket, pulled out his wallet. "Marissa's ten now. She's ten years old now. Here's her picture."

He flipped it open, and Phoebe looked down at a dark-haired, dark-eyed little beauty. "She's gorgeous."

"She looks like her mother." He put the wallet away, held out a hand. "Thank you, from my sister."

"Life's a strange ride, isn't it?" Liz commented as they walked the wide path back to Phoebe's car. "You changed the direction of his life. Never met him, never spoke to him before today, but he's doing what he's doing, maybe is what he is, at least partially, because of what you did one day five years ago."

"Maybe. It's just as true that due to someone's perception of what I did some other day, two people are dead."

Liz followed the direction of Phoebe's gaze toward the house on Jones. "Do you want to go in, check on them?"

"No. Let's go talk to the husband, just to tie this one up. Then we'll try Brentine."

Delray was a quiet, gentle-eyed man. After five minutes, Phoebe decided he'd have a hard time squashing a spider much less killing a man in cold blood.

She had a much different impression of Joshua Brentine.

He kept them waiting twenty minutes in the reception area of his river-view offices. Clouds the color of angry bruises roiled in from the northeast, Phoebe noted. A wicked storm was just waiting to happen.

They were ushered in by Brentine's glossy, narrow-hipped assistant to an office with a wide view of the river that had been furnished more as an elegant parlor than a place of big business.

The mix of elegance and power reflected the man, to Phoebe's mind, who looked as if he'd been born wearing a perfectly cut suit. The burnished hair waved back from a high, aristocratic forehead; the hawk-sharp brown eyes didn't mirror the smile his mouth offered.

"Ladies. I apologize for keeping you waiting." He rose from behind an antique desk, gestured to a seating area with curved settee and wing-backed chairs. "My schedule is well packed today."

"We appreciate the time, Mr. Brentine. I'm Lieutenant MacNamara, this is Detective Alberta."

"Please, sit. I'm forced to admit I have no idea why I've warranted a visit from two of our city's most attractive public servants."

"The bank robbery which resulted in the tragic death of your wife has come up in a current investigation."

"Is that so?" Settling back in his chair, he looked politely puzzled. "How so?"

"I'm not able to divulge the details of an ongoing investigation. According to the information in the file, you weren't in Savannah at the time of your wife's death."

"That's correct. I was away on business. In New York."

Phoebe glanced around the office. "You must travel extensively, given the nature of your business."

"Yes, I do."

"And the bank where your wife was killed. Am I correct in saying that wasn't the bank you used, at that time, for your professional or personal businesses?"

"No, it wasn't. I don't understand why this has anything to do with something current, Lieutenant."

"We're just confirming details, and I certainly apologize for the necessity of bringing up a tragic event that caused you such grief."

But you don't appear to be touched by that, Phoebe thought. Not like poor Falk, reliving the death of Brenda.

"Witness statements agree that Mrs. Brentine did have an account in the bank. That, in fact, she came in that day to withdraw all her funds and close that account. Maybe you could tell us about that, Mr. Brentine, as it was over three years ago. We haven't yet been able to access the bank records on that transaction."

"Tell you what?" He rolled his shoulders. "Angela had a small, personal account of her own. Mad money, you could say. A few thousand dollars. Some terrible twist of fate had her deciding to bank that day, at the very time of the robbery."

"You didn't know about the account?"

"I didn't say I didn't know about it. I said it was her little piggy bank, so to speak."

"I'm sorry, I'm just wondering why the wife of someone in your enviable financial position would need a separate little piggy bank."

"I imagine she enjoyed the independence."

"But, according to the file, she wasn't employed during your marriage."

"No, she wasn't." He lifted a hand from the arm of his chair, a palm-up gesture she recognized as impatience. "She was very busy taking care of our home, being a hostess, working with charitable organizations. I'm afraid I can't help you any more with this, so if you'll excuse me—"

"But to withdraw all of it, at one time," Phoebe persisted. "That's what stood out for me when I read the case file in conjunction with this other investigation. That's just puzzling."

"Unfortunately, neither you nor I can ask her."

"That is unfortunate. I expect she was going to buy you a present, or splurge on something foolish. I'm always splurging on something foolish if I get enough money in my hands. I bet she had a couple of close girlfriends. We women do, and we tend to tell them these silly details we don't tell our husbands."

"I fail to see what that detail has to do with anything."

"You're probably right. I'm just going off on a tangent. It just niggles me, I suppose. I hate not to know. Well, if you could tell us where you were last night, that would be helpful, and we'd be right out of your way. After eleven last night?"

He said nothing for an icy ten seconds. "I don't like the implications of that."

"Oh, there's no implication at all. I apologize if it seemed otherwise. It'd be helpful if you'd verify your whereabouts. Otherwise . . ." Phoebe looked toward Liz.

"That would niggle both of us," Liz said with a big smile. "Then we'd be taking up a lot more of your valuable time."

"I was at the theater with a friend until after eleven, then we had drinks. I got home about one this morning. Now if there's anything else—"

"Just one little thing. The name of your friend. Just to tie this up so we won't have to bother you again."

"Catherine Nordic." He rose. "I have to ask you to leave. If you have any other questions, I'll contact my lawyer."

"That's not necessary. Again, I apologize for bringing up difficult memories. Thank you so much for your time."

As they walked back through reception, Liz glanced toward Phoebe. "Didn't like him."

"Why, neither did I! Self-important putz. And wasn't it interesting he didn't want to tell us anything about his dead wife's friends or that bank account? Tell me, Liz, if you were married to a very wealthy man, why would you be socking money away in your own account?"

"Security, should said wealthy husband decide to dump me or vice versa."

"And if the marriage was in trouble?"

"A girlfriend would know. I get a whiff of something else here. Cold-fish husband, and a controlling one you bet your ass—so you've got to sneak money into a separate account—a husband who's out of town a lot while you're kicking around arranging flowers and taking lady lunches."

"Affair."

"We are not only attractive public servants, but cynical ones."

"Hmm." Phoebe ran it through her head as they rode the elevator down. "I don't see the dead wife as the love of his life. Strikes me as he's more or less x'd her out like he might a canceled meeting. But if she had a lover . . . maybe one she was planning on running off with. Broke open that piggy bank."

"Wrong time, wrong place. Her shooter and his cohorts are doing life, but that might not be enough for a brokenhearted lover. Have to blame somebody."

"And everyone got out alive but her. I didn't get a medical team in, not in time."

"Couldn't," Liz corrected. "I read the file, too, Phoebe."

"If someone was in love with her, if someone was eaten up by guilt that she went to the bank because of him, 'couldn't' wouldn't mean squat. Let's track down Angela Brentine's friends, her hairdresser, her personal trainer. The kind of people an unhappy woman talks to. If she had a lover, one of them knows."

"I can get the best friend." Liz took out her phone as they crossed the lobby and stepped outside. "I've got a friend with the paper. I'll ask him to pull up the report on the Brentine wedding. Best friend was probably maid of honor, or certainly in the wedding party."

"Aren't you handy to have around?"

"The guy I used to live with thought so, until I showed him the door."

Glynis Colby was a long beanpole of a blonde in jeans and a linen shirt. Her photographer's studio claimed a corner of the third floor of a re-habbed house near Greene Square. Various props, including an enormous teacup and an army of stuffed animals, were stacked around the walls.

She called her assistant—a little guy with a streaked ponytail and a cherubic smile—Dub when she asked him to get everyone a cold drink.

"I still miss her. It's been three years and counting, and I'll see something and think, I've got to call Angie. But she's not here."

Here was the emotion Joshua Brentine had lacked. "You were friends a long time?" Phoebe asked her.

"Since we were fourteen. Glyn, Angie and Dub—the unholy trinity. We were going to be famous together."

"I know your work," Liz put in. "You took pregnancy photos of a cousin of mine. They were gorgeous. Then she came back with her little boy. You've got a good reputation—deservedly."

"We do pretty well, right, Dub?"

He gave her hand a squeeze after he'd set down glasses. "Angie? She was the sweet part of the heart."

"We had this concept," Glynis continued. "Angie specialized in wedding photography, I'd do pregnancy and children. A fun way, we thought, to generate repeat business. Plus, she just loved doing weddings, had such an eye for them. And Dub . . ."

"I'd run the business."

"I was under the impression that Angela wasn't working at the time of her death."

"No. Joshua didn't like it. Or us." Glynis slanted her gaze toward Dub, wiggled her eyebrows suggestively. "Bad influences."

"He hated me more," Dub put in. "Homophobe."

Glynis poked him in the arm. "Oh, you just like to be number one. He hated me just as much. I was the slut."

"I was the gay man slut. That trumps. He met her at a wedding she was working," Dub continued. "Big society deal and a huge coup for us."

"We'd only been in business for about eight months."

"She was beautiful. Really beautiful, and I meant it about the sweet."

"And she had enormous charm. Joshua swept her right off her feet." Using both hands, Glynis made a broad, swooping gesture. "Acres of flowers—heavy on the pink roses she liked best. Candlelight dinners, romantic getaways. Six weeks later, she was engaged. Three months after that she was Mrs. Joshua Brentine."

"Then it started." Dub's mouth tightened as he picked up the story. "He pressured her into quitting her work. How could she snap pictures—as he put it—at weddings when, if the wedding was important enough, she'd be a guest?"

"And she had a duty to blah, blah, blah," Glynis said with a shrug. "She gave it up, gave it all up for him. She adored him. He didn't like her socializing with us, so he made it difficult. Manipulating's a Brentine specialty. So we'd grab lunch now and then, and she wouldn't tell him, or we'd have dinner when he was out of town."

"Dangerous liaisons," Dub added.

"When did she start the affair?"

Glynis's eyes widened at Phoebe's question. "How do you know about that?"

"Why don't you tell us about it?"

"It wasn't sleazy. It wasn't like that, *she* wasn't like that. Joshua had to have everything his way. He wouldn't let her be, and she got more and more unhappy. He expected her to be available round the clock for him, but he could do whatever he damn well pleased."

"Easy tiger," Dub said as he rubbed Glynis's shoulder.

"All right." Glynis took a long breath. "All right. She was miserable, and he wouldn't give way on anything. He wouldn't consider counseling, and nixed therapy for her when she got depressed. She didn't have any money of her own by that time. Everything was in his name. When she came to realize divorce was going to be the only way, she'd come in here a couple times a week, more if she could manage it. She'd do setup, darkroom work, digital manipulation, anything we needed, and we paid her in cash."

"She met someone. She wouldn't say how or where or who, but she was happy." Dub pulled out a blue handkerchief, handed it to Glynis so she could wipe her eyes. "The light came back into her."

"When did the light come back?"

"About six months before she died. She called him Lancelot, her pet name for him."

"How'd they contact each other?"

"She bought a preloaded cell phone. His idea, right, Dub?"

"Yeah, she said that he knew how to do what had to be done. Listen, the men responsible for what happened to her are in prison. What's the point of dragging this out now?"

"It's going to help us on another case. Anything you can tell us about the man she was involved with could help."

"Well, I think he had a place on the west side where they'd hook up." Glynis glanced at Dub, got a nod. "I saw her the day before it happened. She was flying. She said she'd decided to move out, to get a divorce. As soon as that was done, she and Lancelot were going to get married. She was going to take what money she had and move to Reno, establish the residency requirements for the divorce. She wanted it fast. She always wanted fast."

"Anything else that you know about him, anything she said about him? However minor a detail."

"I think he worked out—seriously. She talked about how he was really built, and worked at it. He was giving her tips on getting stronger physically."

"Blue eyes," Dub remembered. "She bought him a shirt one day, said it matched his eyes. Blue rugby style. Nice. And he cooked."

"That's right, that's right. She said how sexy it was to watch him cooking dinner. I remember it surprised me, because he didn't seem the type."

"Why not?"

"Everything else she said, or the impressions I got, said ultra machismo. To be honest, I was worried about her. We both were. He seemed like the polar opposite of Joshua, and we wondered if she didn't fall into all this as a kind of reaction. Hot-blooded, tough, physical. Blue collar."

"Why do you say blue collar?"

"Sometimes she called him her blue knight. Maybe it was the eyes, though. But I got the impression he was a working stiff, you know."

Or maybe the blue was the uniform, Phoebe thought.

"He was really pushing her to leave Joshua. He didn't like the idea of her sleeping with another man, even though sex had become a non-issue between Angie and Joshua. She said it made Lancelot crazy to imagine it, and I think she liked that part. It made her feel sexy and vital again. But it felt like another kind of manipulation to me."

"She needed a breather," Dub said. "Some time to get Angie back. But this guy, he made her feel like a goddess, like she was indispensable and indestructible. Nothing bad would ever happen to her when he was with her. He'd promised."

"But it did," Glynis said softly. "The worst happened."

"He never contacted you after her death?"

"No."

"Where are her cameras?" Phoebe asked.

"I don't know. She kept them at the mystery man's. She had two, and for a while I checked eBay, the pawnshops, the secondhand stores. Just in case he sold them. It'd be nice to have them back, those pieces of her."

"You'd recognize them?"

"Yeah, at least if I had my hands on one of them I would. She painted this little pink rosebud on the bottom of her equipment. Like a signature. Pink roses were her favorite."

"Pink roses like on the grave where Roy was chained." It was energizing, Phoebe thought, to have that much confirmed. "Lancelot's our guy."

"Yeah. Now we just have to find a blue-eyed hard-body who can cook and lives on the west side. Or did three years ago."

"Add in cop. How does the cop from the west side meet the sad princess from Gaston Street?" Closing her eyes, Phoebe tried to think it through. "She did charity work, attended snazzy events. A lot of cops moonlight as private security. And let's see who's turned in their papers in the last three years—cops between thirty and forty because he's going to be young, and he's not going to have time to pull tours while he's planning his revenge."

"If we're walking down the right road, she would've had that second cell phone on her when she went into the bank. Her personal effects would've gone to the husband."

"Yeah." Missed that step, Phoebe realized, and nodded appreciatively at Liz. "You're right, and if so, he'd have checked the incoming and the outgoing. He'd know. Better let him simmer first, take this other angle. Then we'll go back on him."

Phoebe glanced toward the eastern sky as she got into the car. The storm wasn't going to wait much longer.

27

"**It could be** other law enforcement, it could be military, even paramilitary," Phoebe said. "But everything points to cop to me. Gary Cooper—sheriff. He doesn't lose, not Grace Kelly or his honor. That's the way it was supposed to be. But on what could symbolize a wedding day, the day Angela Brentine was reclaiming her independence, taking the next step toward becoming her lover's wife, she's killed in a gun battle. Killed by the bad guys, sure, but also—in the subject's mind—because I stood by—the townspeople—and didn't take action, or didn't allow action to be taken. Guilt by cowardice is part of the theme of the movie."

"You were neither guilty nor cowardly," Dave said.

"To him, I'm both. And he's obsessed about this for three years. Plenty of time to work it all out. Lancelot not only cuckolded the all-powerful king, but was Guinevere's champion. He saved her when Arthur could or would not. This guy sees himself as the hero, more importantly, Angela's hero. And he can't accept the failure, or the fate. There has to be blame. I'm to blame.

"Next, the grave where he killed Roy. Jocelyn Ambucean was a young bride-to-be. She died days before her wedding, drowned in the river during a storm. She was, it's said, running away to Tybee Island and her lover rather than go through with the marriage arranged by her father. He likes the symbols—angel watching the grave—Angela—the grave of a woman running toward true love, the pink roses. He likes giving me clues. He wants, at the end of it, for me to know why. I have to know why for it to matter enough."

"I'll get the names for you."

"Joshua Brentine. He's not going to want to admit his wife was cheating on him. It's insulting and demeaning. His pride is worth a lot more to him than the lives of two strangers, or anyone else who might be a target."

"Admitting isn't the same as confirming." Dave cocked his head. "If he believes you already know."

She smiled. "No, it's not, thank you for reminding me. I believe I can make him think I have more than I do."

"I'll call down, see how long it'll take to get the information you need."

"Thank you. I'm just going to call home while you do that, let them know I might be late."

She stepped out, had barely pulled out her phone when Dave stuck his head out of his office door. "Computers are down in Human Resources. New system, apparently. Could take a few hours."

"Well, Jesus, aren't there paper files?"

"And going through those doing a search like this would probably take longer than waiting for technology to flip back on. Go on home, see your family, get some dinner. They're going to let me know as soon as they're back up."

"All right, all right. Why don't you come on with me? Have some of that dinner, too?"

It was tempting, but she looked exhausted. "Rain check. I'm going to grab a little time at home myself with a beer and the ball game. If you're right on this, it's going to break for us, and break quick. Go recharge a little."

The minute he stepped outside, Dave cursed himself for not tapping Phoebe for a ride home. Even with only three blocks to go, he'd be lucky to get home on foot before the storm hit.

Hell, while he was at it, he might as well curse himself for not taking her up on the dinner invitation. He wanted to see how Ava was holding up for himself. Wanted to see . . .

Lousy timing, again, he reminded himself. She, all of them, were in the middle of a crisis.

She'd been engaged the first time he met her. He'd had absolutely no business falling in love with her. None. But he had. Hadn't done anything about it, he reminded himself as he hunched his shoulders against the wind. Stayed the family friend. Good old Dave.

Talked himself out of believing he was in love with her, after she'd been married a few years, had a baby. Yeah, he'd talked himself out of it, and gotten married himself.

And Ava got divorced.

Lousy timing, right down the line. With a healthy portion of guilt on his part. Because no matter how much he told himself he'd wanted to make his marriage work, no matter now much he told himself he'd tried his best, he knew there'd always been Ava.

Now, just when he was beginning to think, to hope, maybe, just maybe, she and everyone in MacNamara House were in crisis.

What choice did he have but to stay the family friend? Good old Dave, who was heading home to his empty house to nuke a Hungry-Man.

Cue violins.

The wind whipped along, sending tree limbs bending and swaying as he clipped down the sidewalk, annoyed with his own self-pity. If he'd bothered to pay attention, he could have changed out of his suit into his sweats at least. Then he could've jogged the distance home while he was wallowing.

Lightning slashed through the sky before he'd crossed the first block, and thunder rolled threateningly in its wake.

He quickened his pace at the next pitchfork of lightning, and decided he might make it home after all without getting electrocuted or drenched.

And at least the wind was cooling things off. The entire day had been oppressive with that heavy, waiting heat.

He could see his house now, imagined shedding the suit, popping the top on that cold beer.

He swung onto his little walkway, bounded toward his door. He heard the quick toot-toot, glanced back. He fixed a smile on his face when he spotted the spiffy red sports car zip toward the curb.

Maggie Grant, twice divorced, wanting to flirt. She embarrassed him a bit at the best of times, but just now, he wanted to get in, shut down and take an hour for himself.

He sent her a cheery wave and kept going.

She tooted again—beep-beep-beep, more insistently. Dave stuck the key in his lock, turned it as he gave her another wave.

"Yoo-hoo! David! I'm so glad to see you. I need the help of a big, strong man."

Ten more seconds, Dave thought. Ten more and he'd have been inside, out of her reach.

"Ah, my phone's ringing, Maggie. Let me—"

"It'll only take a minute or two. I've got all these bags. I don't *know* what I was thinking. The rain's going to start pelting any second. Would you be a hero and give me a hand getting all this inside?" She popped the trunk, sent him a melting smile. "Please?"

"Sure." Sap, sucker, stoop, he berated himself. "No problem."

"It's going to be a wild one." She shook back her hair. "Kind of night you want to be cozied up with a friend and a nice glass of wine."

Now he was going to have to avoid the wine, and the friendship, Dave thought as he stepped back down to the walk. The first fat drops of rain pelted down. The wind slapped, shoved, and he cursed as he heard his unlocked door slam open. For one second he hesitated: finish the damn good deed, dash back and shut the door. Even as he pivoted to do the latter, he spotted the man standing across the street.

Blue ball cap, sunglasses, windbreaker.

Then the world exploded.

Phoebe didn't know how to feel when she saw Duncan's car outside her house. One part of her was relieved—now she knew where he was, and that he was safe. The other part was just plain pissed that he'd been so uncooperative that morning.

Then she stepped inside, out of the fury of the storm, and heard her daughter's delighted laughter. It was hard to keep a good mad on when she heard her daughter happy.

Then she walked to the parlor and saw Carly, Carter and Duncan sprawled on the floor playing Monopoly. It looked like Carly was slaughtering both men.

"I can't have landed on you again," Duncan complained. "These dice are loaded. This is bull . . . malarkey."

"You were going to say the *s* word."

He smiled thinly at Carly. "What *s* word?"

"Bullsh—"

"Carly Anne MacNamara!"

Carly stifled a giggle, then looked over innocently. "Hi, Mama. I'm beating the pants off Uncle Carter and Duncan."

"So I see. Where's everyone else?"

"The women are in the kitchen, where they belong." Carter sent her a toothy smile. "Get on back there, woman, and make us a snack."

"Oh, what kind of snack would you like?" She walked over, set down her bag. "Just let me"—she rapped her hand at the side of Carter's head—"see if that knocked any sense into you. And nobody's going to be snacking on anything this close to dinner. For which, I assume, you plan to stay," she said to Duncan.

"An invitation has been issued and accepted. Going to smack me upside the head, too?"

The glint in those dusky eyes warned her he still had a bit of a mad on himself. Well, fine. "We'll see how the evening goes. I assume, too, you got all those oh-so-important things done on your schedule today."

"I did. How about you?"

"Inroads."

"Why are you mad at Duncan, Mama?"

"That may involve quite a list. So for now, I'm going to run upstairs and change. Carly, after you're finished trouncing these two, why don't you see if you can help set the table? That means the men will be clearing and seeing to the dishes."

"What part of KP does she get?" Duncan asked Carly.

"I'll be . . . answering my phone," Phoebe said as it rang in her bag. She pulled it out. "Phoebe MacNamara."

Her color simply vanished, as if a light had been switched off in her face. Duncan was already getting to his feet when she got out the next shaky words.

"What happened? How . . ." She turned to walk out of the parlor. "How bad is he? No. No. Where? I'm on my way."

She had her game face on, Duncan noted, when she turned back. But there was fear lurking in her eyes. "I have to go."

"But you just got home."

"I know. I'm sorry, baby." She leaned down to give Carly a hard hug. "I'm sorry. Would you run on back and tell Gran not to wait dinner for me? I'll be back soon as I can."

"Did somebody get hurt?"

"Uncle Dave had an accident, so I need to go check on him. Right away."

Tears swam into Carly's wide eyes. "Is he hurt really bad?"

"I hope not, and they got him right to the doctors so they can take good care of him. But I have to go, baby. I'll call as soon as I can. Run tell Gran I'll call soon as I can. Carter," she said as Carly dashed off.

"I'll take care of it. Don't worry about us. Car accident?"

"No." She gripped his arms. "Stay inside. Please. Make sure everyone stays inside. I'll call."

"I'll take you."

She didn't argue with Duncan, simply ran to the front door and through. "They took him to Memorial. He rigged Dave's front door. The son of a bitch rigged the front door on Dave's house. That's what they think. They don't know . . ."

"We'll find out."

"He's alive." Phoebe closed her eyes as Duncan whipped the Porsche into the street. "He's alive." She turned her phone over and over in her hands as if she were afraid it would ring and tell her otherwise. "He had to get inside the house if the door was rigged. He had to get inside Dave's house."

"He's not going to get inside MacNamara House, Phoebe."

"He doesn't want to." Fear, grief, guilt stirred an uneasy mix inside her. "It's not going to be like that. If he'd wanted to get in there, he wouldn't have put me on alert. He's got something else in mind. But he wants me wounded. He wants me hurting when it comes down to what he's got in mind. And oh God, Duncan, I am."

She burst through the emergency room doors, her badge already in her hand. She held it up to the first nurse she saw. "David McVee."

"You need to check with—"

"No. *You* check. Now."

"Lieutenant."

She spun around and bulleted toward Sykes. "Where is he? What's his status?"

"They're working on him. Can't get much out of them, but I talked to the paramedics who brought him in. Broken arm, some burns, lacerations. Head trauma—there're some worries there. And there could be internal injuries. I was still in the house when the call came in. I followed the ambulance in."

"I want two guards here in the ER. Two guards wherever they take him."

"Already done." Sykes nodded when Duncan came up behind Phoebe. "Lieutenant, there was a witness. A neighbor. She was shaken up some, got a few cuts. They're stitching her up."

"I want to see her the minute she's out. Detective . . . Bull, I need someone I can trust over at Dave's, talking to the bomb team, the CS people. I know you don't want to leave him." She reached out, squeezed his hand. "I promise I'll contact you the minute there's anything to do. But I need someone I can trust on that scene."

"Okay. Okay." Sykes scrubbed his hands over his worried face. "You let him know I'm around. Cops all over the place in here, so you let him know we're all around."

"I will. Thank you."

"Why don't you sit down?" Duncan said when Sykes headed out.

"I don't think I can. I'm good at waiting, but I need to know . . . something. I just need to know." Her hand vised on Duncan's arm when she saw the gurney and the medical team.

She lunged forward. There were cuts and burns on his face, a gash at his left temple. And blood on the sheet that covered him.

"How is he? Where are you taking him?"

"You family?"

"Yes."

The young doctor continued to move at double time toward the elevators. "He's going into surgery. He's bleeding inside. Somebody'll let you know as soon as he's out."

Phoebe signaled the two uniformed officers. "They go where he goes. You wait outside the OR. I'll be there as soon as I talk to the witness."

She stood back and watched them push the man who'd been her father most of her life into the elevator.

"It's the best trauma center in the city." Duncan laid his hands on her shoulders. "One of the best in the state. He couldn't do better."

"No. I wish I could fall apart. I wish I could just fall apart until they come to tell me . . . We should've put cops on his house. Anyone who knows me knows what Dave is for me, what he is to me."

"Take a minute." Gently, Duncan turned her into his arms. "You can fall apart for a minute."

She let herself cling, let herself shake. He was holding her, good, solid arms around her. "I'm so scared. I don't know what to do I'm so scared."

"Just hold onto me until you figure it out."

"Don't go anywhere, okay?" She gripped him tighter. "Will you stay with me?"

"Of course I will. Phoebe." He put a hand under her chin to lift her face to his. "I'll be right here."

She sighed, and laid her head on his shoulder. It was such a comfort, she realized, to have someone else be strong. To have someone else be the one who was right there.

"I thought I forgot how to need somebody to stay." She eased back. "Lucky for me I remembered when the somebody can be counted on."

She spotted Maggie coming out of a treatment room. "That's Dave's neighbor." Phoebe blew out a long breath. "All right. Here we go." She took two steps forward. "Maggie?"

At the sound of her name, Maggie jolted, looked over. Then, bursting into tears, all but fell into Phoebe's arms. "All right now. Hush now." Even as Phoebe looked around for somewhere marginally private, Duncan had a hand on her shoulder to steer her and her charge toward some chairs.

"Y'all sit right here," he told Phoebe. "I'll go hunt up some coffee."

"Good, that'd be good. Maggie, I need you to stop crying. I need you to stop." Firmly, Phoebe pulled back to take Maggie by both shoulders. "I need you to stop and talk to me."

"David. I think he must be dead. Oh God!"

"Well, he's not. They took him up to surgery. They're taking care of him. Don't you start going hysterical on me again. I mean it. I need you to take some good, deep breaths. In and out. You *do* what I say, you hear? In and out. That's right. That's better. Now, you tell me what happened. Right from the beginning."

"I don't *know.*" Tears still streamed as Maggie fluttered her hands. "I swear I don't know."

"You tell me what you do know. You were with Dave, at his house?"

"No. Yes. I mean to say I'd been out with a friend—you met my friend Delly when David had that barbecue last summer? We went out for lunch, and a little shopping spree. I'd just pulled up at home, right before the storm, and I saw David."

She covered her face with her hands, but Phoebe yanked them ruthlessly away. "I know you're upset, but you're going to keep talking, keep telling me. Where was Dave when you saw him?"

"Going up the walk to his front door. I beeped the horn, and he waved. I thought how he could help me carry my shopping bags in, so I beeped again, and got out right quick to hail him. It was thundering, and he was already unlocking his front door. But he turned around. He's such a sweetheart."

Fighting for patience, Phoebe stuffed a wad of tissues in Maggie's hands. "He didn't go in the house?"

"He . . . He was coming back to help me. His door blew open. That's right, I remember how his door blew open. That wind came up so strong, and I guess he'd started to open the door before he turned back to help me. Then, oh my God, Phoebe, the door just exploded."

After mopping her face with them, Maggie twisted the damp tissues into ropes. "I don't know exactly, I swear to God, I just don't. I fell—it was like being shoved. I fell down. My knees got all scraped up, and my arm—" She held out her arm to show the bandage. "Five stitches. But David . . . David."

"Here you go, Phoebe." Duncan came back with coffee. "Ma'am? I thought you might like some coffee."

"Oh, isn't that nice." Instinctively Maggie pushed at her hair. "Thank you so much. My goodness, I must look a fright."

"You look just fine," Duncan assured her as he set little tubs of cream and some sugar packets on the table between the chairs. "I didn't know how you like your coffee."

"Plenty sweet," Maggie said. "Oh, and you got the pink kind, too. Are you with the police?"

"No, ma'am. I'm just a friend. I'll leave you to talk to Phoebe."

"Oh. Oh, could you stay? I can't help myself, I just feel more secure in times of crisis when there's a man around."

"Maggie, this is Duncan. Duncan, why don't you sit down? Now, Maggie, how long was it from the time the door blew open until the explosion?"

"Oh goodness, I'm not sure. A few seconds. Maybe five? Ah, he stopped. Yes, that's right, David stopped and looked back when the door slammed open, and I think he started to go back and close it. I think he'd just started to take a step or two back toward the house when . . . Oh my God, Phoebe. If he'd gotten back—"

"He didn't. You calling him out to your car to help you saved his life. You think about that, Maggie. You called him away from that door, so he's upstairs getting fixed up."

"Oh my." Her face ran the gamut. Shock, horror, relief, pride. "I didn't even think of that. I've been so mixed up and scared."

"You said you were out this afternoon. Did you notice anything, anyone, before you left?"

"No. I meant to leave at noon, but I was running a little late, so I didn't leave till about quarter after. And that Delly, she gives me such grief for being late, so I was in a rush. I can't say I was paying attention, so I don't think I'd have noticed anything."

"How about during the morning?"

"I was inside all morning. I was on the phone with my mama awhile, which is why I was running late. That woman can talk. Then I dashed out and drove on out to the mall. I was barely late, but Delly gave me grief nonetheless."

With a long-suffering sigh over that, Maggie sipped her coffee.

"Maybe you looked out the window while you were talking to your mother," Phoebe suggested, "or saw an unfamiliar car or someone you didn't recognize when you dashed out to go to lunch."

"I don't guess I saw a soul around the neighborhood this morning— one of those hot, oppressive days where nobody likes to walk around much. Oh, except for the UPS man."

Reaching out, Phoebe clamped her hand on Maggie's wrist. "Where did you see the UPS man, Maggie?"

"Just coming down the street."

"In his truck?"

"Ah, no. Did I see his truck? I just don't remember. I was in such a rush. I barely took a minute to wave at him and call out to ask if he had a package for me."

"I imagine you see the UPS man several times a week around the neighborhood."

"I suppose I do. This wasn't the usual one, though; this one was younger and cuter, so I yelled out my name, too, when I asked if he had something for me. He said no, ma'am. Not today. Then I just jumped in my car and lit out."

"What did he look like, Maggie?"

"Well, he had dark hair and one of those scruffy little beards. Good legs. Strong-looking. I do tend to notice attractive young men," she added with a smile for Duncan.

"How tall?"

"Hmm. I'm not sure. Maybe five-ten? Not as tall as Duncan here. Had a build on him. The regular UPS man, and he's a sweetheart, but he's on the plump side. This one looked like muscle."

"How old?"

"Goodness, I didn't get a good, close look." Maggie patted her hair as if it might help her think. "Thirty-five? Maybe a little more."

"Would you recognize him if you saw him again?"

"I'm not sure. He was wearing sunglasses. Well, my God, Phoebe, do you think he had anything to do with what happened to David?" Her hand slapped to her heart. "Why, he could've killed me on the street! I was only a dozen feet away."

"I don't know, but I'm going to want you to work with a police artist. I'm going to have an officer take you into the station house, and the police artist will meet you there. You sit here with Duncan while I take care of this."

Maggie sat blinking while Phoebe sprang up and hurried away. "Well, sweet baby Jesus. I sure wish you had some bourbon to go with this coffee."

"Next time," Duncan promised, "I'll bring a flask."

Once she'd arranged for the police artist and Maggie's transportation, Phoebe rode up to the surgical waiting area with Duncan. "There were no new carriers on that route today," she told him. "And no deliveries on that block until after two this afternoon. She saw him, she spoke to him. But he wasn't worried about that."

"A guy can grow a beard or shave it off." Thoughtfully, Duncan rubbed his own chin. "Changes his look."

"We've got a good artist. He'll reconstruct both ways. He had to know we'd get a witness. If not Maggie, someone else on the block could easily have seen him. He's smart enough to know that, but he's not that worried about it."

She walked straight to the nurses' station when she got off the elevator. She showed her badge. "I need to know if there's any word on Captain David McVee."

"He's still in surgery."

"I need someone to go in and check, to give me his status. Please."

"I'll see what I can do. If you'd go into the waiting area, we'll let you know."

There were half a dozen cops she recognized already in the waiting area. She made the rounds quickly, then positioned herself in a corner where she could see the door. "I need to make calls," she told Duncan.

"You want coffee? You didn't drink any downstairs. I'd ask you if you want some food, but you're going to say no, so I won't."

"I could use a cold drink. Apparently being scared makes everything hot inside me. I could use something cold. And, Duncan," she said before he stepped away. "When I can think straight again, there are a whole bunch of things I have to say to you."

"Would that include any comments or complaints about me not falling in line when so ordered?"

She worked up a smile, widened her eyes. "I have no idea what you're talking about."

"Good." He touched her lips with his. "Then I'd like to hear them. Be right back."

She had to call Sykes first and arrange for the canvass of Dave's neighborhood to add in the fake UPS deliveryman. She wanted, badly, to talk with the bomb squad and crime-scene supervisors herself, and had to remind herself she'd sent Sykes for a reason.

And since she couldn't will a nurse or doctor to come in and tell her everything was going to be just fine, she steadied herself, pulled out every ounce of optimism and made the next call.

"Ava."

"God. Phoebe. Is he—"

"Dave's in surgery, and from everything I know it's going well."

"Surgery! Oh my God, what happened? How did it happen?"

"I can't get into that now, but I want you to know, and to tell everyone, he's being taken care of."

"I want to come down there. I want to see for myself. Carter, we had an awful fight about it. Phoebe, you can't expect me to stay here while Dave's hurt."

"I have to expect it. I'm sorry. He'd expect it, too. He'd insist on it. Ava, I promise you, I *promise* you, you're the first person I'll call when he's out of surgery. I need you to take care of Mama. I need you to take care of everyone there. I'm depending on you."

"That's an awful thing to say to me." Tears drenched Ava's voice.

"You know I will. But . . . please, tell him, tell him when you can that I'm—we're—praying for him."

"I will. I'll call you as soon as I know anything more."

Nearly another hour passed before they were given the stingy report that the surgery was going well.

An hour later, Sykes came in to give her a more inclusive one. "Trip wire on the door. Five-second delay."

"He wanted Dave to get inside. Better chance of killing him if he was all the way in." In a futile attempt to relieve the pressure in her head, Phoebe massaged the bridge of her nose. "What did he use?"

"Same as with Roy. Blew out the door, the front windows, part of the damn roof. Turned the living room into the third circle of hell. He'd been three feet closer, we'd be waking him, Lieutenant."

"He's going to have to buy Maggie a truckload of flowers, then deal with her trying to get him naked. How about the canvass?"

"Most of the people on that block work during the day. Got one witness, guy who'd taken off to meet his plumber. He was watching out for him and saw the suspect walking up the street. Description's vague. He didn't really see anything but the UPS uniform. But the time matches Maggie's statement."

He puffed out his cheeks. "Firefighters responded fast, and I'd guess they saved the house. But, well, Jesus, LT, it's a hell of a mess."

"He loves that house," Phoebe added.

"I know a guy," Duncan put in. "He does good work. I could ask him to take a look at it, if that would help."

"It might. One less thing for Dave to worry about." She glanced toward the doorway again. "Yeah, it might help. Do we know how he got in?"

"How it looks is the back side window was forced open. He gained entry that way. Back door was unlocked, so he likely left through that, and didn't bother to lock it on the way out. That—"

He got to his feet an instant after Phoebe. It had to be one of the doctors, she thought. He had that weighty look about him.

She stepped forward. It wouldn't be rank that had her taking the lead. Every cop in the room knew it was personal.

"Dave McVee," she said. "I'm Phoebe MacNamara."

They'd stopped the bleeding, and saved his spleen. He'd suffered a bruised kidney, a broken arm, two cracked ribs and a concussion as well as lacerations and burns.

But his heart was strong. The doctor had told her his heart was strong, but she already knew that.

She sat in the chair beside his bed, waiting. And remembered how he'd sat with her, so long ago, while she'd waited for her mother.

"They tried to kick me out," she told him while he slept. "They don't know who they're dealing with. I'm not leaving until you wake up and say my name. Once you do, I'll know for sure you're okay. Got a lot of cop blood being drawn downstairs. They're lining up to give a pint since you got greedy and took so many transfusions. Maggie got a look at him—you're sunk there, darling. You owe her so big."

She picked up his hand, pressed her lips to his fingers. "We all owe her so big. I'm having them fax me over the composites. And we're going to hunt this son of a bitch down like a sick dog. I swear it." She took a hitching breath. "That's nonnegotiable. I need you to wake up, Dave." She pressed his fingers to her cheek. "I need you to wake up and say my name."

It was another half hour before she felt him stir, those fingers moving in hers. She popped up to touch his face.

"Dave. Can you open your eyes? It's Phoebe. Wake up now and open your eyes." When his lids fluttered she told herself to push the call button for a nurse. But she wanted a moment. "Dave, there you are. It's Phoebe."

"I know." His voice was thin and slurred, like an old drunk's. "I heard you. What the hell?"

"You're all right." She brushed at his hair, watching his eyes slowly focus. "You were hurt, but you're all right. In the hospital. Got some bumps and bruises, so you lie still. I'm going to call the nurse."

"Wait. What . . . it was raining. Was it raining?"

"Hell of a storm."

"What happened?"

"He rigged your front door. He got in your house, Dave. I'm so sorry."

"Door blew open." He closed his eyes a moment, a line of pain and concentration digging between his brows. "I remember, the door blew open."

"You were being the good neighbor, going down to help Maggie with some bags. So you're okay. Not every good deed gets punished after all. You're going to be fine."

"I saw him."

"You . . . what?"

"I saw him." His fingers tried to tighten on hers. "Across the street. Door blew open, and I stopped, and I saw him across the street."

"Maggie saw him earlier, so we've got a couple of composites. We'll—"

"I know him. You were right. Smart girl. Always were a smart girl."

"Dave, Dave." She sharpened her voice to keep him with her. "He's a cop? You're saying he's a cop?"

"SWAT. Was SWAT. Burned out? Transferred? Don't know. Can't think back. Walker? No, no, Walken. Had a beer with him once, retirement party. Beer at the bar, talked about the ball game. Walken. Walken," he said again, and looked into Phoebe's eyes. "Go."

She dashed to the door, called for a nurse. "He's awake, and he's starting to hurt. You." She jabbed a finger at the guard on the door. "You don't move from this spot, you hear? I don't care if there's an earthquake, a rain of frogs or the Second Coming, you don't budge until your relief arrives. And nobody gets inside that room you don't check their ID and go in with them."

"Yes, ma'am."

"Duncan." My God, she thought, it was something to have a man who didn't leave. "I bet that Porsche can really move."

"Damn right."

"You're about to put that to the test. I've got a name," she said, and rushed for the elevator with Duncan beside her.

28

Walken, Jerald Dennis. Phoebe had the full name after a five-second conversation with Commander Harrison. And with Harrison pushing the buttons, she had Walken's last known address within three minutes.

"He won't be there." She snapped her phone closed. "He's too smart for that. He won't be there, but they'll send a team in to make sure of it. He'll have another place by now. Another place where he's dug in deep. Go here," she told Duncan and rattled off an address.

"What's there?"

"He was tight with Michael Vince, trained with him, Harrison told me. I want to talk with Michael Vince. Well, God!" She blew out a breath when he whipped around a corner. "You know how to drive, don't you?"

"Make a hell of a martini, too."

"You can mix me up a whole batch when we finish this."

"Gin or vodka?"

She laughed, just put her hands over her face and laughed. "Dealer's choice. Duncan, when we get there, get to Michael Vince's, would you wait for me? Would you call my house and tell them that Dave woke up and I talked to him? Would you tell them he's all right?"

"I'll tell them. I'll wait for you."

Tears stung her eyes. "Oh yeah, a whole bunch of things to say to you later."

Vince lived in a trim little house on the near edge of the south suburbs. He opened the door wearing a pair of blue-checked pajama pants and an irritated expression. The expression went neutral when she held up her badge and gave her name.

"What's the problem, Lieutenant?"

"I need to talk to you about Jerald Walken."

"Jerry? I haven't seen him in years. He moved to Montana. What's this about?"

"I'd like to come in a minute."

"Sure, but we just got the baby down—again. I need to keep it quiet. I swear, the kid hears me scratch my ass two rooms away."

"How old's the baby?"

"Six months. He's teething, which means me and my wife aren't getting any sleep. I've been on with you on some crisis situations. That Johnson deal, that was a hell of a thing."

"It was. Do you know how to get in touch with Walken?"

"No. I never heard from him after he left."

"I heard you were friends."

"We were. I thought we were." With a shrug, Vince sprawled onto one of the living room chairs, yawned hugely. "Sorry. Have a seat. Jerry was supposed to be best man at my wedding, but he took off two weeks before. Didn't even tell me he was turning in his papers till it was done. Sent me a fucking e-mail—'scuze me—an e-mail a couple days later, said he was going to find his soul or some such crap. Two weeks before my wedding, he's going off to find his soul. I'da figured he was just drunk if I hadn't heard he'd left the unit."

It was apparent that the guy was dopey with sleep deprivation. Phoebe remembered those days—nights, endless nights with a fussy baby. "Did Jerry drink a lot?"

"He could tie one on. You do the work we do, you need a little release."

"What about the married woman he was involved with?"

Vince pokered up. "What's this about?"

"You were on the Johnson situation. It was Walken who fired that shot."

The sleepy eyes sharpened as he came to attention in the chair. "No fucking way."

"You heard, I'm sure, about the incident in Bonaventure. It was Walken who chained Roy to that grave and killed him. Captain McVee was seriously injured today."

"McVee? How? What happened?"

"An explosive was rigged to the front door of his house. Circumstances swung in our favor, and Captain McVee not only survived, he saw and identified Walken. Now if you know how to contact Walken, you need to tell me so we can bring him in before anyone else is hurt."

"I don't. Christ almighty. Jerry?" Vince slumped back in the chair. "Captain McVee said it was Jerry?"

"He did."

"Jesus. Jesus. He'd been on the edge the last few months on the job. Sometimes the edge works for you, but . . ."

"You had some concerns?" Phoebe prompted.

"Yeah, I guess I did. But, you know, I had a lot going on myself, the whole wedding thing. We didn't hang out as much after a tour. But he was a good cop. Jerry had a cool head on the job. Could be hot off it, but on? He was solid."

"There was a woman."

"Yeah." He blew out the word. "He got tangled up with her, and it was like all he could think about. Had this idea they were going to head off together out West—where men were men, and all that. Get themselves a ranch in Montana. I figured that's what they did. He and the woman took off to Montana."

"What was her name?"

"He called her Gwen, or Guinevere. He kept her to himself. I worried . . ."

"What did you worry about?"

"This doesn't feel right, Lieutenant. I gotta say, it doesn't feel right. He was a cop, a teammate, a friend."

"Captain McVee was in surgery more than three hours."

"Okay." Vince scrubbed a hand over his jaw. "Okay, okay. Listen, it was just when he'd had a couple too many or he wasn't able to see her for a while that he got jumpy. And maybe sometimes he went off on a tangent."

"Such as?"

"He talked about how it'd be easier to just put a bullet in the guy— her husband. He didn't mean it, and he'd get right off it again, talking about how they were just going to wait until they had enough money put by for the ranch. Already had a name for it."

"Camelot?"

"Yeah, yeah, 'cause she was Guinevere. He was crazy about her. She was probably stringing him along, and that's what sent him off."

"No, I don't think she was stringing him along. Other friends, family?"

"He got along with everybody in the unit. Thought of them like brothers. He'd even say brothers-in-arms, you know?"

And not a single police officer had been hit when Charlie Johnson's body was riddled with bullets.

"Family outside the job?"

"He had—has, I don't know which—a mother and stepfather, but they weren't close. I think he said they'd moved out to California when he was in his twenties, and he stayed here. He got along," Vince repeated, "but I'd say, except for me, he was kind of a loner. I think he was put out some when I hooked up with Marijay. My wife. Then he got tangled with this woman, and that was it for him."

Phoebe got to her feet. "If he contacts you or if you see him, you need to contact me immediately. You understand that?"

"Lieutenant, if he did what you're saying, he's got to be out of his mind. I've got a wife and a baby. You can believe me when I say, I hear from Jerry, you'll hear from me. I won't take chances with my family."

Phoebe pulled out her phone as she walked out of the house. She saw Duncan leaning against his car, hands in his pockets, looking up at a sky where stars were trying to light through the thinning clouds.

She leaned back against the car with him while she spoke to the team commander, then to the hospital to check on Dave's condition, and finally to Sykes to bring him up to date.

When she was finished, she pocketed her phone and stayed where she was another moment, looking up at those persistent stars.

"You're an awfully patient man, Duncan."

"Most things are worth waiting for."

"In an awful way, that's what Walken thinks, too, and he's been waiting a long time for this. The man in there? That was his closest friend. In fact, reading between the lines, I'd say he was Walken's only friend. A loner who got along, hot-tempered off the job, liked to drink, didn't much care for it when his friend got engaged. But he hasn't once gotten in touch with his only friend in going on three years. He has no friends now. That's the way it is for him. That's the way he wants it now.

"We have to dig him out, because he's somewhere in this city. This isn't what I do, not what I know how to do best." She pushed her hands through her hair. "So I have to be the patient one, and wait for others to do the real digging."

"I liked to play baseball when I was a kid."

Confused, she looked over. "Sorry?"

"I liked to play, and I could wing a ball out of far right and pinpoint it to the cutoff man, even right into second. And I could run like the wind. But I had a bat as green and limp as old celery. So I had to depend on somebody else to hit in the runs. We do what we do, Phoebe."

"I love him more than I did my own father." She rubbed damp and tired eyes. "I hardly remember my daddy. Horsie-back rides and tickling and how he smelled of Dial soap. But I can't hear his voice in my head, and I have to look at his picture now and again to keep his face in there. When I think of fathers, I think of Dave first."

"Come on, baby." He took her hand. "Let's get you home."

"There's nothing more I can do tonight. Just nothing."

"You'll get some sleep, then you'll figure out what to do tomorrow."

"You're going to stay with me." She got in the car, looked up at him. "You said you would."

"Sure, I can do that."

He expected to bunk in Ava's son's room again, so Duncan was surprised when after peeking in on Carly, Phoebe took him by the hand and drew him into her bedroom.

She pressed a finger to her lips as she closed and locked the door behind them. "You're going to have to be very quiet while you make love with me."

"You're the noisy one." He backed her toward the bed. "But if you get too carried away, I'll just gag you."

"Try this instead." She rose on her toes, found his mouth with hers. "God." She let out the word on a sigh. "God, God, I want you all over me. Inside me, around me, on me and under me. I want to be surrounded, Duncan. Surrounded so I can't think of anything else."

He eased her down on the bed, brushed the hair back from her face. His lips brushed her brow, her cheeks, her jaw. Then they sank into hers.

He could feel her relax, inch by inch. A little tremor in the shoulders, then a melting. Her arms lifted so he could slip her shirt off and away. And his hands ran down her sides. Bumped into her gun.

"Ah, I think you're armed and dangerous."

"Crap. I forgot." She tapped him back so she could roll, unhook her weapon. She set it, in its holster, on the nightstand.

"You don't just leave it out like that, with Carly around?"

One more little flutter to the heart, she thought, and cupped his face. "No. I have a lockbox, top shelf of my closet. But I think, as the door's locked, it'll be fine there for a little while."

"Okay. Let's see, I think I was just about . . ." He pulled her back. "Here," he said before his lips took hers again.

They spoke in whispers as they undressed each other. Then didn't speak at all.

He surrounded her, just as she'd asked, with touch and taste, with heat and motion. In the dark, her hands and lips slid over his skin, and she found what she needed.

Little thrills rising to gnawing aches, aches soothed back to silky pleasures. Time ticked away, and maybe those stars were burning now—but she didn't need their light. All the terror and tension of the endless day drained.

She lifted to him, and he could hear her sigh and sigh as he filled her. Then it was she who surrounded him, took him in, trapping him in that glorious heat until he was swamped.

He could see her eyes gleaming in the dark, watching him watching her through that exquisite merging of bodies. The thrill of skin to skin, though the rhythm stayed slow and easy, rise and fall. And lips met with a quick and fresh hunger to muffle moans, to swallow gasps.

When the rising peaked and the fall was a dive in the dark, he pressed his face into her hair, to draw in its scent like breath.

She should get up, stow her weapon so she could unlock the door. But, God, it felt so good to just lie there naked, body to body with her mind all fuzzy and her heart still thudding.

How had she done without this for so long? The intimacy and pleasure, the *contact?* How had she done without him? The conversation and support, the humor and understanding. Wasn't it amazing that at this point in her life she would find someone who fit? Just fit—body, mind, heart.

Maybe she was feeling sentimental and shaky, under siege and out of control. But she'd found someone who helped keep the ground steady under her feet. Someone else who could answer the questions or point the way—because, oh Jesus, she hadn't realized how tired she'd been of carrying the whole load alone.

"You make me feel sturdier, Duncan."

"Good. I think."

"It's very good, for me." She ran her hands down his back all the way to his ass and back again. "Very good. Maybe it's just postcoital euphoria, but right now I feel like I can handle what's happening, and what has to happen. It's going to be all right because it has to be."

He said nothing for a moment, then trailed a finger over her shoulder. "I rehired Suicide Joe."

"You . . . Hmm."

"Phin's going to be pissed, but it's just part-time. A few hours a week. He's not so crazy, and he's getting therapy." Duncan lifted his head, looked down at her. "You save lives, Phoebe—you saved his.

That's what you do. How many people can say that? That saving lives is what they do. Yeah, it's going to be all right."

"I don't know if I want to save his. Walken's. I've never felt that way before, as if—even for a moment—I wouldn't regret someone's death. All these years, I've never drawn my weapon on anyone. I've never discharged it outside the range. But I know I could, I know I wouldn't hesitate, if I walked out the door and he was there. It doesn't even weigh on me, Duncan, the knowing that."

"Why should it?"

"Because it's not what I do. All those years ago, when Reuben had us, I thought if I could get a knife from the kitchen, or somehow get the gun away, I'd hurt him. Kill him if I could, for what he was doing to us. Keeping us scared and trapped, that blood on Mama's face, and the fear on Carter's. That's the only other time in my life I felt like this. But when it was over, when it was done, I was so relieved he wasn't dead. He'd go to prison, and that was good, that was just fine, but he wasn't dead. No one died in that house. I don't know, when this is over, if I'll feel the same."

"I haven't picked a fight in . . . well, that little scuffle with Jake's stupid cousin doesn't count, so in fifteen years or so. Haven't cracked my fist into anyone's face or gotten that rush of whipping someone good and proper. But if I had the chance, if I could get my hands on Walken, I'd beat him bloody. And when he was done, his eyes rolling back, I'd beat him some more.

"It's not what I do, Phoebe, but knowing I would doesn't weigh on me, either."

She stared at him because however calm and easy his tone, she knew he meant it. He had that in him. "Well. Well. We're just a couple of violent individuals, aren't we?"

"Somewhere in there. The difference is we don't set out to be. Tell you what, if you get the chance, you draw on him, and you hold the gun on him till I get there. I'll beat hell out of him, and when he's down, you can give him a couple of good kicks."

She snorted out a laugh before she could stop it. "God, that shouldn't be funny, and it sure as hell shouldn't make me feel better. But it is, and it does. And with this current mood, I'm going to put that gun in the lockbox where it belongs."

She wiggled out from under him, picked up the gun from the nightstand. Then blinked against the sudden light when he switched on the bedside lamp.

"Had to see." He tracked his gaze over her, a lazy sweep of dusky blue. "Naked redhead with a gun. I believe that's stirred me up enough I could go another round."

She only shook her head, walked to the closet. "A few hours ago, I wouldn't have believed I could end the day here, like this. Life is a strange ride, as someone commented recently."

"I like the ups and downs of it. Which reminds me of something I was going to ask you. When this is done, how about taking a few days off, taking a little trip with me?"

It was hopeful and human to project, to plan, Phoebe knew as she took down the lockbox. She smiled a little as she imagined Paris or Rome, Tahiti or Belize. "I might be able to swing that. Where'd you have in mind?"

"Disney World." She dropped the gun into the box with a little thud, then simply stood in the closet, staring at nothing.

"You want to go to Disney World?"

"Big dream of mine when I was a kid. I used to sit in bed and think about it. It all seemed so happy there. Color and music and fun, life-sized cartoon characters walking around. Never got there, not when I was a kid. Been a couple times since, just to say I did."

Carefully, she set the box back on the shelf. "And was it happy? All you wanted it to be?"

"Yeah, I guess it was. If you come out of the Country Bear Jamboree with a frown on your face, you're hopeless. I figured Carly'd get a charge out of it, wouldn't she? It's got to be about the best place in the world when you're seven. At least I thought so when I was."

She stepped back out of the closet to study him. He was sitting on the bed, buck naked, his hair all tousled, a dreamy half smile on his face as he thought, not about the City of Lights or Roman holidays, but magic mountains and flying elephants.

"You want to take Carly to Disney World?"

He turned his head, shrugged. "You can come, too. I'll buy you some mouse ears."

There was a threat hanging over them, she thought. It was very real, and it was very close. His connection to her put him every bit as much in the crosshairs as it did her. But he thought of taking her little girl to Disney World.

She walked to the bed, sat beside him. Taking his hand, she looked into his eyes. "Duncan." And love moved through her like a sigh. "Duncan."

His dimple winked. "Phoebe."

"Would you marry me?"

"Would I . . . what was that?"

His hand jerked, just a little, in hers, and she saw the coordinating shock on his face. She didn't mind either. "You're the best man I've ever known, and that's going some since I have Carter and Dave in my life, and they're such good men. You make me laugh, and you make me think. You're generous and you're smart—which is an important combination since one without the other is almost always annoying. And your innate loyalty is something I respect and admire."

"You forgot the sex."

Now she smiled. "No, I didn't, not for one quick minute. Since I'm being so complimentary, I'll tell you I've never had better, and it does, of course, factor into this proposal. My life is complicated, and it's heavy with responsibilities. You're the only one I trust enough to ask to share that. The only one I love enough. And I love you, Duncan. I love you so much.

"Wait, wait," she said quickly when she saw the change in his eyes. "I need to finish. I love all the things about you I've just said, and all that was the bunch of things I was going to tell you tonight. The proposal, that wasn't on the map. But then, well, I got lost in Disney World."

"Disney World was the kicker?"

"Oh yes, yes, it was. I know we haven't known each other for very long. Just since—"

"St. Patrick's Day."

"St. Patrick's Day. So you'll probably need to think about it, and God knows things need to settle down, but—"

"Where's the ring?"

"The ring?"

"What kind of half-assed proposal is this?" he demanded. "You didn't get me a ring?"

Her breath came out in a whoosh. "I've been a little busy."

His sigh was patient, long-suffering, and quite a bit exaggerated. "I don't know as I can take this very seriously without a ring. But I guess I can make an exception, this once." He leaned down, met her smiling lips with his. "I was going to ask you in Disney World."

"You . . . Really?"

"I figured on getting you dizzy on the teacups, or weak-kneed on Space Mountain, hit you while your defenses were down some. Of course, I'd've had a ring."

She shoved him back on the bed, rolled on top of him. "I like things clear. Is that a yes?"

"You had me when you walked into Suicide Joe's apartment."

Her eyes narrowed. "As far as you knew at that point, I could've been married with six children, or a lesbian."

"Then I'd've pined for you the rest of my days. But I'm a lucky man. Been on a streak for a while now, and it's been heading straight toward you. You had me, Phoebe, the minute you walked in, and from that minute I've been sliding into love without even looking for a handhold."

He tucked her hair behind her ear. "I don't mind complications, and responsibilities are just part of living if you're doing it right. We'll do it right, you and me. So yes, I accept your ringless proposal."

She laid her lips on his, then rested, cheek to cheek. "I haven't even started on the complications. I have to live in this house. I can't—"

"I like this house. That's not a complication, it's a great old house on Jones Street."

"My mother—"

"Is great. If I couldn't get you, I was going to go for her. She likes me." He trailed a finger down Phoebe's spine. "Women tend to."

Phoebe shifted to look down at him. "I'd expect . . . I'd need you to be a father to Carly."

"Piss me off if you didn't. Relax, Phoebe." He drew her down until her head rested on his chest. "You don't have to negotiate this. It's a done deal."

"I'm so happy. It seems strange to be so happy when so much is wrong."

"Whatever's wrong, we'll fix. That's something we're both pretty good at."

"It's nearly morning," she murmured with her eyes on the window. "It's nearly time to start again."

"Close your eyes awhile. Close your eyes while you're happy, and get a little sleep."

The next thing she knew, the sun was beaming into her eyes, and her daughter was banging on the door. Thank God she'd left it locked.

Phoebe gave Duncan a good, hard shake, got a grunt in response, before she sprang out of bed. "Just a minute, honey."

"Mama, why is the door locked? Mama, are you okay?"

"Fine, fine." In a flurry of motion, Phoebe rushed to the closet and yanked out her robe. "Just fine, Carly. Why don't you go on downstairs? I'll be right down."

"Your door's locked, Mama. I'll go tell Gran."

"No!" Sweet baby Jesus. "No, no, just a minute." Moving like the wind, Phoebe dragged on the robe as she bolted out of the closet. Yawning hugely, Duncan stood beside the rumpled bed lazily pulling on jeans. At a loss, Phoebe put her finger to her lips, then, unlocking her door, cracked it open an inch.

"I was sleeping, honey. I got home very late. I'll be downstairs in a few minutes."

"But your door was locked."

"Yes, I guess it was. I'll be—"

"Duncan's car's outside. But he's not downstairs, and he's not in Steven's room either."

"Oh. Well. Why don't you go see if Ava wants to make waffles for breakfast?"

"Is Duncan in there?" Carly shifted right and left to try to see through the narrow opening. Phoebe shifted left and right to block her. "Did he sleep with you last night?"

The child was a dog with a bone, Phoebe thought. Before she could speak, Duncan said, "Busted," and eased the door open. "Hey, Carly."

"Hi. Mama's door was locked so I couldn't come in."

"We got home very late," Phoebe repeated.

"How come you slept in Mama's room?" Carly asked Duncan.

"And aren't you full of questions this morning, before I've even had my coffee."

"You said you have to ask questions," Carly reminded her mother. "Did you have a bad dream, Duncan? I sleep in Mama's bed sometimes when I do."

"Actually." He gave Phoebe a poke in the arm to shift her aside. "Let me ask you a question. How do you feel about your mama and me getting married?"

Carly's eyes narrowed on Duncan's face, then tracked to her mother's and back. "Because you're in love and want to sleep in bed together?"

"That's right."

"You'd be my stepdaddy?"

"I would."

"Can I have a new dress for when you get married?"

"That would be a priority."

She smiled, and Phoebe recognized the slyness. "My friend Dee got a stepdaddy, then she got a new baby brother named William. Can I have one of those, too?"

"Could be a sister, but we can name her William."

With a giggle, Carly shook her head. "Girls aren't William. We could get a puppy first, and name *him* William, then——"

"You're pushing your luck, kid," Phoebe warned.

"We're having a conversation here," Duncan said to Phoebe, then hunkered down so his face was level with Carly's. "I'll see what I can do about that. If I pull it off, what're you going to give me?"

Carly's face went pink, then she touched her lips, very primly, to Duncan's cheek.

"Little peck like that, for a baby and a dog? You MacNamara women are tough."

She giggled again, and the pink deepened as she hooked her arms around Duncan for a hug, and gave his cheek a noisy, smacking kiss.

Not once, Phoebe thought as she stared down at them, not once had she seen Carly and Roy hold each other. Not once had she ever seen her little girl grinning in her father's arms.

"Now that's more like it. I'm going to grab a shirt, so I don't make the women in the house swoon when I come downstairs." He set Carly back on her feet. "We'll be right along."

"Okay." She dashed off, shooting him a dazzling smile as she ran for the stairs.

"Guess she approves. Now we'll see what Essie has . . . What?" Panic streaked across his face as he turned and saw the tears sliding down Phoebe's. "What'd I do wrong?"

Her throat was so thick she could only shake her head as she wrapped herself around him, held tight. Tighter. "We got along without you, you know," she managed. "We got right along. But, God, oh God, things are so much better with you."

"Happy crying." He let out a little breath of relief. "I get that."

"Very happy."

"That's good. So . . . how about that puppy?"

29

The timing was perfect, and the location—that had come about largely due to luck. Or maybe, he thought, it was fate. It was Angie looking down, guiding hands.

It would be today.

A pity, a goddamn pity, pieces of McVee hadn't flown all over Barnard Street. His slut of a neighbor had intervened there. Bastard had flown some though, he thought with some satisfaction. Oh yeah, the bastard had done a little fucked-up Superman.

It had taken all the willpower he'd had not to yank out his nine from under the windbreaker and put bullets in the son of a bitch and the neighborhood slut where they lay bleeding on the side of the road.

But as satisfying as that would've been, as *right* as it would've been, it could have cost the rest. And the endgame was in sight.

Better if McVee died, and there was always the chance of that. Better yet if there was time and opportunity to take out the boyfriend, just for good measure. And it was a damn shame he had to abort the plans to stake out the pansy-assed brother in front of the house where they grew up—with a vestload of explosives.

Cowards, a couple of dickless cowards is what they were, hiding out in that house, behind the women's skirts. Not worth his time, Walken told himself, not worth his trouble.

He continued to load his gear with careful hands.

They'd be looking for him now. Let them look. In a couple of hours, they'd know just where to find him. And he'd be where he wanted to be, doing what he'd planned to do.

Before he was done, everyone would know Phoebe MacNamara had killed an angel, just as sure as the bullet. And when it was over, it would be fucking over.

"He turned in his papers and moved out of his apartment. He had two months left on his lease, left a check to cover it." At Dave's bedside, Phoebe went through the checklist. "He had two credit cards at that time. Neither have shown any activity in these three years. He's contacted no one, not his best friend, nor his former commanding officer. He had a checking account, and a savings account totaling six thousand and change, and a safety deposit box. He cleaned everything out on the same day he quit the department. There was an oh-one Chevy pickup registered to him. He sold it, for eight thousand cash, to a Derrick Means, in the same apartment building. We're checking that out, but don't expect it to go anywhere. Also registered to him were a nine-millimeter Smith and Wesson and a thirty-two Remington semi. His friend knew him to own a hunting rifle, with scope, a thirty-thirty, and a twenty-two pistol which had been his father's."

"Likes guns."

"Yes, he does. He's a trained sniper, and had training in explosives during his time in the army. He also worked with our own bomb squad before he requested and received the transfer to SWAT. He's somewhere in or around Savannah, but as far as we know, you're the only one who's seen him."

She lifted her hands. "I don't know what to do. I negotiate, I don't investigate."

"A puzzle's a puzzle, Phoebe. It's all pieces."

"I have some of them. He blames me for Angela Brentine's death, maybe because there isn't anyone else to blame. He was on the team that day, Dave. He was on the incident where she died. His scope trained on the bank, waiting for the go. We didn't know the names of the hostages, or the injured. He didn't know she was in there, dead or dying, while he waited outside, while all those hours passed."

"Ineffective. Impotent." Dave nodded, then closed his eyes as the slight movement stirred pain in the base of his skull. "Lancelot didn't rescue Guinevere."

"That's what he can't live with. That he was there, waiting while she bled out. While I had them wait, while I talked her killers down so they walked out with their hands in the air. They lived, she died, because of decisions I made. That's what he believes. That's what he has to believe. But it doesn't help us find him."

"Why'd he go after Roy?"

Think it through, Phoebe reminded herself. Empathize. "The connection to me—we had a child together, we were married. Husband— a symbol. Harder, much harder, to get to Brentine than to Roy. And Roy was mine. He wants to destroy what's mine, as I destroyed what was his."

"Not just the woman." Dave reached for the water glass, then settled back to sip through the straw as Phoebe picked it up, held it to his lips. "Thanks. Not just the woman," he repeated. "His self-image was destroyed. Didn't save the day. Followed orders, hung back with the rest instead of walking solo out into the street for the showdown."

"But this time, he is, he will. Moving up the line," she mused. "Roy, then you. Everyone knows we're close. And that I'm a negotiator because of you. Therefore, I was at the bank because of you.

"Do you want me to call the nurse?" she said when he shifted, when she saw pain tighten his face. "You should rest, you should—"

"No. Keep going. It keeps my mind busy. You call the nurse, she's going to come in here with a needle and take more blood. I swear, being in a hospital's like being in a den of vampires. They never get enough of your blood. Keep going."

Wishing she could do more, Phoebe tucked and smoothed his sheets as she spoke. "All right. The dead animals, to defile my house, to under-

mine my sense of security. Snake, rabbit, rat. He's probably based outside the city. Somebody's going to notice if you shoot a rabbit otherwise. Smarter to have a place outside the city, quiet, secluded. Nobody's
going to bother you or notice you overmuch, not if you keep to yourself.
Get along," she said. "Like he got along with his teammates. A house,
a bungalow. He'd need transportation. They're still checking on how he
got to Hilton Head."

She turned to the window. Urban sprawl, she thought, so roads led
to suburbs, and suburbs gave way to swamps and woods. Bridges rib-
boned their way to islands.

So many places to hide.

"Every cop in the city, every cop on the islands, has his picture. He
has to know that. He has to know you lived, that you saw him, and that
we're looking for him now. I see he's got two choices—to cut and run,
or to finish. He won't cut and run."

"You need to be ready when he comes at you."

She nodded. "I'm trying to be." She turned back. "I never asked how
you felt this morning."

"Glad to be alive."

"I've had to tie the rest of the family down to keep them from coming to see you. And I'm under orders to put *you* under orders to come to
the house when they spring you from here so Mama and Ava can spoil
you while you recuperate."

"Would that include peach pie?"

"I can guarantee it. When are you going to ask Ava out on a date?"

"Excuse me?"

"When are the two of you going to stop sending wistful glances at
each other's backs? You're both grown-up, divorced people. I don't
think she got any sleep last night."

"Well, I . . ."

"I don't know how many times this morning she asked me about
you, or argued with me about coming to see you herself, or told me to
tell you she was thinking of you."

"She's a friend, she's been a friend a long time."

"Dave, my mama is your friend." Exasperation eked through enough to have her fisting her hands on her hips. "Are you going to lie there on what might have been your deathbed and tell me you feel the same about Ava you do about my mama?"

"I don't think—"

"What do you want?" She approached the bed again. "I know how to find out what people want in emotional and stressful situations. If you're too flustered to tell me—and it's awful cute to see you blush—I'll tell you. You want to ask Ava out for a romantic, candlelight dinner when you're back on your feet."

He stirred again, but this time Phoebe could see it wasn't about pain. "It happens I was thinking about her—about that—when I was walking home yesterday. Before. I was thinking the timing for doing that was lousy."

"Timing's lousy on most everything half the time." Smiling down at him, she brushed at his hair. "I asked Duncan to marry me. He said yes."

Dave's mouth opened and closed. "You're full of surprises this morning."

"I surprise myself. I love him like I've been waiting to find him my whole life, just waiting for the rest of my life to start. You'll give me away again, won't you? I'm betting this one sticks."

"I'm betting it will, too." Reaching up, he gripped her hand. "I'm happy for you."

"So am I. You've been waiting, Dave, an awfully long time. Ask Ava out to dinner, so the rest of your life starts."

When Phoebe walked out of Dave's room, Liz pushed off the wall.

"Thanks for giving me some alone time with him."

"No problem. How's he doing?"

"Well enough to settle my nerves on that score. I want to thank you again for pairing up with me today."

"Another no problem. This Walken tried to kill one of our own. There isn't anyone in the department who isn't invested in this. He can't hide for long."

"And he's not going to run." She stepped outside into the swampy heat. "That storm didn't cool it off any. Just made it wetter."

"Summer in Savannah. Love it or go away. Go ahead and take it," she said when Phoebe's phone rang. "I'll drive."

"I think it's him." She held out the phone so Liz could read the display. With a nod, Liz stepped away, drew her own phone. "Phoebe Mac-Namara."

"How's Dave doing?"

"He's doing well, thanks. You screwed up there."

"No. Variables, Phoebe. You know about variables. Shit happens. I know you're looking for me."

"You don't sound upset by that, Jerry."

"Not. You won't find me until I'm ready. You wearing a vest, Phoebe?"

As her heart jumped, she shoved Liz down behind the cover of the car. "It's too damned hot for a vest, Jerry. How about you?"

"I think I could've put one in the back of your head, and the brunette's. But I've got other plans. We'll be talking."

"He was here," Phoebe said. "Watched us go in or watched us come out. I don't think he's here now." Could've, not could, she thought. She looked down, saw her weapon was in her hand. The hand was shaking, but it held. "Back of the head. Going in. He's not here now."

When her phone rang a second time, her heart stuck in her throat. "It's Sykes," she told Liz. "What have you got?" she asked him.

"Airport Budget rented a Toyota to a Grimes, Samuel, last Thursday. It was dropped off in Hilton Head Saturday afternoon. I'm looking at a copy of the driver's license. It's Walken. Darker hair, glasses, but it's him. Used a Visa. The license lists an address in Montana, but the credit card's got billing going to one on Tybee."

"That's the one. Relay the situation and the address to Commander Harrison. Liz and I'll join the team there." She climbed into the car. "What's the address?"

Ma Bee smiled a smug smile as she shifted the kitchen phone to her right ear. "Does this mean I'm finally going to get me some white grandbabies?"

"Technically, you'll start off with one who's already seven. Then we'll see what we can do. How about helping me out on the sparkler?"

428 | Nora Roberts

"I do love shiny things, and my taste is world-renowned. I guess I could give you the benefit of my renowned taste in shiny things."

"Today? I've got a couple of things, then I could swing out and pick you up, then we'll swing back in and—"

"Don't I have myself a fine car sitting right out in the driveway? I can get myself where I'm going. So where am I going?"

"I figured if I didn't find it at Mark D's on Abercorn, I'm not going to find it anywhere."

"Mark D's?" She let out a long whistle. "That's the high-dollar mark."

"I got high dollars. And it happens I made a call, and Mr. D himself would be pleased to meet us and show us some of his more exclusive designs."

Now she hooted. "Aren't you the one?"

"She is. I was thinking maybe I could find something for Carly. And there I'm out of my depth. Something that'd suit a little girl, but would maybe move on up with her. I figured it being a package deal, I could . . . you know, make it a package."

"You're going to be a fine daddy. What time do you want me to meet you?"

"I think I can get there around noon. Buy you lunch after if you do a good job."

"I'll be there. You bring those high dollars, boy, 'cause I'm itching to spend them for you."

She hung up, literally rubbed her hands together. A glance at the clock told her she had time to spread the word before fixing herself up for a trip to Mark D's.

The tactical team was already in place and moving in when Phoebe arrived. It was a good location, she thought with a look around. Well off the beach, older house, a little run-down.

For the second time that day, she drew her weapon as the team broke in the front door with a small battering ram.

"No car," Harrison commented. "No bike, no scooter."

"No Walken. He's not here, but now he's got no place to come back to." She waited, blood pumping, for the all clear.

"Lieutenant." Sykes jogged over. "DMV came through. He's got an oh-six Escalade. Got the tag number. APB's going out."

"You do good work, Detective."

"We're clear," Harrison announced.

He'd likely rented it furnished, Phoebe decided. The furniture was old, cheap but serviceable. He kept it tidy, she noted. No clutter, no fuss. The bed was made with military precision, and on the table beside it stood a framed photo of Angela Brentine and a single pink rose.

Thought of himself as a soldier and a romantic, she concluded as she took notes.

"Second bedroom's locked," Harrison told her. "Window's covered. They're checking for booby traps before they take it down."

"Spartan, wouldn't you say? Military neatness. The bare bones of a field HQ. We should talk to the landlord, anyone in the houses and cottages round about." She moved to the closet. "His clothes are still here, neatly hung."

"Toothbrush, shaving cream, basic toiletries in the bath," Harrison told her. His face was hard, his eyes somber as they met hers. "He isn't running."

"No." She heard the crash of the second door going down. "But that doesn't mean he's coming back."

"Lieutenant?" A member of the tactical team came to the doorway. "I think you'll want to see this. Found his nest."

When she walked across the hall, her blood went cold. Photographs papered an entire wall. Her face, over and over, in every possible expression. Photos of her standing in front of her house, talking with Mrs. Tiffany, walking with Carly in the park, standing with her mother on the veranda.

The whole family on what had to have been St. Patrick's Day. One of her moving into Duncan's arms the night they'd had dinner on his boat. Her sitting on the bench, like Forrest Gump, in Chippewa Park, alone, then with Marvella. Of her shopping, eating, driving.

A shudder ran through her before she looked away.

Across the room was a large head-and-shoulders shot of Angela, with candles and bud vases of pink roses crowded on the table below it.

She studied the workbench, a long table, shelves. On them, meticulously arranged, were a laptop computer, a police scanner, chemicals, wires, what she thought must be timing mechanisms, tape, rope and tools. She spotted the shotgun, the rifle.

"He took his handguns."

"He's got a couple of wigs, glasses, false beards, makeup, face putty," Liz said as she crossed over. "No journal. Maybe on that," she said with a nod toward the laptop.

"Why didn't he take it? Why didn't he take what was important to him?" Because it shook her down to the bone, Phoebe kept her back to the wall of photos. "Switch locations at least. He knows we have his name, his photo, and someone's going to point us here."

"He couldn't have been sure we'd ID'd him until he talked to you," Liz pointed out.

"He stays a step ahead. Why is he suddenly a step behind? Expensive equipment, easily portable, just left here."

She picked up a camera, turned it over, saw the painted pink rosebud. Angela's camera.

"He planned to come back for it."

Carefully, Phoebe set the camera back down. "I don't think so. I think he's done here, and that we're exactly where he wants us to be. But where is he?"

She stepped to another wall, covered with photos of Savannah. Banks, shops, restaurants, museums, exterior, interior.

"He doesn't waste anything. Everything has a purpose, even if it's thumbing his nose. So why does he take these?"

"And where are the others?" Liz wondered. "He's taken some down—you can see where he had other shots up."

"If he took them with him, he needed them. He takes pictures of places because the places have a purpose, or the potential of one. Targets. These are digital shots, aren't they?"

She turned back to the laptop. "We have to get in there, find the files, find the ones he took with him. That's the target." As it churned, she pressed a hand to her stomach. "I think he gave himself the go, the green light. Today. I think it has to be today."

She looked at her watch and felt the chill as she noted it was ten fifty-five. "High Noon. We've got an hour to find him."

Duncan shoved his hands in his pockets, jiggled loose change while the structural engineers, the architect and Jake swarmed over the warehouse. "We have to move this along, Phin."

"You set the meeting, the inspection."

"Yeah, yeah, yeah, but that was before."

"If you think Ma's going to mind poking around a jewelry store on her own awhile if you're running late, you've forgotten who you're dealing with."

Duncan pulled his hand out of his pocket to check his watch. Eleven-ten. "Maybe I should call her, tell her to make it twelve-thirty."

"She's probably on her way, especially since she's meeting Loo." Phin grinned at Duncan's blank look. "If you don't think Ma got on the horn and starting blowing the news the minute she hung up with you, you're not thinking, boy. Then again, I guess a man about to buy an engagement ring's not thinking."

"You did it."

"Yeah. Working out pretty well for me, too." He gave Duncan a slap on the back. "Business, Dunc. Ma and Loo can entertain each other just fine if you're late. Loo said she was taking a full hour lunch, and was prepared to make it two if need be. So God help you."

Phoebe paced outside the computer lab. One step ahead, she thought. He was still one step ahead. "Somewhere that means something to him, in association with her. It's more personal than something associated with me."

Her family was safe, she reminded herself. Inside, guarded and safe. Hadn't she checked twenty minutes ago? Hadn't she talked to Carly, to her mother, even contacted the cops on duty?

"The bank where she was killed is under heavy surveillance. If he tries to get in, we'll have him."

She glanced over at Liz, nodded. "And he'd know that. Still, if that was his target, that wouldn't stop him. He'd assume he's far enough ahead of us to hit it before we're in place. But it's the obvious target, and that concerns me. I think it's somewhere else. A restaurant where they met, a hotel, motel, even one of the parks. It needs to be a statement, Liz."

Pacing, she tried to find the pieces. "Blowing up a man in Bonaventure, *that's* a statement. Attempting to do the same to a police captain mere blocks from the station, that's another."

"Big, splashy. I get that. And this is the biggest, the splashiest." Like Phoebe, Liz stared through the glass walls of the lab. "I get that, too."

"City Hall, courthouse, the station itself?"

"All on alert. But if it's personal, the way you're thinking, those don't fit."

"You're right. You're right. He can't get to Brentine, and Brentine isn't his issue, either. She was leaving him, Brentine's superfluous."

"Security's stepped up at his home and office in any case."

"How long is it going to take them to find those files? Even with him deleting them the way he did, they're still there somewhere. That's what they always say. Damn it, we've only got twenty minutes till noon."

At ten to twelve, Ma Bee and Loo strolled into Mark D's, anticipating an afternoon of shopping and a celebration lunch. Ma had donned her shopping shoes and a breezy purple dress. She had put on her going-out-special lipstick, and had spritzed on some of her favorite French perfume.

"I could've handled this expedition, you know."

Loo gave a snort. "You think I'm letting you have all the fun? You've done this before with all your boys. But it's my first chance to have some input on an engagement ring. Don't you love this place?" She gave Ma a little elbow bump as they stopped to look around. "All these glitters, and everything all hushed and reverent."

"So they can charge more."

"Sure, but that little black-and-silver box from Mark D's? That *says* something. When Phineas gave me that bracelet from here last Christmas, I squealed like a girl. And he got awfully lucky that night."

It was Ma's turn to snort. "I don't see a new grandchild for me coming out of it."

"We're thinking about it."

"Think faster. I'm not getting any younger." She looked up at the trio of crystal chandeliers. "But you're right, it sure is fine in here. Let's have a little look-see before Duncan gets here."

Arnie Meeks was bored out of his mind. He was, in his opinion, nothing more than a glorified doorman, standing around while tourists and rich Savannahians came breezing inside. The tourists were a pain in the ass, mostly, just coming in to gawk. And the rich—bitches mostly—had their noses in the air.

Like they didn't squat to pee like the rest of their kind.

The old man could fix this. Resentment bubbled up inside his throat at the thought of it. Push the buttons, pull the strings, grease the palms, he'd be back on the job instead of standing around waiting to roust shoplifters.

And in the weeks since he'd been stuck on this humiliating duty, he'd had only a little action in that area twice.

What he needed was for some asshole to come in and try to rob the place. Now that would be a fucking dream come true. He'd take the bastard down, you could bet your ass on it. Take him down, be a hero. Get on TV.

Get back on the job where he goddamn belonged.

He saw the two black women come in and curled his lip. As if that old lady in her thick-soled shoes could afford so much as a cuff link from this place. The young one was hot—if you went for the Halle Berry type—and had a slick look about her. So maybe she could dig out a platinum card.

Probably just more lookie-loos, Arnie decided as he watched them gawk around. The way he saw it, more than half the people who came in the doors were lookie-loos.

He did his own scan.

A dozen people wandered around the store, drooling over the displays. Three clerks—who made more than he did with their fucking commissions by kissing ass and talking people into buying what they didn't need—manned counters or unlocked cabinets to take something out.

The place was manned with security cameras, with alarms. Even the back room, where he knew the man himself was planted today, in anticipation of some deep-pocketed client. Arnie had heard the buzz on that.

Deep Pockets would be escorted into the back, so the hoi polloi couldn't watch him playing with the sparklers. Or if he *wanted* to be seen—and some of them got off on that—they'd set him up at the special table in the corner.

Patsy, the blonde with the rack, had told him that Julia Roberts had shopped there in the back room. And Tom Hanks had, too. At the special table.

Maybe he'd move on Patsy, get a little action there. His marriage was in the toilet, and the way things were going with Mayleen—thanks to that bitch MacNamara—he wasn't getting anything there either.

Time to scout the field again, pick himself a new heifer out of the herd. He knew by the way she looked at him—the way she made sure her ass wiggled when she walked away—that Patsy was up for it. Maybe he'd take her for a little spin some night after work. See how she handled in the sack.

He looked over as the front door gave its little ding as it opened. He saw the brown uniform and cursed under his breath. A pain-in-the-ass delivery.

He stepped toward the door.

Loo pulled out her cell phone when it played "Jailhouse Rock." She winked at Ma when she read the display. "Hey there, lover-boy."

"Hello, gorgeous. You there with Ma?"

"We're here admiring a whole buncha diamond rings. Where are you?"

"Running behind. On my way, though, with this leech on me I can't pull off. He insists on coming along."

"That leech about six feet tall with eyes like melted dark chocolate?"

"He's about that tall, anyway. We're just heading cross town. Probably take a good fifteen minutes yet."

"Take your time, and tell that brown-eyed man I've got my own eyes on a pair of ruby earrings that are going to set him back a bit. Another fifteen, twenty minutes, I bet I find something else to set him back even more."

"Then I'll take my time. Why should I be the only one spending money today?"

The time was clicking down toward noon when Phoebe was able to see the photos. She hung over the shoulder of the computer technician.

"Some of these were on the wall. Prints were left on the wall. Some of them weren't. This motel."

"Over by Oglethorpe Mall," the technician told her. "You see he's got shots of the outside, the lobby and this room."

"They used that room for trysts when it wasn't convenient to use his apartment. And this restaurant—I know this place, little Italian place. That's out by the mall, too. Not in the heart of things, not places they'd likely run into anyone in her husband's circle. But they don't feel like the sort of places he'd target. They're not what you'd call important, like Bonaventure. Not a statement like— Wait."

She gripped the tech's shoulder as he panned through the file. "Wait, that's Mark D's."

"Inside and out, back and front. I don't think they allow photographs inside Mark D's."

"No, security, insurance. No, they wouldn't want photographs. Pictures of the back door, the front door from inside and out." In her belly, muscles tightened. "I want cars over there now. Right now. Liz, get ahold of Property, find out what jewelry was listed in her personal effects. And, Jesus, let's get his credit card records for three months back from Angela's death. Good work," she said to the technician. "Let's get the hell over there."

Six minutes, she noted as she rushed out. Six minutes until noon. Maybe they weren't too late.

"Hey, buddy, when are you guys going to get the word that deliveries are supposed to come in first thing in the morning, before the customers?"

"Just following orders." He rolled in the dolly with its three large boxes. He turned deliberately into Arnie. "Just like you're going to do, unless you want to take a bullet in the belly. Lock the door, asshole," he ordered as he clamped a hand over Arnie's weapon. "I've got an S-and-W nine shoved right into your navel. The bullet's going to make a hell of a hole out the other side of you, if you don't do now and think later."

"What the fuck do you . . . I know you."

"Yeah, I used to be a cop, too. Let's do it this way." Lifting the gun, he whipped it across Arnie's face and sent him down. Even before the first scream, he was turning, both weapons in his hands. And he smiled as, right on schedule, right according to plan, some good employee hit the alarms that set them shrilling. And locked the place down.

"Everybody on the floor. Now! Now!" He put a series of rounds in the ceiling, shattering crystal. There was plenty of screaming as people dove for cover or simply dropped to huddle together on the floor. "Except you, Blondie."

He aimed the nine at Patsy. "Over here."

"Please. Please."

"Die there or come here. Five seconds."

With tears already streaming out of her eyes, she stumbled toward him. He hooked one arm around her neck, put the gun to her temple. "Want to live?"

"Yes. God. Oh God."

"Anyone in the back? Lie to me, and I'll know, and I'll kill you."

"I . . . Mr. D." She sobbed it out. "Mr. D's in the back."

"He's got monitors back there, right? He can see us right now. You'd better call out, Blondie. Because if he isn't out here in ten seconds, he's going to lose his first employee."

"There's no need." Mark stepped out of the back room, hands high. He was a small-framed man in his early sixties, with a dapper white mustache and a head of waving white hair. "There's no need to hurt her. No need to hurt anyone."

"That'll be up to you, for a start. Over here, cuff your boy, hands behind his back."

"He's hurt."

"He'll be dead, you don't get it done. I want everyone to empty their pockets—one at a time—starting with you." He kicked the shoulder of a man in a Hawaiian shirt and khaki shorts. "Everything out, turn the pockets inside out. Anyone reaches for a cell phone, a weapon, a fucking stick of gum, I shoot. What's your name, honey?"

"Patsy. It's Patsy."

"Cute. I shoot cute Patsy in the ear. Pockets, now," he snapped.

"He needs medical attention," Mark said as he knelt beside Arnie. "I'll unlock the cases. You can take whatever you want. The police are on the way. The alarm."

"Yeah, it's handy." He heard the sirens already, cutting through the high ring of the store alarm. Quicker than he'd thought, but that was fine. "You're going to turn off the alarm, Mark, but you're not going to abort the lockdown. You got that? Screw it up, and Patsy's brains are going to be all over your nice, shiny floor. You." He kicked the first man again. "Up. Roll that dolly to the northeast corner."

"I . . . I don't know which is the northeast."

Walken rolled his eyes. "Right rear, fuckhead. Move! You, you, drag that worthless dick back there with it." He back-walked with Patsy, then shoved her to her knees. "Get some shopping bags, Patsy. You're going to pick up all this junk people carried in here, put it in shopping bags and put the bags on this counter. Everybody else, facedown. Oh, not you, Mark, sorry. Northeast corner. I'm watching you, Patsy. You be good, now. Pick up the phone, Mark." He nodded toward the one on the desk. "Call nine-one-one. You're going to say exactly what I tell you to say. Nothing more, nothing less. Understood?"

"Yes."

"Good." Walken tucked Arnie's weapon in his belt, ripped open the top box on the dolly. "You see what's in here, Mark?"

Mark's white face went gray as he looked in the box. "Yes."

"Plenty more where that came from. Make the call."

30

Phoebe was minutes from the jewelry store when the alarm went off. She stood within sight of it, with the crisis team already moving men and equipment into positions when the nine-one-one call was relayed to her.

This is Mark D, and I have an emergency. There is an armed man holding me and sixteen other hostages inside my store. He has guns and explosives. He says if he doesn't receive a call from Lieutenant Phoebe MacNamara within five minutes from the end of this call, he will shoot one of the hostages. For every minute beyond that five-minute deadline, he will shoot another. If anyone other than Lieutenant MacNamara attempts to contact him on this phone, or any other, he will shoot a hostage. If there is any attempt to enter this building, he will detonate the explosives. Lieutenant MacNamara has exactly five minutes from now.

She reached for her cell phone. "Give me the number inside."

"Communications is nearly set up," Harrison told her.

"I don't want him to know that, or that I'm already here. The less he thinks we know, the longer we can stall." She punched in the number passed to her, sucked in a breath, then punched to call.

"This better be Phoebe."

Answered first ring, she noted, and scribbled down *eager/anxious to get started.* "It's Phoebe, Jerry. I'm told you want to talk to me."

"You and nobody else. Anyone else calls in here, somebody dies. That's the first term."

"No one else calls you, talks to you, but me. I understand. Will you tell me how everyone's doing in there?"

"Sure. Scared spitless. Got us some criers. One guy's going to have a hell of a headache when he comes to. If he comes to. Hey, I think you know him, Phoebe. Arnie Meeks? You've danced with him before, right?"

Her rapidly scribbling hand jumped. "Are you saying that Arnold Meeks is one of the hostages, and that he's injured?"

"That's what I'm saying. He's also wearing an accessory. Just like the one I made for Roy. You remember Roy."

Not someone she loved this time, she thought, but someone she detested. And a damn clever, vicious way to up the stakes. "Are you telling me that you've rigged explosives on Arnold Meeks's person?"

"Oh yeah. A whole shitload of them. Any move on the building, and I blow him and a hell of a lot of others to hell. I don't figure you'll mind much about old Arnie, right? Guy messed you up, didn't he? Coward's way. How about if I pay him back for you?"

"You don't sound as if you want to do me any favors, Jerry. Can we talk about you and me, and what you do want?"

"We're just getting started. You'd better get things set up fast, Phoebe. I've got a little work to do in here. You call me back in ten."

"Get the com up," Phoebe snapped. "Commander, I need Mike Vince here, right here."

"Done." He ordered it. "We've got a partial visual, a count of ten hostages on the floor. We can't confirm if there are seven more. Internal security has locked down the building. There's a device rigged to the rear door with trip wires."

"Don't try to defuse, please. He'd know. It would give him the excuse to kill a hostage, or set off the rig he has on Meeks. What he wants most is to play me, to pay me back. We need to let him do that, as long as we can."

He'd left a tidy house, she thought, and roses for Angela.

"Commander, he's not planning on coming out of there alive. It's a suicide mission for him, his sacrifice. And his way of paying me back. The loss of seventeen hostages, including a man who injured me. I know what he's doing. I need time to wind this out."

"Com's set—negotiation control's in that ladies' boutique up there." Sykes gestured.

"Okay, I need everything, every scrap we have on him, everything we know or think we know. I need Mike Vince sent up as soon as possible. I need you with me, Sykes. I talk. Nobody talks to him but me," she continued as they hurried toward the boutique. "I need you to feed me information, to let me know if I go off on the wrong angle. He wants to play this out, too, so he won't rush it if we don't rush him. You help me interpret, help me listen, help me with every goddamn thing. Because he knows how this works, and he's waiting for me to make a mistake. He's salivating for just that."

"He's got nothing to lose, Lieutenant."

"No, he's already lost. What he wants is for me to sweat, then blow the whole thing—including himself—to pieces. This isn't a negotiation. But the longer he believes I think it is, the longer we have to get everyone out alive."

"You think he knew Arnie was security there?"

"Yes." She stepped into the boutique where her base had been set up amid thin summer dresses, pretty accessories, high-end handbags and fashionable sandals.

"I think it must have thrilled him to find out Arnie was on the door there. I think he saw it as a sign that he'd chosen his last stand perfectly." She stripped off her blazer, tossed it aside. "We already know why he's in there, what he wants. But we play it out. Start the checklist."

She sat at a table cleared of stock, pressed her fingers to her eyes. "He's cold, rational, committed. He's suicidal. He wants to die. This is another kind of suicide by cop—but a specific cop. Me. I fail, everyone dies. My failure's his motive, but that doesn't go for him unless we establish negotiations, unless we talk, play the game."

She checked her watch. Ten minutes exactly, she told herself. If she called a minute before, a minute after, he could use it as an excuse.

She ordered herself to clear her head, to find the calm. When Liz came through the door, Phoebe was counting down the last two minutes. "Your guy Duncan's just outside the perimeter, with his lawyer, Phineas Hector. He says he has to talk to you, right now. It's urgent."

"I can't—"

"Phoebe, he says he's got two people inside. He says he knows two of the hostages."

"Pull him in, fast."

One minute, fifteen seconds, she noted when Duncan and Phin came in.

"He's got my mother in there," Phin blurted out. "He's got my wife and mother in there."

It was like a bare-fisted blow to the throat. "Are you sure?"

"They were going to meet me there." The fight for control was obvious on his face as Duncan stood shoulder to shoulder with Phin. "I talked to Loo on her cell a few minutes before twelve because I was running late. They were inside. They were waiting for me. Jesus, Phoebe—"

"They're not hurt. He hasn't hurt anyone but the security guard." But her hands had gone clammy. "They're smart, sensible women, and they won't do anything to get themselves hurt."

"If he knows who they are . . ." Duncan began.

"He doesn't. He couldn't know they'd be in there. He isn't looking at them. It isn't about them. I need you both to go stand back there. Don't say anything, don't do anything. He doesn't know who they are, my connection to them, and that's vital to keeping them safe. I have to call him back. He can't hear anything but me now."

She signaled as Mike Vince came in. "I'm not asking you to go outside. I'm trusting you to let me do my job. You trust me to do it. Sykes, ADA Louise Hector and her mother-in-law, Beatrice Hector, are inside. I'm calling him back," she said to Vince. "I want you to listen. You have anything, anything at all to add, to help, any question, you write it down. Don't speak. I don't want him to hear your voice."

"Christ, Lieutenant, Christ, I can't believe Jerry would do something like this."

"Believe it." She shoved a pad and pencil at him, then made the call. "Right on time."

"What can I do for you now, Jerry?"

"How about a car, and a plane waiting for me at the airport."

"Is that what you want, Jerry?" She read the note Sykes put in front of her. "A car, a plane?"

Fifteen hostages, cuffed together in a circle. Explosive device in the center of the circle.

"And if I did?"

"You know I'd try to get it for you. Might be able to swing the car. What kind of car would you like, Jerry?"

"I've been looking at those Chrysler Crossfires. Gotta love the name, and I buy American."

"You'd like a Chrysler Crossfire."

"Might. Loaded."

"I'll try to get that for you, Jerry. But you know that you'd have to give me something for it. We both know the way this works."

"Fuck the way it works. What do you want for the car?"

"I'd have to ask if you'd release some hostages. Anyone with a medical condition to start, or children. Jerry, will you tell me if there are any children in there?"

"I don't do kids. If I were going to do a kid, I'd've done yours. Had plenty of opportunities the last couple years."

"Thank you for not hurting my daughter," she said as her blood ran cold. "Jerry, are you willing to release some hostages if I can get you the car you want?"

"Hell no." He laughed himself breathless.

"What are you willing to give if I can get you the car you want?"

"Not a fucking thing. I don't want any goddamn car."

She curled her hand around a bottle of water someone had set in front of her, but didn't drink. "You're saying you don't want a car, at this time?"

"Could've put a pipe bomb in yours. Thought about it."

"Why didn't you?"

"Then we wouldn't be talking right now, would we, you stupid bitch."

Mood swings. Conversational tone, then adversarial. Drug use?

"I understand you want to talk to me. So tell me, Jerry, what can I do to help resolve this situation?"

"You can pull out your piece, stick the barrel in your mouth and pull the trigger. How about doing that? I'll let all the female hostages go if you blow the back of your head off while I'm on the line. I want to hear it."

"If I did that, we couldn't talk anymore. You told me you wouldn't talk to anyone but me. If anyone else tried to talk to you, you'd kill someone. Do you want to talk to someone else, Jerry, or to me?"

"You think you're going to build a *rapport* with me?"

"I think you have things to say to me. I'm here to listen to you."

"You don't give a fuck about me. You didn't give a fuck about her."

"I understand that you blame me for what happened to Angela."

"You let her die, same thing as killing her. She bled to death while you fucked around with the men who put the bullet in her. I had the shot. In the first hour I had the kill shot, but didn't get the green."

Lies. Probably believes he had the shot now. Needs to believe he could've saved her.

"None of us knew she'd been so seriously hurt, Jerry. They lied to us, to all of us. None of us knew Angela was hurt at all in that first hour."

"You should've known!"

Fury. Grief. "You're right, Jerry, I should've known. I should've known they were lying." She read the next communique that came in with a runner. "I understand you loved her, and she loved you."

"You understand *nothing.*"

Agree with him, Mike Vince scribbled on his pad. *Don't say you understand or you know. Only make him madder.*

"How could I, really? You're right. How could I understand that sort of bond? Most people only dream of having that. But I do understand that you were going to be together. You should've been together, Jerry. You should've been able to run away together and be happy."

"The fuck you care."

His voice was calmer, and she nodded at Vince. "I guess, well, I guess I've dreamed of having what you and Angela had. You know things weren't good for me and Roy. He never loved me the way I think you loved Angela."

"She was my goddamn life. If I'd taken that shot, we'd both still have a life. You saved the men who murdered her, but you didn't save her."

"I failed her. I failed you. You want to hurt me, I understand that, I understand why. But how does what you're doing now balance the scales?"

"They can't be *balanced,* you fucking cunt. Maybe I'll shoot this asshole Arnie between the eyes. Does that balance the scales for you?"

She picked up the water now, but only to rub the cold bottle over her forehead. "Killing him isn't going to hurt me, Jerry."

"I want you to beg me not to, like you did with Roy. Hear that! Hear that?" he shouted as someone screamed. "I've got my gun pressed dead center of his forehead. You beg me not to pull the trigger."

"Why would I, Jerry, after what he did to me? After I thought about doing it myself if I could."

"You know what they'll say about you if I do it?"

"Yeah. They'll say maybe I didn't try hard enough, maybe I didn't put myself into this because, underneath, I wanted him to die. I wanted him to die hard. But you know, Jerry, I don't care what they say about me. You pull the trigger, he's gone, and it changes the situation out here. It takes a lot of the weight off me. You know how it works. You do a hostage, Tactical steps it up. So you want to pull the trigger? I don't lose a thing. Is that what you want, Jerry?"

"Wait and see."

He cut off the line, and Phoebe dropped her head in her hands.

"Jesus, Lieutenant," Vince managed. "You gave him permission to kill a hostage."

"Which is why he won't." Please God, don't let her be wrong. "If I'd asked him, begged him, not to do it, he'd have done it. And he'd strap the rig on one of the others."

She pushed to her feet when Sergeant Meeks burst in. "You think I didn't hear that? You think I didn't hear you invite him to kill my boy?"

He lunged at her. It took Sykes, Vince and Duncan to put him down, hold him down while he cursed at her. "My boy's in there because of you. If he dies it's because of you."

"He's not in there because of me, but if he dies, yes, that's mine. Get him out. Get him out of here."

"When are you going to talk to him about the hostages?" Phin grabbed her arm. "Why don't you give him something, give him something so he'll let the women go."

"I can't—"

"My wife, my mother are in there. For God's sake, for God's sake, you need to get them the hell out."

"I'm going to get them out." She couldn't allow herself to see them—Ma Bee's dark, steady eyes, Loo's slow, sultry smile. "I'm going to call him back, and we're going to work at this until everyone's out. Phin, you have to stay calm. If you can't, I'll have to have you removed. I'm sorry." She looked from him to Duncan now. "I'm sorry."

"You'll get them out." Duncan reached out so their fingertips touched. "You'll get them out. Phin, your sister's out there now, and the rest of your family's coming. You should go out, be with them."

"I have to know what's happening." Crumbling, Phin covered his face with his hands. "I have to know something."

"I'll come out and tell you," Duncan assured him, then turned to Phoebe.

"Yes, that's fine. Go out with your family, Phin, let them know your mother and Loo aren't hurt. We'll keep you informed." She signaled to an officer. "Escort Mr. Hector to his family. If he needs to come back in, he should be escorted back in. All right?" She rubbed her hands up and down Phin's arms, felt the muscles quivering. "You go, help your family. I'm going to help your mother and Loo."

"I can't lose them, Phoebe."

"We won't lose them. Go on now."

"How am I supposed to feel?" Duncan said as Phin went out. "They were meeting me in there."

"He's responsible. And I'm responsible for getting them out."

And that's what he'd wanted all along, she knew. Everything else had been building to this.

Showdown.

"Can I get some coffee in here?" Phoebe called out as she rubbed at the tension at the back of her neck. "And more water? Duncan, I have to ask you not to tell Phin anything I don't clear you to tell him."

"I got that. What can I do to help?"

"Listen. You're good at listening." She looked up at the board Sykes had posted. "His emotions are all over the scale. That's typical for this first stage. He wants the negotiation, that's our advantage. He doesn't want to come out of it, so that's his. I'm not calling him back." She turned toward Vince. "He knows how to reach me, he knows how it works. Action, right? He likes to take action, make the moves?"

"Yeah."

"It gives him more of a sense of control, of authority, if he makes the next contact. Let's give him that. Let's wait."

"Got the credit card report," Liz strode up quickly. "Five-thousand-dollar charge, Mark D, two weeks before the bank robbery. He made the minimum payments on it until he went south."

"Bought her a ring in there, that's what he did." Phoebe pushed through her notes. "Got the property list, the personal effects. She had diamond—yellow-gold band—ring on her person. White-gold diamond-crusted wedding band in her purse. Not on her finger. She was wearing Walken's ring when she died. Bastard Brentine. He knew it. Maybe not before her death, but he damn well knew what had been going on when he got her effects. And he stonewalls us."

She scribbled, highlighted, circled. How could she use it? Should she? Time would tell.

"He thinks he knows me, but he doesn't. I know him. And you know him," she said to Vince. "A lot of the men out there with guns pointed at that building know him. He wants to work me, but we'll be working him. He won't allow himself to relate to any of the hostages. They have to remain meaningless to him so he can do what he means to do."

"What does he mean to do?" Duncan asked.

"Kill them all. Kill himself and all of them."

"Oh Jesus God."

"To strike at me, personally and professionally. How can I ever do this again if I fail to save those people? How can I live with it? That's what he thinks."

Pacing in front of the situation board, she stared at the phone, willing it to ring. "The press and public opinion will rip me to pieces. That's what he knows. The connection between him and me will be made known, and the bank incident will be picked over again. I'll be disgraced, and useless as a negotiator, and I'll pay, finally pay, for causing his lover's death. That's what he thinks. And he'll die, in a spectacular and symbolic way. I'll have killed him, just like I killed her. That's what he wants most of all."

She turned to look at the clock. "We're not going to give him what he wants."

"Offer him a trade. He knows about us. Offer to trade me for two of the women. For Ma and Loo. I'm a bigger win for him, and then—"

"He wouldn't take it. And neither I nor the commander could allow it, Duncan."

But he would give it, she thought. He would risk himself for love.

"Duncan." She spoke softly, so he could hear her heart under the words. "I know what they mean to you. I know what you're feeling." And it was killing her.

She turned as the phone rang. "All right. Here we go. Hello, Jerry."

Inside the bank, Ma patted the hand of the woman beside her. "Stop crying now."

"He's going to kill us. He's—"

"Crying doesn't help."

"We should pray." A man across the circle rocked gently back and forth. "We should put our faith in the Lord."

"Can't hurt." But Ma was putting a good chunk of her faith in the men outside with guns. "Hush now," she repeated. "Patsy, isn't it? Hush up now, Patsy. That woman he's talking to? She's smart."

"How do you know?"

"I—"

Loo squeezed her mother-in-law's hand fiercely, gave a quick shake of her head. "She sounds smart. She'll find out what he wants, and everything's going to be fine."

They circled each other for more than an hour before he broke communications again. "He's stalling. He wants to string this out, make it last. There's something he wants to make me do, but he's not ready yet. It's under there, I can hear it under there."

"He's enjoying it," Duncan told her. "He likes telling you no. No food, no water, no medical supplies. He's cruising on it."

"Agreed, for now."

"He's not going to let any of them out." Sykes sat down beside Phoebe. "He doesn't want anything in exchange, and if he did, he knows that releasing any of the hostages is our advantage. They can give us inside intel, make it simpler to shut this down."

"They can't get a shot." Vince walked over to the situation board, gestured to the sketch of the interior of the store. "He's in this corner, northeast corner, and there's no shot. That's why he's there."

"He's been on the other side," Phoebe concurred. "He's familiarized himself with the layout, with the angles."

"They need to go in. Back door's the only way. A frontal assault gives him too much time. They need to deal with the explosives on the rear door."

"And if they make a mistake, if he's got an alarm on it, and it goes or blows, he'll end it."

"You have to get him out of the corner," Duncan said, and Phoebe turned to him.

"Yes, I do."

"If they can't get an angle on him, he doesn't have one on them."

"That's right." Phoebe closed her hand briefly over Duncan's. "That's exactly right. I need to talk to the commander. I need to know where to move him, if possible." She signaled to Sykes to make the call. "They have to let me know when they're going to take him. I know that's not how it's usually done, but they can trust me not to let him know it's coming. I have to move him; they have to know that's coming."

"Got it." Sykes turned with his radio to signal the command post.

Shoving her hair off her damp neck, Phoebe paced, tried to put herself inside the shop. "He's going to have to let them use the bathroom at some point, unless he wants a big mess on his hands. And he doesn't. One bathroom, employees', right in the back room." She narrowed her eyes at the sketch. "How does he plan to work this? He'd have thought it through already, have a system ready. That's why he doesn't have all the hostages in the circle. Holding one back to release another. He doesn't have to move or interact with them to handle the basic function. But it's going to be distracting, and he'll have to be alert. He won't want to talk to me while that's going on."

She nodded. "And we're not giving him what he wants."

Time, she thought, to start playing him. She picked up the phone, called.

"Better be you, bitch."

"It's always going to be me, Jerry. You know how this goes. No lying to a hostage-taker, it puts the hostages at risk. No saying no to a hostage-taker, it pisses them off, and puts the hostages at risk. I'm supposed to empathize with you, be supportive of your feelings, listen to your demands and complaints."

"Yeah, you were damn sympathetic with the bastards who shot Angie."

"Angela was a beautiful woman. She loved you."

"Fuck you. You don't care about her."

"You've made me care, Jerry. I'm in love with someone, maybe you don't feel I deserve to be, but I'm in love. So I understand how Angela felt about you. I understand something of what you're feeling, because if anything happened to him, I don't know what I'd do."

"You don't know what we had."

"You had something special, something once in a lifetime. She was wearing your ring, Jerry. She was wearing it when she died."

"What?"

"The ring you bought her in the store where you are now. She must've treasured it. She must have been thrilled to wear it. I wanted you to know that, Jerry. I called to tell you because it proves to everyone she was yours."

"Everyone can go to hell."

"If something like this had happened to me, I'd want everyone to know what we meant to each other. How much we loved each other. I think you want that, too, Jerry. I want to tell you that I do know it." There was a long beat of silence where she could only hear him breathing. "Roy never loved me, did you know that? He never loved me or the child we made together. Can you imagine? Now that I have someone who does . . ."

She looked over at Duncan, met his eyes, so she'd feel it only stronger, so it would come into her voice. "Now that I do, everything in the world is different. It's stronger and brighter and clearer. Was it like that for you?"

"She made it beautiful. And bright. Now it's black."

Grief, she wrote. *Tears.* Careful, careful, she thought. If she tipped him too deeply into grief, he could end it all now. "She wouldn't want the black for you, Jerry. Someone who loved you the way Angela loved you wouldn't want you in the black."

"You put her there. I'm not leaving her there alone."

"She—"

"You shut *up*! You shut up about her."

"Okay, Jerry. I hear that I've upset you. I'm sorry. You know it's not my purpose here to upset you."

"No, it's your fucking purpose to talk to me like I'm an idiot until I come out crying with my hands in the air. You think you can play me? You think I'm going out that way after I've come this far?"

"I think you're preparing to commit suicide, and take those people with you."

"Is that what you think?" he said, and she noted the smug satisfaction in his tone.

"That's a big statement, Jerry. And a big black mark on my record. But we could spin it, you know how it goes. It's overkill. Seventeen's our count. A lot of people for you to deal with, and a lot to take down. Now, if you were to let the women out—"

"Come on, Phoebe. That's a lame pass."

"It might seem like a lame pass to you, but I've got to do my job here. I guess we both know it's time for me to ask how everyone's doing in there."

She rubbed the back of her neck as they took each other through the dance—requests and refusals for food, water, medical attention.

And the clock ticked off another hour.

31

Duncan stood outside with Phin, a few feet away from the rest of the family. "They're okay. Nobody's been hurt. She keeps him talking, keeps working him around. I swear to God, I don't know how she does it."

"It's been nearly four hours now."

"I know." He could see the snipers from where he stood, see them on rooftops, in windows, doorways. What if they opened up? What if Ma or Loo got in the way of a bullet?

The idea of it had him lowering to a crouch on legs that had gone to water. "If it was money—God, why isn't it about money? I'd—"

"I know." Phin hunkered down beside him. "I know, Dunc."

"Phoebe, she . . . She keeps bringing him back to the hostages. Asking how they're doing, talking to him about letting some of them go. She asked if we could have their names, but he doesn't know, doesn't care. I don't know if that's good or bad. I just don't know."

"It's taking too long."

"I don't know that either." He laid a hand over Phin's, linked their fingers. "Take care of the family. You take care of the family, and I'll go back in, see if there's anything else I can find out, anything I can do."

Despite the air-conditioning, the air in the boutique hung hot and thick. The door opened and closed countless times as cops pushed in and out, so the steamy heat crawled in and set up shop. Sweat gleamed on Phoebe's skin as she studied the situation board, read over her own notes, made more. In a desperate attempt to keep some part of her cool, she'd snagged a tortoiseshell clip from a display to yank her hair up.

She chugged down water as she stared at the red X's marked on the layout of the jewelry store. Kill marks, she thought. Move him to any of those locations, and Tactical had the green light.

"We've had experts move in at the rear door," Harrison told her. "Examine the rig there. They think they can defuse it and circumvent the alarm."

"But they don't know."

"They're pretty damn sure."

"Because they're getting impatient. You know as well as I do everyone's wanting to move, to act. That's the danger of long negotiations. I need more time. He's going to have to move those people soon. Bladders only hold so long, and that's our best option."

"Sergeant Meeks wants to know how his boy's doing. You can't blame him."

"He won't tell me." Phoebe swiped one of the baby wipes Liz had passed her over her face to mop up the sweat. "Tell him I'll try to find out next round."

"If you don't move him within the next hour, I'm going to let the bomb squad take that rig. He's not coming out alive, you know that. Bringing him down's the only way to minimize casualties."

"I'll move him, damn it. It may take a little longer, but I'll move him."

"It takes much longer, you'll make a mistake. That's why you work in teams, Phoebe. As long as it's only you and him, you're going to tire out and make a mistake."

"He wants me to make a mistake. And the theme of this party is he doesn't get what he wants. He's not ready to end it yet, because he wants something from me first. And until he is ready, those people are as safe as we can make them. I'll know when he's ready."

Harrison walked out as Duncan walked in. Phoebe lifted her eyebrows as she spotted the bags of takeout.

"Figured food would come in handy."

Even the thought of eating made her nauseous, but eating was necessary, and might keep her from making that mistake. "You're my hero."

He set the bags down, where they were attacked by cops, then moved to her. "Whose turn is it to call?"

"I'm letting him make the move."

"Okay." He rubbed her shoulders. "I talked to your mom. Everyone's all right there, some worried about you. This, ah, siege is all over the news."

"That's one of the things he wants I couldn't stop." She let her head rest on his shoulder, rested her mind there. "I haven't had anyone take care of me in a long time. I could get used to it."

"You'd better."

"How's Phin—and the rest of them?"

"They're terrified. I'm not." They both knew it was a lie, but it was a comforting one. "I know you'll get them out safe."

"What do you hear when he talks?"

"He goes up and down, right and left, but . . ."

"But?"

"Under it all? I guess what I hear is satisfaction."

"Yes, you listen well."

Ma Bee's back ached, her head throbbed. Pretty, blond Patsy had given up crying and was now curled up on the floor with her head in Ma's soft lap. There were murmurs and whispers among the hostages—something the man in charge didn't seem to mind, or maybe didn't tune his ears to hear.

Some of them dozed, as if they might open their eyes again and find this had all been a strange, awful dream.

"Phin must be so scared," Loo said quietly. "Livvy. He wouldn't tell Livvy. I don't want her to be scared. Oh, Ma, my baby."

"She's fine. You know she's fine."

"Why doesn't he *do* something? When the hell is he going to do something?"

"I don't know, honey. But I gotta do something. I gotta pee."

There were murmured agreements, even a few weak laughs.

"I'll ask," Loo said.

"No, let me. Motherly type might have better luck. Mister!" Ma called out before Loo could object. "Hey, mister! Some of us here need to use the facilities."

They'd called out to him before and been ignored. But this time he turned, the phone in his hand, and looked at Ma with dead eyes.

"Been hours now," she reminded him. "Unless you want a big puddle down here, you're going to have to let us use the bathroom."

"You'll have to hold it awhile longer."

"But—"

He raised the gun. "If I put a bullet in you, you won't be worried about pissing. Now shut up."

He'd had a schedule, and he'd slipped up. Hour three break was when he'd meant to shuffle the hostages, one by one, into the toilet. Whether they wanted to go or not. But he'd forgotten, and now it was time to make the call, goddamn it. So they'd hold it until the next break, or they'd piss themselves.

Fuck them.

"What if I want ten million dollars?" he said to Phoebe.

"Do you want ten million dollars, Jerry?"

Listen to her, he thought, butter wouldn't fucking melt. "Let's toss it out there, kick it around."

"All right. What do I get for the ten million if I can get that for you?"

"I don't shoot a hostage in the head."

"Well now, that's a negative response, Jerry. You know if I could, and I can't promise I can, but if I could convince my superiors to approve that ten million, there'd have to be a more positive quid pro quo."

"What if I said for ten million, I'd think about releasing the female hostages."

"You'd consider releasing the women if I can offer ten million? That's worth talking about."

"I bet it is."

"The thing is, Jerry, you've got an injured man in there, too. You did tell me Arnold Meeks was injured."

He looked down where Arnie slumped, dried blood on his face, tape slapped over his mouth. And explosives strapped on his body. "He's had better days."

"Before I can approach anyone about the money, I have to be assured that Arnold Meeks is alive, and his injuries aren't life-threatening. You know who his daddy is, Jerry. I've got some pressure on me here."

"Cocksucker's alive."

"I appreciate you assuring me he's alive, but I'd have more muscle if I could hear him tell me himself. If I can pass along I've heard his voice, they'll get off my back and you and I can concentrate on the important business."

"Fine."

He set down the phone, stepped over, leaned down and ripped the tape from Arnie's mouth. Arnie's blackened, bloodshot eyes rolled up. "Say hi to Phoebe, asshole." Walken snatched the phone, held it to Arnie's ear. And jammed the barrel of the gun under Arnie's jaw. "Say this: Hi, Phoebe, I'm the cowardly asshole who kicked your murdering ass down the stairs."

Arnie's eyes, full of rage and terror, stayed on Walken's as he repeated the statement.

"What are your injuries?" Phoebe demanded. "How bad are you hurt?"

Arnie moistened his lips. "She wants to know about my injuries."

"You go on and tell her, fuckhead."

"He pistol-whipped me across the face. I think my cheekbone's busted. I'm cuffed, and he's got a goddamn bomb strapped to me."

"Is it on a timer? Is it—"

"That'll be enough," Walken told her. "Now about that ten million."

"You want ten million dollars to release the hostages."

"Ten million to release the female hostages."

"Ten million to release the women. How many women are there, Jerry?"

"Eleven. That's less than a million a head. Hell of a deal."

"Eleven women, who you'd release if I can offer you ten million dollars?"

"Stop fucking echoing. I know the drill."

"Then you know that I'd have a stronger chance of getting you what you want after a show of faith. If you'd release some of the hostages now, including any of those injured or with medical conditions, I'd try damn hard to get you that ten million."

"Ah, screw ten million. Let's make it twenty."

"You're yanking my chain, Jerry."

He let out a laugh. "I thought about killing you, Phoebe. A thousand times."

"If you thought about it, why didn't you do it?"

"A thousand ways. A bullet in the brain. Much too clean. Grabbing you like I did Roy, doing you like I did him. But I don't like repeating myself. Beating you to death, or keeping you alive for days, just putting holes in you. But then it'd be over for you, like it is for Angie. You don't deserve what she got. How about this, you come on in here. Just you, and I let them all go. Every one of them."

"You know they won't let me do that."

"You come in, seventeen people live."

"You'd trade all the hostages for me. Is that a real offer, Jerry, or are you yanking me again?"

"You won't do it. You're nothing but talk."

"But if I would?"

"They wouldn't let you. You think I'm stupid? You think I've forgotten how it works?"

"I don't, but have you forgotten that you've got Sergeant Meeks's son in there, injured. He's got pull. Is it a real offer, Jerry? Me for all seventeen?"

"I'll think about it. But you're going to do something else first."

"What else would you like me to do?"

"You're going to go out there, in front of all the cameras. You're going to give a statement on how you killed Angela Brentine. How you're responsible for her death. How you cared more about running your mouth and playing big shot than saving her life."

"You want me to speak to the press, Jerry, give a statement about the death of Angela Brentine?"

"You're going to say exactly what I tell you to say, exactly when I tell you to say it. Then we'll see about the money and the hostages."

He hung up.

Before she could rise, Duncan pulled her right out of her chair. "If you even think about trading yourself, I'll knock you out, lock you up until you get your senses back."

"You thought about it when it was you."

"It's my mother in there, the only one I've ever really had. And screw this, I'm not debating or arguing, or anything else. You're not going near that building."

"Chill out," Sykes ordered. "She's not trading herself. We don't work that way." He looked hard at Phoebe. "Not ever. This isn't Hollywood."

"You bought it." She jabbed a finger at Duncan, then at Sykes. "You know better, but you bought it. I promise you he did. He wasn't expecting me to consider it. He was screwing with me again, and I threw him off by giving the demand any credence. He bought it, he's thinking about it. What he wanted, expected, was to get me to agree to make the statement. Or to refuse. I do either, it's over. That's what he's waiting for, my public confession. But now he's thinking what it would be like if I came inside. If he had me in there. So how do we use it?"

"Show of faith," Sykes said.

"That's first. Get him to release some of the hostages—and before there's any agreement or refusal on the statement. Because that was his green light. We stall. Put us on the same side on this issue. I want to go make the statement, but they're dicking around on it. I want to go in, but they're stonewalling. I'm trying to work it so he gets what he wants. I'm frustrated because it's taking so long to get the go on it. He's used to following a plan, an outline." She looked at Vince.

"I guess, yeah. Ah, it's training. You have to adjust, sure, to think on your feet, but it's all within the outline. You train for variables. But he likes . . . order? I guess that's the word I want. He's not real impulsive. He'd rather figure it through."

"He's doing that now. Does he want to go through with his original plan—blow it all up, himself included, while I live, disgraced but breathing? Or, if he gets the opportunity, wouldn't he rather take it down to the two of us? The hostages aren't anything to him, but they're everything to me. That was the idea. But to be able to look me in the eyes when he sets off that bomb, that's going to be tempting."

"He's tired," Duncan added. "You can hear it in his voice. So are you. He probably hears it in yours. He's getting closer to ending it."

"Yes, he's closer, bringing up the press statement, that's his lead into the final stage. Now this has given him something else to chew on."

"Activity inside." Sykes held up his hand for silence as he listened to his radio. "No visual on the subject, but the hostage identified as the owner is untying two of the women. Got a clear view. One hostage, female, black, middle age, walking toward the rear."

"It's Ma Bee," Duncan murmured while fear closed a vise on his heart. "It's got to be."

Ma walked back to the bathroom as directed. She moved slower than she needed to, even hobbled a bit though it hurt her pride.

He made her leave the door open, which seriously offended her sense of propriety. Still, she peed like a racehorse and looked around for a weapon of any kind while her grateful bladder emptied.

She wasn't a fool. He was going to kill them all. If she could hurt him, even a little, she'd have some satisfaction on the way to Jesus.

But there was nothing to grab. A bottle of liquid soap, a little dish of potpourri that wasn't worth the throwing at the man's head. In any case, he had that damn gun in that security guard's ear.

She shuffled out again, kept her eyes downcast as if cowed. "I'm Beatrice. They call me Ma Bee."

"Shut up, get back in the circle."

"I just wanted to thank you for letting me go first, before I embarrassed myself."

"You don't shut up and go sit back down like I tell you, you're the last one who goes."

She did as she was told, but she'd seen he had another gun, and more ammunition, in one of the boxes he'd wheeled in. More important, she'd seen what she thought had to be the detonator.

"Has to be the bathroom break," Sykes told her. "The way they're moving from the circle to the rear, one at a time. First hostage is back. She's . . . Tactical says she's signaling. Signing. Three handguns, one rifle, ammo, detonator, rear right corner with bad guy, injured guard."

"Count on Ma," Duncan whispered.

"Get us the hell out of here," Sykes finished and pulled out a smile.

"I'm calling him back while he's moving them back and forth, while he's got to divide his attention. Let's push him on the deal."

The phone rang, three times, four. Just as she was worried he wouldn't pick up, his voice snapped on. "I don't want to talk to you now."

"But, Jerry, I wanted to tell you about the deal. I can't promise yet, but . . . If you can't talk to me now, I'll wait and tell you later."

"What? You're not going to snow me, tell me you're going to make the statement, make the trade, just like that."

"I'm not trying to snow you, just keep you in the loop. I don't want anybody to get hurt. The chief doesn't like the statement—politics, you know how it is. But I'm working on it."

"Politicians like their scapegoats. You tell the chief if he doesn't give the go on it, if you're not in front of those cameras inside the hour, we're down to sixteen hostages."

"I'm going to tell him, Jerry. I'm going to tell him that all you want is for me to make a statement about my responsibility for Angela's death, and you'll let everyone go. Is that right, Jerry?"

"I got a change of plans. You come in. We'll use one of these camera phones for the statement, transmit it. That's how we're going to do it."

"You'll trade me for the hostages, is that what you're telling me?"

"You come in."

Still not going to let them go. "Arnie's daddy's pushing for it, like I expected he would. I haven't even had a chance to think it through myself and he's banging his fist. Jesus, he's a hard case."

"You burn, his asshole son doesn't. No-brainer."

"For him, maybe. I just want to talk to you, Jerry, I just want to find a way out of this. If talking to me face-to-face can help . . . But you know they want something up front. How many would you give us?"

There was a brief hesitation, and in it Phoebe read the lie.

"You in, they're out. That's the deal—if I decide to make it. Keep your eyes on the ground like I told you!"

"Sorry, what?"

"Not talking to you."

"I was just . . . hold on, hang on, they're bringing me something." She clicked the phone to mute it, and prayed she was right in going with her gut.

"He's not going to let any of them out, even if you could make the deal. You're tired," Sykes continued, "maybe you can't hear—"

"No, I can. I can hear it. Tell them to move on the rear, but not until I signal. To move in, front and back, but not until I give the go. You're right," she told Sykes. "He's not going to let any of them out for this. But if I can move him far enough away from the detonator, they can take him—maybe take him alive. Go in, front and back, they can take him. On my say."

"What are you doing?" Duncan demanded.

"Taking a chance. Jerry? Sorry, Jerry, you know how it gets. Jerry, I've got her diary. I have Angela's diary."

"You lying bitch, she didn't have a diary."

"I'm not lying, Jerry. You know I have to be able to back up what I say. She was a woman in love, and she couldn't tell anyone who you were, or the way things really were between you. So she wrote it down. That bastard Brentine didn't tell us about it, just like he didn't tell us she was wearing your ring when she died. Had to save his pride and reputation. They got a warrant, and they found it. She called you Lancelot."

She heard his choked breath. "Read it to me. Read it, so I know you're not lying."

Phoebe flipped through her notes so it sounded like flipping pages, and pulled out the information she had on Angela. "You gave her pink roses—they were her favorite. She's got a pink rose pressed in the pages here. She loved when you cooked for her, loved to watch you."

"Read it. I want her words."

"Tit for tat, Jerry. I want to give you her words, but you have to give me something."

"Read a page, and if I know it's her words, I'll let a hostage go."

There, she heard truth. "Let five hostages go, I'll read a page. She wanted to build Camelot with you. Let five go and I'll read it. Let them

all go, and I'll find a way to bring it in with me and you can read it
yourself."

"You bring it out where I can see it. Nobody goes out until I know
you've got it."

"You want me to bring it out? I can try to work that. If I bring it
where you can see it, what will you give me?"

"Three of them. Bring it."

"Three hostages go out if I bring her diary where you can see it? Is
that right?"

"Now!"

"Let me clear it. I'm going to start down there with it, and try to
clear it on the way. I'll have to call you back on my cell. Is that all
right?"

"Do it now."

"I'm on my way."

She shoved up, grabbed her cell phone. "Somebody get me something that looks like a diary, a journal. Nothing too big. I want you
patched in," she told Sykes. "When I say: *It's all I can do, Jerry,* that's the
go. Exactly those words, Bull. I won't say them if there's another way, if
I believe we can talk him down or take him alive."

"This do?" Duncan offered her a fancy address book with an em-
bossed red leather cover he'd grabbed off a display.

"Perfect, unless she hated red."

"How did you know he'd go for this?" Duncan asked her.

"It's personal, intimate. Something that was hers. Her speaking to
him, and something he hadn't factored in. He'll trade for it, there's a
good chance he'll trade for it. I need to coordinate with the commander."

"I'm going with you as far as I can go," Duncan added. "What's to
stop him from just shooting you the minute you're in view?"

"He wants the book. More, if he gets a bead on me, they'll have one
on him. He shows a weapon, they'll end it. He's distracted, people are
moving around. He hasn't stopped the bathroom break. He's off his
stride now, churned up, and he's made a mistake. We have to capitalize
on it. Commander, I can move him away from the detonator."

She explained her plan, shrugged into the vest someone passed her. "Once he's away, I'll keep him there, or, if I'm lucky, bring him closer to the display window. When the rear door's clear—"

"We'll take it from there. You move any closer than I've cleared, it's over, we sweep you out."

"Understood." She turned to Duncan. "You can't come with me."

"You'd better damn right come back to me." He gripped her hand. "Not negotiable."

"Deal." Her fingers tightened on his, and in his eyes she saw both his fear and his faith. "I love you," she said, then walked away.

He might take the shot, she knew, if he was quick enough, smart enough. Odds were against it, but she hadn't been completely truthful. She ordered herself not to look back, because Duncan might see the lie in her eyes, and the fear with it.

His mother, she thought, his sister. His lover. What happened in the next few minutes would determine if any, or all, of them came back to him.

She pulled out her cell, called Jerry.

"I'm heading down now. You need to get the hostages ready. Three hostages, Jerry, that was the deal."

"I know what the damn deal was. I see you, I see it, before anybody gets out."

"You see me, but you won't see Angela's diary until three people are out. You have to work with me, Jerry. You'll still have fourteen. You didn't know how many people would be in there when you planned this. There might only have been fourteen to begin with. You're not losing anything, and you're proving to me you keep a deal. I show it to you for three, and I'll read you a page for three more. Then we'll talk about the trade. That's a fair deal, Jerry."

Lies, she thought, she was full of lies now. Did he hear them?

If she failed, could she live with it? Could Duncan?

She heard the chatter through her earpiece. The rear rig was booby-trapped and set with an alarm. It would take time she wasn't sure she had to bypass and defuse.

Work with what you've got, she reminded herself.

"Tactical needs to see the three hostages, Jerry. They've got me blocked; they won't let me through until they seem them."

Movement. Three females . . . moving toward the front.

She got the nod, stepped out from cover. In the swampy heat, her flesh goosebumped with ice. "I'm here, Jerry. First part of the deal. Now your part. Let them go."

"I don't see you."

"If I come any closer, Tactical's going to swarm me and push me back. I'm at the southwest of the building. I can see the display window, and make out one—no, two people standing just to the right of it."

"Stupid to wear a vest, Phoebe, when I'd put one in your head."

The awful amusement in his voice stripped all the moisture from her throat. "I know, but rules are rules. Let them out, Jerry."

"I want to see the diary."

She kept her hand behind her back. "I kept my word, time to keep yours. Then it'll be my turn again."

The locks clicked, the door flew open. People ran or stumbled out, weeping, shouting, "Don't shoot!" Cops in body armor rushed to pull and drag them to cover.

Out of the corner of her eye, Phoebe saw Ma Bee, and sent up a quick prayer of thanks.

Duncan's mother was safe.

"My girl's still in there," Ma shouted. "He's hiding behind her, hiding behind the others. He's got the detonators. He's got two of them."

The prayer died in her throat. She watched a wild-eyed woman come forward and shut the door again.

"That's three. Show me the book."

"All right, Jerry. Tactical needs to clear the civilians out of the inner perimeter. That's a clear." She brought the book from behind her back. "I have Angela's diary."

"Open it. Open it and read. That could be any damn thing."

"I need three more hostages." And though it went against her heart, she followed training. "I need the injured man with this group, Jerry."

"Fuck him. He stays, just like the rest. Want to see him, Phoebe?"

She saw the movement, and Arnie stumbling forward as if he'd been shoved. His face was gray, the blood on it dried to black. As Roy's had been, his torso was imprisoned with the bomb.

Through the barred glass, his bruised eyes met Phoebe's.

"You read, or I blow him. Going to take a few other people out and bring serious hurt to the others. But what the hell, I'll blow the big one, too, and that takes it all. You read *now* or it's done. No more negotiating."

She opened the book, stared at the blank pages. Women in love, she thought, spoke the same language. So she read from her own heart.

"I know what love is now. How could I have thought I knew before him? Everything before is pale and soft and foolish. Now, now that I know love, the world's bright and strong and real. He makes me real." She closed the book. "Send three people out, Jerry, and I'll read more."

"No more out! No more. You read what she wrote. I want the cameras on you while you read what she wrote."

"Jerry—"

"Fuck you!" He screamed it out so all his rage seemed to fill Phoebe's head. "You read what she wrote, then you're going to give the statement. You do it now, you start it now, or I pick one and take her out."

Phoebe stepped a little closer, got the sharp order through her earpiece to stop. Looking past Arnie, she could see part of the line of hostages. And she saw Loo. So tall, Phoebe thought. All that gorgeous hair. Such a good shield.

"I'll read it, Jerry."

"I want to see the rose, the rose she put in it." He was weeping. He was lost. "Ask for a goddamn hostage, I do one. You understand me? Ask for another, I pick one and put one in the back of their head. You show it, you read it, you tell the goddamn world how you killed my angel. Then it's done. Then this is done."

Death, his longing for it as much as his lover, vibrated in his voice. And he would take, she knew, fourteen people with him.

With her gaze steady, she turned the book, flipped pages. "She saved your rose."

"I can't see it."

"I'm holding it up. I'm doing what you want. I can't come closer, they're holding me back."

"Two steps forward. Everybody, two steps! Hold it up! Goddamn it."

She shifted, turned the book only a fraction. In her mind she saw the red X's on the sketch. She saw him shove Loo's head to the left so he could get a better view. And meeting his eyes, just for an instant, she said, *"It's all I can do, Jerry."*

Go!

The sound of the shot cut straight through her. She barely heard the screams, the shouts, the running feet that followed it.

She watched Loo run out, on her own, and straight for her. The force of the embrace knocked Phoebe back two steps. "Oh God, oh God, oh God. I thought I was going to die. I thought he'd kill us all."

"You have to get clear now, Loo. You have to move out of this area."

"You saved my life." She drew back, gripped Phoebe's face in her hands. "You saved us all."

"Ma Bee's over that way. You need to get clear, go to Ma Bee."

"You saved us all," Loo repeated as cops hustled up to pull her away.

Phoebe dropped the book, turned. And there was Duncan pushing his way toward her. "How did you get through?"

He held up a laminated ID. "I stole it." His arms came around her. "I love you. Still a bomb in there, right? Let's get the hell out of here, let's go home, let's go to Acapulco."

"Yeah, but for now, let's just move far away from the building with the bomb inside."

"Your hand's shaking."

"Yours, too."

"Not just my hand."

"I have to sit down, Duncan. I have to find a quiet—quieter—place to sit down for a minute."

She moved through the aftermath with him, nodding, acknowledging those who congratulated her. Good job, nice work. Then she stopped short when Sergeant Meeks stepped into her path.

He said nothing, simply looked at her. Then he inclined his head and strode away.

"He ought to be on his knees to you," Duncan muttered.

"Not his style, and I don't give a damn anyway."

Duncan led her back to the boutique, nudged her into a chair.

She breathed out. "Can you give me five here?" she asked the rest of the team still inside. "Five to clear my head, then we'll finish this up."

"No problem, LT." Sykes jerked a thumb toward the door, paused on his way out. "Hell of a job."

"Yeah." And in the relative quiet, she breathed in again as Duncan crouched in front of her.

"Honey, you look like you could use a drink."

"I could use several."

"I happen to know an excellent pub." He lifted her hands, kissed them, then just buried his face in them. "Phoebe."

"I was never in any real danger. Not me."

"Tell that to my guts."

It was so cold in here, she thought. How had it gotten so cold? Only her hands were warm, where he'd kissed them. "Duncan, I've never discharged my weapon. I told you that. But I killed a man today."

"That's bullshit."

"I did. I gave the go on the kill shot. Not officially. But everyone involved knows I maneuvered him into position and gave the go. No choice. He was going to—"

"I know." He kept her hands gripped in his. "I know."

"I couldn't find another way, so I'll live with it. I used the love he had for Angela to manipulate him. And I'll live with that."

He picked her up out of the chair, then sat with her cradled in his lap. "It wasn't love. It was too selfish, too self-serving for that. And you know it. You were smarter than he was, that's what it comes down to. And you were braver at the heart of it. You stood out there, and he hid inside, behind innocent people."

He turned his face into her hair, pressed his lips to her temple. "Don't you sit here and feel sorry for him, or sorry for your damn self either."

"That's telling me."

"I got a hell of a woman here." He sat, wrapped around her, stroking the cold from her arms. "When Mark D's back in business, we're going in there and picking out a ring."

"I can't afford Mark D." But she managed a smile. "I never thought about why they were in there, Ma Bee and Loo. I never thought about the why—I couldn't let it in. Oh Duncan, you were meeting them so they'd help you pick out a ring for me. If you'd gotten there before—"

"Not thinking about that. I didn't, and everyone's out. Safe. That's the priority, isn't it, in your line of work?"

"It is. And I have to do the rest of my job now."

"I'll wait. After you do that job, make sure you tell whoever you need to tell that you're taking the next three or four days off."

"Why?"

"My woman just saved the lives of seventeen people, so what are we going to do next? We're going to Disney World."

She didn't smile. She let out a quick, shocked sound that became a rolling laugh. "Oh God, thank *God* I found you."

"I found you," he corrected. "I'm a lucky guy."

She put her arms around him, put her head on his shoulder. He gave her peace, and solid ground, and that shoulder to lean on.

She was damn lucky herself.